Until the Sun Breaks Down:
A Künstlerroman in Three Parts

Until the Sun Breaks Down:
A Künstlerroman in Three Parts

III. Blue Fields of Heaven

Joseph Nicolello

RESOURCE *Publications* · Eugene, Oregon

Resource Publications
An Imprint of Wipf and Stock Publishers
199 W. 8th Ave., Suite 3
Eugene, OR 97401

www.wipfandstock.com

PAPERBACK ISBN: 978-1-7252-6980-4
HARDCOVER ISBN: 978-1-7252-6981-1
EBOOK ISBN: 978-1-7252-6982-8

02/24/21

Ludwig Wittgenstein from Philosophical Investigations by Ludwig Wittgenstein (Author), Joachim Schulte (Editor), P. M. S. Hacker (Translator) By permission of Wiley Blackwell, 2009.

Bernard of Clairvaux (tr. O'Donovan): *On Grace & Free Choice* (Cistercian Publications, Inc., 1988). Copyright 1977 by Cistercian Publications © 2008 by Order of Saint Benedict, Collegeville, Minnesota. Used with permission.

III. Blue Fields of Heaven

Justification by experience comes to an end.
If it did not it would not be justification.

—WITTGENSTEIN

The first freedom is thus a considerable honor; the second, of even greater power; and the last, of total happiness. By the first, we have the advantage over other living things; by the second, over the flesh; while by the third, we cast down death itself.

—BERNARD OF CLAIRVAUX

Reality and Reconciliation

SING, O GODS OF the plague, thou seamstresses of Hamlet's mill, the boy-girl semioticians, and the girl-boy who eclipses dialectical reason; thy Milky Way on acid, and the Bacchae reincarnate, thy proem and thy holy seed; sing, O muses, as thou hath before for philosopher kings and eye-less seers, down through Ficino and unto my platonic lyre, psalmodies catastrophic, caught here between two eternities (the One); sing O holy ghosts, thou that lay waste to that which is unneeded, and say, whatso-ever can be destroyed by the truth, shall be, on earth as it is in hell; O Holy Spirit, ye catalogue of ships and women, through to the beginning and end of time, sacrificing the planet in one fell swoop on an altar con-structed by the calling of the gods, and render me thy poetic servant, prince of the muses, author and finisher of aesthetic mysticism.

~

Across the massive, sleeping land, nostalgia dying, breaking down in a half-bottle Rocky Mountain blizzard, reincarnated developmental continuity and toothless news-clippings, a celebrity here and a skull there, and ahead again to unfamiliar aluminum, distant locomotive whistles, gleaming white fields racing to the blinding sky, accursed air dropping in temperature until Philadelphia, Arch Street, 15 degrees, where vacant streets and buildings were familiar in a disfigured sense, their architec-ture casket-colored passing by in its stilted, distended whirlwind.

The bus left and returned to the town, traversing through decayed highways, past a sign for Quakertown cast in well-carved sheets of icy rust. William's exhausted heart was bursting with arrogance and con-tempt, curtailed by the fragile state of his mother and the morose sense one gathered driving along the empty highway sleeping straight through to the town's arterial roads. Where once the martyred slaves of time had stood out, they now blended in together quite well in their furious glances of frivolity and ignorance; the condemned culture consisted of obese bodies and brainwashed minds. It had not been a nightmare. It had been the turned millennium burning inside. Their dimly colored rowhomes presented a persistent, mounting sense of meaninglessness at once as William walked through the long parking lot. Dripping windowsills of melted ice glowed beneath the moon wrapped in ribbons of gray and brown.

It seemed long ago William had ever walked through this town, had attended its schools, had fallen in love along its rivers, and yet his hatred for the town was crystalline as ever. Terminal, sleepless spells sifted through his body and mind; he felt as if he were suffocating as he listened to the snow crunch and echo beneath his boots and felt alleviated by the hallucinatory sense such unrecognizable street signs, closed storefronts sifting in and out of preemptive sight and foreign recognition and amidst such dim surroundings knowing that his stay would be as brief as possible.

He had yearned to stay long enough to ensure his mother financial stability and to do so with a simple heart. But he knew at once, re-arriving in the winter night, that it would require too long an effort to adapt to Jerusalem for any sort of significant financial accumulation to transpire. Had the pilgrim ever felt it home he would have readapted, although alack and alas, the outcasted sense with which he had been looked upon in years prior seemed now magnified; and although it was a town of living people, he knew, those people were composed of reflective blue lights and dying dreams.

To the left he looked up to the old, sloping hills of Jerusalem University, to the singular clock atop contemptuous bell tower, and walked away to his mother's car. The hills broke beneath the bells of the chapel and yet had lost all semblance of nostalgia, like the imagination drained from a creative mind. He deliberated the old library just for its nocturnal scent of ancient books and dusty, tattooed mahogany, but even in daydream he felt lost within a foreign museum considering the revisiting any of the past and all its sculptures with no meaning on display that one longed to touch, if anything, although the sculptures sat encapsulated by bulletproof glass.

Shadows cast in a way that William could not see Ms. Fellows' face but her gloved hands upon the steering wheel of her old charcoal sports car, paint peeling beside pluming exhaust. He wished just as her face came into perception that she would drive the car far away sometime and leave Jerusalem. Sadness rushed through the docile streets cloaked in the bitter channel of sleet and wind, pellets tapping against tin roof tops and windowpanes.

Then a smile stretched across William's exhausted face as he stepped into the car to see his mother had not aged a bit. She had not been young for some time, but the tone of her voice had filled William throughout the country with agonizing, tragic images of his mother's proud New York complexion being absorbed from her face; to the contrary she appeared bright and smelt of a crackling fireplace as she and William embraced.

"You'll see it's temporary and I got you good and set up," Ms. Fellows said. "Uncle Martin even came by with the boys—you know Angelica divorced him—did I tell you that? Did I tell you that?"

He was back alright, though not quite home; home had nothing to do with staying still and everything to do with the experience and imagination, with new places, with chaotic bliss and the revolution of everyday life far away from the past. Ms. Fellows drove to the new apartment making plans to buy a Christmas tree, a new desk, a bed, wood for the fireplace, and between sentiments interjected her longing to hear all of William's travels, and what had happened where, and how Uncle Martin was to lend her a lot of money. She had a paranoiac tone in her voice and emphasized the temporal nature of the apartment. William did not mind at all. He could think of nothing better to do than receive Uncle Martin and his children, in from Philadelphia, and lay down for a good while. He had a feeling, for a moment, that his mother would be alright.

But at the same time a hallucinatory tint was formulating upon the most ordinary things. The feigned innocence of suburbs is of course part of its psychological unraveling; but what the pilgrim had considered perfectly normal for the past 200 or so days all at once hit him like a powder keg of sealed information. As was noted by Strauss, thought William, there must herein transpire a coded language that went back thousands of years, but would be tougher to carry out orally; the art of writing lent itself to layers, where as any speech-genres hoping to carry out a similar task must at the very least subside far from spontaneity. Before he had lived life on his own terms while seeing the country, conceptual wanderlust had been balanced by the university library and Octavia's aesthetic theories, among other things, late into the teenage night. Then came Gideon, Helena, and a handful of friends, all bound by geographical destitution. Now that the pilgrim knew wanderlust, rather than the idea of wanderlust, an oscillating interior light, or shadow of a blessed realm, dwelled with him. He had less seen a place, a state, or city, than had reflectively come to consider that all of this was a vision that took him on, and would drag him back for a second round: so must it be in death, that the apex no language was ever formed to comprehend is solved in mystery.

"My memory cannot go as far as my intellect," he wrote to Octavia, "crowned as I am with future leaves—a spark that erupted in flame, uplifting the world's lamp, with an angel's eyes infused in my imagination—in time I shall return to your little words, which are oftentimes smiled rather than spoken. For there are gods that call from beneath the sea, who conceptually disintegrate and remain all at once, and which no tilting of the ecumenical ear can muster: one must offer oneself up to the muses, which through the mutation of historical consciousness became the unity of contained beatific multiplicity, in the Trinity." Absorbing the delirious sterility of Jerusalem, the windowside pilgrim knew now that all natures lead into one; that the sun is on a leash, and the great chained sea of being in great haste does what she will with men, like fire falling from a cloud. And his thought summoned within him at least two days of rest, an isolated ascent up the University mountain, Augustine's *Confessions* and Petrarch's *Invectives* in his pocket, and nothing else. "But the age is so disgusting that it demands that man know *it*, rather than itself; and therefore I can no longer acquiesce, my dear Octavia; I cannot forgive it, for it knows precisely what it does to me and mine. So witness me my love when I abscond one last time to say, sing to me finally, O muses, and let the chips fall where they may: sing to me, in calling, ye of the Celts, the Vikings, the Romans; sing to me, damned, that I might one last time run the gauntlet, before I vouchsafe my life in the One, having purged myself of manifest sickness, and make something of an Augustinian turn, O Lord, should ye let me, a helpless orphan, and the relinquished essence of nihilism." William sensed a ladder that formed from the mind to the heart, that was a little larger than the entire universe and yet contained in one; twenty-four texts swam through his mind like little embryonic dreams. Ms. Fellows, preparing paper plates and plasticware, looked upon her pilgrim in a way that brought him back to childhood out of the corner of his eye, as one feels when returning to a locale of one's youth after time spent elsewhere memorizing other streets and places,

These downgraded living quarters were the third floor of an old-fashioned stone building repainted white with ashen awnings across Main Street overlooking the old diner that was now boarded up after, explained William's mother, having burnt down in a grease fire. They were still working on it, that scorched slab of three graffitied crosses.

Minerva and the Argonauts

PAST THE REINSTALLED ALUMINUM doorway Ms. Fellows led William through a cramped, bare kitchenette to the hallway. She had arranged for herself a new bed, clean as an advertisement, and a set of indistinguishable paintings hung on either side of the hutch. She'd sold everything, Ms. Fellows explained, during the worst of the legal incidents.

"The IRS or oh, there was a time a sheriff came with forms, policemen knocking at my door—I suppose sadly that Aristotle and St. Thomas did me unwell then."

William contemplated such men,—the former—their souls stripped from their bodies via costumes and uniforms and lapel pins which glowed in the dark, waddling upon bowling-pin legs from prison cell to townhouse doorbell handing out forms and reciting speeches, equatorial weaponry stout in its bemusing circular single-file line. Every day was a costume party for these abhorred masonic oafs. But it was also a trap to despise them all; and thus the good life did not so much demand the obedience of laws in the city of man, but an exterior life that maintained authoritative anonymity, rendering chaos and mayhem a beatific gift of the inner life. One had to be invisibly serene, obedient as a Benedictine out in the public square, so that one could violent in original in one's hidden work. He wished he had been there for any of it. He would have—

William's room was more or less a walk-in closet, nothing of his possessions remaining but the small library, the old stacks of portfolios and magazines, a second-hand desk with an ovular holder at its corner, front leg cracked and replaced by parallel bricks, the dust of which sat sprinkled in a trail that appeared to lead to the air mattress.

"The man said you used to be able to put an inkwell there," Ms. Fellows said. "I saw it in the thrift-store and had to pick it up. It's all just temporary, dear, but imagine that! Like the old times, an ink well for rough drafts of assignments!"

Beside the portfolios and at the foot of a slight closet with its doorway which led to wall with steel tube inserted, he sat upon the barest of mattresses propped up by some Proustian pillows, a yearning to fill the cubit with frankincense and myrrh, cuddling into a collection of woolen navy-blue blankets. He absorbed the warmth of the exposed gray radiator while Ms. Fellows carried on the conversation by means of readjusting and flattening the blinds of the window; and the scent of the fireplace came from an elderly man's bungalow across the street, his mother explained, whom Ms. Fellows helped with daily items in exchange for a little stipend.

William opened his blinds with fear all of the town would be on its docile display before him when to his subtle pleasure he found the river beneath him, some distance away, vague trajectories alongside the forest of fallen pine needles, and a small creek visible through the light of bare trees frozen over and reflecting beneath lantern, sifting in the breeze. Drops of rain trickled upon the river.

Something within the bath of light, his mother readjusting the blankets and quilts behind him, allowed William's soul to relieve itself of hatred. He clicked on an old lamp and found solace sitting down beside the window splashed with frost. He could hear old Uncle Martin shuffling up distant stairs, one by one, his boys rushing and singing with grocery bags swishing and crashing together just behind him. Perhaps hard times were not such a bad thing for a little while and would serve without question at bringing one closer to nature, to the mind. Thus the door swung open and the children leapt inside, Uncle Martin whistling behind them.

His appearance was breathtaking; he'd gained at least 100 lbs. though had always been obese, wore black trousers and white top with new running shoes of orange peel and navy-blue gum. His hair was near all gray and yet he was not yet 40. His eyebrows were in constant motion as he turned away to end a conversation through the blinking headset attached to his cellphone, kept within a leather holster at his side, concealed almost by his sagging chest.

"You're a grown man!" he shouted, stepping to shake William's hand.

"I win!" cried the boys. "*I* won!"

"No you didn't!"

"Boys," Ms. Fellows said, kneeling to their height. "Do you remember your cousin William?"

The twins were five now and most definitely did not. Their mops of blonde hair shown to and fro as they looked on at William in silence, clutching Styrofoam army jets and a canister of toys.

"I've got presents for you two."

William returned to his room, rummaged through his bag for a packet of peanut chews he had bought in Baltimore. The boys' faces lit up, tucking their jets and figurines away to hide beneath the table eating candy.

"That's that," Martin coughed, heaving and readjusting his pants at the waste to and fro. "So, you've made it back in one piece, William my God— I'd never have recognized you! It's been too long, God—It's been too long!"

William told Ms. Fellows and her brother innumerable tales of the states, the origins of the names of the land, and paraphrasing George R. Stewart did his best to accept their penetrating, unreal eyes and observations, the reoccurring longings and inquisitive anticipations over a plain pitcher of sweetened iced-tea, Ms. Fellows stirring the ice cubes into one another and sharing looks of astonishment with Martin.

At once he came to notice, or at least to believe, that he could accept certain frivolities and tragedies in most people, and that if a man were to grow fat, bald, do nothing about the mole beneath his nose from which dozens of little curling black hairs sprung from, relate one's first-hand experiences to an array of popular movies and sitcoms, then a tragedy was all it could be. Everyone had been taught to have multitudes of dreams and very few people would take the necessary steps to follow such unseen paths in a predictable world; this, also, did not exclude the rich, and William absorbed it as the boys tugged his pants cuffs beneath the kitchen table, making faces and giggling, sneaking Peanut Chews.

"You see it," Martin proclaimed, uplifting the clicking window blinds and pointing to the blue, misty light overcast upon the old steel mill.

"God," he refrained, pointing to the cursive title towering before the town's iron heart: "Isn't the casino just one of the most beautiful things you've ever seen in your life?"

"We're hungry!" whined the boys.

"Come on William! Tell daddy to make all the food!"

"Everyone hungry? I got filet mignon, beer, wine, soda, potatoes. We'll have ourselves a regular ol' feast," Martin smiled to his sister.

The children leapt into the air, crying out into song, rushing off with their fighter jets and parachutes to William's room.

"You've got two handsome boys," William said, pouring cherry-spritzers and two pints of beer. "And I wish you all the best."

Martin turned to William, wiping his brow and extending his bare, clammy hand once more. Nike Sports Casino glowed behind him.

"Thanks bud, I mean it. We *all* been having hard times. We'll all have to stick together."

William smiled to think his mother would be alright whenever he'd set flight once more and the fresh food sizzled in pans, the voices elevated once more by drinks and cogitation. He thought of old Harold Smith, Phil Cohen, Heather, and all of San Francisco, and life went on.

After dinner he took his drink to the fire escape and wrapped in his peacoat called Octavia at once, his heart satiated with the indescribable joy of sudden proximity, a burning sensation within his blood he had not felt since he'd read Ignatius Loyola's *Spiritual Exercises* many years back, aglow with obfuscation.

∾

"Hark thy herald!" said Octavia, her voice warm, familiar amidst the piercing winds breaking through the rustic side of the apartment. "You need to get a phone already! The trip!"

"I will, I will—I'll tell you all about it. Four, five days from now what are your plans?"

"You strike me as a happy man; there is nothing so refreshing. Nothing, I don't work on the weekends. You know it doesn't matter anyway. Let us advocate what is right and just, here across the burning field of years."

"I'll come this weekend. What's today—Wednesday."

"Come tonight!"

William contemplated, opened his mouth to speak.

"I know," Octavia reflected, "You need rest. You'll have to see my new apartment too. How do you *feel*?"

"It is strange to come, gazing out into the frozen silence of the winter, you know, everything familiar and nonsensical in its own right. I think what surprises me most is how little I feel surprised at anything any longer."

"I miss you so. I understand."

All of William's memories of New York City and the east were rushing through him when Anaheim cut across Main Street in a leather jacket.

"Octavia—I'll call you right back; Anaheim is walking by just now!"

He ran down the staircase and out to Main Street. Anaheim looked at William with an instinctive shock which turned to confusion. An airplane drifted overhead, and within seconds Anaheim's mood collapsed into a strained malice.

"My name's Vishnu."

He began his poetry at once.

"Where have you all been? Where have I been? Nothing can kill me now but loneliness. I'm going home and going to bed. I hate this life."

"Come out and have a drink with me," William said, unable to believe the severe look dripping from his glazed eyes. "Let's go have a martini."

"They don't sell martinis around here, ya big dummy."

His coat swooshed as he turned, and returned trekking north, smoke pluming and evaporating behind him in rich, twisting bursts. William walked to the stairwell downcast and amused at once.

"What did he say? I haven't seen him in years."

"He didn't want to have a martini with me. I don't know if he recognized me. He seemed sedated."

"Well."

"How is it in the city?"

"A little rainy, quiet, perfect!"

"I'll take my mother's car on a drive into a city. I love that feeling of driving to a city."

"Do it! Wait—you drive—since when?"

William reflected upon Anaheim, and that unbearable exhaustion that had been carved by some inconceivable force of furnished wrath into his once young gleaming face. He looked like an old man, an old man of all but 28. He had had enough transpire in his life to qualify him for death. William feared to see anyone in the town at all. What could they have been up to? Nothing.

There seemed two options: To break away from the mutated symposium, or disintegrate within that betrothed, parallel affair of anguish and convenience.

"It must be so happening on Main Street now," Octavia said, "Almost as great as San Francisco I'd imagine."

"Yea," William sighed with optimism, repeating himself. "There's a fine view of the casino through our kitchen window."

"Oh, God!"

"But enough, enough—it's going to take us days to catch up! Days of staying in bed and long nights out, and oh despite everything, I missed you and New York and God know we'll have to do as much as possible—I won't be around very long."

William's imagination swam with the colors of Octavia's words. Lying down, but unable to sleep, he took a shortcut down through the soundless, ghosted town square, the Hotel Jerusalem all that looked somewhat alive, with its plump piano player transforming the cocktail-sipping crowd of ten before a can of orange soda and a tumbler glass filled with mixed nuts.

These are the little waters before the sea, the pilgrim said to himself out on the sands, but still I must undertake a second pilgrimage, with neither Helena nor Octavia by my side, in order to perceive just what precisely lies in the mimetic balance: that latch of light which unlocks itself, and until it is confronted I shall feel like a sea-toiler who has no one with whom to discuss experiences. Minerva and Apollo rage against she who says in that blithely infectious voice to fix the mind on God, and so I'll so I'll spend warmer winter days beside the old creek in town, immersed in ancient texts and the meek serenity of duck families, dissecting the glittering winter light of water with little swimming lessons. William had to halt his reason to engage in contemplative silence, listening to the wind, on the edge of giving thanks to He who had severed him from the world. From the city of orgies and the deconstructive echelons of reason, fixed in faulty premises, which every morning destroys itself, into then the fountain of artistry which steps in and corrects men, who had forgotten the stupidity of their conclusions. There the spirit moves behind invisible gates of so many eyes in a threefold mirror, the spirit's echoes the accumulation of salvation lost, clouded by the ones obsessed with quantitative, numerical lives alone. One cannot conclude that the second volume of a two-volume set is ever rich enough to announce the first no longer exists; there is instead forever something missing, working with one of two volumes, as evidenced in religious concerns for a planet that shall and deserves, in the end, to expire. Above and below, the organs of earth, as the waxen seal signaled souls contained in dust, the body against carnality and its bondage is the body that shines in earnest, its sacredness and familial potential the ire of the evil world; blessed is one who seeks goodness day and night, transcending the generative principle, moving from shadow to reality, in having come to abhor the conceptual world's mindless vanity, but draws up the vindicated shield of tradition against the enemies of perfection. We are all Tom Thumb at some point or another, two weeks old and invisible within a clenched fist; such is the duty of *Logos*, the rejection of political religion and the resurrection of the flesh called the pilgrim's name, as in a thunderclap and three ferocious bursts of lightning. Such were the pilgrim's thoughts down by the river.

Repose and Vertigo

Two days later it was nine degrees outside, the weekend before Christmas, as Nielsen and William entered Philadelphia. Nielsen had arrived upon Main Street and stood out in the drizzling rain in a brown corduroy suit. As William approached him, he noticed the rain falling seemed symbolic of the impending news, that there was no impending news.

They spoke little along the car ride into the city, with Nielsen apologizing for his brother's recent departure, inquiring seldom as to William's travels, at last explaining he had for some months been on anti-depressant medication and was attempting to ease himself off of it.

The surrounding architecture had a perplexing dismalness about, one unexplainable unless one had read Gerard Manley Hopkins on hashish in San Francisco, rectangular clods of tall unattended tombstones blackish-brown shades of crumbled brick, suspended decay; they had been discussing the beauty of the Bay Area with such exuberance upon the last stretch of highway that Philadelphia seemed a baron prison more than a city upon arrival. William kept the conversation rolling with unyielding description as to avoid any further topic.

The meeting seemed doomed for the get-go. Nielsen's terminal depression did not jell with William's tales and looming departure to New York. Nielsen's move to Philadelphia seemed, at Hermetic glance, a validation Nielsen longed for in the strange, reccurring stalemate of his life: as below, so above. Hell is less other people than a demented spirit patient beyond belief. He'd been having 'A Hell of a time,' he'd been explaining, but that he would have to eat and have a drink before any of it could be discussed. He seemed the moment he refrained from speaking to slip into despair.

Out on Dickinson and Avenue of the Arts the wind made one feel frail, as if dressed in tatters, when it pierced through to your skin. Nielsen ran to his room to drop off groceries and insisted at once he take William for a stroll down Passyunk Street.

Winter-lights and Christmas wreaths were strewn upon the street-posts, creating a maze out of the whistling whirlwind breaking through the long, empty street.

"Now I feel better," he admitted, clicking the door closed behind him. "Tell me of this voyage, the bus ride. I seldom heard from you at all while you were out there. I didn't know you were taking a bus."

"It was a long, sleepless time," William said, "And a fun thing I will never do again, poverty permitting. Strange people, woodcutters, drug addicts, factory workers and young parents introduced themselves, offered drugs and drinks, but I couldn't bring myself to accept. I had neither headphones nor socks. I have absorbed the land. The whole time I thought. That was all I did. Planned another escape route. I thought for three days straight. It was very refreshing."

Nielsen eyed the tinsel wreaths upon the streetlamps and walked, breathing, then transfixed upon the dampened sidewalk. Phantoms and Eskimos of the Art School paced down Dickinson texting and running their fingers across iPads.

"Look at her," William insisted. "Doesn't she look just like Medusa?"

Nielsen spoke of his brother, Carson, Anaheim. Everyone seemed so sad and useless. There was little to do but play along; with the town, the townspeople, to hear the morose speeches on University life, on the working life, the lack of desire to get up and go again.

They sat down in a small Mexican restaurant and ordered coffee.

"My brother said the whole situation at the house was rather, oh, egregious," he began. William wondered what had ever come of his farming novel and observed Nielsen take two pills from an orange cylinder. He felt less beside an old friend in a familiar city than beside a ghost in a haunted house. And Mother Nature is but the landlady of this house.

"Of course," William said. He understood wisdom and positivity were not going to be allowed. "The whole thing was bad. Nothing good came of it."

"I think Carson has lost it."

"?"

"He is so annoy*ing*." He pointed to a windowside family passing around an iPod. "In ten years the mobile phone and the computer have managed to shatter the human psyche, the sense of reason. And these people, they are so slow here—"

"Let's grab a beer after this," William said, thanking himself. That was the way he would make it through. One would either drink oneself into sobriety or follow God into the land of imminent wisdom and martyrdom, to give God back the creation he had made, thy self, and offer up obedience and service to His Will. For now, however, it was the prior.

A live banjo-act emerged and began Spanish love songs upon the multicolored blankets spread across the corner of the restaurant. Rosary beads clicked to and fro as the cowboy played his songs. What was Passyunk Street without ducking into the pub, anyway?

"But," Nielsen began between songs, dropping a sugar-cube into his cup, "I feel as if my psychological condition has grown severe, worse. I can't see myself functioning in school. I feel as if I am acting all the time and one day I'm just going to fall to the ground screaming and be carried away."

"Now why would you go doing a thing like that?"

Boots progressively, hideously stomped against the floor to the rhythm of clapping hands.

"But Carson, he's lost it, but I understand it." William looked around the room; there was no liquor. "Listen," Nielsen said, "It's simple; Carson needs to use people. For him, conning people is a way of life. He ripped me off, he ripped those other people off, and I never gave the guy much more thought than that. You can have a smoke with him and look at his—interesting paintings and that's it. What do you think, man?"

He found it astonishing that at the end of the day their conversation was guided in the direction it had been heading when William first ran into Nielsen years prior. He could not understand that such people, with or without potential, could go on into the future while remaining damned to the irretrievable past.

"I think that I don't care about any of this at all," William admitted. "I don't understand how you think that I could. I don't even know what the hell you're talking about."

"Well, no, no, I just wanted your opinion," Nielsen said, concealing anger. His eye squinted once, twice, and the steaming food came out on enormous pastel-orange trays.

"When do classes begin again, the middle of January?"

"I think so."

"Are you excited?"

"No, not really. I'm kind of regretting the whole thing."

William knew not what to say. So few people, he was coming to find, weren't a matter of circumstance; a lot of people worked well in situations although one could not imagine himself with them a lot of other places. For Nielsen, and many others, it was Jerusalem; envy and pity were womb-lodged twins, bound by the brittle limb of experience sought and never sought at once.

The band wrapped up. A dozen tattooed acolytes tipped cigarette ash into the motion-activated proximity of sprinklers, meant to dispel the homeless, in one moment laughing hysterically and in the next solemnly regurgitating newspaper headlines about 'justice.' The gray sky turned a starless black and an automated lamp cast its glow upon veiled women pacing through the markets of compressed awning, dented cans, and warped stickers strapped to crumb-laden plastic boxes waving in the filthy wind of heaters.

"I want to quit drinking," Nielsen said. "I don't want to go to the pub. You see—"

William came to a stark realization: Heaven and Hell are the basic metaphors to the process of life. We live and die, witness falsehoods and truths, feel pain and bliss, and yet there is an option. Nielsen began to speak of the Tenderloin, to deliver a speech on its insanities and its paradoxes, and William realized at once that Nielsen, with his ecru turtleneck revisited, would absorb the bad and the obnoxious from each place he went in life. For him, there was darkness and darkness alone. Nothing was bright; it was but awaiting inevitable darkness. William pitied him, a notion encompassed by indifference, and for the sake of securing his own path in life. Had everyone always been so downcast, had the winters always been so cold?

"I've burned all of my bridges," Nielsen said, with violent and clear abruptness.

"Well one's got to burn bridges sometimes in order to stay warm—"

Before William could finish Nielsen tore his card and receipt from the waitress's tray, flipped the table over in a collision of shattered glass and porcelain, and stormed back outside to his apartment, like a moth drawn and quartered on a discounted burning bulb.

William covered the tab with embarrassment and felt he would never see Nielsen again.

On his way back out an incredulous old man in a wheelchair stopped him who had been listening in on their conversation.

"San Francisco Cali*fornia*," said the man, readjusting his bent Phillies cap. "Now why would you ever even go to such a *place?*"

He went down to the bus station, arrived in New York at midnight.

Octavia stood at the Port Authority in her long black coat and took William into her arms. They held each tightly, swaying, to the overhead tune of the string band.

～

Some long, uneventful three months of vintage postcards, theological and philosophical interlibrary loans, and penniless midnights inebriated in hindsight though devoured by boredom at present, broken up by the odd case of beer and pint of vodka. William took a dishwashing job and a job at the historic hotel and the first months' pay from either job went to the new apartment and Ms. Fellows for the deposit money. William found that at a certain age you could avoid anybody by staying away from the local bars and thus he did so with ease, dried out, and resumed his studies with New York on the weekends.

At night his heart beat fast, as if it were trying to tear itself from the confines of his chest. His body had grown so accustomed to impulse and motion that physical relaxation seemed terrifying, wherein mental relaxation seemed as a faded myth inscribed upon a long-discarded envelope.

The old, darkened rowhomes of generational steelworkers stood still in residential rows, fused together by the glowing blue light of television sets within each window.

Beyond the houses stood the cemetery with its ashen tombstones spreading and duplicating across the enormous, sloping field a quarter mile by a quarter mile and filled to the brim with graves. A single mausoleum stood at the brim of interconnected concrete walkways beside the single-story Catholic school. The flags stood frozen in the night with their remanufactured simplicity in tow, and specific flags seemed as if upon an ovular stage, beneath the varied spotlights interjecting from the mausoleum. The twirling lights of streetcleaners swept through the snowy pathways.

He felt like he should have been online although he wasn't, and it was then a matter of frivolities and cores. The basic front contained little substance in that its substance came second; the latter, rather than sheer rebellion, was the genuine necessity of individual growth even within the blackest midnight of the soul:

'For the outsider the universe is life, life is the universe, and all sight seen. The rest of the world, if they are to acknowledge the outsider, often make as if to imply he has choice in the matter. Their laughter is often outrageous at first, quite deafening, although with time it dissolves like gas from a burner. In the end the outsider is right, and often worshipped after his death, because most people live external lives and purgatorial internal deaths.

'It is inane that this question, contradiction, is seldom answered, although its answer is simple. The visionaries of our time go on ridiculed not because they are funny or strange or different, but because in their eyes and thoughts is the impulsive registration of the falsity of the world at large, and the knowledge that our world at large is hallucination.

'There is just the individual, the luckiest of whom are born in hospitals and die in hospitals, and it often takes the death of an outsider for the world to commend him. This is because the outsider knows the entire world to be dead from the beginning, and the entire world to be Hell from the beginning, and appreciates moments unlike the others in their lives, whereas most people have been raised to believe that repetition is the answer, that individual substance is a dangerous thing.

'The difference is seeing the fury and chaos of the universe each time you cross the street as opposed to waiting upon a green light. A band of outsiders is often too sweet a deal, for the richest inner lives are anxious; perhaps they are brilliant. But worse than the two is those who derive their experiences from books, for they are purgatorial. They are less presumptuous than repetitious.

'One must get out, get up, unplug the electronic arteries, and live—'

"What about this Saturday—2:00 pm?" Octavia suggested. William could feel the waves of pleasure surge through his body and mind with the subtlest pronunciations of her words.

The town was insufferable, so he'd plot out his escape for spring and would arrive West soon and leave thereafter never to return.

~

He arrived on time to the million luminous lights of Times Square revolving in their ominous way. Octavia stood out amongst the thousands of disjointed passersby racing forth to the next stand, the next intersection, the next entrance, the next entranced body.

When her hands met his he felt again the waves rush through his body the way a chemical kicks in at once, and Manhattan fell apart around him. He looked into her light, intelligent eyes, then to the other downcast, cynical eyes, and felt the best he had in months. Winter would soon come to an end.

"What is this news, then," Octavia inquired, as they began a long walk down 9th Avenue.

"I'm going back to San Francisco soon," William said, lighting a cigarette. "I've got my mother all set with money and not a reason to remain east. I'm going to take the train and meet Phil Cohen somewhere, anywhere."

"Where are you getting the money?"

"You know I've got two part-time jobs."

"Working for peanuts."

William took slight offense:

"If I haven't got enough by the time our date arrives, I'll steal it."

"Don't go stealing money now."

They crossed the street.

"They pay a college graduate seven dollars an hour to set ballrooms overnight in hotels, another seven to clean out old teacups with two Irish buffoons and a few other worthless characters. I tell you—" He allowed himself one, two deep breaths. "These sorts of jobs where there's nothing to do, and if you sit down to rest your feet someone runs out screaming with ladles and pots and pans and fat wives telling you never to sit. The other day no one was coming in because of the hail and so I sat down to write a letter to Harold Smith. Some man in a full-blown kilt came out to scream about cleaning out dirt from between the tiles. I told him that was not my job. When he said nothing, I followed him to the back and observed the tiles. There was no dirt between them. What sort of people are these?"

"I don't know, William, I just don't know. You need to be pickier. Why do you even take these jobs?"

He knew he was becoming dull and abandoned the topic, alleviating the tone of his voice:

"Manhattan is the one place in the world you can fall in love every two minutes with someone studying the sidewalk. You look beneath them, then, to observe their shoes as to see how you can take them, when there between their legs is a homeless man without teeth or nose carrying around a dead crow in a disheveled coffee cup. I feel at home nowhere else but Brooklyn and San Francisco."

Wind swept up their long black coats as newspaper peddlers with coal-colored teeth sifted through crowds of tourists clicking buttons on binoculars to the idiosyncratic tune of sirens colliding with doorway-sized dominoes falling through the performance-gallery entranceway.

"Is that the news? That you're going back west and that you'll steal if you have to? You came here to tell me that?"

"Why are you acrimonious?"

"What?"

"Rancorous."

"Speak English."

"Bitter."

"I'm not," she said, in a reserved, metallic tone of voice unlike her own. William knew from experience that it was nothing he had said or done, but that the strange overtones would continue unless he enquired as to her mood.

Several policemen stepped from an enormous truck with machine-guns attached to their bulletproof chests. Comprehensible thought sifted, albeit unbalanced, through William's mind. He was neither shocked nor ashamed, but to the contrary, speechless, as if he were alone at the edge of a mountain.

"You don't even ask me how I am. You arrive and talk about yourself."

"I didn't mean it that way. I figured we were beyond the preliminaries. We speak enough now, don't we? I know you better than I know myself. I can tell when you're upset."

"I've been rejected from that gallery back there twice," Octavia admitted. "It's nothing you did. I thought we could walk past it today and I could tell you I would be there soon, but this morning they sent me a nice e-mail explaining I didn't make it."

"What are they doing there anyway but playing dominoes?"

"I know," she said. Her sharp pronunciation of the term seemed to absorb the tear from her eye, scraping one's watercolor soul like polished, sharpened glass.

"You're . . . no other girl I've ever met who's even more striking than her art, and in the attractive way, the subtle way. Don't let those bastards bring you down."

"And you're positive that you are done with that other little girl?"

"Octavia!"

She sniffled. He took her hand, observed the emerald ring, and kissed her upon her palm and fingertips.

"Don't even mention any of that. If you didn't mention it last week, why would you mention Lolita now?"

"I just want to make sure you are not complicated. After you left last time, I felt bad about the things we did."

"Why did you feel bad?"

"Because I thought of that girl, see now I can't even recall her name—" She pointed to the subway entrance. "I never met her, that she never knew about us, all of it. I thought of myself when I was young like her and it would have broken my heart."

"Why even mention her name?" William laughed at the abstraction, and let his laughter ascend over the mutating sounds around him. "She's out in Los Angeles right now; I could see that caricature of an original person, waiting on a four-hour line to get Quentin Tarantino's autograph or something. She was good once and later became worthless; Dreiser knew it well. I cannot thank her enough for deporting me from Hell."

He blew a kiss to the Hudson River.

"I thought you two might get back together," Octavia said.

"I can tell you're upset when you begin talking nonsense and bringing up the past."

"Don't you like to recall past loves when you're feeling down, just to emphasize the feeling?"

"No."

"?"

"That girl's going to end up as a roadie for her brother's Strokes cover-band until they're 30-something, end up unmarried, and drink themselves to death in a vacuum-bag of a kitchen just like their mother did."

"You don't think that."

William stopped her on the street and held her arms.

"If you look into anyone's eyes, whether you're permitted or acknowledged or otherwise, you can nearly see into their future."

"I didn't know she had a brother."

"The plump gay one with the shark earring."

"You make me laugh. What do you see when you look in my eyes?"

William accepted her romanticism. The city in the winter was cruel, remote, yet never more beautiful, and through it one could decipher the good people from the bad.

"I see my best friend." He put his hands around her shoulders, looking into her dark eyes at the turnstile. "And what do you see in mine?"

She paused a moment, looking into his eyes:

"The world."

William kissed her and decided it'd be better to take a cab, stop into the shops along the way.

"To the Williamsburg Bridge and across and fast!" he shouted at the driver.

"I didn't think you could have meant you were upset by my decision to pursue myself, my furies, by any means necessary."

"Your responsibility is to your art. Everything else can do, which is good, because it shall. The grass fades and the flowers wither. You'll do anything you can if you're the least bit serious. I wish there were more I could do to help."

William responded, kissing Octavia's collar bone:

"As long as you're behind me I stay afloat and in the path of my future if everything slips by the wayside, all caution thrown to the wind, I'll speak your name within my heart to make sure we stay intact. We have dreams, you and I, in a world that doesn't sleep well enough to understand them just yet. We keep trying to get back them but are interrupted by explosions, and worse, false excuses for them."

"All great historical sequences begin with art," Octavia said days later upon departure, the steps of Morgan Avenue. William repeated her words and kissed her goodbye.

~

The pilgrim revisited the moonlit paths to the carnival when it came about and found this time around no Ferris wheel but a caged elephant in its place, no sparkling entrancement but senile men and women of all ages with heavy, sagging skin eating sardines from dented, oily cans, talking to themselves beside vats of boiling water, and helium valves ascending skyward.

~

The days broke down into collages of labor, thievery, letter writing and extended solitary walks. Long-dead flowers rose again to the tune of distant cries and love and laughter the way memories sift and flicker throughout the mind as if speaking for all of life and one carries on without knowing nor caring why. Fresh paint was applied to the fences and mechanical hands waved like little bronze bars beneath old-fashioned clocks.

Successions of letters began pouring in from the west online and hand-written. The hand-written letters were the best. He read each word, each fragment vibrant in its own way and glowing with ideological rebellion, inventiveness, the gilded western spirit which drowned the dreary country in baths of golden light. That kept you going, all of that, when times grew troubled.

～

"She's living like a bum with an old Chinaman," she explained, stepping down from the bus. William walked around her, through a maze of collapsing tents, pottery exhibits, tapestry tournaments and to the brick entrance of the Irish tea-room. Mel the Owner was still in Dublin. The room was chaos. He took his brogue and his delusory self-image and set them in an enormous trunk and took off.

"Don't know when he'll back," Nell said. His eyes looked as if reddened discs slouching toward the sun. "Four minutes late, milady, could ya type that into the database? Yellow, yellow."

He bolted upstairs while miniature bells clicked on his kilt and boots. Waitresses reread People magazine and on disobedient days negated to Newsweek.

Bleakness held the overhead orchestral strings together amidst unfilled eyes and plates of margarine and jam crashing together within overflowing sets of steel sinks. Fruit-flies zipped through the restaurant as the customers swatted their hands north, south, east, west in intervals, compass ends guided to the troglodyte tranquility of worn-out portraits of foxes, bluebirds of the mountains, watercolor mugs of Guinness. He deducted the four minutes from the database and added another nine hours and fifty-six minutes for it was the simplest way to make extra money rinsing out mugs, mopping floors, in order to pay off library fees and then return across the street hours later to the hotel which was busy. April from the café walked by. She had just seen Carson's girlfriend. Heroin and a black eye. Poor girl, ragdoll, distant mug never to be completed. Several parties had taken place last night. Rental chandeliers and hypothetical photography.

Man in an auburn suit conducting traffic, another breaking hard-boiled eggs with silver teeth. Businessmen, businesswomen discussing diet soda with tycoons and baboons. Ten million dollars' worth of asbestos. Condominiums and abandoned shopping malls. Spiral staircases dressing gown the exploiting of silicate minerals; Quebec; visual criticism; muscovite; mussels; New York clam chowder soup; swaying gray mop water setting sail Tropicana box.

Three men with gleaming shaved heads; menthol cigarettes; trumpet transcriptions; the hollow ballroom; excuse me; thank you; thank you; excuse me; laughter breaking from curtained corner; toothless autograph collectors beaten in alleyways; get high on the roof; parking space, where; clean a room of two-hundred tables and reset; long mirrors; vulgar display of power; climax on Wall Street; 'I'm high;' live bands began; some waited on lines a mile long to get to the bar; someone lit a cigarette; it was like dropping a match to a pile of thousand squirming ants; 'Flashes of orange;' stalled bodies; structured silken quilts, liqueur, lacquer, the seventh commandment, foreign regiment, southern men in bucket hats throwing money at cocktail mixologists in crumpled balls; through empty hallways; repeat; repeat; Montaigne, Rabelais; then Auerbach; the bus terminal at dusk, garbage trucks rumbling up and down the vacant streets, funnels of putrid fog and sewage, a man dangling from coat racks smoking torn cigarettes, familiar; unfamiliar, parricide.

Anaheim, pacing the sidewalk, his face and hands light blue with scars. "I thought you were in California." "I came back for more money." "What do you need money for?" "To leave again." He did not (Unspoken) recall his unspoken arrival. "It is a shame what they do to a man in mental homes. One of the doctors told me if I ever talked, talked about it outside they'd burn my house down." He sat down, coughed, and stood straight as an arrow. "You've got to get out of here. Anywhere. They will crucify you here. There are two kinds of people; the clinical-insane and the private-insane." He burned his palms with cigarettes. A blue jay tilted its head upon sharpened black gates. Seduction is less a matter of hard-fought discernment than it is Gainsbourg plus Lynch divided by wine. "Stigmata now, as I know is all, that once and for all, the revolution is a race to the grave. And I don't want to leave my mother's home again. I don't want to create anything. It's over, useless, done, dead; this town will burn to the ground. The ground of the universe. Lacerated harmonies. You heard old professional acrobats beat his girlfriend, his girlfriend beat him, and isn't going to prison. Special tonight at nine. He's going to a psychiatric ward. You can't care there, you're done here—I'm boring you, what did you just get off work?"

He spoke with stunning conviction heightened by the initial hour. Allegorical fire burned somewhere within him buried beneath copyrighted quicksand of pharmaceutical drugs. "I have a joke without an answer: How many pharmacists does it take to kill wisdom? Inimitable drug warfare. I sing, I sing," he sang:

> *Sarveśām Svastir Bhavatu*
> *Sarveśām Sāntir Bhavatu*
> *Sarveśām Poornam Bhavatu*
> *Sarveśām Mangalam Bhavatu*

"How long you worked there?" "A little over a month." "My brother worked there. The Carnation Revolution. He quit, he told me that such places do not maintain souls but kill souls, that day I lost my faith in work; there was never an impenetrable God to begin with and you cannot go without entrances." He said nothing. "Go explore everything, the countryside and cities, intimacy for everything, our stagnant period longs for sentences to come and devour it; every great period: preludes in agony; dismal epilogues; Trollope is my name; history depletes itself but not mon; I have faith in mon; ravenous appetite; Mon; devour everything in your way; the perpetual orgy; Trollope, Trollope, I long to hate you and love always. Never read a word. Mon."

"And what'll you do, O comrade?"

He sang:

> *Sarveśām Svastir Bhavatu*
> *Sarveśām Sāntir Bhavatu*
> *Sarveśām Poornam Bhavatu*
> *Sarveśām Mangalam Bhavatu*

He lit another cigarette and spoke through thick clouds of smoke which broke in tunnels to the riverbeds rising beneath the fenced cliff and attributed to his pastel voice its permeated undisclosed lisp. Clicking horse-carriages made their way up Main Street. He switched his attention from the bookshop to the horse to William with lethal intensity. "I am psychic. Everyone we ever knew around here is doomed. I know Nielsen will never sit still until his torment is immortalized, and then he will burn it and pick up painting or the guitar. He's a rich boy, a typical degenerate. Look at his shnoz. A most prescient reciprocity, revolutionarily wretched. Pity is a pity, no? A social construct is a social construct is a social construct. Pitiable. When the sheltering sky collapses then I shall awaken, perhaps, from my slumber! Aren't you afraid of Hell? No. Eternity is Hell and I've swallowed the moon. Is madness the truth, William, and can the truth be untrue? The world won't listen until its timing, chaos, is off, on. Simultaneities: Now is not the time. Throw everyone under the wagon that gets in your way. The right interval just must be struck."

He began to sound like a military operative. William knew not what he meant by much of his words nor when he was joking although he was enraptured as always by his unyielding conviction in something, anything, different, and William's foot fell asleep. "Well I think no one can say much at all to anyone if he hasn't been betrayed and willing to admit he's been betrayed in taking no further steps backwards. Avoid admittance, magnetic drift toward the unreal:

> *Sarveśām Svastir Bhavatu*
> *Sarveśām Śāntir Bhavatu*
> *Sarveśām Poornam Bhavatu*
> *Sarveśām Mangalam Bhavatu*

"I feel dissatisfied with everything in my life at once, you see—I went to New York, broke down, I had three good friends on 6th Avenue from years ago. Two lived together, the other a trust-fund type who lived there who had never been laid and was obsessed with psychoanalysis but the sexual inexperience coming from his tone of voice made him a bad unbearable person comparable to if you were to consider discarded expired dog food or the dead dog himself. I spent a few days with them; the city had no use for them. The highlight of their lives was attacking everyone and everything at once, inside, while the city and the world went on around them, without their docile observations, their aphasiologies, their forced anguish. It was a sad affair. Their observations were most pathetic because they attacked the functioning in a city within which they could not function. I wanted to go to bars and see the men and women raving of politics and art and life and death! My friends had grown steadfast and laconic in contagious mental disintegration writing Christmas cards in digital halls of digital mirrors, crying upon Yacht-Club balconies. The hollow men are most often full of themselves. Paris does not exist. I couldn't even stay on the couch. Suicidal, working sixty stoned hours a week, making filmic renditions was the sanest one of Superman with his old-man lover whom he claimed to be using and then I watched their short film and realized he was being used. On holidays he'd masturbate into a glass and feed it to the toothless man, who as a child had been raped with a corncob but we've already discussed Mr. Magoo. Have you ever felt so bad for someone that you'll never talk to them again, less spite than logic? The lost souls of the New York Night. It is a good thing no one cares." Cars passed through the brick street. The horse and buggy turned out of sight. Steam rose from the river. "I have to go," he said, and left, turning at the edge of Main Street and pacing microbial into the tunnel that led to the west side of town while William watched him dissolve and felt as if he were drugged watching him disappear holding onto something it was almost a shame the way the working hours suffused and made sense at the end and where did all of the highways go once they reached an end? Had they let Picasso upon adult amusement park rides? Hadn't they let a legless war veteran on a ride and he fell 250 feet to his death? Someone had said that on the rooftop. The Brown Jug. Where did these people come from, where did they go, and why did the village idiots make more sense in their fractal moments of clarity than anything anyone else had ever said off the top of their head?

William was exhausted. He cradled the manila envelope to his breast although he had no desire to open it and then his mother was driving to work as he stepped inside. Slept upon deflated air-mattress, counted pennies, dreamt of Melody Nelson. 'A dead fly floating in wine, and all of that time I thought it was fragmented corkscrew.' Sad boys and girls kicking half-inflated soccer balls across packed parking lots. Once walked through the cemetery, kissing all the way to the graves. Where was she now, when once the western skyline had been unfathomable? The river shone, and the air itself tasted like champagne, smelt of a book that hadn't been touched in decades; bliss. O Abigail Blake, what was that sadness that brought young people to suicide, as if long-term self-destruction weren't brisk and stylish enough any longer? What is that feeling of walking alone through graveyards and libraries?

He took his phone from his pocket, crossing the bridge, observed its gadgetry, and threw it into the river without watching its slight impact. All the restaurants, shops: closed until Tuesday. Neon lights of a casino; futility. The recollection of black coffee in bed; bliss. Love is a blind date in the desert of the real. The bells of cathedrals. Cold gates. Weathered couples pass by. Flags whipped and disarrayed in fluttering, crumpled slogans. Her thoughts were made of color. Grey streets; her visual famine. Cars come colliding through silence screaming bloody murder mocking, imploring, delegation, fumigation, homeless men falling from locomotive trains while reaching for mouthwash. Steelworkers' homes; compacted sawdust.

He speaks of gin-mills in the sundry, liquid afternoon, his voice is sterile and even more alluring with time. Reconciled blue lights, roaring drunk, reconciled blue lights, roaring drunk. The emaciated fountain. Mother whale's eyeless perfume; on Earth as it is in Heaven, the next heaving corkscrew unto exhalation; the cold gate was locked when he turned for home; black iron bars; the light of living dreams; uphill to the day; the disconnected thoughts of lights of thought. Cavernous realms, dissociated through the plasmatic suggested. Cervantes in pursuit of the White Whale and yet seen on the unassuming stamped steps of prison-complexes. What had he seen? He awoke, dressed, washed his face and read the postcard. Buy a pipe, says Percy, as did all the masters; good for thought.

He awoke, opened the pamphlet: The Catatonic World—Anaheim. Dedication and all. Gentleman.

Middle-afternoon, retracing morning steps nothing doing save the girl, exception, he walked back across the bridge. Digital whores, commonplace spades, bloated men playing banjos. Four dollars tonight. No alcohol or drinks outside allowed. Nor permitted. They've begun to underline, William noticed, curling his typographical mustache; in his pocket a stolen twenty dollars, there must have been some, something, they've begun to underline. The local businesses are using propaganda. Across the bridge, words burned into ground, ineligible names. He was online a moment and saw the beautiful girl's blog whom he had always wanted. She had been straight edge when he knew her and he always admired her sense of style. She worked for Burger King and painted portraits. Someday, he told himself, I hope that she reads my mind and sees through my leather jacket and understands the internal absolute of my soul and perhaps had admired me always from a distance. Offered to take her on a date to the city; no reply. Women these days. Women those days. Women all-ways. The truth will set you free, Prof. Booty had said, retrieving Schopenhauer's essay from his library.

He crossed through traffic at 2:56 pm, opened the heavy brass door.

Dark corner, you recognize at once, K. Lang. Tobacco-stained fingers. Broken teeth. Spousal abuse. 15 drunken driving counts. He claimed to hold part-time jobs to pay court fees. He cleaned toilet bowls by day and drank 35 beers by night. He broke into hysterics each time he ordered drinks, and his liver protruded from his chest like a leech. There he was, in the dim corner, looking away, in the dim corner, with so little on his mind. Swaying wooden doors. Cigarettes broken in half. Burned fingernails. Acrid walls. Wind whistling. Forget the swan, the swan has passed, and the present moment which then must also become the past, for the present could never be the present lest it implied it was here but to disappear.

Colliding voices and smoked out air hung like liquid gallows at Your Fiction Within. William felt in the trance of brutal insomnia that he was awakening from a dream within a dream by being dangled by his feet twelve stories in the sky from a bridge of bent bronze, overlooking an upside-down desert of helium nitrate-induced desert sands, scorched across its scalp. Clear mouths: saturation. White combs, old maps, old pictures, record sleeves, shades of paint which weaved a sort of cultural flashback of structuralized gazetteers, for they were no longer familiar in any way but finality. Exposed radiators moaning. Space heater; its un-plugged wire creating a cursive L. Bronze liquid dripped into the pint glass. His eyes burned like the wick of an opaque candle. Eight flat screen television sets were turned on at once. Sing with the stars. Win $5,000. Credit card companies. Eleven faces familiar fixed upward at the television screens. "I've seen this show. It's hilarious." Obesity epidemic.

"Do you remember the night the space heater died out?" through laughter. The man beside William looked over through a ragged, dim, acne-torn face of exhaustion, his slanted eyes packed with crisscrossing lines of blood which may as well have been rust. Faint; if one turned his ear a specific way one could hear once more the faint satellite radio station analyst speak in the tongue of tape loops.

William's beer was set down before him upon a blank coaster. He paid, placing an extra dollar beside wet oak. The bartender tore the bill from the table and crammed it into his jogging pockets. No more money for you, Thou Walrus. He looked around him recalling the days wherein his temples were going to split open igniting a sort of faint mental evapo-ration following the eruption, the days William became more conscious of things and felt even more so, therefore, looming consciences. All around waiting to be ruined with the weight of whiskey. Call El, looming departure, Money, 'In a voice that rustled.'

Nobody moved. Sound ceased to break into the bar.

"Turn up the volume."

"Musikfest? When are you starting loading this year?"

Carson: My temples pulse as if gongs that send sickening waves of neurotic trembling all through my shaking stomach, vertebrae, veins, blood, all of the soaked-up atrocity within me, the soft factory of per-sistence that feels as if it's had enough; for once my mind and my body mesh together and neither will any longer discuss which comes first, for the Time being.

Heroin: Whatever you like.

William took a slight sip of his ale. To the right was a new computer, lifeless, though strands of microscopic neon interject themselves into the corner of his eyesight. Fragmented light broke through the cavern. For a moment he stared at the small fossilized object contemplating a trillion images and alternate personas disavowing an entire generation which had dived head-first into its waters, trillions of images of drowning men and women and for a few years an ironic notion was the get out jail free card, though it has run its course he felt. He felt justified, drenched in bitter tears. Then he laughed, because he could. Boiling hotdogs for everyone.

William titled his head in the direction of the voice but could not match, sync a face up with the voice.

"Stop worrying," a tattooed voice barges in through the daylight of fallen leaves. "Just stop."

Quick, on observance of the bathroom, plain yellow-white walls like teeth, patterned like teeth, chipped like teeth: 'Out of toilet paper.' A little bit on the floor. Nobody cares, no reason to.

What Nielson would have said:

"I hate America so much I'll never leave!

"And the problem is being an enemy of the world looking in on the problem, most people think you have two options for everything but you have about ten thousand and I can think all day long of millions of problems though the solutions I know are singular and temporary as the night within which such thoughts are acted upon in a vast haze of stampeding lust and some of the buildings have enormous television sets on the side of them, ah America you commercial, you commercial with violent producers who keep their citizens, or viewers, alive in a— ruined tradition of neocapitalism under the mask of Democracy, annual juggling of imagery, look at me now leaning against your newspapers and listening to the radio. Nothing further is needed beside a man who works himself to death and surrounds himself with useless objects; that is everything, from romance to insanity, all of it control; , the voluntary self-enslavement of man, the film itself. Though I hate my times I must go on because these bodies around me make up a desert too brutal to resist. Drunk and stoned it was more momentary, this vision, but now I am sober and here it is asleep somewhere behind me."

In walked a familiar brunette, an MFA in the arts. What place hath she here? Free money. What now? No, look away, you and your brain take a drink. A drink for your brain. Brain for your drink. Sober a moment never. Man had said he felt more intoxicated sober than any other state and now we understand:

Iron and steel will bend and bow,
Bend and bow, bend and bow,
Iron and steel will bend and bow,
My fair lady.

William could see that thin set of underwear set atop an imported rug. Those were hers. Such sights have no idea what time it is; what day of the week it is moves beyond etymology into archaism and is revealed a symbolic retraction. William was daydreaming as she walked in the door alone on her phone. Strange to see someone for the first time and be struck with an avalanche of potent memory. Persuasive domination, nonphysical contact. Mutiny on the bay. A thin man wheezed on whiskey glasses; eyes watered with accidental blue smoke. The bartender checked on him as William slid back up in his chair to the dampened, carved beer upon oak. The men beside him breathed, spoke in tongues to themselves. His glasses-lenses had filled with the flashing, cluttered neon shining down from above. Domesticity: Disability to weave toward possible advantages prevalence through the colossal consistency which is defamation this was all unnoticeable to me until flailing strings began to flash before my eyes the dreams are of dreams the bodies asleep beneath light hum of distant air conditioner come summer come now the paralleling draped nudes around us beneath blanket, casualties of chemical war, the war, the war. What happened to the war? I put it up my ass, why now no you know why. Message in a bottle.

Someone went first, someone went second; the second came. Lungs interrupt the journey: "Man I have never over two dollars in my pocket. I do not care. Do you know what I mean? I do not care." He seemed honest enough, a good chap, as they say, and he readjusted his basketball jersey and smelt of misplaced caviar. Rotten fruit. Failed attempt. Children every other Saturday.

Phantasmagoria: he'd laughed at his apparition.

Reoccurrence: Amorous memories of the girl gone. Her blog.

Delirium: Could he save her? She could never leave her emptiness behind.

Fruition: *All the sad women.*

Culmination: Beyond his figurine accomplice mouthfuls of razor wire raveled by the hands of gravity whence was it neuro-linguistic programming after all?

Incapacitated: She leaves.

Spinning barber-shop bulb through parenthetical windows.

> *Build it up with silver and gold,*
> *Silver and gold, silver and gold,*
> *Build it up with silver and gold,*
> *My fair lady.*

In through the door swung K. Lang. He'd left? A fine reception. Wrack the mind open timeless let it barge. That last paycheck concerning cups of tea will be sent in the mail, thought William. Ought to have it mailed out West. Also the check from the Third Reich. Voluntary storm troopers. The terminated contract. O Heavens. He drank from his cold pint glass.

Laughing voice goes from groan to glee: "Thank God it's Friday."

"That makes sense."

'Traced the running text of screens, languages without mouths then to roar toward green lights, rage through the reds, and the yellow lights of life must then in turn become nonexistent because blah there is no time left to talk, to dream, to think alone without seeming insane, the obsolescence of everything around the small pocket of artistic vision blah blah an unreal heartbroken wreckage like cannonballs blah smashing one in the face every time one would step outside blah and blah oh blah, a voice that a-way but blah he could not break blah down the linguistic compounds in time, blah the blah black blah second blah between the commercial blah with the news anchor and the commercial with the fast food above said blah , "Don't blah sometimes blah you just blah want to blah?"'

Dramatic opera music: Fine for drunken daydreams brought alive.

William drank down his drink further and said to himself: "I am finishing my drink," with the golden ray of San Francisco on his mind. He looked away from Lang, noticing that beautiful woman had already gone. Perhaps she had been given the wrong address.

The middle-aged woman with large breasts and brown ponytail three seats down from William smoking a mentholated 100 cigarette sat beside a young heavyset man who'd rolled his feverish eyes at the second-rate actresses' inability to hit a proper D note on the Madonna song, 'Like a Prayer,' which was odd because the television set airing that television show was muted, alas, the woman's strong back was of sweat as she turned to William. She smiled as he observed the wet-white spots of perspiration. She made a movement with her left hand relatable to rattlesnake's flickering tongues, spasm dear limbs, using her right hand to reach diagonal of her another man, who blinked his eyes and swallowed a pill with either sparkling water or gin and vodka. The verdict? Gin. With? Icicle bricks made of tonic-water. Explain the fizz: Alka-Seltzer.

The last man, who was facing the other last man, clad in purple-grey mud-addled jumpsuit, was holding a torn edition of the Jerusalem Times with the title bearing the homeless report.

"The study found," the bartender laughed, in a mocking voice. William laughed also.

The ruptured, sweating men swallowed double shots of vile russet exaggeration and began a conversational debate concerning something, when in stepped Michael Kahn with his date, a girl?

He turned around, his eyes widening, smile spreading. William returned the favor. The three walked to an adjacent table beneath Christmas lights and bold paintings of bald eagles. Michael ignored those around him without knowing; William did so on purpose. He equated them with spiritual ruin and perfunctory masochism in the sense that they spoke of nothing but leaving the area, though never did one leave the area, then when one left the area they were despised. Good for him though. Proof-readers from such romance-novel firms. Oratorical mansions: William attracted to Michael's date, whom he recognized from somewhere, and it was in her plainness. Off with your pants!

"I missed you," said Michael. William and his date shake hands, mutual looks of curiosity and familiarity.

"I'm Danielle." Her hand was soft like plush decorum. The way legs look in the dark air when the pantyhose comes tumbling down the up-hill waterfall. How could such a thing exist? (Leather jacket before plain denim outfit, a plain haircut, no fraction of makeup, no piercings, no tattoos). William had the nerve to look at her.

Danielle, without any admittance of her strange connection with William—perhaps a single, distant hallway and nothing more—asked him, "What are you doing now, or for the summer?"

"Nothing all that much," William admitted, lighting one cigarette with another. "Returning west. I must taste the last drop of desolation before I, in my Dionysian fashion, render negative theology to the concept, and therein recapture paradise."

A vivid image of standing in a crowd of smoke and neon lights out front of Casanova on Tuesday night's Mission Street passed through his mind, prompting a subdued shudder. Goosebumps ran across his arms, legs, back, neck.

"A lot of people looking for jobs seem to congregate in bars," Michael said with brief, melancholic laughter. He pointed with his eyebrows to tablefuls of students.

"I figured you would be working for a high-end paper by now," William said. "Your article was the best all year around."

"What's that to say about you? I thought you were going to edit the New York Times."

"Either I've changed or the world's changed since then, though I have said this before over a similar glass—less changes than we'd like to think. We learn from history that we do not learn from history, including our very personal own. But yes, though even at that point in time I knew somehow, someway, I'd end breaking free from it all."

"Someone told me, right, that you were in California. Just went up and left with a woman. I had no idea you were back."

"I'm trying to figure it all out," William lied. He felt uneasy lying in front of Danielle; her calming, inquiring eyes widened above the pint glass of beer.

"I'm a dinosaur," hacked an ancient man before him over his shirtsleeve. He held up his curled, sausage link of an index finger and projectile vomited into his lap. "I don't like that dinosaurs are extinct, though, and that the cockroaches are still around." He slammed his fist down on the table. His empty jar spun like a detached, spiraling coin.

Danielle became drunk within thirty seconds.

"We were talking about the University earlier," she explained.

> *Iron and steel will bend and bow,*
> *Bend and bow, bend and bow,*
> *Iron and steel will bend and bow,*
> *My fair lady.*

K. Lang took a seat where William was sitting and ordered a pitcher for himself and drank from the pitcher its entirety. He gazed about the darkened room with the look of Atlantic City shining in his encapsulated eyes. The disheveled bartender waved a furious finger at the man in jumpsuit, he threw his newspaper over his shoulder, the distant pages palpating like the wings of crooked, stuck birds, like packs of infant penguins at birth, each rustling out into the wind of automotive breeze, fluttering and then going on toward distinguished branches of a frozen dome, the stray papers rustling home toward the caked linoleum floor as if glued, as if magnetized, whereupon palms against forehead he smiled, letting down his hands, overlooking the litter, letting down his hands that was all before laughter, against his will he searched stumbling for a recycling bin reciting one-line jokes, monosyllabic pleas unheard, mocking, retrieving the forty-something pages with his tongue out panting and everyone pointing and laughing with tombstone teeth around him. K. Lang crawled through the doorway with his car keys in his hands. Alcoholics saved him this time. Declamatory directions.

"In memory of my feelings," drank Michael.

They adjusted the sleeves of their shirts and sat still. Danielle mentioned her roommate.

Michael Kahn:

"I don't like know about her. She was walking on a tight-rope for some-time. Now she has fallen right off."

"My parents are coming into town from Pittsburgh tonight." Gust of cold wind; man wearing black and red gloves wheeled keg of beer across tiles. He and Michael glance at one another.

"We wanted to have a drink beforehand," smiled Danielle, "And yours is out." She tapped a turquoise fingernail along William's drained glass. "I'll buy you another."

"Oh, it's—"

Michael interjected: "Shh, William, it's OK. I missed you. We will have another drink before we leave and then promise to stay in touch. The casino's coming in, I'll be one of the first cab drivers on the streets. I'll give you a ride! We'll make the best of things. We still never made it to New York either—we always used to plan weekend trips, remember?"

William swallowed guilt and forced a smile. Michael Kahn—Cab driver of the suburbs; Spinoza in the backseat. The young men watched Danielle order a pitcher of beer. She was like a golden ring found in the wreckage of a multi-car pileup. William suggested this analogy to Michael and Michael agreed.

"The direct essence of solemnity," whispered Michael. There, that was Michael Kahn. Less frantic, but himself, nonetheless. "Behind those masks of men picking up paper emotions from the sawdust ground but we can feel it, something or another."

"John Smith quit the band!" Michelangelo screamed, pouring an entire pitcher of beer over her pretty little pelican head.

Her there passing, rejected her once, twice maybe in one way or another like a squirrel chipping away at imitation meat. Stunk up the whole room. Weaseled in with pharmaceutical eyes, worn lips through which sentence spilled forth like closing garage doors, bad attitude, rather have decayed teeth than decayed dreams, pint of rum at midnight. Mop bucket.

Drawers opened and closed behind the bar, silverware clanging around in unseen drawers below the pristine voice before clanging guitars glasses breaking together reflective with inanimate soliloquy. Forty dozen centuries of stony sleep.

"That man drinks much whiskey," Michael suggested, more than announced, pointing to a desperate man guzzling from a plastic bottle as if it were water. Danielle came back with the pitcher and the three of them filled their mugs.

"Family into town."

"How is your family doing?"

"Family into town."

They drank on, eyes wandering about the smoke-filled room, creatures of the night spending summer days inside, dim doorways eager to listen but agreed *chacun pour soi* to continue this-that later on, the dispensing of physical frustrations, who's who, and she was smiling her white-toothed glee and made the most sense of all with her simple untied shoes, blinked, the instinctual triviality of eager pursuit. Then everyone at the bar took off one shoe and sat by the dozens wearing one shoe, comparing athlete's foot and corns, blisters and scars, structure and scent, laceration and inflammation, waving one shoe about the room, including the bartender, who removed one shoe, and swung it round like a lasso from its lace. A middle-aged couple stepped moments later through the disquieted entranceway and were pelted with dozens of pairs of shoes.

"Make a plan to get my shoes back on after dinner and romp back up the street, make checklist of people to call, charge phone at T-Mobile store, refuse to look at the clock, between the Casino and the University."

Danielle waved one last time from the door. William waved back and had the table to himself. They had meant it when they said one last drink. Rare. Cannot tell if that is respectable or not; the way I feel inside? The latter.

The love-sanctity of routine, William thought, is tragic but it'll do. I am a young man, and whether I was an old man or infant I would be alive thus dying—then death must be beautiful its own way, wherever it leads, implicative of life. Do not fear shadows—for shadows recognize light.

He stepped out and lit a miniature cigar. Phil Cohen confirmed to meet in Reno, Nevada. Now they were talking. He rubbed his hands together, cupped them, and breathed warm breaths into an open crevasse, warming the rosy tip of his nose.

"I want to go home but there is nothing at home," he explained to El. "I'm always at home. Comfort becomes dangerous and I want to drag myself along the street and be a witness to life long enough until I am not longer being dragged but running, sprinting as fast as I can and otherwise."

"Just wait ye comrade," El stomped his foot. "Mustard and I shall meet ye in the desert. Let me e-mail you cheap ticket prices. You stay with me as long as you need." That then was a real man. William knew he meant it, to offer a hand, and William knew that in the future he would reciprocate Phil Cohen in any which way. A month in New York City— some fine day.

'Phil Cohen—I can recall meeting ye as if it were yesterday—O this drink—too sweet a treat. Sit upon broken walls somewhere between Nob Hill and North Beach. Oceanic winds. Conviction in life.'

"An oversexed lack of debauched sleep always seems to put me in this mood."

Was she saying that? Her? Now, who is she? She won't look my way. When did I even walk back inside? recalled even hanging up or walking in through the doorway. Well. Not unless it's while returning from the bathroom, say, say can ye see? A lot of the greatest looking seldom get laid and vice versa. Found that out in the city. Wanted some of them so and when we at last lay together post-mortem they were the saddest women I've ever met in my life. The pharmacist's sons and daughters of the world still believed in film and television. Attractive boys, beautiful girls. Manic composure: political defiance. Thank you, sir: defilement.

'It's as if I forget where I live, but not out of memory loss. I do not want to go home and twisting, squirm through an agonizing dehydration process. I want to roam around where the sights are insane and the sounds are too loud to ignore, steal water if need be, anything but feel folded as an accordion waiting for the workweek to begin. The floodgates have been let open and there is no turning back now. I want to live and to talk and to smile until there's a collapsing of the lungs I always assumed to be or not to be colossal—to the contrary, as the weeping child. I want so much to happen that I wonder now I wonder then I wonder if I shall dare try to remember it all; I want to remember that whenever I could I breathed, listened, shouted, tasted, smelt, heard, motioned, relayed everything fathomable and unfathomable, and that I did not let the gaping misery of most things ruin me. I want to ascend beyond what it means to be common, for I disavow the situation which prompts something such as commonality to exist.'

Dreams cut through William's mind as he sat alone unable to long to do much else but raise his hand to his mind amidst cranial, desalinized overture. One in which all of San Francisco was rendered unrecognizable by another catastrophic earthquake.

Dream sequence, dream sequence, we put importance to our dreams: Hath thou not known the mind does not stop thinking with sleep? The mind moves as the tongue maneuvers. Swallow thirty spiders a year I heard. Now how did someone find this out? Confetti, corner pocket, in the chair.

His response to all this negotiation was a deep, deep breath, a tilting of the glass as an overhead chandelier lit for a second shining off of the ovular glass, channeling the warm breeze running through anyone's hair providing an unspoken sense of hope, hope, hope. Hope for nothing, rather the feeling, lack thereof come morning my love. My love and I see through the sky, and still we smile so often.

There was nothing on the floor then but an envelope from the public library and an ounce of cigarette ash. The smash of distant glasses against a silver sink and a flood of fifty-eight voices in between songs.

"But if one drifts in and he looks suspicious we'll, um," with contempt, "*Call.*"

"Yeah well," prolonged gargling uranium-enriched cough, "If a man—ACK—man keeps to himself when need-be and expects nothing from anyone (ACK) let him succumb to pleasure! Habits are habits because our voices are like Hell conquering, conquests, you know what I mean? You know I'm drunk," he laughed, reinserting himself upon the counter-top, "When I can't care anymore. This town ain't so bad. Hell, you wanna do me a favor, then, gimme a wiener before I die of starvations. Gimme, Giovanni, a frankfurter! ACK."

Entrance country-western voice, like amber bed sheets:

"Hell Yar," shifting, Werner Heisenberg, shifting, Auergesellschaf, shifting.

"Hell Yar first inning."

"Thar he blows me arse. My arse blown to smithereens."

The short man noticed William was eyeing him over and shot a vicious glance back. He made a gun with his hands and shot at the absent sun through the ceiling.

A quarter-block away, he explained extending his belly and yawning sheds a wave and meandering, punched the number-by-heart into a dilapidated pay-phone and leaned upon his stick. Young men ridiculed him in foreign tongue. Cavemen these days. The short man answered his phone and marched out of the front door. Door lodged open with the Yellow Pages still wrapped in cellophane.

"There are nines times," gurgling fatal voice of the cracked shadow of-a-man clad in varied torn rugs, "Yee-hoowaw, shoosh, DAME, I mean tens, tens, tens times as many men in wheelchaysh or pushingsings shopping cots alongsla nica blocka th' Soufside than th' 's zew within a wawk from front to backa in any megamartsuoomahk't pharmacy du-plex, mahn, WOOO-EE-E-EEE-E."

All this through proximity they bespoke the history of the world.

William drank his beer and then there was a glass-full left in the pitcher; he poured it into his glass. Optical illusion in the gal beside him. Knew her from somewhere. Still it would never work. In a town like this no one can ever become happy.

Sideways, mispronouncing binoculars since last millennium, the student ghosts exchange Torah for *Aurora*. Chabad versus the Company. I must say me lad th' ladder looks a lot like me with stick, cloak, and virtuous detestation burning behind black sundials, giving the rat a wrong number and vanishing. O Lord, what are days? Their plays reek of odium and clink, vanish, back en route, o'erseas, toward the Land 'o Hermeticism. Wish me luckless! Good move life had cracked down into singular moments if but one could battle nauseated ruins. Prolongevity. K. Lang swallowed at his amalgamated, red-rimmed-round plastic cup.

Thin man stuck his head through the slot of an open door, screaming, "GET OUT NOWW," gargling screams through broken cigar-teeth "AH," but then those clicking heels moved, click-clack-clack-clack-clickalak-calos-dicl-click, sputtering plastic along the concrete ground sudden invisibility the bartender barged gloved hands like pliers into an auspicious junk drawer with his sweat-stained back to an alleyway where brown liquids rumbled down the road in a silent blast of glistening turbulence never to be seen again he stumbled back and knocked over a bag of groceries at once the drunken patrons leaned over the table to offer help his groceries (Three Macintosh apples, Packet of Steak-Um's, Frozen Ellio's and Tombstone Pizza ('What a name'), Two-liter of Diet7-UP, Case of Canned Ravioli, Powdered Cups of Shrimp-Soup, Four pounds of Chop-meat, several packets of chicken gizzards, gallon of Whole Milk) rolled and tumbled wrapped logs down the river while bus swung right-hand turn toward the river before a wail of horn walloped any pending silence into frenzied blast-boom of a mechanical grunt a steel groan the electric announcement of an unquestioned barge and a yellow light ahead continued, weaving and twisting what a poor position in life, she offered with her booklet of matches, what a poor position in life someone sang:

> *Give him a pipe to smoke all night,*
> *Smoke all night, smoke all night,*
> *Give him a pipe to smoke all night,*
> *My fair lady.*

Someone ran screaming down the street with a gleaming machete but by then all attention was fixed upon the food. No cigar.

A young wait Octavia was saying something about relegation, or Piccarda, I can't remember, insomniac dreams whence odd-looking type straddled himself along the bar and debated—running cable television programs with a similar-looking counterpart. Nike sneakers. Ignore them by any means necessary.

"What left is there to do, wait to get it done?"

Picket-sign: looking for signatures and then go home.

"You are a thief, a liar, unrespectable!" K. Lang approached him and spoke for the townspeople. "You are a thief, a liar!" He set his cup down and looked at William. "You are an egomaniac! A liar! You are *gay*! When I see you on your bike I throw garbage at you and call you a faggot! You are a terrible person!"

"I am?" William asked, with an inadvertent absent air. He felt confused at this sudden proclamation although he could not bring himself to feel surprised. One of the finer things in life was contempt from the pitiable; then one may be, at least, be amongst the outskirts of something good. "What ought I do to change my life?"

"It's too late! Too late!" His dull eyes reddened, his plump body quivering as if on the verge of seizure. "I've been waiting to tell you this for so long! I am a real man! This is what a real man looks like!" He made an impressive muscle with his arm and took out a knife. "I'm going to kill you!"

The bartender rushed over and took the knife away. K. Lang lunged to his stool and began to weep. D.U.I. D.O.A.

'Eternal misery longs for the destruction of light; lighted souls can never be so bothered.' In retrospect, William gathered, it made sense, had always made sense, and people were capable of very little sense. 'Worst was in that they believe the politicians and the Gods were holding them back, when in the midnight of the soul they knew they were to blame. In conclusion it is much easier to blame one's opposite than one's self. Symmetry in chaos, conformity in the abstract, disassociation in borrowed automobiles; O heavens, the symposium let out, screaming women, O but if this privilege you scream of existed you would be censored, fined, or destroyed for referring to it; you'd be committing gasp hate speech! O lassies, thou wouldst be a terrorist each! That ye and untold parrots deflect envy shortcomings hatred proves in dream tavern a supple non-existence... and what that proves, O hopeless whores, defective Aristotelian seed, is what ye face alone, that collective nightmare ye shall face in Times New Roman!'

William left the bar hobbling on invisible crutches.

He walked to the café. He sat down. He finished his coffee.

He walked through the streets of unfashionable automobiles, broken-brick stores and shops, the occasional horse and buggy, and the sun was beginning to set at last. He had remembered Abigail as he'd once forgotten her, for she had been diagnosed with schizophrenia as a teenager. This made her social recognition blasphemous although William did not care. Abigail had long since encouraged him to keep distance for the sake of his own social withstanding. Years past and she grew evermore dysfunctional. She was beautiful with beaming blue eyes and pale freckled skin and he recalled her from the old art exhibit. Once she worked at a restaurant she would always work at, where one evening she sat outside smoking alone, and William's heart-rate rose as he stepped closer to Abigail in his memory, whom now looked harrowed, older, even from the distance of life and death.

He sat down beside her. She turned his way shocked, frozen, then eased up as he smiled to her and she returned the look. They caught up, but two such minds at sunset—one drunk, another worn-out, and on a few pace-quickening drugs—tended to cut to the chase. Cutting to the chase had been the origins of their romance some summers past; an ability to lay beside one another all night long stopping sporadic words for a deeper, glorious thought which one could then toss into the tender night to retrieve at later dates. In the middle of nowhere nothing save the past and death are interesting; and as the latter is unspeakable, one who is ungrounded is thereby damned to that pathetic myth of the past.

He ran across the street to purchase pistachio ice cream and returned before her cigarette was out cold.

Pistachio Overture:

"Well, Billy, the enveloping paranoid magnitude of the street is this, if you know what I mean: You are invisible, and I am trampled beneath humanity's inconsistent consistencies."

"Let me digest that, Abigail beloved. Last saw you where, the art gallery? What a shame that was, what a shame to end all shames with shameful beginnings. You were with that strange man."

"Many strange men. And you were with what's her name."

"I was."

"Always together."

"Always."

"Like we once were."

Pause. Facial reflections in the windowpane. Pause.

"Anyways."

Her smile was bright, her mind was bright, the street hazy, and he could look nowhere but into her pale eyes, big gray clouds above moving faster as seen through building-tops and cable lines, faster thy become and into that good night, orange contours broken forth from the enraptured sky, those glittering last instances of the sun above them then, the shadows of birds beating across the scorched atlases of burgundy cement and burdensome reputations.

"But then I suppose, how are things, here? What have you been up to?"

"Oh, leaving soon. Leaving a-gain. Seen enough of those fair-weather friends."

"I like live here," Abigail replied, pointing over her exposed, freckled shoulder through the window of the restaurant. "Tonight, is a slow night." They peered into the dining area, hands cupped around one another's eyes like binoculars.

'To see how the other half lives and turn back around toward the street less disdainfully than bored with that program.'

"Where have you been applying for work?"

"Everywhere."

Gazing into the distant sunset now twinkling upon the still summer river while cinematic smoke ascended larkward. 1946 was the tone of her voice.

"Formulaic, no," she exhaled, squinting, "With age each transition— it's been years, God . . .—seems to I guess, near depths, for me, even the transitions which take a lifetime. The puzzle of this," Abigail said, outspreading her arms again toward the casino, its architectural avidity, "Life and what it ought to be, what life could be, and what life is, is no universal theory; all universalities imply impossibility. Methodological relativism is justification's milk carton bereavement. I see attributing anything with a sort of universal theorem as a base, contrived way of provoking an insatiable argument those being questioned cannot answer . . . just bitterness, I don't know, I'll stop talking, I go to school and work and feel like a drone. I never get to talk to anyone. I smoke two packs of cigarettes every day, each one a melancholic enchanted recapturing of the unknown. If they outlaw smoking I will move, yes, because sometimes you must stand up for your soul . . ."

She finished her cigarette and exhaled toward the ground with the bent lipstick-filter, blinking. Seemed to William just then as if her break was over by the way she sighed and though she'd spoken what she'd wanted to there wasn't enough time. He would need to spend more dream-time with her to absorb her mind though were he to spend more time with her there would be implications although she looked so very depressed as if awaiting to be crushed by something anything and seemed as if she may return to Art School and he hoped that she would and be glorious once again and all he could do was visit her grave and it pained him so inside.

"I'm done, I've decided, with school, also," she said.

He expelled the possibility of her return into the institution. But do angels visit persons? Or do persons—all of them who claim to have seen angels—lie?

"Tell me a nation's idea of the afterlife, and I'll to you its temporal future. Laugh it off; many long to perish laughing. But I believe it is, yes, impossible, Abigail, and pardon me if I am drunk, to decipher between a crushed ant and an assassinated president . . . and implications are not a person; the concept of matter is not matter; the backbone is not the body, so to feel incomplete without something is not to cease existence because in life deprivation and extraction are basic forms of menial puncturing; to not die is to live. The individual decides his own fate in a free society though the free society is nonexistent outside of varied basements and bedrooms of peripheral intoxication—"

"No, no," she grew excited, lighting another cigarette and stuttering through profane, mentholated smoke, "I wonder of happiness these days, don't you, I wonder why it is impossible, but Bill I know why it is impossible, because everything is momentary, fleeting," she sullen said, a gorgeous ray of sunlight reflecting off a passing cyclist's spoke which caught her cheek, soft peach-fuzz glimmering in the wee evening of worn window, apron flickering, suit jackets, everything passing through, and spectral Spring was over, their love was over, but he said nothing and she looked up at him with a mind filled with the joyous remembrance of romance past and without preconception William responded to her lips:

"Let's walk down the street, Abigail Blake, let us walk down the street today."

They stood to walk and he felt her eyes upon him, remembering him, and the couple walked to another intersection, one out of managerial sight, there then more alone, out of sight of obligatory anchorage as Abigail sat upon a circular flower pot of concrete, her soft brown hair filled with wind, tousles along her delicate shoulder and she began once more to speak her eyes widened with budding insatiable anxiety troubled, a lost look in her face, a new lostness which was everywhere and as often covered with some portable electronic device although upon acknowledgment William thought each look of finality is frail and daunting and though they hadn't spoken in years, nothing but now that exactitude could seem natural to either with all of the sky's withering-down process casting all of the shopping center land and all of the imaginations of those who walked forth upon the battered hills with white-orange rays of fleeting light and grime black puddles shining with filthy sifting rainbows wandering as if open mouthing tongues staring into pixilated sets of somersaulting photographic lenses O God Octavia please stop these dreams in waking life I've underwent since seeing Anaheim! Saint Francisco—pray for me!

"Something wretched is happening, Bill," she said, whispering, as if on the verge of tears, lighting another heartbroken cigarette, beetle buggy, lime green, to think she'd never known Anaheim—Give her the packet?—backed out of a driveway beyond her shoulder, she able then to

confess some sort of intricate catastrophe she knew no other to comprehend, "And everyone is aware of it, and at times I feel the reason Americans are not exterminated is because we haven't yet finished participating
in our own literal enslavement, our own hypnotized means to an end,
sleepwalking toward the edge of a skyscraper top, but well, I know we
once spoke of things like this, I don't know, but when the soldiers spill out
into these streets, their commanders will have announced defeat. This is
the notion I find a shred of solace within, because there will be so much
blood running through the streets in tides of screaming memories and
torn flags, at this point the soldiers will begin committing suicide at an
even vaster rate than the War on Terrorism has induced. What we're told
is alarming, those suicide-numbers, and it's not even half of the truth.
Something wretched . . . a total lostness, I see it everywhere," she said,
William transfixed within her words and the way she dragged her cigarette and batted her eyelashes.

"Do you know what I mean?" Abigail asked, looking lost into his
eyes, his heart breaking, breathing inward he pondered, sighing, with the
old wafting Camel clouds creating chemical closet dramas:

"An emotion exists," William suggested, "And in order to infiltrate
the public—though I must say that in the language game we are damned,
even a term such as 'Public' implies helplessness, foolishness, when in
reality we're talking about 99percent of the country—with a new reality,
pseudorealities must be prevalent, marketed as the way like all advertising
displayed at incomprehensible rates; you know, my dear Abigail, my lost
love, all the wars are predetermined. From oh, who knows, WWI and forward. Once you figure this out you get to the philosophy of money. Then
the dream merged with another in sleep paralysis, yearning melancholic:

'Whether or not the imagery instilled within the nationwide mind is
staged, it must be ingrained, singed, into the public mind, and the deterioration must be labeled progress. The more absurd the proposition, the
more hammering into the mind will occur.

'The image is the emotion. And the image—our generation's emotion—must be presented in a mathematical way but also a perverse way;
the image must be patterned into a flood of colorful data as to make the
individual defend not his or her self, but to defend the image-emotion.
The means by which this is done are simple:

'In order to wage a subliminal-invert global war, the enemy—the
suspect—must be all humanity. The phantom must be a tendency. The
nightmare must be bland and contradicting, for most people are bland

and contradicting and despise what they cannot understand. Terror is a human emotion. Humanity cannot win over an emotion-enemy; he can then denounce alone his own freedoms as the bitter years pass by first like nightmares, then bad trips, each one more a lie than the last. Thoreau said, "Most men lead lives of quiet desperation," but for one hellish reason or another, time won't let me."

"Agree!" Abigail shouted, glancing at her phone, "I agree!" She wrapped her arms around William, and they kissed atop the flowerpot, her denim behind upon his lap like an instance of a corkscrew. William placed his hand upon her rosy cheek: "O, I knew you when we were so young. Ghostly pale, the first to give me your body while the others were in school. You led me to the places I did go; for there is the greatest lie of all, you said, and this is one who claims that life makes sense." She pulled away, gazed into his eyes. "You've said it, you've said it you've said it," and for one moment Abigail Blake's face wore the equivalent of an entire generation's collective dropped jaw. William looked down to the surrounding garbage and flowers. Abigail pulled him back against her body against and they kissed one another in the bursting mausoleum wind.

"What are you doing after work, Abigail?"

"The town's best people are meeting for an art exhibit."

"Oh?"

"In a phone booth."

Then without further explanation she ran back up the street. William followed her to where at the doorway her manager awaited. He handed Abigail a note, refusing to look at her pained eyes any longer, and set off in the direction that held together the sun, setting beyond an old-fashioned railroad track rusted, running beneath the bridge, and the glittering waters beneath.

Abigail disappeared into the crowd. The sun went down and it felt as if the planet he stood upon were somehow behind him, charm disarmed and like a hurricane coming down side streets stepping into Blue Suede Shoes Vintage Clothing, stealing a cloak, mitre, returned outside to silence, some birds debating thrice-torn bread, Diet of Worms, and at last and in at the university library, then ahead home to rest.

"Look at thou," he spoke to his reflection; "If thou art not setting the world on fire, what art thou doing? Do ye wait for a cannonball or what, man?"

It'd been a long day in the Olde rustic town, and William longed at last for a glass of water. After that an ice-cold beer, and Shostakovich at ear-splitting volume.

"That . . . was the most insane dream I have ever had."

O Octavia, my Beatrice; without ye I am nothing... now exteriors begin to give way at last to the first and last and always, interiority.

~

But before the liquid sound and symphonic fury commenced, walking to his abode with packet in hand, William was astonished to run into the sister of the ghost, Monica, as he thought that he had sighted her through the library's polished transparent glass, but had brushed it off to poetic misremembering. Now, however, he was drawn to her, this veiled figure, magnetized by vision, guided by memories of mirrored semblance:

"Break thy vow through impulse to that world of current affairs, for they are the works and chronology of slaves and vipers, you who are condemned and saved at once.

"I was her opposite; she was, well, Abigail, and I am just a lowly vestal virgin, guarding the four-walled flame of a sacred heart on fire." She spoke to William of the archaeology of the oath out along alien streets, a crowded alleyway, and demure byways. His mind burned with the first and everlasting wisdom, the fire of love, through which he could feel that icicle that was his heart melting into resplendent mush, reminded of Octavia and the Golden Gate Bridge at sunset—*Ave Maria*, she said, and took off down the lonely path.

Anaheim's Packet,
Dedicated to William Fellows

"I CANNOT HELP BUT be haunted," William said to Monica, with whom he had caught back up, "by the fact of so many of the damned are themselves victims of violence, technological and ideological violence. Could I have once had, if not answers, then at least clues, in Plato and the Platonists? Octavia said to me it is metaphorical, this Platonic business, a bow that occasionally strikes the rim of its target. But if I always knew that the *Timaeus* would not save me, how then did it, and what does it mean to be saved? Hegel's Force, Schopenhauer's will and representation: force and will converge in sacred texts, like the flowing of a holy river."

"Sometimes a boy works on the expansion of a debased copy of the categorical imperative, William; you stand at the foot of truth in doubt."

He stood perfectly still before the nun with sparks of love in her eyes.

"I am downcast, left standing 'neath the entranceway with the warped footwear of Ignatius of Loyola or Samuel Johnson, with three dollars in my bank account, fifteen in my wallet, and three volumes of Ficino's *Platonic Theology* awaiting me at home—but now only the sight of Octavia, and the light of truth she is after, calls me the way Ficino and the rest used to do."

"You, in turning to Octavia, shall say that the things you can see have differences that do not exist, and more generally that the things that one could not see had in fact tangible differentiations, evident where such things were evidenced. For all of the life of the mind, you are guided to her body like a panged magnetic, sore and distressed, and a half-full cup at the edge of a counter in a little room on the edge of a town that has undergone the aftereffects of a little earthquake."

"So I am beginning to understand that the saintly woman's body compliments my own, and that it was right and just to join parts, achieve ecstatic union in birth, which is, well, the idea of the concept of the etymology of the word in English that is called 'life.'"

"I'm not quite sure what you mean by that. Some want Theresa of Avila alone. Others want George Eliot alone. Others still want neither. But I seek both. I am unsure what else to tell you. Also, I'm sorry to be blunt—but could you kindly donate to the Discalced Carmelite Nuns of Jerusalem?"

He smilingly found himself lost.

I.

A Poem Regarding the Psychological Effects of War on Eternal Human Emotion: Terror
Or:
Prolegomena to the Cusp of an Infinite War

> *Stripped him first of common sense*
> *Then thrust him toward the deafened trench.*
> *Load his ego with what's never been done*
> *Load his polished, sunblack gun.*
> *Whipped him till the sun shone blood*
> *Upon this throne of bone and mud.*
> *From which an aerial clarity cracks*
> *Then survive now son; the money back.*
> *Speak now of that which happens most*
> *Pale imitations prevail beyond the host.*
> *Imitations which crack the global whip*
> *Where all seems well none is equipped.*
> *Though they'll have slain the mother's child,*
> *You should have seen his brother's smile.*
> *Of oral retraction and entertainment,*
> *Amused, abused, equatorial death.*
> *Stripped them all of common sense,*
> *The sky admiring its wind chimes lent.*

∾

Two months passed into spring.

"How's the money coming along?" Ms. Fellows inquired. She was making coffee.

Before William could answer she handed him an envelope with five-hundred dollars in it:

"Anonymous contribution."

"Toward?"

William counted the money astounded and began tying his shoes.

"You getting back to California without difficulty. Your uncle helped out more than I had expected, and things are picking up at work—"

He felt sure this money had come from someone else although it may have come from Ms. Fellows and he did not long to puncture her elation.

"If you ever find out who the money came from tell them I thank them."

"But of course. Perhaps you can quit one of those jobs now. Oh, and a package came in for you." She pointed to the left-hand side of the bread-basket atop the refrigerator. A package from Phil Cohen: Pipe tobacco, corncob pipe, mixtapes and the notice to call whenever a date came about to meet in the desert. William ran downstairs and out into the streets. They hadn't looked so beautiful before.

The money was good. He cashed out his account and held onto a thousand dollars plus four hundred beneath his mattress in the room and went out and bought a nice bottle of red wine for he and his mother.

"The hilarious thing about that," El explained, "Is I'm on the web-site and if we meet that weekend, we'll make it for Hot August Nights, a hotrod show and all around bender."

"As long as you go undistracted from your work and see fruition as a possibility, even in death."

"I'm on a block O lad," El solidified. "Ye in for thee Hot August Nights?"

"Sign me up, m'boy! I'll get the ticket tonight."

"I'll look into the rental car—that'll be easy enough. Then we begin again!"

. . . return to Saturnocture. Little silver-gold medallion, working pin in place, outside of the vacated chapel: IHS. Swig.

Homeward bound.

To Saturnalia—gulp.

II.

Empty Streets

In the beginning there was the impossibility of the present moment,

the idea, and the passing facial relief maps of petulant and bewildered unhappiness.

There was the byzantine reflection, the archaic message, the secular rumination.

There was the suffocated structure of the future, the sightless end, the dissolving arrow.

He felt his fingertips press against his palms. There had been no company but broken-down moments upon reflection of which one cringed, extending his hand, to-ward his body.

In the beginning gas broke from a burner, plumed unto the decaying sky, and all of the poetry of life had admitted itself disintegrating.

She arrived on time, her headlights dim, lest commit crime, she let him in.

Shoulders to the breaking brow, they spoke of childhood and now, they spoke
laughing, of making vows, yet cried and died inside just a little.

Her quilt was ashen with the dream, that once he'd admit what he'd seen, and
with a voice of kerosene his turquoise language altogether made her ill.

She took her pill, swallowed the child, just to break his porcelain smile, the
smoking slits of which dissolved in cream.

Spring had come the winter done, the funereal bulletin begun, and all the while she played his rib-cage like the xylophone.

Mutation, quarrel, incineration, the listless psalm's pronunciation,
he would not stay nor would he go, when in the country one must know,
to break
    away from anchorage, to take the orphan from its crib, to pronounce
the spiraling wicker in one's mind.

The stage set for pronunciation, laden with an amputation, the interlocking hands broke beneath the sand of telephone wires
    and dreamt of goldmines.

She explained he may have been too young, she and her recurring
tongue;
    Conducive wands of obligation, membranes entranced by recitation,
    That same mouth had taken him in, when the winter graves would
go begin,
    To stand in meteoric eyes of death, having grown bored with ever-
lasting breath.

She explained the way the world was, knew quite a bit concerning
love, yet to the
    contrary he laid down still, the way the dispossessed must build,
upon that opaque
    bridge of bricks, an envelope dismissed, all that she could love was
what
    she'd learned of love.

And when it came she saw through windows and through rain.

(Broken Breath)

John took his blue overcoat on ; if you won't slip away then I'll dis-
miss thee.

There's men downstairs who are playing darts, exchanging bandages
and wordless art;
    The room is filled with oxygen, and when I knock they let me in.

Music passes by yourself; with a loaded shelf.

A man spoke benign of mardi-gras, pearl necklaces and bras; the wine the wine was more than fine, followed by ripe Clementines;

He saw in no one what he saw within himself.

Here one sits with diplomats, who've garnished their tonic intact, beneath metaphysicians' bulbs, the tank and bells tie belts and toll.

This one then will be on me, our allowance after-all is thee; apostrophized to

death by fire, the glory of thy tainted choir.

We thank God he had not been home, and taste his body to the bone, reseat

such mouths bursting with foam, awaken dehydrated.

Not yet, no, this goes down slow,
a life in ruins turned to cloves, of Scottish fields
and reminisce, of Forster's memorized first kiss, we take now bliss yet lean,
forget, the unvanquished corn-cob truculent.

Now what would you do for a deal, considering we ought to steal, alphabetic
delirium and ardor, preparations for the parlor—
No not I, with clinking glass, having graduated the memorizing class, having
ridden the ivy's wild ass, unknown and yet unheeding.

'She hanged herself for a thrill, having first rolled down dew-dampened hills
'And still I wish I held her in my arms.'

For what is there but bronze reflection?

Memory and symmetry?

For what is there but recollection?

The internal extinction of time, of such echoing, entranced lime, and still I say I swallow lest ye candle light.

Empty your pockets, William:
Morals, said the Rimbaud of Jerusalem, Are for cannibals.
Ballardian, summer cannibals.
Amen I say to you Amen.

O and now you look my way, having dampened such a day, we leave here for home in disarray, and that is all that matters

The psychological apocalypse, perfection, bereavement unto disconnection.

(The Foreshadowing of a Lucid Dream)

You, there, with the rich father. You, there, with whom no one bothers.

You, there, you're pretty. You, there, you'll buy the city.

You, there, in pre-torn clothes. You, there, blowing your nose.

You, there, your father's land. You, there, with vein-wrapped glands.

You, there, amidst the voices. You, there, curmudgeons moisten.

You, there, laid light tonal. You, there, another photo.

You, there, with paper eyes. You, there, he mimicries.

You, there, you're just like her. You, there, your life's a blur.

You, there, with abstract money. You, there, a taste of honey.

You, there, with self-images. You there, crusading pillages.

Have you not seen what I have seen? Are you prone to dissect a dream? Are you the blinds upon the windowpanes? Are you, there, deranged? Absence is such the crumpled gallows, we elevate yet still prove shallow, regurgitating bones of burning marrow, take my hands straight as an arrow.

> Alms for oblivion, Good Miss
> Now just connect, then reminisce!
> Hollow is her name,
> Now what follows is a film:

> > You dislike popular films you say,
> > You speak in weak ironic ways,
> > I lay you at the close of day,
> > You're more depressed than a dead body.

> > The atheists turn the burning wheel,
> > Within which nothing's found concealed,

> > Projections of heretical sleep,
> > Your martyred direction retreats,

> > Saturnalia, psilocybin, disassociation.

~

He hung up his suit jacket and stopped for the last time into the public library. He gathered philosophical, theological, critical, neurophysiological, historical, and poetic texts. He flipped through the hackneyed pages as children read multicolored golden-brimmed books with their mothers in the quiet Friday evening as sunlight came in through the large windows. He observed the old whiskered men in bifocals reading crumpled newspapers over crossed tweed legs, black socks interwoven with faint patterns of roses; financial pallbearers lined amidst the asthmatic dust of answering machines; terminal pathology, and away, to San

Francisco in troubled times; to work little but on that which is one's own, in the gilded hour of revelry and ecstasy.

Complexities of the future bound by curiosity, wisdom, depression, fate; such complexities he could call his own.

Signification: Impulsivity, feverish rationality.

He returned his attention to the table. Ralph Waldo Emerson, page something or another:

'All diseases run into one; old age.'

He could feel the air enter his nostrils, his brain and his lungs. His heart skipped a beat; he felt it, and again. He thought of breathing. He set his face into his palms and breathed deep, swallowing, looking to the back of his eyelids. He grew conscious of the tongue gyrating within his mouth. He felt terror until he asked upon what grounds.

He knew there was an answer, accepted himself, and then understood the answer:

Heightened consciousness may well be feared in our human complexity of melancholic opposites.

~

III.

Between Mothlight and the Others
(As Gomorrah Fell, They Longed to Rape Angels)

I must say, he says, it's been awhile, and all of our neighbors are growing furious as they start packing.

Do you consider moving on, ever, perhaps at breakfast?

No, no, says the next man, for whom am I appointed but to I?

'Take the sequences down by heart, we'll ridicule the lesser art, we'll scorch the falsest seminars, we'll admit the boredom of the stars, and yet the universe resembles the brain cell.'

Having a drink with you, I may not show, but that's because I know you know I couldn't fathom any better.

Dying, that one says absorbing darkened rum, what does it mean?

One man turns and roars with laughter: 'The truth was that he's what we're after.'

Reality, he smiled; O that myth!

One woman held her finest specimens to the disco-light,
Human molars in delight,
He let her vocal chords take flight and for a moment all were one.

There's far more to this and that you know, yet it's at times difficult to show, the way I feel when I'm walking down the street, those corners at which I'd once retreat, but yet to what, and so through tears why, why turn away?

Something someone else might say, their lips and linens made of clay, and still we go on disenchanted.

He's saying through blown-out candle smoke something profound, his eyes and mouth are circling round, swallowing the world whole through sound, the sound of whims far less profound than our chicken with its head cut off.

Oh but now I see
It's coming through

There's a loft he's got for me and you

Forty others meet us there
It's best to arrive unprepared

In so we are surviving.

IV. SYMPHONY OF THE NIHILISTS

Yet in this retired café
There is a constant path, burning,
Just before autumnal parks.
Surrounded by cheap wreaths and
Broken blue smoke rings twisting.
Outside the rain is gentle, harmless
The sunlight unlatches its belt
And another lover looks him-her in
The eyes beyond bullet-proof glass:
Elevator avoiding her jaw
Him, her, I hate him, her
And I am off, or in, as you will,
Without traced choices

Echoes of Life

(No more Death)
You know him, her, you hate them
When the cardboard lives cave in—
Now cancel thine forbidden mouths.

II.
Using the looking-glass reflexivity
To his advantage, another Red Man
Hits the floor, curling his dampened toes.
Another bridesmaid hits the deck
And the front-page news is of cold
Nuclear concern once more: She, he,
The agony of Hollywood, sheds four pounds, kids;
The propagandists slit their throats at once with keys,
Claiming too late they knew not what they did.
Journalists arrive with razor-wire and teeth
Flash bulbs: sky rocketing ecstasy—
Down into Hell—
Below the miner in the mirror
Strikes something undeniable;
Tomorrow morning comes around
Well-worn rope, well cut dope, well one hopes:
The noose torn in two
We start anew.
Now take my arm, and since it's you

And since I've not seen you in so long
'Before this then?'
You sung her song.

III.

Gas-blue smoke floods the room
A deli man picks at newspaper
Cinnamon toothpick, checking
His rusted watch frozen in time as
His ice cube is melting a throbbing telephone
Screams theory and bloody murder until
The welcome sign flips its face.

We leave.

IV.

Dream fragments connect.
That ancient chandelier sways beyond stained
Glass symbolism window and then the
Yellow explosion reads the final diary
Entry of another lover I'd known and
Danced with before her existent tears
Were apprehensible, she whispered,
'Sálvese quien pueda,'
Out of boredom,
Everybody cries.
And thus the sky, soaring,
Becomes all the more boring.

V.

Tip of the iceberg—online, reincarnated
There is so much more in yr eyes of angel,
But no, it is nothing, there is nothing but the

Text me

'So much more beyond grave's recognition
'Reconciling in the stream of cosmopolitan presence!'

Yes, I love you, yes, it's the weekend, yes you're a very smart girl
With your framed degree and locked-up gown
How men must pluck at your mind like it's a flower
And how your mother must cry across the country.

Hand in hand, found amidst tremendous strobe twilight
Ecstatic nativity of lights in skyscrapers covered
By the invisible tears of imported window washers
The angular chrome came through your pillar legs
As the limp rag grins at concrete lamps soundless,
Deafened, the dozens strutting 'round, complexities
Upon a dead-end street, cradled, connection, construction
Of nothing whatsoever;
Now the concrete mends its surgical tires
Behind he, before she, rectangular voices
Of anchorage, of amputees, of the illuminated city
At dawn, behind me, the waitresses' daughter nibbles
Egg, milky, Caribbean archives?
Cerebral, well,
Triplet, well?

O, then we upon the oak weep vivacious,
Because you insist life is tragic
And I insist you've heard that elsewhere,

As I swallow the world whole through language.

VI.
And all of the photogenic questions begged
To taunted avail in tormented years
Your veil was at once stiff with tears
Ashen fixtures in the closet
'They are hiring minimum wage;'

Bent backward observing, listening,
In a crowded street, spray painted:
Paradise.

You break away discreetly; I listen to the foghorn.

VII.
The architectural hangmen step out with scotch glasses
For a curtsy, beyond the red velvet curtain
That marvelous play thus far, tragic,

For friendship is a trapeze act, lost in
The future, the ship in its bottle—message to
Infinite sea, content, Atlantis shrugs, Atlas twists
With broken shoulders—And yet once I was so humble—

She took speed and spilt rye on my fresh chess board
Hath the bitch no manners after dawn?

Grand buildings spilling open with vomit
Grand Street department stores, crawl out of student loans,
Crawl through the wreckage,
Architects of the flesh, the city unreal
Youth, Youth, Youth
A short-term goal, Melville's beard
Milton in a corduroy handbag
Vomit spills from the window-panes
"Reveal thy dreams truth"
Insanity sits still, peanut-elephant brushes
I tell you in tidal waves, here me now, mental vomit
Brain City
Vomit breaks in seas from the bridges
Against the fears of a clouded crowd
Shape and size in time and style;
We're walking now in horror.

Get thy martyred bearings:
Proper manners from thy delinquent arms!

For once we loved, now we mourn, as
Living isn't so difficult, wide-eyed
The long term nocturnal, tonight

And tonight by skylight, longing
Proselytized high hopes, thronging
Yet you see it on the horizon now you know it to be true
To have prosthetic eye, cosmological keg,
And still to uproot gods by their cork-legs,
For tonight alone shall not perish but survive.
And when I speak your name I know I am alive.

VIII.
We arrive in rags
Looking high and high (And high)
Lend me your cannonball
And I'll walk across Rome
Finding some suite to call home.

Teach me how to cook and sing
At once our lives will be intact

Tugboat turns, of events, make
Ambience out of the teenage spine, savage
Tipping over of the hour glass hollow, hate
"Laden, longing, mauled, chain-reaction," illusory

High and high, like a film

She was a queen when she swallowed manners
He was killed when he told the truth
She was righteous to have attended the viewing
He was insane to have denounced the noose
She was a nightingale who tied him loose.

High and

To sit on your bed while we rob
The bank of Earth, in love,
The ocean beyond, lust swallowed whole, again, we arrive in
gold.

IX.
We can hear them on the ceiling and
If we don't share this can we, may we, tell the truth.

My false gesture:

The nitrous skylight is born
Candy cigarettes evaporate
Save chest pains for the comedic
Woes we'll transplant into song
Sung,

In our rags,
Short little numbers,
The violin swallows its seismic ankle

We still despise the dreaming moon,
The appearance of several guillotines;
Encore, encore, Bay Bridge; stoned.

The drunk stands still.

X.
Still

The wicker cradles creak,
The street-sweeper sifts

Still

Cremated, joyous affair
All I'll never know for now

Still

Realizations, tile floors,
Seas of voices, tours of hallways
Realizations, tile floors

Still

World standing still
Creaking toward past
Hydrogen errors revisited
The look in their fatal, final eyes as they walk across the bridge,
Gasp of breath, foreign tones

And we must live before we die.

Still

Hallelujah, Hallelujah sings the choir of Catholic youth

Still

Silent hallways, the dresser drawers of America

Still

Hidden beneath countless library counter-tops, silent marble,
go down,
Bags of heroin, burning bushes, gadgetry, inception

Still

There are no nations, only saints and poets

You explained so without precision in our drunken hour;
Don't give me your body
till we're far away from the concept-world.

Still

So let us stay drunk forever, and let old age jump into the fire,
longing,
Still—for you,
'O muse.'

Still.

Yet you, yet you, you're going to sing now aren't you
Beautiful genius, beautiful genius

XI.
Drawer split wide open
Splintered cigars on fire
Vacuum cleaner, pop-culture
Sucking contagious mind ash
From beneath the noble chair
For the land of the free and the home of the brave
Can a mirror get out of bed?

Every so often.
Another Whitman aesthete
Slips between the sheets
Beneath this relayed head, head.
We've got no other option.
Three dozen recognitions and still
I feel more ill than I did in the future

Now let me explain, let me explain
My emotional life stands somewhere
Far away in the nearest coliseum.
So kiss me before we consider such gates of freedom.

XII.
Having dubbed the language opposition as
"Far too many breaths,"
And you consider yourselves
O, the sorrows of gin?
No, Floyd, she's sort of joking—

Oh now I didn't know that you quit smoking—
The colossal vibration composed of automatic doors
Tonight's special is murdered whores
Pregnant tellers in aborted banks
Ventriloquist digital fascism
And yet you still beg for convenience

For you are I:
You hollow men, you women,
You drive your cars and speak of linens
You eat chicken bones and speak of cancer
And your foggy eyes contain no answer
Status, status, that's the word
Ignore all else that you have heard
And take those knives out of your ears
Eternity's piggish nuns adhere.

Sit down my love, sit down there,
And please stop reaching for my hair
It's not my hair? Then oh, my mind?
You know we always make the train on time.
Some people don't mind discussing the weather,
One hundred voices crash together.

Then the fat, oil-faced jester
Speaking televised tongues will cease speaking

Nobody cracks a smile in such demise
Of ancient tradition, of asshole stench
The kitchen clacks with glassware

"I will blind your ignorance with visions of no man's land
strung out in electric chairs," said the last genius who had chosen to sit right there.
"Do not attempt getting in touch I am in touch with synchronicities indescribable."

She spoke of him whence we gasped for air.
And while capitalist conversion is considered freedom
Such bodies of legs of feet of boots coming in the exit door
Curse it broken and stuck, with nocturnal feet arranged upon
the floor.
We hold rooftop hands; for this world, too, shall terminate.

V. EPITAPH

Tiptoeing out of Hell
Shrouds of Earth break
In the fierce winds of
Funeral homes and
Of sullen clocks of autumnal wiry hands

Looking back on the
Thousands of days
He, she having escaped thus far
(Chords and hands excluded)
Christ cannot contain me
Satan cannot contain me
Playing with fire, young renegades
Without a prayer left, saved
Ancient knees and nobody thoughts,
Whereupon what body derived of
Water and what paths you've
Not laid even eyes upon we have
Leaped through, memorized,
From creaking towpath
To creaking towpath, beyond splintered woe
Cramming notions into gambling
Minds of old and new alike
Let us congregate in and out of dreams
Within the gilded slots of distinct reason
Jammed machinery, echoing into the Void
                        Final

                Final

                Final:

Upon this fragmented isle
Of broken-glass clay
Nihilism sways forth by night
Dementia settles in by day.

A multitude of one man
Spits forth from Brooklyn Bridge
The last ember of his dream
Composed of plain cartilage.

The silence of dawn fell forth
From the sky like lukewarm pantheists
Whence his pale hands shook
The blackened world's last psalm.

The winter wind of the sea drove
He and another out of Hell, and into
Litmus inauguration; dreamt elbows
Upon the oak of an ashen generation.

Within the burning field of years the
Guillotine retrieves its corporeal tier
Which swaying commands the innocent
Mind, Metropolitan Avenue, crystal clear.

"The night is a room with smoke in the air.
The day is the way that she unties her hair."

Don Guy having stepped from Purgatory:
Melancholia, last night's theorem; midnight
Mass, his prostitute having witnessed skyscrapers
Implode then into rustic sight.

We stand together at dawn, our bodies gone,
Battle-lines drawn, the Bridge of song,
O Brooklyn spleen
Here, now within the city as one can love
None in the city none but the city loveless
Brooklyn spleen
There was the world, which went blackout West
Brooklyn spleen
Our images like boulders falling from some mountain,
As water breaks from your fountain,
The river runs, past Houston.

CODA

His name was Vishnu Donatello
He had a friend named William Fellows
Read everything & thrice Othello
Some called him a thief and liar
In bad humor, through mouths far drier

Than the dull Atlantic, the frivolous sky
And he made it out his way while
The catatonic world died.
If you look closely it's a love story,
To save my life I had to bore thee.

Invisible Ships

FOR ONE WHO HAD so often lamented the death of literary culture in America, William knew not what to do with this long poem a friend of his had penned. At the very least, it seemed wise to visit Anaheim, poem in hand, even if just to begin with "I have just finished reading it." The thousand splendors of Augustinian immutability in light of illusory prospects of meaningless fame and subjectively linguistic power instilled within the one who had for so long sought to unpack their conditions; but now a seed had been planted within him whereby he came to know that persons sought neither to be understood, diagnosed, nor spoken on behalf of, unless it entailed political religion; his little soul, and its vague musings in a journalism of integrity and truth, gave way to the peace of understanding the misunderstood: that he could not even speak on behalf of his own heart, let alone the world's: let me know myself, yea, as war rages onward across the splintery globe.

But when he arrived at the old home he and Nielsen had spent so many hysterical evenings in the recent past, the house was vacant and up for sale.

Snow came down at sunset now in a blanketing stream of eternal light, uplifting the spirit, the freedom of the will and the trove of good-ness, and bitterness fell from his soul like an archaic rite or language. Now one could walk with a headful of poetry through the cosmos, as one who loves art loves life, and the other types of persons do not even exist. The pilgrim stopped to pet the last Kantian in town, a dog named Bobby, glancing at inquired by its owner of the crimes of lukewarm leaders.

"These are not men but silly sheep, poisoned with appetites for the mind-rotting distraction and hatred of poetry," said William. "I have no television set, nor computer, and I thank God every day the screen on my phone sits at the bottom of the riverrun, past Eve's Pet Shop and Adam's Tavern. God bless your dog, the last Kantian of Jerusalem."

From there he ran into a new parish priest at the nearby Catholic Church, out shoveling snow over a cigar.

"You read the blessed, and follow Thomas Aquinas to begin, as the saints are linked in ways to God: do not go venerating or conflating them, as you would not settle for a millimeter of the hair of my head were you expecting my entire person to arrive, now would you?"

This is our station in the sphere of technological slavery, thought William, that we move from Machiavellian moments into an unfolding of Absolute Knowing.

A Congregation of Hypocrites

HE KNEW CONSCIOUSNESS OF such equations could deliver him beyond fear and trembling and felt mechanical agony corrode within his heart ambling one last time through the sliding doors.

Who was that little cross-eyed librarian who'd never look his way, William wondered. He had seen her for years with her photocopied William Butler Yeats passages extending from her linoleum purse and she would never look his way each time he stopped to think and scratch his head of greasy golden blonde hair.

What did she think of the city? What did she think of the surveillance camera dangling before the children's room dangling before the entranceway's rubber strip of walkway?

Pretty young women laughed upon the ledge. He'd known either one amidst varied circumstances years ago. Troubled childhoods. Laughter through smoke. He longed to approach them and bid farewell but he had already done so at separate sunsets long ago. Rippling ponds, pennies tossed within Chinese garden. Trees, blossoming, October in Vermont.

They walked by and bid farewell to another young man. Behind them the automobiles continued across the bridge from stop light to stop sign to car-lot to storefront to driveway to garage. Distant mountaintops. We speak of that which we ought to shout because in the cells of our tinny-tin hearts we know too well we've got everything dread wrong was the look of her downcast eyes as she walked through to Moravian College campus.

They passed at the crosswalk: "Hyperbolicsyllabicsesquedalymistic" playing from loudspeakers o'erhead; in pursuit of the white whale. Cultural sterility. The blood of whales, they looked away. City Hall spills suntan lotion to the cracked concrete.

Bowties, tailored suits, glossy cigars, harpsichords, observing an old photograph alone in the afternoon the beautiful melancholia of that which is unlike anything else. Not registered to vote. Bandaged finger. Mobile updates from death beds. Whipping the wounded; vacant, answerless looks. Where have you been? I missed you although I would never like to see you again. Anyway let me say that I miss you because it is expected of me but in the deepest part of our souls we despise one another (Words within an anguished first); few people have much in common I consider as you dissolve into the unfathomable night. And what was your name? So much so the search engine intercepting thought, double, replay, so as nothing is to remain retained any longer. Cannot depend on yourself; unfashionable. Cannot consider yourself; selfish boy. Cannot have faith in yourself; jugular atheism. Cannot jump ship; monomaniacal mouths. Cannot breathe; megalomaniac's kiss.

Up this street, have forgotten all the street names so well. Saw in documentary years ago, no, it was a foreign film, the old barns from World War II filled with hair. The Room of Hair.

Hologram, presentation, proliferation. Left, rather. Every town is the same: Familiarity. Every city is different although few are admirable enough to encompass that eternal unfamiliarity, inquisition. Everyday people. Brown paper bag and the sun.

Syntax: myriad. Rook, king, premeditative extinguishing, implicative, coming first, who came, the question the answer. Someone came first. Four librarians. Merry spinsters. Still never compliment me on my books. What does it take?

Creaking stools, long picnic blankets blue and white, and wrapped-up rectangles barcode.

"Marianne," one pouted.

She was the young cross-eyed woman.

"Call storage at once."

"Yes," she held the phone to her breast with a smile.

A creaking voice said: "Excuse me."

The bags beneath his eyes, he found, added a sort of adulterous touch to his youthful face. His outfit was in place. His hunting boots fit well. Across surfaces that one could describe voices with. Through lead grates in the gravel ground a cracked compass from specific clockwise angles—Sundial. He'd seen something like it on Lorimer Street outside of the café with an old-fashioned typewriter in the window.

"Betrayal is a fine champagne," the plump man boasted to the girls looking skyward through the citadel. Rome. Romeo. Cell. Cellular. Acropolis. "And pride was his vice, you see, and pride is a worthless lifestyle, girls. I never understood people who claim to be proud all the time; they're often the very people waiting like jackals for the opportune moment to jam their stinking opinions down your throat. Ha-ha-ha-ha! Where is he now? I must be nicer! New Year's Resolution—Broome Street to be kinder! 11:37 AM January 1 2011."

"Dead, I believe—dead in one form or another."

He rubbed at his temples and thought again to the old café. Years ago. That downcast stretch he could recall arguing with Octavia Savonarola. That was it. He disliked the café. Smoking was so bad that now everyone sat with glowing apples in their eyes. This was something? What sort of something? New art scene: Polaroid of a baby carriage. Don't kill lungs; kill mind.

Of what rules, ye Bard, doth vision sunder itself from an eternal prolegomenon to any future acceleration, and why is ye G train running so off-kilter?

Flaccid air, sexless starvation, metaphysical minivan mothers, fathers of the future unite and go home to Trenton. The drugs the taste buds fade away and everyone just begins swallowing. Thy kingdom come thy will be done. Expectancies of loss, longings for the anticlimax. Thoughts like ash, drifting against the latched window before the television fireplace. Our secret fence, slanted neon, through the pathway unto the cafeteria. Glossy oak. I remember you.

Wind chimes for sale, half off; tis the problem with being born, nay, anguish of anxiety as she returned the blows by walking through the streets.

"The sign of a true hero—"

Through bushel extended the Chinese garden, pale pebbles and benches of Plexiglas, slowed down by serendipitous streams of laugher, who spoke of The Wild One, the Algerian Civil War, The Idiot—And to just watch the rain pelt. They put him on suntan lotion mailing list.

All at once it all made sense, that nothing made any sense. Both sides of the equation, the country, seemed loathsome just for an amalgamated moment:

Though it read otherwise in Greek, Socrates was known today for saying 'The unexamined life is not worth living.'

William shuddered with a chill, as the thought formed:

'Socrates means nothing now, for I know too well that life without Christ is not worth living. That is the truth., that is my way of life.'

Cartesian machine malfunction. Give me to drink. Next.

Public Assembly Warehouse is hiring. Who cares? Blow the place to smithereens.

"Had a relative who made both the mallets and the wigs; you bet your ass I've got a clean record!"

"I have no idea how they got my e-mail address," she explained. "Clever, send me digital junk mail all day long. Suppose they'll remove me if I ask. Just too lazy. I can dream, can't I? Good karma, by God, good karma."

"We open it this Friday—First Friday. A new restaurant is opening also!"

"Mexican place. Danny Trippet. Owns that other one on the South Side. Ate there once. Alright, I guess. Pricey. Service awful. Should have stayed home. Durn-it. Well at first it wasn't too awful. Music was too loud. Charged for chips and salsa. Thought that was in Manhattan. Hur-hur. Durn-it."

He cracked his knuckles.

~

Also transpiring amidst the local chaos were reports coming out that a dozen local businessowners and academics were suspected of running a terrible web of political collaboration and embezzling, as well as admissions scandals, in addition to sexual engagements of the most extreme, inhuman kind. That it all came crashing down at once gave credence to theorists who suspected more than occasionally that power was obtained less through good fortune and ethics than subjugation and blackmail, either end of the spectrum fueled by surreal acts of genealogical money laundering. For the time being it brought the townsfolk together: the ones who despised academics and liberals all along, and also those progressive investors were not above taking part in a primal game of cops and robbers. A number of the names were familiar to William: R.X. Cornvoid, Muffy Ouch, Hooker Priestly, and Tyrone Pudendorf were names that he recalled, if he could not quite put a face to. One of the non-academics a local café owner named Justin Milk was supposedly on the run.

The pilgrim was out taking a morning stroll with coffee, contemplating a three-act play on the affair, when a particularly drunken professor, who emerged from a dirt path beneath an old barn George Washington had once slept in and some fenced off, sacred plumes, whom everyone in the town despises but apparently put up with because he 'had connections', crawled out from the wreckage, catching his breath on a bench.

"It's me, Prof. Mahler. Early's son—no, I'm trans. How dare you— well, I'll get back to that, and how absolutely dare you—but how then do we get the police force to turn against them, when we have been publicly despising the police all our lives? What? Who does he think he is, Justinian?"

For all their talk about Roman history, William observed, they fail to comprehend that history is fiction in so much as philosophy is a literary genre. You have your standards, he longed to say to them, your sacrosanct politics, your transubstantial propaganda—I give you that.

"You're like my brother, Pallas; I need the ride *immediately*. I've been sleeping under a barn all night, don't tell me how it's tough! But he's dead, and so too are your minds! You get me out of here or my beloved mother will die from sorrow!"

Now I know how Satan felt, how Lucifer felt, how Milton felt writing it down: you people drive one to it. Behold, behold: what is sovereignty? Is sovereign a matter of making the exception?

"I'm offering twenty dollars to whomsoever can play a song for me in my melancholic hour, it is called "Lucretia, My Reflection." Yes, I'm drunk, thank you for asking. Thank you for acknowledging my fame and contributions . . . but this yellow-orange liquid within this glass has convinced me to willingly embalm that fame. You don't understand me? If you do not understand a man at his most dense, you don't deserve his clarity," said Professor Early's son.

Fame—even local fame—like a constitution, is an indication. Borne of extremity, it can at best offer indication amidst the tide of whatever causal extremity comes next. The Rhone is a line, like quarantine.

"Ptolemy it all to Heaven. Brutus and Cassius art exhibit—get me a cab there, I have $500.00 on me right now."

William had seen enough. But before he turned homeward bound with his coffee he pondered if the Zodiac had indeed become a watering hole for fascists, like he'd heard somewhere. Fried food and cigarette smoke at nine in the morning; he tilted his ear to the hole in the door instead of stepping inside.

"But more disgusting still are the types of people who must make illegal simply telling the truth about them; such is the hallmark of genetic shipwreck. It's scattered all through that long novel called history, cockroaches occasionally demanding that home-builders understand them, tolerate them, celebrate their creativity and inventiveness . . . meanwhile they erode the pipes, the walls, the cabinets, and are worse still disgusting to look at. Damn you all, I've had enough of this whiskey, laugh at me, berate me, do as you will—but vengeance is the Lord's! And you do not hate me; you hate reality!"

"No, sir—we hate that you are saying this crazy stuff in front of us. We hate your hate speech. Bring your bigotry elsewhere. If you want to watch the news, have rum with breakfast, and stay peacefully, you're welcome. But otherwise you've got to go, man. Goodbye!"

I should not be surprised, thought William. The writing was on the wall. When one has moved from genuine astonishment to having to constantly pretend one is astonished, one is in a lonely place; one is duped. I wheel myself one last time westward, in order to ensure mutual excavation—the little planet with its two little cities, one for man and one for God—well, now you see the yellow lilies bloom out in the world, while in the screen-world it'll be time to vote before you know it, voting as Americans do for sodomy and infanticide on the one hand, usury on the other.

But then he received checking his email at Jerusalem Library a message from Octavia:

'O Romeo! Poor boy, my pilgrim, traversing the rubble of character and fate; lend me your hand and I'll be your pickaxe.'

∽

Later that day William returned to the Zodiac to see if this Oswald Mosley live program was literally running from sunrise into midnight. But when he arrived it was another scene entirely.

"What are you," one woman began beside him, ashing her cigarette on the warped tile floor. William looked up and was surprised to notice the face; he further noticed her words no longer carried any sort of structuralized artistic compound; such passion she had once given off seemed absorbed by the bruises on her arms and face. It was late in the evening when he ran into Carson. Her pale cheek was swollen. Carson, meanwhile, staggered ahead as if possessed captain leading his last two confidantes to an unbeknownst plank. He had developed a mechanical limp and torn bits of his leather jacket—sliced in reedy portions as if with razor-wire, splotched with brief collages of worn-out paint.

"Take no prisoner," he mumbled through the dissolving embers of a cigarette before replacing it with a fragmented roach. He lit the roach and for a moment William heard his lips burning. Carson removed a magnifying glass from the inside of his jacket and exhaling, looked up at William through it, enlarging his glazed, widened eyes of blood.

"Aha! Mother—I went we—California—No, an apartment, this I have now and what I'm doing—Ah! You look handsome. Well, we're just visiting. No home but here and there," and for a few blocks carried on this way, coinciding drugged utterances with palpated answers to questions he would have enjoyed William to ask him if William could find the thing to say. Carson scaled the edge of the bridge and jogged across the steel barricade.

The girl swayed about the sidewalk giggling. William realized in an instant that Carson could not speak of the future. It was the look in eyes through magnifying glass, or the violence with which he inhaled smoke, that made all this clear.

"Bep!" Carson yelled through cupped hands, wrapping his arm around his girlfriend, "And then, then, we, he, ha, yes! Yes! Can we, now no? My brother shipped out to Afghanistan yesterday. Call him later."

At that very moment the night encapsulated the sky and the street save one lost child had halted any, all potential activity. Lights lit up within nameless buildings and whispers of a holographic chain-link fence for a holographic concert followed suit.

"What are you doing?" Moll Flanders asked him. She was unable to conceal her pathetic, raspy laughter while ahead Carson whistled Tombstone Blues, running his scarred hand along the torn black gate of the towering, abandoned asylum.

"I work too much," he said. "Work, work too much. Where can I get weed?"

"Has to happen sometime, I mean we've all got to work a lot at some point. The longer you try to escape it the worse it will be in the end," she began in voice less constructed of human thought but rather from pushing a button on an automated machine constructed by her boyfriend. Before William could say anything, she continued, "Do you work tonight?" He felt as if he were being dragged through some ominous Day of the Dead ritual, and that the nightmare would not cease.

"No," with immediate regret.

Carson shot his face around once more; within his pointed head a fire raged out of control. He wiped hair from his eyes and said, "Then you're in luck; we can go have a drink and see old friends and talk and yes, tired, no, that time we, then, a mime show in Philadelphia," and he collapsed into a bad cough.

He regained his composure upon the ledge, his girlfriend massaging him. "Come on with us, to the bar! We have an all-star lineup, William, you see: Failed artists, prude sex columnists, trust-fund types, and attractive fashion-majors that you know make for good company in the sense that we can learn firsthand the way on how not to live or think, and perhaps a one-night stand and free drinks in a celebration in this big, this big mask! The mask of celebration! By reuniting in we will be escaping the void!"

"Get away from these people," William thought to himself. "Mind not the times but the eternities! Die rather Soon, soon. I am no longer angry but saddened and still I long to be free, set in flight once again."

William longed to see his old friend have a complete nervous breakdown, perhaps get laid, and could keep his fingers crossed that Carson's girlfriend would stop talking.

He knew it best to go home, rest, but an unidentifiable pressure Carson brought with him everywhere had its hold on William, and through a large open window he recognized familiar faces, adjacent chairs and did not know quite what to think, for by then the man who'd led him here could no longer talk at all.

The glasses shone beneath fluorescent lightbulbs glittering liquid, flickering metallic frames inexpensive food inexpensive quality for ex-lovers revisiting Darwin, here were a few. 89 total that night he realized; three arrived.

The preliminaries: Weather ambiguous organs touching sacred in an imagined world such as the actual think about flirting but not yet until the second or third rum. This one loves making out; what else, though? Doth she seeketh a family? There is no road, but I seek to dispense my seed, shake sweaty hands, smiling flushed faces, and return to Sir Thomas Browne and wine. Excuse me while I kidnap the sky! With such a pagan whore? For the greater glory of God, she must repent! Nothing is new is a matter of momentary agony never the past actualized. She was saying all these things everyone had heard before. Columnist spoke out of line concerning a dull city she felt isolated enough to call her own. Everyone in her car later we'll drive to the river and strip. Forgot those two still dislike one another. She & I. Rather have them detract. Negative people. Update through phone expelling into the database of the world the minute chemical details and textures of lipstick past. Bodies falling blind through the solitary familiarity that would allow them in. O how magnificent they all were then a passing group. Ethereal. Pregnant with fatherless child, overweight to the point of another outbroken plague, death of brain, had to shed laughter beneath the dim disdain of a shuttering bulb I know yes my God right he said that to me to you were there well of course it was my he was always like that I hate him he isn't that bad you knew him too right what have you been of right I forgot here try this it's not bad yeah it's alright summer is here it feels good to be home is boring but everything is oh my God boring wait what did he say nothing look at you strange joke yes in the trunk of my car strange sense of humor you look well enough to ignore awakened already then next morning alas tomorrow mother down the hall dislikes when he comes over so we've been going but now how are you need batteries for camera update laughter update tell all the world everything at once tell all the world nothing each molecular breakdown prompting forth another much more singular moment like vomitous ponds pouring through the well of clattered health those languages that beggar-remoteness of their lives don't mind him things have gotten much better he always does this did you hear that history teacher died another caught amidst adolescent bodies of the adolescent hands he once shook hello read about it in the newspaper grandmother then arrested for standing at one place in the street too where right there on Main Street long what a shame the policemen carry guns with them at all times that does things to a collective frail nervous system to begin with but right already getting excited the revolution will not be sober and taking on the world let's wait until midnight for that any plans to return well perhaps the problem was that my ex-boyfriend took me to a party yes sure get another one night when earlier in the day it's good it's fun you should come down more often he was having sex with her on the couch that I sat on all night terrible shameful grotesque ironic apologize well of course I slapped him in the face when he cried I don't believe in pacifist culture human animals deserve a good smack sometimes if they never get smacked they cannot comprehend pain conciliatory pain which is the theoretical Janus of pleasure which cannot exist without its opposite pain ever think about that how something cannot exist without its opposite that's what our generation never seemed to know poof and it's gone like a photographed birthday cake candle so sad safest word choices reorganized the banter-nell docks as dismantled compasses thrashed at the last breaking switch of the program the channel something strange about him tonight stranger than usual tell now that he's gone what happened to your

eye what happened to your innocence what happened to your dreams of
life and art and reconsidering acquittals because it takes one to know one
now that's something for a photograph them there photographs with telephones send them through computers presenting ourselves in thousands
of collected images unconscious pre-language Maritain responding to the
terrifying void which prompts such avalanches wish he was him there
drilling a hole into the wall squint of the eyes fixated on solving the pearl
necklace curved along the exposed top of her chest her eyes then would
always remain within his memory though he wanted to weep instead her
battery died and high that song spun by heart and such of the moment
reflecting aloud with the melancholic types who unbuckled their belts just
once upon a time though it wasn't such as such films then melancholic
shades of phosphorescent seasons whence que salgan a la que siguió mu-
riendo como los aviones forjado luchando en el cielo nocturno del verano
tragar vidrio humo inhalantes flickering light streamed down with time
money thrown against a dampened table-top she like a leech biting a nail
thinking somehow cannot present myself false shall not present myself
at all he went for a long walk last year and came back sound that prurient mind within precious-trotting head left money on the counter and
he came back drugged as for once for all for the gates of freedom he approached through a rich sifting cloud of smoke he looked upstairs ill as he
raised a paltry, concealed glass.

"We must talk, now," enticed TPSC, looking into William's eyes.
"Why are you not on Facebook?"

"I consider myself well beyond it and consider few of the living de-
served of my day to day life, if anyone," he announced, contemplating
further arrogance. "I consider myself superior to the idea. Nay, consider;
I live it. I am that I was, and I was below, as shall be above, come future.
O my little bird, abracadabra, come experience this liberating servitude.
Thy vagina is good because it is so rare! It is not a conscious decision!
When I contemplate such a way of life, I find myself unable to indulge.
Did you not say you'd buy me a drink? Irish whiskey. Could you lend me
ten dollars?"

Inferior: Genius as novelty-item.

Attempt: Deconstruction, *finis*.

William, as the night was well underway, leaned in to kiss a former
lover on her rose-petal lips.

Out of the corner of his eye he noticed a single hand raised high in the
air which shone the way a guillotine's blade shines just before it falls. In that

very second of inebriation he looked into the eyes of his old friend who sat before him whom with he had been discussing a good number of things:

First, he noticed her dropped jaw, then the terror in her eyes, and then a silence of the senses overtook him before giving way to the sound of shattered glass as blood filled his glass lenses at once. He felt air rush in through a puncture in his forehead as blood spewed forth the way water would out of an unlatched fire hydrant. For the first time in a while sympathetic, terrified people took him into their arms as he just as soon slipped into unconsciousness.

He awoke in a hospital in the all-white room wearing all-white garments with nothing comprehensible about him but a small window through which the sun was either rising or setting.

His mother came into the room and they could agree it was a shame what had happened though it was accidental; the dead were burying themselves and any rage within William was submerged into an oblique energy although he felt ill at giving anyone a chance, but then his train departed thereafter. He would leave Jerusalem on a scarred note, albeit definitively so. If he could not have his leg blown off, he could at least have his pale forehead lacerated.

His mother returned to work after farewell. At home he waited a moment and with a bandage wrapped around the twenty stitches in his forehead he threw his bag over his shoulder and rode his bicycle back downtown, got onto the Philadelphia bus, slept the way through, and was ten minutes into that morning when it struck that he was now upon the escalator heading down to the tracks.

Memories recent and distant poured through his mind in the station though the vivid reality of his near future and his exile and the shape of things to come outweighed each fraction of the past.

Two hundred people waited before the old, brown tile walls while operatic voices swam overhead.

'With death always just around the bend then death is never real as life, for life which is now shall live until death is accepted as relevant within life across those burning fields of years, to go forth and let the rest collapse upon itself, that which is not being built.

'I seek that realm whereby there is no more death, where He has wiped away every tear, and still until the clarion call I shall return again, exchanging rattlesnakes for small town stupidity, excess in place of comatose, vile bodies!'

Zig-Zag Wanderer

HE BREATHED AT LAST and smiled within the sea of a hundred rushing bodies, and then there was the distant rumble of a battery-ram and the train was pulling in. He had his bicycle in a cardboard box and tucked it away along with his luggage, taking a window seat. Anxiety, futility slipped away like sand through an hourglass; on the other side of life, or somewhere unknown, never gone but out of sight. Sunlight streamed inside the car through an array of trees creating a flickering, hallucinatory effect to which William fell asleep.

He awoke to a suit-cuffed feminine hand. He took his face from her padded shoulder and looked up in shock. The train was jam-packed with broad, silken shoulders separated by fresh newspapers and pulling into Washington, D.C.

"It's fine," said the older, professional woman with whimsical eyelashes. Dyed hair and liquid bipolarity, wind knocked an empty egg cart across the ribbed column, as she seemed neither angry nor glad though dispersed, her attaché following her stride to the gates. All the civilized world rushed and paced in anxious streams around her. She broke away, marching muscular calves. William looked through the skylight of the station and then to the exit-door. It was a three-hour wait to Chicago, where the California Zephyr arrived, and he felt at last as if slipping away from some delirious past and projecting once again into the future. The air tasted fresh once more.

He slung his bag over his back and wiped sweat from his forehead stepping out of the porcelain station through the entranced maze of passersby and into the city.

Another train took off and there was so much more than routine, and man was limitless, he who had by hand built those thousands of miles of iron, spike, and the furious confirmation of life, totality, handkerchiefs of blood in the summer, ah! William pondered cutting through the hot, fresh-trimmed park, and where was Octavia just now in her cutoff shorts and tank-top just always moving with a lust for life and her vision of the individual! Precious Octavia! The one William would miss out on the east after all, he knew, for the others had forgotten the vital ingredient to contempt is self-dependence, and he knew he'd never see her again whence the sound of hammers coming down upon spikes chimed from beyond brick fog. There was a mob scene chanting at a political rally; he laughed at them all, the dead burying the dead. Renascence boiled within his calibrated heart.

He thought of Phil Cohen in the summer morning roaring out to Reno, to embrace the solitary and fleeting moment of abandon, relinquishment amidst the hopeless land! Calibration!

And with that exited the station's property.

～

The late-morning air was serene, not yet stifling, and nearly as fresh as the Bay's. Perhaps because it led there. Men and women talked and slept on putrid mattresses out in the streets, shielded by torn wooden fences amidst the astonishing poverty with the White House just beyond one's shoulder. Of what means, what ends, beneath what sky, did the homeless of America breathe, go on? They'd been young once, that much was known, a sight unseen to devastate the most roaring optimists.

"Quart mane, a penny arven," disjointed, cried out some black dwarf with bleached blond hair; his prosthetic eye was half-way inserted, drooping hollow, flickering like moth wing, his face torn with acne scars, his mouth twisted in a ribbed, ashen circle. "What 'bout you?"

At the corner of the slight intersection there was an octagonal island. Behind it stood the chalice-white buildings one sees on postcards or in the reflection of passing, televised tinted windows of jet-black automobiles.

Beside the coffee hut and terrace there was a little bar. The interior proved twenty television sets playing the same commercials aired in a monotonous synchronicity. The place was empty; there was a counter in the corner for people-watching set between dozens of autographed plaques and trophies. The air-conditioning was on and the faint air smelt of soap. William drank beer and listened to the older men make jokes concerning the bartender's enormous breasts. He tuned out and studied a travel guide:

The Cardinal line would be one of valleys, countryside, mountains, riversides and skylines by afternoon into the next-morning traversing through Virginia, West Virginia, Indiana, and Illinois.

From Chicago it would be Iowa, Nebraska, Colorado, Utah, and Nevada. He recalled a blizzard in the mountains last winter in a sort of psychological abyss although he could not feel pain any longer. He thought again of Phil Cohen, approaching Berkeley at dawn, and whatever Nevada had in store for the two.

There were few people he'd let know of his return and the prospect of getting down to work in Oakland seemed better each time the daydream crossed over. Oakland had a sort of hummingbird-solace to it in parts, upon Colby Street, and seemed the best place to return to, to work at, with the city experience of the weekends across the water.

Through the bathroom mirror one could wash up and look out over the land which led to the Washington Monument. William wondered what was happening in there at one moment, another, and lost interest before long.

Jerusalem, all that it had come to symbolize, was a bad dream. There was some sort of psychological war going on in the country that seemed uninterested in being neither won, lost, nor named. Perhaps it was the world. He had several beers at the counter and wrote several letters within his mind. Euphoria burst through his blood like ecstatic cries coming down an infinite, well-lit tunnel.

He picked up a pint of Old Grand Dad at the deli for good measure and made it back to the train station; he felt the scar on his forehead and felt as if wounded in battle, the suburban trenches, the plague of irrationality, the diseased convenience; soon, some fine day, there would have to be a rebellion, and all great historical moments begin with the mirror of language, and a long drunken ride into the night.

∽

"It was she who rendered me that lightness in the gravity of time, a glass of water in the pits of Hell. O, I could no longer bear those Adamic tracts, those seminars of providence and progeny!

"You see estranged nature and a species at odds with reality, and exilic paradox of insight—our old friend Milton himself had written, 'he who destroys a good book kills reason itself.'" "My heart still has its knots, as it is unclear to me still why God made anything at all—let alone so many cemented minds!"

"O William, don't you know you can question forever and never receive the answer? Jump all life long, until your knees are powder; have you once ever grown closer to flying? Listen to me and pray upon the sacred mysteries, for we see grace move in as it moves away from itself; one loses everything and realizes nothing of value was lost."

"Your speech is like a well, Octavia, from the days of Lot."

~

Through automatic doors an enormous cauldron, an abandoned cathedral of a train-stop wherein dozens of coal black motors droned in each direction creating an industrial symphony which brought each man and woman mute beneath, within it. Patterns of pluming black smoke cut across the iron archway rhythmic and rushing through the looming, metallic interior draped in layers of unrecognizable debris. Broken-down trains and unrecognizable pieces of fractured, discarded steel lay in heaps beyond a maze of twisted fences, dusted platform panels, radiators slouched atop disheveled razor-wire, abandoned lots of crushed orange triangles and cylinders interwoven with caution tape flickering before towering circular fans. A light shined at the end of the tunnel, the blaring horn just commencing, mitigating beside the metallic rapture.

It was late at night in recondite Chicago, that democratic city of unspoken and thus uncured disease of death; the train had arrived earlier than expected. Another light shined in the distance of the sightless dark and like a set of golden eyes the California Zephyr approached, its echoing horn colliding, resounding within the increasing, voluminous abstraction.

Trancelike voices connected as the towering train advanced, swallowing each instrumental cry whole in a roaring elegy of guided light before glistening tar and the oil-streaked concrete.

"About Goddamn time!" cried the youngish hobo, snapping shut an antique pocket-watch. The crowd began to push ahead. William stood at the end of the line, sober from another long sleep.

Upon the nearest bench a young mother awoke her child from a deep sleep. He rubbed his eyes with miniature hands and outstretched them across her knee. She pointed ahead to the train, kissing him once.

"Hey!" he bolted right up. "Hey—we!"

In his wondrous flash he attempted to lift all three bits of luggage from the deck; he couldn't have been older than six.

"Is that the train to see papa and mama!"

"Put the bags down!" She rustled a tan hand through his dirty-blonde mop of hair and took a denim-striped conductor's hat from her purse and placed it atop his head. The train advanced to a stop, its final diffusion echoing through the labyrinthine cavern.

Dust broke from the nearest array of lamp lights and dwindled to the tracks. The front lights of the California Zephyr lit up some unforeseeable space before it. Passengers filed out. A stream of clipped tickets and weary voices flooded around the conductor, the attendants.

The boy leapt up and down while his mother attempted to drag their luggage ahead. The muscles in her frail arms and legs protruded as savage mixtures of people waddled through doorways cutting around her through uncovered coughs and monosyllabic utterances. Their eyes darted from electronic schedules to the blanketing soot beneath their pounding feet.

"Let me give you a hand," William said. The little boy stopped leaping to overlook William. He turned his head sideways:

"It's alright mister."

"Oh thank you," she exhaled. She had a dark Midwestern beauty to her in that one was less drawn to a specific feature or set thereof, but rather drawn to the plainness of her body, her face, her downtrodden look of relief, her large ceramic teeth with attributed a rare beauty to her physical subtleties. In her plain white dress, black tennis shoes, and uncombed shoulder-length hair she seemed to un exude a complete disregard for fashion therein creating her legitimate own. Summon the source of self—all hail Hillbilly Thomism!

William walked with the bag making small talk with her as the young boy bashfully guided him to luggage department.

"Where you headed, captain?" The attendant took the bags. The girl looked through her purse for the tickets.

"Green River!" peeped the boy, handing in his ticket.

"Good luck, sir." William pointed to his cap. "Get us along safe!" He tapped the boy once on the head.

The girl turned to William as he followed her up the steps and spoke in an unrecognizable drawl:

"How 'bout you, sir?"

"Out to San Francisco," William announced. The words fell from him like honey. He overlooked the Chicago terminal for a final time, the reflection of the endless aluminum train shining in the overhead rafters and reflectors. He took his ticket clipping.

"Be a long ride for all of us! Be seeing you!"

An innocent, fragile beauty cast a glow upon her face, one incapable of sorrow. William looked to her eyes, her chest.

"Goodbye."

"Goodbye, mister!" waved the boy.

"Goodbye!"

"All aboard! All aboard!"

Thunderous voices resounded in the tunneled space of heating motors and reemerging horns and lights.

William looked to his left, watched the mother situating her son beside the window.

"I can't do that now—"

He took a seat beside the window. The last door clicked shut.

His train began to make its way ahead, rumbling at once and automatically taking off at an accelerating pace. In no time the sky, or lack thereof, was all one could see. The skyline of Chicago disappeared beneath a blanket of stars, reappeared, and burnt out like a comet.

He combed his hair to the side and took a long drink of whiskey. The feeling within him he could relate to none save the rawest love, the rawest power, for the highest power was to realize its temporal futility and throw it into the fire; to think once more, set in flight, of where this train was to take him and all of the frantic parade encompassed by distance, measured in friendship, he knew not only were it possible to die with love in one's heart, but better yet that to live one's own way was the product of an unspoken, channeled love for all the surging, infernal existence, and no longer did life have to con itself with cruel elegance.

He drank and length and took down panoramic notes throughout the night, pressing across the dying light of American land.

~

Sunrise christened the mountains having passed through its ceremonial light-purple hue, descending to a bath of atmospheric pale blue, parallel to the past having birthed the future unknown and its contextual, disembodied exercises as through slight, dried fields and anonymous towns of sawdust counters and general stores broken signs swung, shrugged before an occasional batch of townsfolk standing beneath hoops of telephones wires, the pole themselves somehow resembling rows of crosses beneath suffused, photographic windmills. Tarped, stockpiled blocks of concrete glistened in the morning dew. An odd fellow in torn blue suit chewed at an unlit cigar, rummaging through a deteriorating lime-green dumpster in a vacant lot. The train rolled thereafter into the old-fashioned, miniature station through a stream of discolored-maroon wooden pillars. Four, five souls appeared to lean against exposed brick, posts curving north, their fingertips caught within the rustic pages of in-herited, leather-bound bibles.

"Galesburg, folks; Galesburg," the attendants glossed the aisleways. Men and women double-checked their schedules stapled overhead. The sun rose over distant plains. He traced his trail on an old map.

The old man beside the dumpster limped past clutching a split picture frame with hands scarred by fire. He sang Louis Armstrong, held a matted handkerchief to his reddened nose, waved once to the train and turned away beside the overpass laughing to himself.

"Excuse me sir, do you have the nothingness?"

The Sabbatean Platonist Takes a Bow

THE BUTLER LIMPED INTO the kitchen.

"You cannot be in here. We are to set the tables, you see, say, you see?"

"I am just drinking coffee. The cavalier bipedal who interrupts my thirst's quenching risks injurious consequences."

"The coffee in the lounge cart is for passengers."

"What is the difference between this coffee and that coffee?" William inquired.

"Porcelain."

The coffee was lukewarm; William drank his without looking at the stout young man. The men looked about the empty dining cart.

"The coffee is not scalding in the dining cart, also," suggested the butler, looking to the concealed windows with a fleeting weariness evoked in the methodical rubbing of his chubby fingers to the tune of his heaving injurious breath.

"Where do you all sleep at night," William said. "I always wondered that."

"Why? No."

"Everyone wonders where the workers sleep on the train."

"I don't know where any of them sleep, or where I sleep, now no, you can't be in here just now," the butler said, jumping at a sudden bump in the tracks.

"I do not want a location. I am just interested how the workers on the train sleep and what stops you from ever just leaping off at a stop in the night and turning your life into an adventure?"

William knew he was rambling and ought to mind his own business when the young butler's voice shifted its tone into one of comfort.

"There are cots, bunk-beds, you see," the man twitched, alleviated by sunlight rushing across the entranceway through a crack in the cardboard. "You just get used to living one way or something or another after some time."

William aimed for his self-esteem:

"Not the chairs though. You are lucky to not cross the country sleeping in those chairs. It is murder."

He took a parcel of newspapers from the stilted stall. The butler breathed, broke into a coughing fit. William restored his glass to the daisy-yellow checkered plastic rack which clicked like cold teeth across each brisk bump and switch in the tracks. The man began to spit upon the countertop, his face enflamed. He removed his cap and scratched at his eyebrow, his balding scalp, taking a napkin from his corduroy breast-pocket. William turned away and went downstairs to the lunch tables.

A grandmother and her daughter in matching black sweatshirts spotted with something like obscure white islands of design sat beside the window, the younger woman rocking the sleeping child within her arms. Her mother spoke in the rasp drawl of a dedicated smoker and moved her repetitive right hand as if pulling from an invisible coat from a hanger. Her robust daughter nodded, silver wedding band upon her sausage finger twinkling beneath overhead light. The steam of their coffee ascended in conjoined wisps, and Rabelaisian wind was broken.

"I smelleth something contemptuous," feigned William, uncapping the water bottle beside him, dampening a curtain, and patting down his twisted face. "Someone here hath broken wind. It was thee, globular harlot; I would bet money on it."

"You don't look so good," the older women said.

"How? Why?"

"You look pale."

"The grocer said that yesterday now, that one over on self-checkout we used to see."

"Not too bad, Laura, but well, listen here; I'm going to take off my coat."

She unzipped her sweatshirt and went to place it on a hanger. The snack-cart man came through the doorway, doing her the favor.

"Thanky you."

William watched her rock the child in her arms.

"Look at that child, look at you, little Jessica! She becomes more beautiful each day, I swear it!"

"She thinking of her daddy right now. Poor Jay. I miss him."

"You heard from, now, from him as of late, dear, I mean?"

"No," she said, looking up with brisk solemnity, noticing her mother's bolted eyes and turning away, "I just get nervous now. Every day is a suicide bomb. When I don't hear from him two weeks I get nervous. People don't think of this war they do other wars, mama."

"Oh shush with your History Channel! What I tell you! Spooked! My baby's spooked!"

She extended her bare, pasty hand, patting her daughter beneath the shoulder-blade.

"It'll all end soon, baby, now you know Jay'll be *fine*! You got to stop *worry*ing!"

"It's all a big lie. All the stories we hear are big old fairy-tales."

"You been saying that all along! Now what's wrong with fairy tales!"

"Well they ain't the truth! Stage blood ain't enough!"

The mother scratched at her scalp, pursing and pulling at her discolored lips, eating the scalp flakes out of her long fingernails. She bit her thumbnail again, recalling her coffee. She smiled, taking a meditative sip.

"Now," she stated, "You just sounding crazy. Like off the medicine. You know Kern's pharmacist a sweet boy. Oh, turn on the little TV, my show's on!"

"I got no service down here."

"Hell!"

"Mama, you ever absorb silence? Nourish your soul? Let it all go through?"

"What the Hell! Sweetheart, you look malnourished, here, now I'm going to get you water! No more coffee!"

"No, no, no, I hate water!"

"Stop that! You can't hate water!"

"Hey kid," the old woman said to William, "Want a little coffee? I bought too much."

"Sure."

She purchased the water, returned. Her daughter did not take her eyes from the child and lip-sang with her eyes closed. No one spoke for five minutes; William rubbed at his temples and eyed the distant mountains which appeared as if dissolving in the rising dust of morning. The woman continued to pick and chew in slashing motions, sipping.

"Now you seemed so happy just before all of this, when we watch the Super-Bowl with everybody and had a wine-cooler and that's it, since then you been a mope!"

"Mama, the Super Bowl was a long, long time ago."

"Don't say you didn't enjoy it. Don't you dare."

"I dint! I loved it! But I been worried about Jay longer'n that!"

They reverted to a whisper which could still be heard above the subtle breakage of turning wheels:

"I said, I told them now there ain't no way the Wolverines win! I bet me five dollars too, and guess what!"

"Guess what, mama, you lost."

"Yes! That felt sad! See, it's all, you know, everybody hurts!"

"Five dollars ain't nothing!"

"Well it seem like it never was." She paused, looking around the car. Her eyes switched up and down in a gradual frenzy, from her grand-daughter to the overhead ventilation shafts. "Raspberry Stoli!" she shout-ed, reaching possessed for something unseen, "I was young once too!"

"Mother," the girl whispered, "Will you just stop? You're embarrass-ing me. You don't ever stop talking."

"Well I suppose if your car broken down on the hill, or even steak dinner—"

"Stop, ma. We know what's next. 'Patterns are a funny thing.'"

"All of that liberal nonsense but oh, girl, Jay get back safe and all that. He made it this far, they'll give him a reward, he's doing the right thing, and that's all that matters in this crazy world my baby, that you do good, get the baby home safe and sound, oh look at you, little baby boy, give grandma a kiss, kissy wissy—"

William detached himself from the conversation with acute difficul-ty, for even the furthest seat was less than twenty feet away. Iowa morning resurrected itself in stretches of turning, synchronized windmills, small hand-built shacks of burnt dirt and satellite dishes, the anxiety of redupli-cating shopping centers, men in orange vests and goggles clearing their lots out with long rubber hoses for the day's work. He contemplated the lounge area upstairs, its skylight, the walls made of window, and yet it was far more soothing to follow the fragmented conversations around him at times than the land. Where did these discreet people come from? Where did they go? Life preludes language, and thus language must go before life itself. And here I am, biting my fingernails over tofu frankfurters.

And though he was reluctant to admit it even within his own mind, a sudden memory of Helena plagued him; and he could not help but wonder, at intervals with agonizing curiosity, what she was doing at that moment, wherever she was. He winced not at her whereabouts, but at her being. He thought of her overlooking the trainside fields of morning, positioned in their lemonade-pink tint, suddenly last summer on his mind, and a tragic sense of life.

Yea, it was most wondrous to travel alone, for too many opinions directed at us in the beggar-remoteness of our lives concern the sanctity of the questionnaire. He thought of her voice and of her interlocked hand within his and knew why at once he hadn't done so sooner: life could not progress without reflection, though it could not develop without going against the grain. Memories of months past, years past swam through his mind, colliding somewhere amidst the common ground of longing and detachment. He felt the sunlight streaming across his closed eyes and no longer believed in the sun; its abstract rays could only add chaos to his thoughts, and the whole business of reflection seemed contemptible, dreary, enervated. The sole memory conjoined to an optimistic, lilting tone, were his memories of adolescence, of college, and of his days and nights therein and after along the East Village, the Lower East Side, Bushwick, Greenpoint, and all of Brooklyn, of Octavia Savonarola. Her bed, retrospectively, seemed the finest ever built, her touch the softest and yet not pliable, her mind on fire in that infernal city. She could make him laugh, she could make him cry, she always had, and she always would; such a rarity is what one may be searching for in that blank, fleeting fracture of meaning. He began to wonder if he had much more than her in his life. He fell asleep at once; his coffee untouched, and knew he'd call her again upon awakening.

"William?"

"You sound less sleepy than I thought you would if I were to get a hold of you! I—"

"No, no, I went to bed! Where are you! It's too hot out, it's bad here. 95. The temperature is too high always."

"I know, I know," William sighed, concealing his almost childish sense of anticipation at the sound of her familiar voice. "I'm in the middle of Iowa on the California Zephyr."

"The train."

"Yes."

"Oh! I've been so busy thinking I've forgotten all about everything. Do you know what I mean?"

The train let out at an undecipherable city. William stepped out and lit his pipe.

"Well that's what good old New York is for, business and forgetting, but now I wish I'd had another night with you before I left! Everyone I know on the East—save you—seems to be destroying themselves or are being destroyed by something I cannot grasp nor erase from my mind. Chemicals, screens, no, it doesn't matter just what, for it's everything. You know I just had to leave, and you know if I ever come back it is to see you in New York. Even my own mother is gone. Everyone is sick in the head. I feel as if I repeat myself to you. I just get excited at times."

"Everyone's at wits' end. So I'll visit you in San Francisco!"

"Oh," sighed William, exhaling into the winds, examining plastic woven ivy wound around the base of an aluminum mill.

An old woman in periwinkle dress outlined its interwoven foliage with a tapping plastic cane which resonated across the dust-swept station of collated, ashen brick-divide. "We'll just get married and do that whole thing."

"Married! William, what's gotten into you!"

"And care for one another and our art," he stood, detecting a serious level of passion in his voice he hadn't foreseen, "And you know what we'll say if anyone asks why we married, my dear Octavia?"

"You make me smile," she said. William overlooked those departing, those arriving, their clicking plastic wheels crossing through concrete pathways. He paused his speech as a distant train horn resounded. She continued: "What will they say?"

"We'll tell them that we got along better with each other than anyone else."

"Oh, stop! I was just thinking of you! You say all of this *now*!"

"But you said it best," William admitted. "You know it."

"All of those years ago," Octavia sighed, as if stretching in bed.

"Because one day when we're older and wiser we'll end up together in New York, pursue our furies by day, hit the town by night. We'll do it in our style, but in a new style, one which wouldn't involve me leaving in the morning to travel across the country, smoke tobacco on scorched wicker benches, but most of all, most important, you know, we'll be together some day."

"What will we do at night if we're tired?"

"We'll order food, stay in bed all night. Call in sick to work. We'll read books to one another and kiss! We'll make sure our lives are spent well. There are too few people one can do such a thing with."

"Stop!" pleaded Octavia, laughing, "We can't go on torturing ourselves, at least not so, and not so far a*way*."

"Tell me then, tell me anything!"

Passersby looked to William as if he were mad, shouting through his thunderous cloud of smoke, and he did not care.

"Well, for one, do you know what I've realized on my nights out in New York?"

"What's that?"

"Here, I'll give you a piece of literary trivia I found in a little book first."

"Please do," William exhaled.

Octavia cleared her throat with deft, unprecedented exaggeration, reciting, *Malcolm Lowery on the Bowery wrote flowery and glowery. He lived by night, drank every day, and died playing the ukulele.* But what is in all this 'glowery'?

"Dunno. One would have to be quite sick to make even one's own epitaph cryptic."

"And then this, the other thing is that sober you're inhibited—"

"Who, little old me?"

"No—no—the general you, the you-you, you see, that anyone, sober, I realized, you're inhibited. With whiskey, enough strong beer, you're uninhibited. Then with wine, you wonder if you're uninhibited."

"What if you," William contemplated, "Drank a gallon of red wine? What would happen?"

"William!" He could hear her poetry book crash against the shelf.

"Then make sure I don't ever do that sort of thing if it's all that bad."

"Yes, but you must, well if you get your work done in San Francisco and it's reviewed well, and you feel like falling over the floor and being ridiculous. I'm beginning to loathe people who are anything but ridiculous."

"The heat of the moment. I am going to write a short book of articles in San Francisco. I'll photocopy the best pages and mail them to you. You wouldn't mind," William said, "Then, if I were to get silly once in a while?"

"Of course not."

"Some day when we are together, I might drink too much wine sometimes after an autumn day in Central Park. And in the morning, I'll still love you, love you more than before."

For a moment neither spoke. He looked about the emptying platform, cast an eye about the people filtering into elevators, escalators, staircases. He stretched his arms and legs across the remainder of his bench as to occupy the stretch of it, lest someone approach him in his paradise.

"It's just sometimes," Octavia sighed, her voice removing William from his surroundings, "Sometimes I wake up ahead of time, groggy, sleepless, and I just don't know what I'm doing. Here, with painting, or anything. I never felt that way with you." William's heart skipped a beat, another. "Even now," she admitted, "Talking to you even the stifled air coming in through my window seems fresh. I always liked when we woke up here together. You don't even remember all of those things you said, all of your hope for today, tomorrow, and mankind, when we awoke with a hangover and had mimosas, listened to records! You can't remember that morning! Those dawns of ours! Singing in the rain, and campus, the university, secret kissing at your mom's house drinking wine! But the mornings in New York!"

"Yes I do," William said, "I remember them all. And yes, those were interesting days. The Boone's Farm works when one is a teenager listening to the Ramones. After that it takes a train full of vodka and chanting from a rooftop to feel any sort of efficient buzz."

"I'm discontented, yet I look back and recall memories with you and my job isn't terrible; I don't feel so isolated; but then the memories fade! I don't know what to do!"

"Voyage west!" The eyes of turned heads fell upon him once again.

"William it's not that easy, here, in New York."

The softness of her voice broke his heart in half.

"Why there? Why ever?"

"It's hard to explain."

"I understand," he said, and knew she would make it West, and then life would be complete. O Harold Smith! O Dolores Park! Melody Nelson—Where art thou—Octavia Savonarola shall arrive!

"But you know, oh wait, let me get this coffee machine on. There, alright. I guess it's, well, in New York everything does not stop happening at once. If I'm depressed here, I don't want to move because it seems more-so that something is wrong with me instead of the city. When things are good here, they are the best. Otherwise I can't explain it, you know, I'll try to visit this fall, when at last things are beautiful."

"You don't have to worry, your thoughts at random make more sense to me than most in concentration. What are you doing today?"

"Café—work—if I can't work as of late, I walk across the bridge, come home, think until I go to sleep. Thinking is a full-time occupation, don't you think?"

"I think so."

"I think so too."

"I've got to get going. Soon enough we'll make love and dance upon the rooftops and sing in the streets of San Francisco and Brooklyn soon, until the sun is so broken down it can no longer stand up and we can dance upon it till the end."

"Yes, sure, but at the same time I'm now remembering to tell you that it is unfair for me to send you messages, letters, and notes around the clock. Would you even answer all of them? Would it not dilute the initial affect? Tolerance is a virtue of prurient beings; I seek not to grow accustomed to your words, but perpetually intoxicated by them. Do you promise to return east? Yes or no, I need to psychologically start preparing myself better for a change of life."

"Yes," said William.

William found it strange that distance, that time could prompt one to speak in such a way and to receive such sentiment in return. Promises, longing, fleeting sadness; perhaps he'd always felt such a way before and was right after-all. Someday they would meet again. His heart pounded at a hazardous pace. He was in love and he had always been and at last, through distance, he had revealed it in his own way.

"Do you?"

"Yes."

"Good."

"Once I've got a steady address, I'll write you a letter."

"And send me pictures!"

"I will," William said. "And Octavia, Octavia—" He sat upright and dumped out his pipe.

"What?"

"When life gets you in that mode, that crippling mode wherein you know not what you will do in the future nor if your past was worthwhile, when you understand the present moment is an impossibility—Summon up the images of things past unto your art and never bend for anyone, my love. Never stop."

"To me, impossibility to paint is tantamount to being buried alive. But there is still worse than being buried alive; and that is being killed without having seriously sought the truth, here where virtue is an abstraction now, one that increasingly decreases in size, so that elsewhere it must flourish, and in essence become itself—but there are mercy and justice, William: these are the cruxes of the new life, and I do not mean this is any vulgar, profane, political sense: I mean a monastic severance from the incidental, and immersion into the scared mysteries. Our task is the simplest, and therefore the most nearly impossible: to turn our backs on that which does not matter. We might have clinical dissections carried out without pause around the globe, but I tell you there shall be no fruits reaped until one realizes that the atom, like all of the elements, is also composed of virtue; a sense of being bathed in the rays of holy light, multicolored cathedral windows on either side of the doorway to the cell of one's heart—a stroll across the greenery and little creeks, familial barns and wild horses."

The pilgrim detected incompleteness in her absence. It turned reflective, serene views of the country into waves of exceptional loneliness, an essence of manifestation that swept through the ancient weeping willow trees, intersecting with statuesque telephone wires along a slight, old-fashioned creek dried out behind him. Crowds collectively pointed to a distant field where a mother horse stood with her tail swaying beside shaded mare. It was out of a picture book. They took pictures, sent them out, and the train was boarding once more.

He unraveled the skin of a fresh tangerine and the Norman Rockwell towns began again to unravel themselves in sifting silent yellow planes, golden wax reversing the reddened sky, patches of grape-white needling across the clouds in a quilt as he readjusted the bandage at his forehead. He propped up the chair counter and made outlines along the map of instances, impressions, ideas.

Then the sun had gone down and there was nothing to see besides one's reflection unless he cupped his hands and pressed them against the glass, or set his weary sights upon the rushing, infinite darkness of—what was it now—Wyomingconsin?

It seemed travel-induced delirium was the most joyous of deliriums whence anxious night and day no longer appeared conquered by the hands of the clock instead entranced, captive to the lucidity of rumbling matter, formations, personal metaphysics, to watch the fractured world pass by through a window-frame of one's own and he daydreamt of New York and San Francisco at once while a rotten apple rolled up and down the aisleway.

The Solar Battery

HASTINGS, HOLDREGE, AND ALL of Colorado racing through with its sequenced cities of orgies, the lights of which fell across the nocturnal windows like sparks with the occasional leaking sonnet, the electric arrow blinking and pointing to and through the sky. For once in his life William overhead another's music that was transitorily agreeable, in Frankie Avalon's 'Venus.' Downtown lights flashed upon the digital, maneuvering storyboard of buildings and advertisements; the last lost souls waved by from their enclosed fence-casings around the calming backyard fires of summer.

At Fort Morgan mechanics prolonged the Zephyr's stop to check headlights as a new track—the Union Pacific Railroad—set the wheels fixed in voyage. Bums waddled around the station picking butts from piles of glass and tin. William stepped down to the station's platform. The air around the exit-way was stifled by blue, wandering smoke, and that irrevocable sense of alcoholic disintegration.

He overlooked his map of America smoking beneath the electronic lantern and let the fleeting physicality of clairvoyance rush through him in a spiral of maddened, rejuvenated spirit. It was far worse to feel alone in the universe whence surrounded by people and buildings, row-homes and arterial streets of cars and headlights and it was far more superior to feel surrounded and guided by midnight's wisdom when at last you were out on your own again.

For the desolation of the universe was much more bearable when set in motion, when alone, looking out at the distant bums hobbling back to the dew-dampened forestry, the set of mechanics groaning amidst clicking headlights and seas of fog like green fuses burning in a dream, the distant mosquitoes and the fireflies and closed-down general store, the shattered compass, the distant scent of torn parcels sprinkled about stoves of sticks; in that case there was nothing available in the immediate world anyway, William gathered, which felt rather nice.

Then he turned around and noticed a familiar-looking woman pacing upon the platform. She at once seemed embarrassed at his recognition.

Her dark hair was pulled into a bun, though she turned at once to her reflection in the car window to attempt further constriction. William observed her fine, simple features, magnified by the lights of the station. She was the mother he'd seen in Chicago with the little boy in the hat. He forgot where she was going and looked away to his map.

She wore a different black dress at the same knee-length as in Chicago. She seemed as if she worked out, retained a very thin figure, and went without bra. William cast glances her way, watching the summer wind press her dress against her body. Each time he looked to his map he read not states and cities and counties but traced his eyes along intersecting lines in anticipation of looking her way once more.

He felt her come hither; she stood for a moment beside him as the cool wind rustled her hair, her dress. He noticed neither crevasse nor indentations and eyed a blurred tattoo of a rose on her tanned foot, nails polished cerise pink. He concealed his nervousness and looked up at her before him in the dark, the disconsolate eyes of a widowed cathedral builder. She hailed him with a wave and bow, greeted him with a waving hand although she stood just five, six feet before him.

"Where is the conductor?" William asked.

"He made friends with a boy in another car. His mom's watching them. I can't sleep!"

"Sit down?"

She laughed and sat down beneath the vestibule lights and in a dialed instant seemed far younger than William had pondered in Chicago. The young mother seemed still as if a teenager, perhaps 17, awkward to himself yet also trying to get beyond it, she capable of some inadvertent charm. Her face was thin, not attractive, her nose hooked, and he tried in spurts to understand his increasing nocturnal attractions.

"He stretches out along my seat at night! He knows by now if he wakes up that his pal's mama is right there, that I'm in the bathroom or getting water." Her voice panged with random pronunciations, the wiry enthusiasm of her voice coming through in bursts as if it had went unused for days and nights at a time.

"He is a handsome boy," William said, recalling the boy had reminded him of faraway childhood pictures. "How old is he?"

"Five."

They looked out upon the becalmed night. She dropped a coin into the coffee-cup jingling like a little oscillating tambourine before them, the coins already within the bottom of the Styrofoam well as if a minute cabaret act or a small and invisible group of tap dancers. "And I'm sorry, what's your name?"

"William," he extended his hand. His was coarse; hers frail.

"Caitlin Forestier," she said, and with an awkward dignity placed her hands upon her hips before tucking them away. "He wanted to tell you all about his trains. All in the beginning he was saying 'I want to tell him with the beard about the trains!' but we didn't want to disturb you. I said, 'Don't bother that man, he looks busy.'"

"Well anytime your boy wants to talk you can bring him by. I don't mind."

They were the same age, they found, as William dropped an unspecified coin into the next cardboard well. Fireflies lit up and down across the platform.

"That is good for karma," William explained.

"I don't believe in karma."

"Good."

"Why is that good?"

"Because it doesn't exist," William said. Caitlin began to laugh with an embarrassment which heightened her beauty. "Where the boy's father?"

"Oh, Davey's dad," she cut her laughter down, grew sullen at once. "He died."

"I'm sorry."

"He's in a better place," said the girl, making the sign of the cross once, twice, whispering psalms to herself. "That's why we're going out to Utah, to my folks' house. Died over in *Afghanistan*. But that's his own damned fault, I told him. No one made you go there. No one *made you*!" She offered mutilated witticisms with a practical rage. "Patriotism! *Yeah*! Now you're *dead*! They don't know we're all just passing through this fake bad life and into the *real one*! Hell I say, Hell is reincarnation! The world on fire!"

"Look," William cut in. "Let's go have coffee. They're polishing off the new headlights, the mosquitoes will murder us out here. We can go talk inside." He stood up straightening his lap, cognizant now that the girl was quite maddened; the problem, then, was that he agreed with what she was saying but not that beyond-the-threshold look in her eyes.

"But the lounge is closed," she snapped.

"Well they keep the restaurant car open all night." He stood. "You can have coffee or water in there and no one bothers you."

"All aboard!"

"Well," Caitlin said, stepping to the train, "Looks like we're going to go anyway! Nice meeting you! If Davey is alright, I'll come by, but anyway, nice meeting you!"

But after said pleasantries William again felt magnetized toward interior development, the affect and interiority of exilic vagabondage, not unlike the monk who keeps his sights set on the monastery even after those around him have stopped laughing at the joke. While he regretted having left behind Guibert of Nogent, he took solace in revisiting "The Lady of Shalott." He did his best to make a bed out of his seat but nonetheless remained awake, eventually trying to concentrate on not concentrating on pondering how precisely one does fall asleep, catching himself as his thoughts took bizarre, dreamlike turns, as in the Sandman arriving, with the intention of giving up this type of self-torture up in some moments. But his mind was plagued with a vengeance of questions concerning history, family trees, and what for so many centuries' worth of books had gone by the name Providence. To this end, with his eyes closed and squirming here and there in the silent coach, he began by considering that all of language is reality and symbol, and thus reality is fiction; hence, he affirmatively shook his pale head, that we venerate poetry because it allows us confront conceptual reality, which is the bare bones of the concept-itself. Therefore, William continued mutely, when I say a thing is unreal, it is likewise real; fiction is less a genre than an acknowledgement of language. It is no wonder persons find the truth in it: for the truth is in it, in recognizing itself as conceptually not-truth. It destroys taboo less because it is insensitive but because taboos exist to be destroyed. Sure, they prevail in times of stupidity; but stupidity must be annihilated too, in order to usher in the new sciences of thought and expression; and, lastly, even if it were insensitive, it would simply be mirroring Mother Nature, who is in essence the landlady of a haunted house. Bored with his once-default of returning to Solon, Xerxes, and Daedalus, William now thought that he might relieve himself another way, one that he had never been alone long enough to take seriously. But this, despite its naughty atmosphere, was not to be: no matter how comfortable he remade himself in the privacy of his Pendleton-tent each time it seemed release was inevitable another thought crossed his mind, a thought discerned despite a spark counteracting with another en route, which he immediately forgot and tried to replace with one of several scenes stored into the hard drive of his erotic memory, now finally, to explosion; but then nothing came of it, either, save the realization that he was not fit to relax, at least now, calmly set down the Pendleton, digging his robe out of his bag. He then meditated on Octavia, ascending the interior castle, telling her in his daydream of an internal lamp, her voice with its inimitable affection offering kerosene—the world possesses one for the whole time, and the next for a short time. But what happened when the world no longer consumed one's mind and body?

He awoke from the evening of inner chaos to a halted foliage evidenced through nascent sulfur: an odd, miniature political rally out beyond the platform and taking place in the parking lot below, stretching into the pitiful public square, and what sounded like 'Death! Death!' There was a young man William could have sworn he recognized from university, in his hand a copy of *Homage to Catalonia*. But even if that was someone from Jerusalem, William knew nothing about him except that according to Octavia he was of a cast that 'rejected the perfect mind and took up astrological coloring books.' All this political psychosis was the reason there were no arts here or there, but ruins, as what lies ahead is past, and what is past lies ahead. He was taken back to the SFPL, Bernard Lonergan, and "higher level thinking"—all that we ever had to do, William sighed, was let one follow natural inclination, or law, eliminating the idea of force outright, and the nations would be left to their own devices—and I say this, and it sounds true, but it is not! There are laws that we cannot see that shatter every utopian fantasy we surmise; and if rationality is obliterated, so then nature runs her course on the annihilators of natural law and reason. "I sometimes cannot tell if I am not yet already in the afterlife. But I seem to have the chance to pray, and there are good works, even if I must squint to the point of sightlessness to see them. It is either that Satan has tricked me, and I am in Hell, and part of Hell is not fire and dungeons but simply a recreation of life whereby I have no idea what I am in for . . . therefore I say the Pascalian wager is on. I must trust in the Lord and discern the good from the evil, and cease concerning myself with the latter. I must live as though eternity is on the line; for it is."

But can there be sexual exploits without self-hatred? It is true I was so squandered that I grew even further lost in failing to comprehend the intuition of the instant, and thus following whimsical leads to negate despair rather than accumulating practical wisdom, summer knowledge, and caring a little better for myself, I was debauched. And I was debauched first and foremost because it rendered me friends and things to do in the evening, and for them evidence to post on computers that we were very happy, or at least appeared ecstatic, although of course we were dissatisfied and sad. Such is the crisis of empirical culture: at its apex nothing more than 50percent of the thing in-itself is ever taken into self-reflexive account. Were I not, he continued, I would never have lived that way; and yet had I never lived that way, I would have never understood the prospect and holiness of redemption, the canon and saints and blesseds, that come to me like shelter in an ice-storm. Therefore I thank God for the experience, as did Mary of Egypt, for now I shall never wonder again what the life of mindless pleasure is all about. Lament is a season, not a tattoo, nor an oily forehead lit by screen. O even crooked leaders and the falsely imprisoned, executions and betrayal: institutional history is full of vice, but what has ever been accomplished for the good by simply talking about it all day long? How one approaches reality is a choice! And I, anarchical poet, desecrator of shores, half asleep beneath the luminous wheel, a canticle of obscurity—here in my heart burn holy fires, burning in the eyes of desert-dwelling nocturnes—and a singular shadow, cone-shaped and swinging across the wall, singing O Melmoth, wandering o'er ye rocks, go home to thy Scotch Rite Cathedral!

The pilgrim walked out among the dazzling sunbeams and riverboat, praying, 'I plant my palmed staff atop thy poisoned flowerbed, crushing poison vines and preparing to light the ground on fire.' But then he would return to a more formal way of proceeding, where golden legend evaporated into mere civilization.

A Wheel of Green, White
and Gold Circles

RETURNING TO THE TRAIN it and his mind set back in motion, having passed a thousand miles, and considering his re-accustomization to the Bay and to the road, and that mysterious sphere where the separate forked paths converged: *I suppose there'd be room for Octavia in our heavenly high court, she who had said, 'It is amazing that we even stayed in touch—how I suffered in Jerusalem! God, how depressing my work made me. One considers staying in academics but likewise considers leaving. Whether I can contribute something or not, is it even worthwhile? We must define worthwhile. And that cannot be done well beyond university gates in today's satanic day and age.' But none else like her; if we are to vanquish time, then let us vanquish things like beneficiaries and doubts as well. I move beyond the shadowy thrownness of the earth into the jubilant movement of cosmopolitan being. Too much ecumenicism is a bad thing, just like wine and ice cream and other temporary intoxicants. For what does it do long term? Erodes all the host knows as true and good. Thus the pathological altruist must reject common sense, because with it he realizes he has dug his own grave; and his guests all these years couldn't have possibly had dogmatic goals of their own, odious syllogisms, could they? One must then reject historiography too! For the world-stage must therein have a script, or scripts, for us actors; and perhaps the most hateful aspect of at least one of the scripts is that illusory prognostication of equality and tolerance, the first a genetic and geographical fallacy and the latter the typeset of enslavement. Master craftsmen good as dead, should all heaven be in vain! We should cease at once replace evenings with screens with, say, Bonaventure, or Thomas Merton: letting genius, art, and practice coincide with silence, exile, and cunning. This is what Octavia called for! This is what vindication for our forefathers called for—nothing less than rejection of vile society!*

Anticipation pressed, rushed through William's chest as he sat in the emptied car alone, within him secret ideas enduring like twinkling seaports at the harbors of cities fast asleep. He sat with his map, his pen, and felt as if he held more than anyone had in modern times. Two dozen rectangular marble tables made out the body of the car. The carpeted walkway led to spare sinks, coat racks, and unmarked entranceways beside the sliding metal doors.

He watched the door handle turn clockwise amidst the accelerated pattern of iron rumbling caught in weightless motion and presented shock with a dramaturgical execution as Caitlin placed her frail hand upon his shoulder.

"He's fast asleep!" she whispered. Listerine. She placed a pint of Gilbey's gin on the table with an unguarded smile and let her hair down; it was difficult to believe she was a widow of any sort with her smile, or with her laughter of cosmopolitan marriages, but it was her smile, of course— one that could end up emblematic of popular films someday. The rushing lights of another station cast down in flickering, enveloped shapes across her fountain of untied auburn hair. William smiled as Caitlin at once set into an animated New York accent:

"Hey Charlie," Caitlin pointing to the abandoned sink, "How 'bout two gin and soda, huh?" Her eyebrows fell to her dropped jaw. "This place has gone to bits, absolute bits! Water, then—two gins with water! Sheesh!"

William watched his new friend dutifully mix the drinks before returning to the table, clad in a vexingly peevish mask.

"Da place has gone downhill, Mrs. Forestier, and oh, who is the gentleman and what happened to his forehead?"

Caitlin sat down before drink, looking over the shoulder, reverting.

"The name's Fellows," William spoke in a Brooklynese tone, readjusting his bandage. "Baron Fellows." He shook hands with the air.

"Here's looking at you, kid."

"Cheers."

"I'm Russian," Caitlin explained. "Aside from my dad's dad, who was French—say, you are sharp-dressed for a ride across the country alone!"

"As are you."

"Do you like this dress? I bought it on Madison Avenue! We were there for Fleet Week. But this, this is a Chanel dress!" She stood and twirled around once, kicking her slippers away, and again on her toes. "What do you like to drink," she sat down.

William took a long sip, summarizing: "I am a seasonal man, a geographical man, thus anytime, anyplace, I opt for whiskey. Then when the summer hits the East I rehydrate with cold gin, margaritas, mojitos. On a rainy Sunday, Bloody Mary. In a triumphant hour, scotch. In the meanwhile, there are the good microbreweries, the IPA. Then by night across the country with a striking stranger," he let slip through it did not alter but heighten their rising, mutual laughter, "I'll have gin and water in Colorado!"

Caitlin propped her feet up alongside William from beneath the table.

"Don't look at my naked feet!"

"I bet my feet are as filthy as yours."

"Don't speak to a woman that way."

"I know."

"And what happened to your forehead?"

"Someone broke a glass back home. A couple of stitches. The road to Hell is lined with adverbs; the road to Paradise is wrought with sin and stupidity, for God is merciful so long as we are honest and willing to risk annihilation for the sake of the Truth; but as for Purgatory, let's just get drunk."

She finished her drink, pouring half of William's into her glass, retaining her slippers and putting them on.

The drinks went down as the train accelerated to weightless speeds through Colorado nocturne.

"People these days are just scared of all the wrong things," Caitlin said, standing to mix drinks.

"Well now that God is dead no one else is afraid to die; they are afraid to live any which way in the Western World vicarious, through gadgets. They stand up for what they cannot define."

His philosophy was wasted. Caitlin stood swinging to and fro at the sink, humming to herself, returning with the drinks. Her narrow face was blushed red.

"He was stoned on the cross, dragged down the mountain," Caitlin began. Her rosary beads were on the table in an inscribed velvet gift-box.

"There are so many crosses though, and twice as many mountains, there are histories of failure, the fossils of exploration."

"I just wish I was a kid again," said Caitlin, turning to the boarded window and away. "I wanted to be an ice skater. I wanted, I had so many dreams as a little girl!"

"Well we'll keep drinking then. Severe drunkenness and senility seem the closest we can come to recapturing childhood, would you say?"

William thought of San Francisco and of Phil Cohen as Caitlin went to speak. Yea, the light that never went out.

"Denver Union Station, folks, Denver Union Station."

The train stopped.

"Quick!" cried William. He leapt to the light switch, turned it down. Caitlin drank her glass and followed William beneath the table.

Voices loomed outside of the still car, inaudible proclamations in the anxious night. Footsteps marched to and fro the windows, the doorway. Caitlin tugged at William's pants, laughing with excitement. He readjusted himself against the wall, Indian-style with bent back. He longed to turn his face to hers, to observe her misaligned teeth he had just noticed while she told a particular tale, for at the perfect time there is nothing more attractive than a set of misaligned teeth.

The table was just high enough for their heads, yet the titanium centerpiece pole eliminated any chance at complete luxury.

Caitlin turned off her exposed knee and against William. At once he felt the warmth of her breath upon his neck.

"They're going to come and *get us*," she whispered, taking a swig of gin. William followed suit, shrugging his shoulders. He had never met a country girl before and here one was beneath the shadows in Denver, Colorado. A young mother and widow. The war. Was she a country girl? A Midwesterner?

"They've turned the fans off!"

He turned to her, wiping a bead of sweat from her forehead with his thumb. She appeared to pay this no mind, listening for another voice, or set of feet, as sets of keys jangled outside of the door and up and down small flights of aluminum stairs where luggage rapped to and fro and into compartments.

"Do you hear anything?"

"No."

The train's pre-departure rumblings started back up again.

"Well," Caitlin readjusted, "I'm going to go check on Davey."

"Of course."

As she maneuvered out of the dining cart William envisioned Caitlin placing her clammy hand to his neck, where she had been breathing. He placed his arm around her as the train began to move and ran his palm along her shoulder, her exposed back, and through her slowing hair, kissing her. They relocated to the aisle-way, he imagined. William lodged the doors with bamboo tray-holders. It was more important than anything to do so before the pressing train tracks in the reoccurring nocturne of approaching dawn—

As she stood and flattened her dress he envisioned them dressing at Granby, she at last went to check on her child; he waited awhile after the train had started back up but the girl was gone and the gin was introduced to whiskey. The pair shook hands, and could cut a young man down to size, make the hideous beautiful and bad music sound alright, and meanwhile the train pressed on along its winding tracks across the country in the still summer night.

As if in a dream:

He lay alone in the room with blinds down and yet shadows flashed across his eyelids singling out any visual assessment of the wallpaper; though he was awake (He could tell because for some time whenever he questioned the reality of dreams, the dream of reality, he knew with absolute clarity if he was awake in that it felt as if he'd been awake all of his life) and wider awake than anything was sleep paralysis, thrashing him, the lucidity of the dream-state dissolving as if quicksand, kicking at a cracked, plastic cup as the jingling keys opened the door, snapping the figurative bamboo tray clean in half.

"Oh my God!"

The clatter of several dozen tin trays intercepted William's disjointed sleep; he vaulted his upper body up at once as if rising from the dead, wild-eyed and disheveled.

"You, again!" cried the plump bellboy, the butler, whoever he was.

William staggered to the man, pulling his old-fashioned pocket-watch from his breast pocket, wiping it clean with his handkerchief.

"You're drunk!"

"Amigo, amigo, will you stop it?"

"I've warned you once!"

"Let me explain!" William shouted.

"What!"

The barrel-chested man reverted his leg, took a step back; William took one step forward. For so long he had been famished, stagnant, fearful he would never make piratical escape from Jerusalem, contrarily lingering on as a glutton for punishment. He noticed a half-full cup of gin on the table and drank it.

"Because, man, all of this world is not good enough for me. In the long run all memory is photographic and if we could no longer tell stories we'd cut our tongues off; one can go on hurt, but well, clad in sexual famine; but one cannot survive a severance from, just to begin, literary history. One must at least have the ability to wrestle, struggle with God, should it come to it; but let him abandon Eve and all of her descendants first, before he even thinks about going mad. Therefore don't lie, amigo, illustrate. And don't become an addict, rather, be a lush. And don't concern yourself with what's real, concern yourself with what's unreal, concern yourself with the heart and soul. If you have balls and cannot do that, or admit that, I suggest you sever them and throw them off a bridge!" His words slurred as the man looked on in horror, his eyes bloodshot, clothing traced with spider webs and dust. William walked past him through to the door, aware he had exhibited some sort of temporal madness. Strange pride rushed through him.

"Hey!" the man shouted, less orderly, and for a moment appeared almost solemn.

"Yes, yes."

"I won't tell on you—just don't break things! I don't care!" The poor man was trembling.

"Come down for a drink tonight," William said. "We'll talk Buddha, Noe."

"I'll be in the bunks," he said with sorrow.

"Forget the bunks."

"I'll lose my job!"

"Fine."

William clicked the door open and wrote a note back at his seat. The sun was out. He walked back to Caitlin's table and slipped it within her hand; she slept beside her child. The note read, in three bullets:

- The tip of your breast is like a poppy leaf.

- Seit mir ein Wind hielt Widerpart, Segl' ich mit allen Winden.

- I hear you whistling 'Mini, mini, mini, mini!'

The limitations of empiricism, or empiricism as the reduction of sensory phenomena, was thus the topic of discussion with Octavia. She said to him, "You touch my perfect body with your mind." She encouraged him to abandon himself to divine providence, to release oneself from the bondage of object-culture and render oneself unto mystical annihilation. "Come to NYC; let us create an authentic philosophical society. You would be surprised: we are not alone: you see the Catholic philosophers have always read everything, and that is what makes them distinct; they are philosophers, and not censorial phenomenalists." O triumph unmatched, death of death, my culture and my people—all the anxious aspects of life and its uncertainty dissolve at the return of her voice, there where the air is itself pregnant, and the semen trees in bloom—listen to the singing lights, where silence becomes this grave, holy verities! Straw Street was no Montague, nor Clinton St., but then neither were Montague nor Clinton St.

He uncorked a little bottle and drink down time, its sweet notes and gloriously spherical burning up one's chest; a sweetness incomprehensible, like driving a Cadillac into a hitherto savage society, magnetized by an unfathomable light of song.

He slept through the Rocky Mountains.

Azurous Hung Hills Are
His World-Wielding

"ABOUT HALFWAY THERE M'BOY!"

Phil Cohen howled at the moon on the other end of the line.

"I got the car ready."

"And how is the Bay?"

"Mimosas, a picnic, blue skies. It's not bad. Noonish. Call me tomorrow morning!"

"Ah yes, ye Mustard, ah yes."

"The countdown," through heaving coughs, "The countdown nears its end indeed, and the hour draws nigh."

The river split open at Glenwood Springs and there was ample time to observe the fading stretch of mountains from beside the tranquil, flowing stream some yards away from the station exit. Caitlin and Davey were nowhere in sight. William followed the overhead directions of another young man to the general store with the dinner counter.

He drank beer at the counter discussing Book Cliffs and Wasatch Mountains with the counterman and overlooking over his proud display of a hundred license plates. He bought beer to go and ran back to the train. Fresh breeze swept through the streets of old-fashioned houses, boarded gas stations, and dried weeds sprouting through cracks in the concrete ground.

Caitlin stood in her rumpled black dress beside a group of conductors in fresh-pressed uniforms. William felt them glaring from afar. Had he not been drinking their looks would have seemed far more daunting, although if he hadn't been drinking, he would have arrived back to the train on time. Everything seemed, or admitted itself to be, comical in the world when drinking during the day. Everyone on the streets seemed so pallid, almost disfigured by mechanical anxieties and fears.

"They were ready to leave without you!" Caitlin shouted. "I told them, 'No! Just another minute!'"

She sat down beside him, telling dozens of stories concerning a popular televised trial and the importance of Twitter.

"As a medium see, they said—"

"Where's Davey," William said.

"He's playing with his friend." An indistinct look which leant toward longing crossed her face. "They just got along so good. He never even asked! He never asked!"

"What are you talking about?"

"Last night! He didn't even know!"

"Oh, alright," he said. "Good. That is polite of him. He is a handsome young man."

"We'll be through Colorado soon!" Caitlin took William's hands for a moment. He gave her a look. "What—you don't *like* Colorado?"

He said nothing and longed to enjoy his beer alone though felt to say such things aloud would warrant suspicion and felt the girl unworthy of a scene. It was a depraved mood swing, but it could not be helped. These things happened. It seemed more honorable to be uptight than to act when one felt down.

"Colorado is nice. I just look to the train ride being over with."

"You don't like the scenery?"

"Not as much as I used to."

"What is the matter?" She took his hand again.

"A man I met at the general store saddened me," he said. "There was something so sad about his lunch counter. The ancient license plates along the wall. When I told him I had to go he looked at me as if he were about to end his last conversation on Earth. I am filled with sadness."

"Oh come on. You're just drunk is all. Drunk and weary."

"How else can one feel traveling the country alone again?"

She draped her arm across his shoulder in a sociable manner.

"Cheer up!"

For miles he felt her eyes upon him. He could not shake the feeling of longing to be alone. He felt idiotic for having ever even daydreamt of sleeping with a young mother, widow, another young father dead in the war, another strange fragmented black sea through which dissolving tinted rainbows run unto another cracked sandpaper coffin.

He knew the problem was that at first it all seemed normal, like any number of things, and when you looked deeper there was tragedy at every corner. That's why you were not supposed to look closer or into certain matters; some things have no meaning to them, the details of which are deemed dangerous; yet there is no danger, there is no nothing, and that then is the threat—all of which makes the world go around is impulsive, hollow at that unquestioned, and so young men will die and others will be born, and at times it takes immense courage to focus on birth, to focus on pale blue rocking horses in shop windows at Christmas time, and at other times it is impossible.

"I lied to you about how old I am," Caitlin smiled. "I'm 19."

"Don't worry. Everything flows."

"No it doesn't," she began. "Something is bothering you. You don't have to say it."

"Alright."

"It was something I did."

"No, no, it has nothing to do with you."

"William," Caitlin said, "I don't want to go to Utah. I want to go to San Francisco."

He understood there was perhaps something wrong with her. An emotional problem. He turned to her and looked over her thin eyebrows, powdered cheeks extending from her thin face, hazel eyes which appeared without lashes, her large ears standing behind a mess of sleep-strewn hair. She was less harmless than helpless.

"You should go someday," he said. "It is a fine city."

Her hand twitched, murmured, and again, in the refracting light of movement.

"You'll never please everyone, William, and so you must at the very least please yourself. Look there, at all the homeless men—how the culture romanticizes warfare and addiction, and then neglects its veterans and addicts!"

"I too thought that poverty was noble; but then I realized that all the professions—doctor, political businessmen, fiddlers, actors, lawyers, the men and women who throw meaningless balls about for a living—that from soapbox of wealth profess the blessed are not *they*, but the masses below, poor and pure; but that this has been a tactic for untold millennia—it seems the consistent thing is to keep the great deal of persons pitted against one another regarding issues that mean nothing in light of eternity's gate; that this and all political history has one crude goal in mind."

"I long to go climb up some northeastern mountains next summer, where the pilgrims prayers and toiled. Women were women and men were men back then. Our present complications are less indicative of cumulative merit than they are borne of degeneration."

"Indeed, my friend," sang William, "I say let one be oneself, lest one should tell me to be anything more. And as for the women then and to-day, I had no father to dissuade me from a lady opening the lock that had contained innocence; but thankfully in good taste was she. Little stray kittens, St. Francis of Assisi, poverty and contradiction—such was our heaven of the sun, and so shall it be when I have concluded my business in San Francisco, and I am with her again and forevermore."

"I can drop Davey off with papa and mama and come visit you, Mr. Fellows. I've never been to California!"

"That would be nice. Don't look so sad. That's where wrinkles come from. Being sad all the time. You ought to call me sometime."

The train set in motion and William pulled his quilt over the two of them. He shared his beer; she spoke:

"We could have a little family," it began, "Of little Russian and Italian and Irish boys and girls running around and we, think of that! Doesn't that sound *nice!*" William felt her large, yearning eyes upon him and wanted to laugh but instead watched the reflection of her phone in the mirror as she typed away. There was something calming, soothing about whispering of drunken daydreams beneath blankets.

"Oh, that just sounds pristine."

"I never have anyone to talk to on the train," Caitlin said, caving into William's arms. He clicked off the light. He'd never thought of a family of his own before. "Oh just hold me for now, I'm so tired." She placed her ear to his heart. He felt as if an old, helpless friend were within his arms and he held her just that way. When she fell asleep he knew she was at peace, away from the reality she had been dealt, and he liked to think that someday he would hear from Caitlin again—not to start a family, but that she had had a stroke of luck and good fortune, and that her child was doing well, and that the war was over.

When he awoke, he was alone. Book Cliffs, he knew at once, tow-ered in the middle of the desert night. There was little sound but snores, rumbling tracks underfoot, headsets, and one's thoughts which ran as the rain began to fall in the desolation of night.

He was on his own again when night passed into morning, whence persistent as that wind which keeps the flag flapping atop Manhattan Bridge in its o'ershadows triumphant delirium kicking clay memories be-neath speeding bullets of buses and cars, so did William's delirious state come to an end as he stepped out into the morning dew and tranquility of Utah. Phil would be departing California soon, and his imagination fixed within the future felt as if conducting some unfathomable, waxen symphony of triumph.

The air had begun to taste and feel crisper as the breeze of a dam rushed through blackberry bushel, the intricacy of birds' nests of twigs; he washed his face in the cold stream and walked about the parks at the edge of Utah.

In 400 miles William would meet Phil Cohen and press onward to San Francisco and begin anew. That pressing feeling of long-awaited realities was upon him. He could no longer sit down and paced the platforms, paced the length of the train. All was set to go. He ran the hot water and took a long shave, plucked from thin, chaotic air, there was Nevada before his eyes, and there then was Reno in its maddened afternoon, lost in time:

"Reno Nevada, folks; Reno, Nevada."

The Tide Across a Map

HE RETRIEVED HIS BICYCLE, locked it to a post, and set out to roam down-town Reno. The hot air tasted of funnel cake and trash. He lit a cigarette of success and watched beneath the old buildings, amidst the closed-off streets of vendors and madmen and madwomen, blinking lights always in the corner of one's eye, searching out the seediest bar in such a town—a difficult task in its own right.

It was a blistering afternoon, and everyone drank on the sidewalks, yelling and singing in choruses of the damned; William leapt right in. There were layers upon layers of old-fashioned buildings, signs, cars, and even several people who seemed as if from another, simpler time. The simple, historic grace of Reno diffused the fever rushing through him. Old couples with canes smoked long filterless cigarettes and spoke of Meryl Streep, Reagan, God-damned liberals, with an intensity as to implode at random—behold, a magnanimous whore—the voices broke across the crowded streets and full of life and yet one walked through downtown while metal guitars were being plucked distant in the circular shadow of cupped straw hats. Broken, rusted signs announced each bar's special of dollar tacos, dollar beers.

William walked through inverted wooden gangplanks and received the message: "Shall arrive in 120 minutes, will call ye when car is parked!"

As gravity precedes language, it was not until then that it all be-came real, when old Phil Cohen was roaring through California at that very moment, the image racing through his head and his racing heart as he cradled an ancient, splintered wooden sideswipe of a doorway and plunged forth into the Dew Drop Inn.

The pilgrim was at once taken by hand by a pair of prostitutes through the cavernous tavern, to a punch bowl spiked with absinthe. And there, with two dozen strangers, he broke into joyous dance of the wise:

arms interlinked, legs kicking, tearful laughter, hobo and millionaire alike, young and old, chanting unknown things with the zeal of thirteen moons.

But it was short-lived.

As the holy dance of the wise broke up, fights between factions concerning the journey of the mind to God in ferocious poverty rendered men marched out back by bouncers.

"But either one emanates from me or I decline altogether: it is not that I choose not to follow, but that I do not follow," the pilgrim said to his new friends.

"Did you hear about the governor—what, was it the governor? I don't know. Somebody ought to tie a millstone around her neck."

"Yes; in the other world millstones were used for another purpose, a most holy relinquishing of evil; but here, amidst the Sirens, from song to song in a bath of eternal light, the flood has ceased and all nagging demons of the temporal, deconstructed past drawn and quartered. Do you follow?"

"No, honey—let's just dance."

William entered a slow dance to Elvis Presley with a woman who looked like she was out of *La Dolce Vita*, black eye, and all. But in the warmth of her perfumed arms he could almost taste the rejoicing, effulgence, blithe, tender day of wandering drunks. As if to confirm his absurd foray, he eyed through the half-polished window, between two unlit beer signs, two rainbows over the mountain, albeit mistaking Elvis as singing '*needles by starlight.*'

Ah yes, smiled the pilgrim, grounded and a soft hand moving to his neck, encounters with the damned. The damned are my people. Spiritual Combat, united with Francis De Sales in this warfare: let his sons grow lukewarm, my song flames forth by torchlight of a hidden world, where new leaves cast their die, and the west wind is both orator and epistle. Armorica rejuvenated, he intuitively crooned, or not, I advocate a mighty shield against the culture of death and its advocates.

"For this I came," he whispered to his dancing partner beneath disco ball, "That I despise the preordained evils and uplift the holy martyrs; I am a man riddled with a torrent of bullets whose soul is none but strengthened by the blows; seeking the One who shall lead us to the true manna, against the errant world, against degeneration," touching her shoulder blade, silken straps, and lofty veins, like ripe blue aquarium tunnels in miniature.

∼

"Twelves volumes, William, Metropolitan Avenue, bookshelf of Saint Victor, Augustine, Chrysostom, Anselm. You should see the collection I acquired!"

"I recall Dante himself had a Joachim, somewhere in *Paradiso*, my love; but I suppose not this one. Does anyone recall the Calabrian Abbot? Let us see to him, my love, after the Apocalypse is over. I say again my dear and must make a fast move and be gone—take thine own unto contemplation, that the next time we are together it shall be for good. They pour jug wine for me in Reno, Octavia, and dance me to the end of love, or time, or whatever it is. O how I feel like a character in a book whenever I drink this particular jug wine: this is all less up to me than to my maker, though the critics pick at their alleyway feasts indeed—my aspirations are sanctity, reunion, poverty, and holy death; if I am not making the angels sing, the rest is kaput!"

He sat between an estranged toothless gambler (Spreadsheets of venues, times, horses, tables, rates and advertisements surrounded his sole glass of seltzer-infused whiskey, fresh and breaking the way a waterfall crashes upon and within several dozen crescent stones at once) and an emaciated figurine with the complexion and nose of the Wicked Witch; William marveled the green hue of her skin, and hadn't known such was possible. Beyond her shoulder an enormous barback swung open tin doors. The patrons rose. Behind the bar was a river; he threw an ossified man, screaming, straight through the tin doors and into the river. At the sound of the splash everyone laughed, raucous and roaring, and lifted their glasses to the ceiling.

The long, horseshoe bar smelt of seafood and burning leaves, the languid breeze rushing in through broken windows. Frantic patterns encompassed all the faces of the dispossessed and put a stranger at an ease unfamiliar. He felt neither wanted nor any less foreign than the Mickey Mouse clock upon the wall of antique trophies. Electric drills ran overhead with meticulous nail-ends appearing at paneling end of each vibration, sawdust, the distant voice of Carlos Gardel echoing from a shadowed pallet of carved and smoked out booths with broken lanterns. Mantelpieces of moose heads and beaded necklaces pieced along the pillars while hammers hit nails between vague voices intersecting with the light accordion, the screeching car tires and sirens of the street a backdrop to singular bliss, the occasional uplifted peppery mustache and straw hats uplifted to the ceiling with a fond memory, or recognition of summers past in moments just like this. The gambler combed at his eyebrows of overgrown weeds. The bartender emerged.

An emaciated dyed blonde from Bulgaria. She took to William. Her otherwise plain white dress was lined with chrome beads and buttons and necklaces of stunning variety draped upon her tattooed chest of colors so vivid one could not feel guilty gazing, her glossy eyes, thin as sheets of paper, in private concentration. Before all of that she had been in Montreal, she explained in charming broken English:

"It was yes; eight years. Today second day. Start last, yes, Monday. Now today second day! Yay tequila!"

William drank tequila with Esmeralda and spoke of the world. Greater variations of sawdust fell from the pummeled ceiling. A woman with her arm in a sling removed the sling and took a shot of bourbon, laughed with a reverberated, bronchitis crackle, and fell to the floor. The barback reproached her, asked her the President's name, the present year, and before long the barback threw her, too, sling and all, into the river.

Unless someone was thrown into the river behind the Dew Drop Inn no one moved, as if within a sort of deranged museum, or a photograph. Ash stockpiled in carved silver crates.

William bought the bar a round, received warm thanks, Esmeralda showed her breasts, and just before the tacos came out a midget fell from the ceiling. He, too, was thrown into the river.

"He just hang on de ceiling like a bat sometime," explained Esmeralda.

Velvet Blown to the Root by Breath

BY LATE MORNING, NEAR noon, the streets were even more jam-packed, outdoor speakers turned away, hash smoke a stream of spurs, toilet bowl hallucinations driving one man to suicidal consideration and the next to another bottle, another nauseating, delusional woman, the sort born deflowered, and another two quarters for another song from Captain Beefheart, though the streets themselves lacked the cut-throat tempo of New York. Yeah, turn up the Beefheart you fachim! There the lost were always on the verge of getting mowed down although it never quite happened, resulting in a learning experience. Fumes of sizzling food broke from stove tops, fryers, vendor carts, the crackle of breaking plastic, creaking roulette wheels and the music from decades past spilling from enormous storefront speakers and out into the hot streets. Children walked along smiling with their candy apples.

William readjusted his bandage, parted his hair to the side, wiping the grease at his pants-leg. The collective faces passing by were all sunburnt and yelling as a firecracker imploded within a forest-green aluminum trash can, endless wrappers and warped, plastic bottles smoldering and burning down at once as the children cheered on, the drunken men and women drifting in and out of doorways.

A young woman stood behind the counter of the café in the rectangular corridor of shops just off of the main street, secluded in its own precipitously modern contour. There was a small sign for wi-fi. Bands loaded equipment through backdoors and smoked weed in the alleyway. William took a seat at the plastic table and had several cups of cheap white wine as the fundraiser for skydiving took place beside him. Trays of peanut-butter cookies and bagels dabbed with tomato and avocado slices were passed around. Another stand sold fine Mediterranean sandwiches, another homemade jewelry, and docile old men in polka-dotted t-shirts sold parachutes, smoked corncob pipes. The rich fumes filled the shaded breeze with smoky scents, propelling him to dream lucid of childhood magazine tobacconists. William felt invigorated and locked into the day as he polished off the last of the wine, making small talk with the building owners and local promoters. His phone vibrated. He did not recognize the number.

"The hour hath dawned," Phil announced.

"Phil?"

Images of Harold, Daniel, Heather, Fort Mason, Polk Street, the Mission, Janine, and everyone else, just to begin, burst through his mind in unfiltered reels.

"Yes, yes, my phone died O lad. I'm at a payphone out front of a bar—what is it—Porkchop Hotel—the car's parked; where art thou!"

He explained.

"Go see Samantha over there, my friend," said the young woman. "We have all of the best whiskeys! We just opened! Always wanted to see California—us—still ain't made it!"

"Hey honey, be right there."

William pondered, the best bartenders were middle-aged women who had once been beautiful with youth and now had aged and used the term 'Honey' in earnest. He looked over her body as she took over for the younger girl; her big flapping ass wrapped, suffocating in denim, and rattled his knuckles mute along the gas-blue tile of the porcelain swirl-grey countertop.

There was El, standing out in the parading crowd upon the street. He'd went on the same, neither pithy nor agonized—a refreshing twist for such a good soul to do so—with his beard and all, and smoked through his middle and ring-fingers, brushing languid ash from his three-piece suit, the clay architectural patterns of old casting a hypnotic, reflective glance upon his sunlit eyes.

"What ya looking for, dear?"

"Oh, you see that man, there, in the beard?"

"The philosopher? I'm kidding, hun."

"Isn't it so strange to watch someone you've come to meet from thousands of miles away just sort appear, when you're contemplating a glass of whiskey and you've decided to abandon all of that which isn't bound to fruition and artistic wisdom in your life—"

Then Phil's hand was upon William's shoulder and the two broke into thunderous laughter, contagious, catching the observant eyes of passersby. The jukebox broke overhead as the two dispersed, embraced once more:

Doctor Ross—"The Boogie Disease;"

Jack Nitzsche—"The Lonely Surfer."

"Ah," El let loose, pulling his stool to the counter. "Paradise regained."

"O," grinned William, absorbing the music and the presence of El, rubbing at his temples, "What a meeting place is ye Reno!"

"Here you go—boys."

"Ye slept at all!"

"No, no, save spaces of two, three hours here, there, though I feel serene regardless. I've seen enough now, I believe, to portray my own vision of this country in an accurate way. People often blame things on the cities or on the towns, when of course both are filled to the brim with mindless slaves regurgitating as fact whatever propaganda they've been sent that afternoon. Useful idiots come in every form, and technological communication enslaves the masses by getting them less addicted to justice than impulse. Democrats are sodomites, republicans are usurers. Destroy them all."

Send that Doctor over here

"Yes, yes," El said, lifting his glass. "And to this: There is no joy quite so awesome as escaping routine, the contradiction, the repetitious imitation, me lad, of life! And wandering far away!"

"El," William said, clicking his glass. "What song is this?"

"Jack Nitzsche. Sign of a fine, quality jukebox!"

The bartender made their whiskey and soda up in pint glasses with whiskey and a splash of soda. It was a good homage to travel. Everyone toasted, banged their fists down upon the table, and roared.

"Tell me," Phil said, "Of what the trip was like!"

The evening was a fine ducking in and out of casinos, country-western bars, taco stands, and hours later after having caught up they walked down the long, winding road before sunset.

"You know the progress," began Phil, "Or lack therein, of this current war in convincing numbers of people that returning soldiers are heroes. That seems to be the most recent effort. You know it's always been that way, as of late it's been a little obvious. But it's most strange, because heroism involves, implies truth; ignorance, more fitting in the core of this case, implies insolence, so then that makes one a fool to find this war heroic at all, to find this war even a war."

"Literature," William replied, "Is the sole thing that accelerates beyond, transcends politics. Politics are a heap of ash spinning down a flushed toilet." He laughed and as the array of television sets announced the decline in American manufacturing, peeled from his bottle the label, recalled tossing a dollar to another dampened table in Washington, D.C.

"I've got the couch all set for you. It's going to be a damned good summer, better than last, if ye can believe it!"

"Indeed, comrade, we shall see that which can die, and that which dieth not. Here is a toast, to the mimesis of ideas and perfection! I count fifteen stars, and shake off the frost of ideological death as though it were dust from my sandals of peace."

Holy lights and sunrise with thee, William wrote to Octavia, *our growth in happiness builds from word to word, morning solitude, discourse and Creed.*

The contingencies of days of heaven, candle wax and a psalm of immutability. Her hand trembled in mine, as I gave unto her my art and vision. For even a king has asked for wisdom, and so a pilgrim may too be peerless. Tell me, O muses, where the shaft of thy intention strikes, and I'll tell you where to go—*I laugh in proximity to these fools, Octavia, namely the women that make me sick; Lord, I could just hate California girls.*

"But we keep alight the flame of hope," William said to Phil, "And did you hear back there the one, a little scribbler, claimed to fish daily for the truth; but it never dawned on her to refine her methodology of fishing, quality of net, furnishing of one's perceptive apparatus! She seemed quite near grieving in that I was at the last minute excluded from the party; what a town is this!"

"Yea," said Phil, "The lady knoweth not that I have Heidegger and Parmenides beside me, and that I choose them over futile comingling in deleterious clouds of feudal politicking, vassals and all—theirs was a bulwark against Judaica, reaching for the heretical stars; so mote it be—in a time of wicked leadership, as the pilgrim sayeth, one must either become a heretic or be driven to suicide. The hour that the ship came in, I stood like a demented, glorious prophet, and one could almost recapture the scent of burning wood and flesh in the auto-de-fa of ages past. I long to go down to the depths of the ocean, through the harbor's mouth at last!"

"Yea," said William, "Such is the dice of drowned men's bones. A glorious peace be unto you and me. Amen."

William absorbed a stream of interior, exterior lights as they walked the roaring half-mile through Reno and drank coffee and whiskey in the rented car. The sheltering daylight sky dissolved to grayish, summer clouds, and the moon could be seen already in the last patch of blue to the west, with all the neon lights racing behind them in the city.

Long Live the Weeds
and the Wildness Yet

THE SIGN READ, THROUGH an unlit swarm of mangled branches and broken panels, Val's Midtown Lounge. William squinted, leaning, polishing off the half pint of Old Crow. The circular iron had a pull on him; moreso did the karaoke inside: Bruce Springsteen—Working on the Highway. Duane Eddy—Ramrod.

"We must investigate this," El said. He smashed a hand rolled cigarette against the broken wooden stairs, William absorbing his delirious bewilderment. "Whoa, ye bard," El cried, creaking open the door, his turning face aglow, "Thy Midtown Lounge with ye broken windows and honky-tonk insanity, I shall stand and deliver in thy establishment!"

"I concur, ye bard of the underbelly." William stepped ahead with an exaggerated limp. He looked in through the cobwebbed window. "The bar looks as if an ancient basement, with old pool hall and everything!"

He walked through the front door of shrapnel, his blissful eyes containing abstract glossaries of the damned. In one corner a man was whipping another with his belt as the bartender cheered on. A young cross-eyed man at the bar greeted William, with the unprecedented kindness of having arrived at an anniversary or birthday party of sorts.

"Th-th-thank, you for coming." He tapped the enormous, leather shoulder of the man beside him in stained, overflowing beard as the overhead singing stopped and programmed instrumentals roared through smoky space. The robust man turned his rosy face, baseball-mitt of a hand to William.

"Siddown! Siddoon!" He let out a roaring cackle as his counterpart attempted to compose sentences, to no avail, with his terrible stutter. "Rita! Rita! Get him a drink! ARGH!" The whipped man ran from the corner began to dance atop the table. He did the shuffle and the Macarena. "Rocky loves to dance," explained the portly man. "Look at him go!"

William went beer for beer with the men, the bartender, upon the broken coliseum of a counter. El broke off into conversation with some visiting women.

The young stuttering man, or so he explained through some sort of happenstance osmosis, had a disease whereby when he awoke he remembered nothing from the day and night prior—neither his plans, his name, nor even year—and had to have maps and post-its about his room. The following day they were to take tubes and beer down to the water and go kayaking with the high school girls.

"I got you covered; you just remind me in the morning. Multitudes, son. Or we could stay up all night. Where are my post-it notes? They even a midget, too, my girl Micro Machines—"

William promised to join come morning with stately, bewildered candor. He stepped out for a cigarette.

The wooden-metal spliced doorway swung once, twice behind him. He sat upon the deck, its dimensions similar to Fort Mason, the overgrown weeds blowing in the wind. Nocturnal breeze swept through streets, the distance collage of music and voices and announcers crashing together with pulsating regularity. The seesaw of exhaustion and enthusiasm rushed through him and in a sense, he knew, nostalgia was disintegrating within him; past and future were a simultaneous void, everything near seemed far away and vice-versa. One could look ahead in his mind the way he did with his eyes.

Beneath the sky of the desert every man was for himself, the hair blowing atop the brain. Electric clocks turned hands advertising sports logos of decades past. It was all a dream, an impossible dream:

Rip Van Winkle conducted the tin guitars with his hands. Shirley Temple skipped into the room attempting to sell an autographed photograph of Bobby Fischer. Round of drinks. Attempted to unglue roguish elbows. Mutiny. Cheers. Whiskey. The bartender was transfixed over his dollar. Happy belated birthday. Rip Van Winkle, the young cross-eyed man explained, was his best friend in the world; "Since it's summer, here you go!" Myriad sluts stained with ash danced alongside old drunks, corner to corner, pointing with elation to the most robust of all, filling shot glass with funereal Bacardi. A Thomistic sphere-edge had been carved out of the table just for his boulder of a cask gut. Metempsychosis. "I like you fellas."

"You boys have fun at the muscle car show?" She placed half a-dozen franks into the mouth of the microwave. "See that corner, every springtime there's a cocoon there you see when we're cleaning the thing because *well*—"

"Where's the TV?"

"Broked."

"Nothing's healthy anymore anyway. A disciplined diet of nothing but heroin, I say."

"Why was I born?"

"Don't know," William admitted.

"Midnight."

Pool-balls clacked. Torn pieces of newspaper swirled about the checkered floor, collapsing at the trampled bookend doorway.

"What happened to your head, hon?"

William ran his exhausted eyes along the charred corkscrews stapled to the hutch. He daydreamt for the last time of the east, of Jerusalem:

'Redistributed syntax; emulation is a shopping mall. Long black coats before the winter sun, that star ineffectual as any other. Cuffed black jeans, heeled boots, shined for a shilling out on the porch, the smell of sand, vermillion temples and confederate eardrums there his teeth rattled like Mexican jumping beans. We see your cylinders. Poor dead souls!'

"Piece of glass—I had no time for revenge!"

"Revenge?"

"You got to come r-rafting! T-teen-n-nay-ay-age p-pussy!"

"Oh Walter come on; you're scaring the boy!"

He brandished a borrowed knife across the counter engraving everybody's initials, physical inquisition, and disco lights spun the words and the world around and around with an outstretched mist.

"We'll see you at the r-river in the m-m-morning! Here, one more she s-says, hurr-ray!"

"Good-night!" El shouted to the women, re-approaching William, and they took off again downtown, with the Midtown Lounge's whole sick crew waving and shouting behind them.

～

Near dawn William awoke in the rental car at once accepting the flask from El, who took a heavy pull racing down the highway, vacant save the occasional truck in its passing lights enveloped by the limitless forestry streaming by in its nocturnal, entrancing stillness.

"Good morning! Soon we reach Oakland! Till surrender, till bliss— we must die!"

William felt his senses deranged and already could see he'd lost it a bit at Val's Midtown Lounge. He recalled the carpeted casinos, a policeman, hot rods, spinning wheels, blinking bulbs, finding a twenty-dollar bill on the sidewalk, his memory a transcription of foggy images, of nocturnal sojourn and transposition.

He rolled down the window, inhaling that crisp beatific air of the Californian night. He let the light wind press across his palm and rush through his hair. Light purple formed amidst the sheltering sky. William washed his face with water from the canteen and took another pull of whiskey.

"Those strange men," he said, "Those scattered lights, retrieval to a casino," the memories dissolved amongst the cascade of darkened, towering trees.

"I won thirty dollars; you found a twenty!" El shouted, his wide eyes on the highway. He smiled and yelled through the window to a truck driver, whose horn bellowed past and onward.

William recalled finding his twenty-dollar bill on the ground in a moment of clear cogitation. At his feet he found the bottles of Budweiser, the half-eaten O Henry chocolate bar. He had a beer and let Californian dawn soak in. William turned his last working eye to the distant Pacific borderline. He adjusted the bandage strapped to his forehead, examined his stitches, and threw the bandage to the wind.

"I've opened my heart to eternity," announced William, letting the wind across his extended palm, "And now all of the memories of the future, memories of the past collide as one and sift through the echoes of my mind as if it were the Grand Canyon—let us digress further tomorrow, Phil Cohen, when reality removes her blouse, the sky there becoming enveloped with that pale shade of blue, to soak it in, and to arrive delirious unto life, O comrade, and soon enough we shall walk Polk Street a-gain. Belayed, cliched, decayed. If we didn't cry, we'd laugh."

El shook his head in wordless redemption, an affirmative gratitude of the vagabond lifestyle as the orange embers of his cigarettes burst across the fleeting gravel.

∾

"The root of the truth is silence, for some the silence of St Thomas. Ardor and brightness shine forth as one."

"You drop clues and mysterious hints about what you're up to, and I must tell you William that it is not very nice. Bad boy! I must ask: how do you think this cryptic, incomprehensible language strikes me? Do you even think? Sometimes I cannot tell if this is sophistry or mania, or whether there are just perpetual depths to these 'sentences of desolation', as you call them.

"My vision," said Octavia, "is nothing more than a touch of that which it is elsewhere; beyond the pre-Socratics, to the realm of the one who sent Him, the *Logos Incarnate*, that we might live on earth and carry out the work crystallized in the harmony of the spheres."

William drifted in and out of drunken dreams, intoxicated further by his summer knowledge that wine was less the answer than the temporal supplement, envisioning Octavia lovely and smiling, a higher salvation unto absolute salvation, the salvific fragrance of her arms, dreaming, when she holds me when I sleep, and I her, or when she stole a glance when we did kiss; how my warm hand cradled her soft neck, softly holding, though I knew not that I ever did so, so was I entranced.

~

"Brandish me a galaxy, and I'll render ye a skeptic."

They neared in on the Bay with sweat breaking across their brows. The kaleidoscopic journey was coming to its close, its destination. William thought of Mack Winter, one arm and a hook, spindles falling from his breast pocket in the heated night, swollen fingers clutching carved glass with velvet bottoms—that was the tale, that was Rip Van Winkle's tale—

"It's all coming back to me now—"

Then it was daylight all around as El beat across the two-lane blacktop, the spherical planet adrift as its youngest inhabitants, stepping toward the glorious sun, peeled windows and ye Pacific regained; William thrust himself from daydream, from looming exhaustion, to shout through the window, recognizing the Berkeley entranceway in sunlit proximity:

"Ye Frisco Bay doth exist, the dust shaken from my boots drifting westward, eastward, salvation and the destruction of time's limitations, serenity, serenity, wayward my sons, wayward! And morning, clear morning!"

Through Berkeley at the break of morning, beyond dawn, exiting the highway and into, upon Colby Street becalmed.

"Ah," El sighed, extending his hand to William and placing his head upon the steering wheel. "Here, at last!"

It all came back to him beside the hummingbird, stepping from the car: the replenishing solemnity of western morning. Carnivalesque had never even begun!

"Ah, heathens of the radio—put on 'I Need a Mars Bar.' Later on . . . a bodega."

Foghorn to foghorn, like godly voices tossed from cosmic tree to tree, in the last seconds of a consul dying of delirium tremens; extended and petite the particles of bodies—

"You, William—arise! Arise and conquer!"

And suddenly he had a fresh, ice cold beer dissolving in his chest, and found himself paused before a towering Oakland church, cast in the shadow of its cross.

"How I would have loved to be there at the start of the Crusades, alongside Peter the Hermit. What a wondrous people! God, how they must look down in absolute disdain. Or worse for us, they do not even acknowledge our corporeal being. I suppose at some point the nihilists shall be unleashed. There is truly nothing new under the sun. It's all so tiresome, until we set our sights on the unseen."

There, if one listened enough to the sonnet interwoven less by stricken targets than unforeseeable vision, one could hear cymbals and grand pianos crashing together somewhere, and nearing, within some foreseeable distance.

Epochal Transformation

IT HAD BEEN ARRANGED for William to sleep upon the guest-couch for as long as he'd like or as long as it took to get situated. Before he'd even sat down in the familiar first-floor of the house El handed William his set of keys. Such was the greatest of odes, the way Western men and women were always so ready and willing to put someone up for any amount of time, to allow life a random shred of enjoyment. The birds chirped outside of the old window propped open by Phil's old edition of Marcel Proust.

Exhaustion shone on Phil's face and William could feel the bags beneath his own as they sipped hot tea at the kitchen table, communicating in sporadic fits and bursts of laughter.

The jasmine tea was hot and put a fresh coating, a lining of armor within, upon William's chest. The waves rushed through his blood in restful streams. Phil's occultic roommate stepped out of his chambers, stretching, and sat down before William with his pipe.

"Well, we're glad to have you. I want to get you up to a brownie a day, for your soul. My research focuses on Philip K. Dick, Dogon, and Sirius. The Statue of Liberty is a strange bird."

"A language of identity and difference."

"Yes, in the pure strumming of an evening guitar, like tranquil sunset, therein is a truth much greater than one would like to admit . . . such is the object of my dissertation."

On television there were rumors of a factory on fire, subconscious etymologies, the device's upholstery clad in ribbons and bows, gemlike beads, a picture of a girl with burning smile.

"Without knowledge I am too without love, and loveless is myself, severed from the journey that never ends . . . I do not need your family history; allow me to observe your choice of words, and let us compare mythologies, and everything else will unravel at the seams."

He stood to tie his belt of human bones.

"Phil tells me you read the Church Fathers? Well, you've gotta read *VALIS*. I'll be at the library till later—I look forward to talking to you, man."

~

The pilgrim was fatigued until he forced himself upward, popping open the kitchen window, pouring a tumbler of wine, and breathing in some gusts of fragrant wind. In no time he'd be sketching out, initiating postcards once more: *Someone knows my family history, but I do not know that someone. The grass fades and the flowers wither, ancestral martyrdom coronated with ceiling fragment shipped here from Cincinnati—there are no equal languages, just as there are no equal combatants.*

Amid a smoky backyard conversation William stood and paced the kitchen as if it were a subway platform in the winter. His words came out jostled, frantic, and then somewhere between. El presented his set of blankets and pillows as the two made plans to explore Oakland by night, and that a job was already secured for William at the new café. First Phil Cohen was to return the rental car, get laid, and rest up at his fresh young woman's apartment near downtown, returning in the evening. They gave a final embrace, solace, and William laid back upon the couch. He listened to the car start up and take off. Tranquility placed itself upon, within each visible item in the room:

The overhead fan with its rattling plastic chains attached to the faded-white, disintegrated ceiling; the warm quilts stitched with golden-maroon clubs and arrows, frayed at the edges; the multicolored collection of books and films; the ceramic pipe upon the marble table atop an island of stapled pages; an unopened ink cartridge; an old wrench bearing rust of last century, of the millennium past; the silence of an old, ironic cuckoo-clock and its strange, yellow-brown baby bird locked atop its weightless plank, wings outspread; passing cyclists turning through shaded streets, ringing bells, the clicking switch of gears, he found himself standing at the window and again began to pace.

He took an unrecognizable book from the shelf and flipped through its crisp, untouched pages, where he came to understand that there is nothing more difficult than to be a stepson of the time; that there is no heavier fate than to live in an age that is not your own. One would have to revisit Vasily Grossman.

But, William knew, stepping outside and plopping down upon the hammock beside a concrete slab contained by carved and chopped trunks of trees, it was the return of fresher colors everywhere one looked which separated the Bay Area from the country, from the world; the interior, exterior of buildings and homes, the editions of books, the hue of even unreceptive wallpaper, the blue tonality of the sky, the richest white clouds sifting through over the ambient acceleration of the Pacific Ocean. And the Pacific sky, one knew, was a most subtle, if not languid, way of being in complete awe and recognition of one's soul, and its forgotten attachment to the world which stood still without even a set of legs.

He fell asleep to the dreamt sound of melancholic guitar strings plucking like flowers upstairs, thinking of what it had been like to be born, to give birth, to die, to live. It was too easy to sulk in the modern world, far too rare to avenge vitality, to beat on in memory of the trapped, the lost, the bitter, the afraid, and the forfeited.

A miniature book of words sifted through him in the last conscious moments, the West rushing through his heart, and the crisp air filling his lungs, his memory, with its rhythmic, luminous flow. Visions formulaic— 'The art of life'—had overtaken the reality of the past, colder than death, and the path was now fixed in place, a sparrow sang on with its precision and vanished, and William felt as if he was getting older, and it felt fine upon a hammock on Colby Street in the morning. For there, when one has the warmth of sun, one will never die.

Adversely, turned the dreaming pilgrim, everything appears equal to the moron, who must rely on surface-level thinking; but peel back the layers slowly and see, that all of life is difference and identity; it is one hopelessly long and mercifully brisk study of physiological literatures of cocoons and butterflies. For there are two choices in life: good books, which lead to interior and exterior good, and servitude, which leads to the opposite.

One makes an aesthetics of life, whispered William, and so must flourish in order to perish with satisfaction . . . life for the harmony of art works . . . one's life is a poem that must die, but only because it lives.

Fate Sweeter Than Wine

THE AFTERNOON BROUGHT ON elevation in warmth and hunger. There was the deli out on University he'd longed to visit in which there was an old man in the corner with multiple aliases who spoke of pleasant things over grilled cheese sandwiches such as the secret history of Jack London:

"One time he come in and use typewriter and yell at top his lungs about his wife left him and no one say anything because Mr. London was loco in that day and he order beer. I gave him private back room. I have own fridge. You know who invented fridge?"

William got his belongings, his bearings straight, showered. He stuck his head out of the bathroom window as hot water rushed down beside him to take a long hit of hashish. He exhaled across the lawn and watched the pluming smoke dissolve against the neighboring chimney.

Life always had its way with reaffirmation, William considered, but far too often did such a notion link itself to the past. There were other far more obscure moments, however, wherein one knew he was on the brink of something fine, entranced within the proximity of the unreal city's permanence.

He put the deli on hold. He took a mason jar of fresh red wine and filled the tub until steam canceled out all mirrors. In the makeshift hot tub he traversed through the once-formidable eons of altered consciousness and alleviated any lingering inspectoral nuances with wine. It was a damned good life if one had the proper, parallel psychological dosage of courage and despair to go for it.

Outside the crisp fields of grass gave off a clear, delicious scent, and surrounding, shadowy blankets of risen trees warranted acknowledgement. He passed it all en route to the subway, thinking of stopping but never stopping, coming into his own the way others come into what is called the world.

He'd managed to keep his mustache intact, now waxed as if tied red strings at the edge of a parcel, wrapping like its copper circles toward his nasal bridge, and with his hair parted to the side and the stitches soon to have fallen from his scalp, he felt as if a debauched prince in his leather jacket and black jeans, his customary Harold Smith wingtips. A young man reminiscent of Daniel Welles crossed William's path on the platform, his cigarette tracing a ladder.

The nine-car BART train screeched ahead at breakneck speed, the familiar stops coming into ascending sight of formulating Friday afternoon, elevating above water and recalling, overlooking the skyline, solidified remembrance as the weight of life rushed through him. Still he had no interest in strict emotion or nostalgic redemption. He had his mind on a bottle of Rockport and hitting Church Street now, and the hell with whatever had been rumored yesterday, and he knew to enjoy himself, enjoy himself, getting back down to work.

'A bottle of Rockport wine and Dolores Park,' thought William, passing through Powell Street—'Then one can die alright, a smile on his face if he feels up for it, and throw those disinclined beneath the wagon.'

He came up for air on the corner of Church and Market. Again it was idyllic in that all was as he'd left it. He came above ground and at once recognized a friend of Harold's standing across from Aardvark Books. Ah, yet how he longed for old Market and Polk with a good song stuck in one's head, but what synchronicities of the city! The air one breathed—to drink afresh whimsical oblivion.

He approached the young man, flaming forgettable character with matching black gauge earrings, nose like an ornamental bulb covered in blackheads, his hair a multicolored beehive and his clothing torn less by time than by machinery, sneering down at his sneakers, and waiting for something or another. It had been Fort Mason where he'd seen him, set by slight ivy and breaking wooden steps, yet William could not recall which night except that he had beat him in chess once.

He straightaway explained that Heather was around somewhere. She earlier in the year lived with Percy, whom Harold had once mentioned, though he was now on Liberty Street in SoMa.

There hadn't been a reliable word on Smith in months. The man attempted to summon an address from the gods with squinted yellow eyes, dilated pupils, in the antechamber of the Milky Way. He spoke in brief of reblogging a reblogged post from his phone.

At the corner men pulled to a yellow light in an old teal Mustang. The theme song from the Blob played from their speakers. They took off in a ricocheting cloud of smoke. William attempted small talk, it proved too difficult a task; the wine store was far easier, Dolores Park far more enjoyable, and he kept on walking ahead.

"And away we go—"

On the sidewalks which led to Dolores Park young people lined the café terraces, street corners, stoops, decks, steps, and rooftops in as rich an abundance as he'd recalled. California was not going under. The news forecasts had been wrong. Either that, or all the jobs had vanished and yet unemployment, inheritance money was still funneling in for now.

At the park's edge there was a patch of grass to sit upon. The old trash cans and recycling bins sat overflowing with empty bottles and swarming flies, a crumpled lawn chair extending to the sky. He took a seat near the tennis courts and looked out upon the sea of voices and bodies, handmade quilts and frothy white smoke and popping corks of 12:25 pm.

An hour and some tumblers of wine later and surrounded by the usual motley crew of painters, designers, musicians, professors, a hand pointed forth with archival finality at William; he squinted across the fields. The man yelled something and stood, leaping over the heads of the young women encircling him.

Daniel Welles began sprinting down the hill, attracting a great current of attention as William sat still transfixed, elated, and he knew that Dolores Park was, at least then, a place where one summoned his spirits. He stood, not canceling out the idea of misconception or hallucination brought on by exhaustion.

Daniel's mustache had taken on such depth as to encircle up and around his cheekbones. Life burned in his eyes. William felt even stranger to not feel shocked one bit; he'd returned to the Bay for such occurrences.

"I knew it!" Daniel shouted, "I knew you'd be back soon!"

He took William by the hand and introduced him to an array of second-hand actors and actresses who passed a jug of wine around and asked approachable questions; everybody knew everybody through someone or another. Projects, travel, the year, the night; there was much to discuss. William found it most remarkable that in San Francisco one was never surprised to feel at home so immediately; it were as if those who had been there all the while knew if you had any sense you would return, and thus when you returned it made perfect sense, and when you did not return it made for something less than perfect sense, and that was an imperious thought.

"Smith and everyone, all of them, are still around," Daniel said.

William noticed another thing he'd admired concerning Daniel: his slightest, uncensored remark commanded respect. No one spoke over him, and seldom did the men and women attempt to speak when he spoke at all. "Everyone's still around!"

He smoked a pipe, readjusted his sailor outfit. It was difficult to ever imagine Daniel as an old man, as he and William caught up, caught breath, applying his old cloth to the motorcycle helmet.

"I was saddened to receive no soup in the mail," William said.

"Oh, oh," Daniel looked away, shrugging his shoulders, "It's all over on that end. No serious relationships for me anymore. No more Sasha, no more anything. Destination: Sanity."

"Nothing could contain you?"

"Nothing at all anymore."

~

Through conversations and endless introductions William at once knew he'd waste no time in finding a room suitable to his journalistic rejuvenation. The weed and the wine were potent by any ferocious means, and yet that chorus of a thousand voices no longer eased his sorrow nor relinquished his position as a young artist or individual in the face of the modern world as it once had, the superhuman daydream of which once had made an awkward personage of him. Now mind and cosmos no longer sought public assistance, or amplified sentences of desolation.

There was no longer an idle, romantic circuit in his mind while the refreshing wind flushed in through Dolores Park, for he knew it was time, to his great relief and sober or otherwise, that his conviction remained the same.

"You know Melody was a good friend of mine," said a nice young girl who'd been listening to Daniel and William speak.

"Is she—dead?"

"Oh no, no," the girl laughed. William looked upon the half dozen of them, their fluttering dresses and strawberry blonde hair—there seemed nothing more difficult in the world any longer than remembering anybody's name—"She just sticks to her old rich boyfriend these days. She used to be a lot of fun."

"Was that the elusive, foreign one?" asked the man with no nose.

"Something like that," William said.

"She's just a nasty girl," laughed TMWNN.

William sighed, pouring a bottle-cap's worth of wine to the dirt. He raised the jug to old Potrero Hill.

Daniel turned away to another group as William and Mary spoke on. She suggested they go to the Gold Dust Lounge by night, and that he'd see a room she'd put up for rent near the beach. William agreed without question as Daniel turned to go. He spoke with apprehension of a new woman he'd met—

"I'll call you tomorrow!" William shouted, jumping up to embrace his friend. "And we'll do lunch!"

He rolled up a spliff. Someone ran out for a crate of beer and another jug of wine as the park became crowded in the haze of the late afternoon.

Then it was dark out, near Union Square.

Within the bar a jazz trio played on at its lightning-pace, the dim interior providing a fine atmospheric calm to the familiar bar. William and Mary drank Anchor Steam in a booth and engaged in familiar tones as if they'd know one another for a long time. He put off finding anyone else till tomorrow.

"Why'd you not tell anyone you were coming?"

"I wanted to surprise everyone. Oh, and I lost most of their numbers."

"What about Facebook?"

"No Facebook."

"*Really?*" Mary asked, spitting her drink at the carpet.

"Oh yes," William sighed, then yelling over the voices: "Oh yes."

"There's all sorts of interesting people coming in and out of the house. You know some of them. You can reconnect," Mary shouted. He tried to get a good look of her but the bar was too dark, and again the day felt as if a festival of excess as the trolley cars clanked by at midnight.

"Oh course," she said, "We'll go have a ball there tonight!"

William felt for the Oakland keys in his pocket and felt secure.

"You know that Melody said the nicest things about you," she said. "I always wanted to meet you. Well we may have met before; you never know."

She was a cute California girl all right. Still there was something incestual about how William could speak with her, how she seemed like a lost sibling or cousin, and began to cause a racket in his mind. He knew to never mix sexuality and real estate. Still, Einstein and Darwin, those great diseases of the mind, made love to their cousins. What was that familiar feeling evocative in rare member of the opposite sex, wherein one feels a societal obligation to pursue matters, and yet within his heart knows he is content with friendship? Parades of people rushed in and out of the swinging doors as seen through blackened, distilled shadows.

William held his manuscript-outlines in one arm with his sleeves upturned to the elbow. He then touched Mary's stocking-laden leg beneath the table before lifting his glass high to the bar's unanimous toast:

To the City of San Francisco!

Roaring drums beat on. William stood to order a round of Fernet before Mary could react to his gesture, set them down upon the table, and observed himself in the bathroom mirror. He thought of his face, washed it clean with cold water, and weaved through the crowd again, his mustache and mind twirling in heightened disarray.

His leather belt was tearing at the buckle from age as he returned to the booth. He found the sign of wear and tear a fine accommodation to the miniature pitchfork-scar across his forehead. Mary went on speaking as if he hadn't touched in her in any way but with his eyes:

"You know Melody used to say you and your friends drank too much." She clicked her fingernail against the emptied pint-glass. "You ought to be careful is all."

"What do you mean?" William found this bit of information trivial and offensive.

"Oh, she said you were all wild."

"Oh Melody, how she had to learn the hard way that there is no nobility, just subjugated barbarism and inbred desolation, high walls and famine, and the laconic technologies of discalced friars."

"Is that so?"

"I feel so good, I'll offer some ideas on how it works," the pilgrim said, "Because there are two roads for the rich and famous, just as every television journalist knows they are so easily dispensable, and it is a fact that I have been advocating idolaters consider for quite some years now. Famous or not, the road leads to a posthumous diet of worms, or dust. Therefore I say let the blind stare; let the legless walk. Now we begin to destroy the appetites of perversion that had caught us off guard, digital trap as it was; and as such Melody really just wanted to tie me down, I who could not stay put. I understand there was one serious writer who took LSD in Death Valley—but I can assure you that it would be better for no other mortal to even try."

"Are you talking about Foucault? I read him in college!"

"Yes, and I believe that was Melody's idea—to emulate Foucault. But emulation is flattering when it is unconscious, appalling when it's not. I had on my mind then Octavia and theological geography, as I have now. You see, dear Mary, I abandoned my multicolored coat for good last year, donating it to a shivering woman; from then on the black cloak was, is all I had a cousin who'd mentioned Augustine's lion to me when I was very little, and rather in love with her; from what I understand she is very poor now, living in Williamsburg as a divorcee. Octavia and I even ran into her around Christmas, maybe even Christmas Eve, but she did not recognize me. I must have been about five years old the last time she saw me, but I also remember her reading to me about the planets and the prophets, John the Baptist and Mars, sharing childhood silences trembling in a cousin's beautiful milk-white arms. But maybe she is happy, and it is I who am not. But what does this have to do with that harlot Nelson? O city of maladies, taking in souls as the body takes in food, races dissolving into the stupidity of time, the city and the novel someday coming to respective ends!"

"She'll be at Della Pera, the hidden bar at North Beach, tonight, you know."

"Is that so? What bar is that?"

"It's in what had been a vacant church," said Mary, "Rather, if I do say so, *resplendent* still with aspects of stained glass. You go through its little circuitous gate and garden path, taking seats before the mutilated stone."

"Let us go there in time . . ."

"But what were you saying about Melody?"

"She is mad I did not want to stick around and do drugs and so she criticizes my drinking. It is no big deal. I'd rather have Dorothy's bottle in front of me than a frontal lobotomy."

"I never see her anymore!"

"Don't you know that, well," William grew flustered, recomposing himself with a deep inhale, "If she referred to us as alcoholics and this or that, don't you know that an alcoholic is someone you don't like that drinks as much as you? That girl was callow—"

"Mr. Defensive!"

"Oh, never mind."

"You're a pretty boy," she said. "You just don't want to go getting a big stomach and be not able to see your penis."

"Any good man would stop drinking if he couldn't see his own knees," William said, adding at once: "Literal, figurative, whatever. Don't tell me you know men like that!"

"Well some in my family," she admitted with a blush, "But I don't want to talk about families. It's like calling someone you know won't call you back."

"I know."

"You do?"

"Yes."

"We've got to go to the party soon at my house. See those gross men over there—they tried talking to me just now."

"Too many statues have mouths," William said, clicking his glass of Fernet against Mary's. The band started back up.

"Let's take a cab back to the house."

They took off, young and alive and arms interlocked, through the doorway and out to Powell Street roaring at midnight, into the taxicab and straight through to the Sunset.

～

"It's a city of orgies," William relayed over the phone to Phil Cohen. He looked over the withered two-story house with gated windows and a garden beside the rectangular picket fence. Mary met him in the basement, which had an entrance of its own.

"Call me tomorrow, ye bard!"

"Used to be a three-car garage," she said, taking William on a tour.

The room was enormous and filthy with couches and desks already set in place. Cobwebs lined the thin windows and the ceiling was thick enough to prevent excess sound. It'd take a day's work to sweep the place up, but one could afford to pace with a neurotic pencil in his mouth quite a-ways if the thoughts were not flourishing, and that was what William wanted; a room large enough to walk around, by any means necessary. The room reminded him of the back of the Chicago station where he had caught the California Zephyr. He sneezed several times, let fresh air in through windows, and tugged the chord of a flickering light.

The sound of the light-rail came and went outside of the doorway with a brief ring of the bell, a slight rumble throughout the interior of the room.

"It picks up right outside, also."

William got along with Mary so well he felt foolish to have made any sort of move on her and all the more foolish to have to bring up the somber issue of money. He leaned along the balustrade and poured Spanish red for two as voices blended together upstairs.

"How about a hundred dollars a month and you can spend whatever would have been added to fixing the place up?"

How anything made sense! His impulses gesticulated toward spitting the wine clean out, letting his eyes bulge, but his thrifty heart prevailed and he attempted to take it, as each day death dies with sleep, and to solidify the deal before morning, interior jubilation and exterior stoicism:

"Oh," William said, "I suppose that would work."

With a shake of the hands and a handwritten contract the massive, disgusting room was his. Had this been a garage once? I suppose the cobwebs and broken glass could be taken care of in a mere afternoon. Still, it is quite heinous, but then again so am I. St. Benedict and St. Ignatius had their caves; let this be mine! Mary went up to the party.

He sat at the warped desk hypothesizing just where to call for freelance work. Nothing came just then, but that's what a stroll to the university library and a long sprint back was for.

"I'll stay at least two years until these manuscripts are done, these essays published, my reputation solidified!" he sang, drinking alone, listening to the baseball game on the radio: Giants vs. Yankees.

He took an old broom up in dance, crooned, swept up broken glass and empty matchbooks beneath the doors leading to the backyard. The fact of the matter was fate, and that was something effulgently whorish to believe in. He felt as far away from the action of the city as he'd felt on Colby Street, with the fine possibility of getting there at a moment's notice. He stayed up until dawn, wrote postcards to his mother and to Octavia, enough red wine to quench the whole summer, and he never even made it to the party. There will be many, there will be an overflow of them, he configured, falling peacefully asleep to the sounds of distant rushing trains, the headlights shining through fog.

From East to West
the Heavens Through

DANIEL WELLES RODE HIS motorcycle over from across town the next afternoon. Seventy-five and sunny. He and William went out for charcoal, steak, and drinks. They smoked a pipe out on the porch and Daniel relayed further information he'd forgotten to relay yesterday.

"Well first off, that Percy character, that is his nickname though—his real name's Brendan White, I think—I believe he's in SoMa, at least I see him at the thrift-store every time I'm there. His ilk is full of grievous words. He goes by Brendan and Percy interchangeably. I think one is when he is stoned and the other, well, otherwise. He asked about you, I figured you two would be in touch."

"I just got a new phone less than a month ago," admitted William. "And still I haven't even bought a laptop of my own. I have the money, but I can't get myself to care enough to buy one."

"Well," Daniel said, tapping the porcelain pipe as the remaining ash scattered across and through the front yard, "I'd like to think that difficulties are often the byproduct of enrichment." He took two cans of Simpler Times from the ice-bucket.

"I could see that—"

Daniel twirled his mustache as if in deep concentration.

"Oh," his eyes lit up, "But oh, yeah, what I meant to tell you—I know a guy from high school coming into town soon, see, he's in Santa Cruz, he's coming through with a pound of weed and a quarter pound of hashish. I'm going to help him sell it and take in a couple of thousands of dollars."

"Brilliant," William said. He further inquired the illegalities.

"I'll call him after we eat. I'm thinking if you let him stay here for a few days he'll give you some money. You've got much more space than me. You'll get something like $600.00 out of it to begin. Just let him store his drugs here; he returns east in less than a week. Weed, hash. We'll get you a card. He is returning to Pennsylvania, I think."

"Where do you know him from?" William asked.

"He's staying with a friend of a friend in Santa Cruz right now, but the ranch was raided two nights ago. The guy is, in a sense, worthless, well-nigh brain-dead, and not picturesque in any sense of the term. His name is Thom Stoykovich. He is a drug dealer. When you look into his eyes you can tell he is thinking about drugs whether he is on them or off them. He'll braid his hair, complain when he speaks, and listen to nothing but the Beatles." They laughed in the sunlight. "He's been studying music theory for years although I've only ever heard him play Beatles cover songs on his steel guitar. Come to think of it, the last time we got together I almost ended up the way of Virginia Woolf."

"Well look, look—I'll take his money," William said, ". . . but you say it'll just be a few days and then he's gone? I've got people to find in San Francisco, Daniel! I've got business to attend to!"

Daniel called Thom, confirmed the details, and made an arrival time for the next week. This, then, gave William time before he felt obligated to stay inside, keep the door locked, and let the drug dealer from Santa Cruz get rid of his stash as William got down to work.

They stepped out to the unkempt backyard, William running his hand through his beard, contemplating eternity and what the upstairs looked like.

"You know a city, a time is a good one when just looking at a fence in the afternoon seems monumental," he said. Fresh air rushed through the yard, twisting and returning the smoke eastward. Daniel dowsed the charcoal in fluid. The pluming smoke rose and evaporated along the rooftops.

"What are you working on, anyway?"

"I'm going to write a short book, a novella I think it is called, one day along Polk Street from Market to Beach, day to night. Series of political essays. I've got a whole portfolio full of outlines I created in Pennsylvania," William exaggerated.

"Yes!"

"I'll explain all of it in detail after we take a ride out through Twin Peaks, Lincoln Street, through the Mission to the main branch of the public library."

"Clement after, Green Apple! Dumplings in the Sunset!"

"Reverence in the city," William said, preparing plates on an old amputated picnic table of plastic held up by a dozen cinder blocks. A subway train passed across the street.

The flawless day, sheer and clear, sifted into a beautiful chilly night. Daniel and William swept out the enormous room of dust, wrapped the wooden pillars with strings of lights, set down a new mattress upon the floor between the desk and the couch. Daniel had given William a newer radio with larger speakers and a brand-new lamp he'd found sitting within his garage.

William spoke with his mother; seasonal depression continued on the east, jobs disappeared, the fraudulent banks ran the country and the world into oblivion as if an insatiable fuse followed by pale fire. Many people had seen this happening in other people's lives and now it was happening in theirs.

Yet in its own way it brought Ms. Fellows closer to Wm., as it brought many people close together, bound by that obscure object of despair. Now, countrywide. For when you put all of your stock into one's skin color or genitals one is left with the perpetual governmental rape of civic lock, stock, and barrel, and nothing in return save a speech designed to distract and said skin, genitals. And to return her definitive understanding of William's rebellion, his exile, and as the opinions of the past tend to dominate the current, there was a new formula, one of broken waves, which had at last reformed between the son and his mother. It was the life that would leave the living astonished were they to soak it in. Everyone was furious and bitter and longing to reject useless positions and temperaments in life. He'd arrived in one piece, she explained, and what was there now but to retain optimism in a darkened heart, to sing the sun in flight? There is no lexicographical escape route here. Sit back and enjoy the ability to sit back. And so they spoke at length, jousting between nervousness and redemption, and at the end of the conversation William felt closer to his mother than he had since his college days.

There were riots in the streets, protests on Wall Street, Octavia explained, though either of them knew any sort of revolution began in far different formats. Mobs of unarmed people with picket signs and pocketsful of marijuana are the sort of thing the enemy can laugh at through tinted windowpanes. That then is not victory but public castration. What, then, is victory, William pondered—and is paradise recognition of that which isn't, the bough that must break, whereby one must have open arms for what causally must fall: the vita Nuova, or new life?

"In our modern age," Octavia said, "the true horror is not just comprehending that it cannot be made sense of without understanding the historical magnitude of abandoning God. The true horror is in sitting down and thinking about what this means."

～

Around midnight William met his roommates, or the people living upstairs.

Aside from Mary two pensive unemployed couples shared bedrooms, all four in their mid-twenties and halfway at work on some sort of ambiguous fashion thing and some photography project or another. One of them looked like a horse, but loved anal sex, so there was that. The other's father was a homosexual. Balzacian. William admired this. No, neither the horse nor the homosexual, but the degenerate nature of the house; it sent a touch of Balzacian insight through his veins. It was not just in literal shambles but in emotional shambles as well. Here one could vanish for a season to read Proust and garner few questions in temporal wake. Speaking of Wake: hadn't someone mentioned Vico? Nay. That was too good to be true. Nico. Yes, alas, that was what the sophomore was on about Pasolini's *Gospel According to St Mathew*. Through the smoke clouds, William managed to offer that he himself sometimes felt like a motherless child. To which the girl said well, yes, and what about fathers? That, said William, is up to exile and future generations—for you see, all the Epics of classical literature end in death—

"But I would much prefer the death of worldliness, or temporal obsession, or to have one shed the mental death of our culture like the skin of a reptile. That shall be the end of the new epic, which rightly summons an epoch in all its unfathomable becoming. There is enough termination in epic and aesthetic discourse; now we need a psychic death that reveals the evil of the age, so that the next may never believe the lies their master ventriloquists tell them, that they'll know in their heart are lies anyhow—"

The housemates were fond of the pilgrim, if perplexed. But then, so were the host of persons he had known last year with whom he gathered now; something was changing. He walked about the old-fashioned house when everyone was out, puffing away, robe-clad, and wearing a mitre made of cardboard remnants, up at last to the kitchen with its window overlooking the city at night. Alas, he came to realize that a view gets old in about ten seconds. What is there to look at for any longer than that? He knew not, and thus drank.

He marveled anyone who kept their projects to themselves. Sometimes it meant one knew what he or she was doing and that she or he would get the job done and if it did not work nothing specific had been proclaimed.

Creativity was more of a conversation than an actuality and they seemed like fine people to see on occasion, acknowledgement without presence. An idyllic roommate.

Everyone was optimistic enough and glad to see the basement being renovated. D. Welles held many of the conversations with his innumerable tales, leaping from seats and countertops, gazing out of the window to distant trains pressing toward West Portal. The shadow of his mustache curled along the wall and there was the beautiful view: Extended miles of skyscrapers, shops, tall swaying trees and vermillion stretches of beach, darkened cliffs and glittering stars as the wine and the spliffs went around and around. William longed to shout how good it was to arrive once again.

Phil Cohen and a dozen others arrived with jugs of wine, fresh loaves of bread and pints of gin, liters of tonic water and half a dozen limes. Everyone was deranged with summer's beginning, had food-stamps, collected free money, blared the song by Patti Smith, and kept a casual eye out for work. America had prescribed itself a moral complexity that did not exist save for neurotic paperwork, and the God in which one once warranted trust was no longer dead but had been laughed into the realm of a discarded joke at best, emerging only ever to seem as if a constructed fairytale in any of his million forms.

Yet who was it that laughed, William wondered. How could it be that there was never an atheist who attacked anything, or anyone save Christ, and who further was less an adept in church dogmatics than regurgitating subterranean corporatism?

The more he thought about Christ, the more he grew anxious in his realizing that His critics were less correct than parroting one retrograde opinion after another. Indeed, the industry of anti-Christ was so commonplace that when one started to notice that it was forever Christ and Christ only under fire—and the mental shape of His critics—one could not help but reconsider the Triune God. At the very least, so many vile bodies abhorred him while claiming to fight all religions; but they never moved past Christ, and thus shot themselves in the foot before the euphemistic race even began, bogged down in ad hominem and Darwinian futility. William never sought evil spirits, but now reflected on his having magnetized lukewarm atheists throughout his time in high school and out in the world. It startled him and gave him much material to set down on his operating table of loose-leaf, and begin surgery with his pencils on the aged, stale bodies of charlatans.

Alas, he still could not bring himself to go to Mass or even bother with religious texts, let alone the Bible. There were times when he was close, like kissing a beautiful girl for the first adolescent time, except that this woman, the church, possessed much familiarity in his memories. He recalled each prayer, response, hand signals, and so on without effort.

"Someday I'll stop in, but when the time is right . . . because this life of atheistic chemical abuse is losing its grip on me . . . it never ends. I shall not stop today, nor even next month, but the mustard seed has been planted.

"God help me," he prayed, going so far as to consider the Rosary and the Pauline Epistles, and other mandatory texts he had not even considered in adulthood. "Perhaps if I remain alive long enough and keep my heart in New York City, that will be a beginning. I am on the cusp of something . . . and I shall learn, even by making mistakes; so help me God."

There was, however, an increased anxiety in the air that came through in doubtful bursts. The countrywide tone could be laughed off, most would agree either years later when nothing could be done or in death, in the possibility that everything one heard on television was complete propaganda. Most people, they agreed in the night, expected of others and the country just what they themselves were incapable, thus making a complex everyday relationship with life which seemed bound to collapse entrenched in a haze of weed smoke and blue light. If there was going to be anything but breakdown, there would have to be a lifestyle alteration. This approximation brought fleeting silence to the kitchenette. William turned over the record.

The war was infinite, one might comment, and the neocapitalistic state began and ended with a subliminal fascism one could admit drunk but not sober. Sober acknowledgement of the condemned world, country, and state seemed mad, so one saved his energies and philosophies for drunken hours; at least in San Francisco there were a good, good many, and still William sat around friends old and new with that awful feeling which comes sometimes from too much fun: Too much sorrow. He told himself to never make decisions at night. Make decisions in the morning. Yea, there was some good left in the City by the Bay. Yet this fuse too was set to make societal contact unto implosion in three, two, one, in a maze of excrete and mountains of needles . . .

Still, as the second night roared on, friends old and new sang beside the open window overlooking the city and raved of films and memories and ate fresh food and downed fresh drinks all night in a room of smoke. William, in his brooding hour, knew it would be wrong to attempt to relive anything at all, for such hypothetical insurgencies could break a man down far faster than anything the natural world had to offer.

There was that fleeting tint of eyes, that great burst and collision of enthusiastic voices that found themselves out west just before it all went downhill, and for that last summer one could find immense value in even the shape of a crack in the sidewalk just as long as it belonged to San Francisco. In the morning—if for some reason one happened to get out of bed before noon—it wasn't uncommon to find a functional, intelligent man or woman, friend or acquaintance, enjoying a half pint of whiskey and sitting Indian-Style upon the porch in stalled, beatific morning hours. The Bay retained its atmospheric tranquility, its angelic resistance to sobriety at all waking hours. Each sign of arrival was refreshing, then, for someone who grew up in New York. There, in Manhattan, slaughter seemed eminent if one were to have an elongated blink upon the streets during the day. In San Francisco one could wander about entranced for a good couple of hours, days, weeks, seasons, or any number of decades, depending on taste and circumstance.

Living quarters were comfortable in their squalor as well as in the excess money it left him. It was a miracle that neither insects nor rodents ever got in. He considered it a studio, although if anything it reminded him of McSorley's with its framed antique news clippings and sawdust, carved furniture and a rich, wooden scent. He stepped away from everyone for a moment to marvel its debauchery, its whimsicality.

"And to think I could have made a clean living at a standard price!" William shouted, overcome by the wine and sleeplessness and the sound of pretty women dancing upstairs. "And to think I ever was weary, and to think, O, to not think—garnish thyself in poverty!"

He loaded up a garbage can with the photographs and shards, replacing one vacant corner with a framed print of Christ calling St. Matthew, and another with Francisco Goya's colossus warring across the lands. These had been sold at a fair price out on Valencia Street, and their respective places in the room's corners fit like the last piece of a puzzle. As for music, he had come to despise most of it. There would be tons of classical albums borrowed from the San Francisco Public Library. Aside from that, he had one album just as he'd had just one last year in Leonard Cohen's first album; this time it was Monk's *Solo Monk*. He'd purchased Captain Beefheart for Melody Nelson, met another woman in Dolores Park, and over the course of philosophizing and neck licking traded Beefheart for Monk, then Monk for Vaughan Williams. All that remained was acquiring Samuel Barber's "Prayers of Kierkegaard", which would prove a journey all its holy, salient own.

Overhead swam the sea of heightened nocturnal voices as the sun crept over the ocean. He took to his glass of gin and looked through the tall rectangular window. He lit a crisp miniature European cigar. He looked out of the window at nothing in particular, considering that he never saw himself having children. What did this mean? Should he let people know? He contemplated this while running through when amidst his longhand notes a revelation crashed down into the plain of his mind the way cars crashed into poles and wrapped themselves around in burning pieces of fractured chrome; it struck him, so he sat down:

How could one get anything done in Paradise? And wasn't Paradise effortlessness? Why bother at work? The life of artistry was a life, after-all; paradise was thought, defined unearthly. He listened to the voices calling for whiskey and the existence of God, others swaying with optimistic pressure; he did not categorize these voices as different from his own—he had stepped out of the room for a moment. If he listened, he could hear his voice in any crowd. This humbled him.

Phil Cohen and Daniel Welles appeared in the doorway singing Bobby Lester, calling William back upstairs with a definitive optimism which made him feel foolish for ever having contemplated brooding. He raced up the staircase at once.

And still, if anyone were ever to inquire his redeveloped level of artistic seriousness borne of anguish he would tell them: 'The generation I've been born into did not satisfy my needs—that generation with surfaces smooth as a girl's hand, and of souls beneath such skin bankrupt as the state itself. Every man and woman for themselves—It is the time of the assassins.'

Beneath golden lights in the living room Mary lay upon the felt couch, her pale legs visible from sudden angles unbeknownst. She placed down her book down, stretched, and yawned.

"How are you," he said. He leant rejuvenated upon the pillar attached to the narrow hallway of watercolor paintings.

"I'll be back out soon. My drink is running low. I've got two pages left in this book." She picked *The Sorrows of Young Werther* back up and extended her hand William's way. "Have you read him?"

"How would I know?"

"Um—because you are yourself?"

"Says who? I read that when I was a little boy. When I was sad that book and *Ethan Frome* always uplifted me."

He walked past the smoldering ashtray, the licorice-gated living room window, and sat down upon the couch.

"All I know of the man is that we've got the same birthday," he admitted.

"You can borrow it soon—How is your room?"

"Oh," William said, "It is all coming together fine." Mary smiled and returned to her book. He thought of refilling her drink. He wondered of the gesture's implications; he was frightened at the prospect of revealing, lest exhibiting, his attractions, and frightened of extending his sexual resume.

A group of teenage anthropologists had made it to the roaring kitchen. Each of the young women wore white t-shirts, shoulder-length dirty-blonde hair and spoke of last year and yesterday at once, university life and the decline of man.

One with the candy-blue Boone's Farm mentioned she'd been raised in Eugene, Oregon; Daniel's eyes lit up at once.

"Isn't it most beautiful to drive through Northern California, Oregon, Washington, as autumn breaks!" He turned to William through the doorway. "Don't think I forget our plans!"

Holy visions of the autumn highway swam through William's mind as he shook Daniel's hand, entranced. The tone of his voice coincided with his eyes, springing with ceaseless fervor, and William knew at once it was another journey to look ahead to come autumn.

People came and went through the house at all hours of the night and day. Everyone was aimless albeit optimistic and save the students no one had much of a specific reason to be there, again or for the first time, no reason other than that unspoken magnetism one could explain so well at dawn, as spoken though a gaze into enthusiastic eyes through a sifting cloud of smoke.

Mary reentered the room with a crate of champagne.

"I'd like to propose a toast!" she cried out, at once engaging the animated room's attention, the bewildered eyes of a dozen glittering bottles. Daylight had come about and shined in stretches of light through the torn paper blinds. Trains broke to and fro before, beside the old house. "To William's arrival and to the summer!" Everyone raised a personal bottle to the chandelier, to the sun, and corks burst throughout the room in a running stream of intoxicated laughter and triumph.

He sat upon the couch with a young student whose name he would never remember, whose face he found both familiar and unfamiliar depending on its tan, supple angle.

"What is it like there, on the East, and all of New *York*! I've never *been* there!"

He rubbed his forehead with his fingers, looking down then to his hands.

"When you're here it feels like a graveyard, and when you're there it can feel like a graveyard. But when it's good it's good, when it's better it's the best, it is the infernal city no one can ever master. It is most charming in that it is not charming. The city will always have a good grip about you or anyone who's lived there, that sense of nostalgia we claim died with a certain age or experience. But right now, yes, it would seem like a graveyard, compared to the morning is San Francisco. I think that realizing you must be in a certain mood to be in New York is like the day you grasp Santa Claus. I wish I still thought Manhattan and Brooklyn and Queens were the world; I was much younger then. And yet, to end it all, when New York calls your name, though, there is no turning back, and you had better arrive on time and looking damned good."

The girl sat bewildered as the pilgrim let the words break through long gulps of champagne. Phil Cohen stumbled into the room, clicking his glass against William's.

"A seven-day weekend," he proclaimed, as the young girl that had been on his arm returned from the bathroom.

William and the girl went downstairs. They shared cigarettes, pulled the blinds, listened to the morning classical radio crackle across the room. Time, be it five minutes or five hours ago, had begun to dissolve at an increasing rate. For minutes at a time he and the girl sat back, laughing with increasing earnestness and vigor, until their throats burned, and all began again with William punching his knees, reaching for his aching temples and chest.

Around 9:00am he noticed she had neither further questions nor statements when another of the young anthropologists came in, untying her turquoise dress with a giggle. She came between William and the girl and sat laughing, attempting to talk in her bathing suit. William and the girl pulled down the straps of her bathing suit with caution as her head tilted back, her lips separating with deep pleasure. They ran their hands along her body, then one another's.

He looked over at his desk and thought of tomorrow; it was already happening. He took the young women in his arms beneath the blankets, to the queen-sized mattress upon the floor. They took their time with one another's bodies, laughing between sips of champagne and tickling. Then it all ended, and everyone grew serious, their bodies in accordance with one another with symphonic erudition.

At last, when everyone had finished at once, no trace of a sound came from above.

~

He awoke alone, which was undemanding and pleasant enough, in a sea of sunlight which ran through the windows and straight through to the unconscious. He stood and looked with exhaustion to the clear blue sky, inhaled oceanic breeze coming through pried open windows. Voices came from outside, from the porch, intersected by closing car doors and passing trains.

There was a pile of records in a blurred corner of the room. Lee Hazelwood had written for and with Duane Eddy. Little synchronicities like that fell from the mountainous mind, tumbling to an avalanche, and one felt obligated to break into the day by any means necessary. It were as if in such contemplative moments, looking to the desk and away, William knew decades down the line all would return to him and he'd never let himself off of the hook for aspiring to do anything but live if he were to do anything but live. Fervent sexuality broke through his mind with an ambiguous consistency in that he could remember their bodies so well, the tones of their voices, hued shadows. He sat motionless, transfixed within his imagination upon sore elbows; he stood to walk, limping, hobbling to the door while buttoning his red-flannel afternoon shirt. Streaks of nail-marks lay embedded across his curling, jet-black chest hair.

'Which in this afternoon light,' he thought aloud, 'Resembles razor-wire.'

He sat at his desk. He outstretched the outlines of manuscripts. He received a text message. He got his pencil and paper in order. He observed the theoretical lithograph.

He lit a cigarette of success and tucked his manila folders away and took a half-bottle of champagne. He coughed, laughed in a frenzied pattern, and walked to the doorway, where thin traces of sunlight broke in across the exposed-concrete ground. His work was done for the day.

"Well, well!" Mary cried from the open window of a brand-new fire engine-red convertible. She wore Ray Ban sunglasses and a one-piece strawberry red bathing suit, stepping to the porch. "How do you like my mother's car?"

Daniel and El sat in rocking chairs with bagged eyes, scratching at beards and the shades of stubble, drinking hangover wine.

"Yes!" El shouted, entranced within the glorious Polaroid-recapturing of an afternoon bender, grace disheveled and euphoric: "Yes!"

"He is alive," Daniel pronounced to the delight of surrounding people, "He is alive! And well! Good morning, sunshine!"

William's roommates waltzed to and fro the trunk of the car with beach-blankets, baskets of wine and crepes, sun-tan lotions applied around the exterior of bikinis and trunks.

"What is happening, with everyone," William said, knowing at once the answer was serene.

"We're going over to the East Bay to meet some friends and lounge around on hammocks," Daniel said. El began to stand with a wipe of foam from his crisp, tar-colored beard.

"Mwahahaha!"

"And *we're* going to beach!" sang Mary. She appeared glowing at William's side, keys jingling around her fingers like a pinwheel. "Because today is going to be the greatest day, the best Saturday! Todo ese Cielo Permitir!"

William sat between El and Daniel. They polished off the champagne and cans of ale from the cooler. He longed for the company of old Harold Smith, even Heather, but cut the idea out of his mind once and for all. Some fine day—

"If we could swim," he sighed, draping his arms across Daniel and Phil's shoulders. "What with ye freezing waters and all, O Mustard—"

"No—no—we're driving to Santa Cruz, the five of us!"

Mary threw her pale hands to the overhead panels; William reached out and caught them and the pair began to dance, spilling out into the streets as subway trains passed through beside them. The street was long and winding with its train lines down the middle and at a specific angle, if one tilted his head the right way within an opiate-dance of instinctual sovereignty and perpetual triumph, one could see the glittering Pacific at the sloping edge of Taraval Street.

El drank his cup of tea and discussed other matters with William's roommates as Daniel raved on in a scorched, raspy voice of a cocktail no one had ever heard of, twirling his keys the moment Mary threw hers to a roommate, tossing his spare helmet to El from beneath the padded wicker chair.

"Well I'm glad we're all *alive* God-damnit," Daniel said, throwing his arms around everyone in sight. William and El embraced. The motorcycle revved up. "Call me tonight or soon! Or we'll call you!"

The engine roared up once, twice, and the raving metallic black bomber helmets took off through transcendental grey smoke in the summer afternoon around the winding corner soaked in sunlight and ahead to the Bay Bridge. Mary's hands dissolved from William's.

"It's my birthday!" she announced.

The motorcycle's rumble fell from auditory recognition.

"Well happy birthday," he said. "I'll buy you cotton candy and all of the games you want in the arcade!"

A stream of wind rustled her strawberry-blonde hair westward.

"That's too kind of you, strange boy of the underworld."

William stepped out to the mailbox to send off handwritten lines of poetry to Octavia, including a nice, cursive page of Dante's *Paradiso*, 17.43–45.

"Indeed have descended into the bowels of materiality, its false extension ushered into the programmed laboratories; soon enough I shall depart San Francisco, perhaps for good!"

She turned to William, her eyes rolled, then tilted northern to his own, the lady's fixed in concentration:

"I just don't understand how his, how Daniel's mustache stays so *waxed*, curled at the ends that way while he drives all over the city! I tell you, William—I swear, I do—it's the closest I've come to reconsidering God in a decade!"

There was a time when this sort of thing would have either made him laugh or automatically propelled him to feign laughter. But now he was just concerned that an unprecedented access to knowledge had coincided with the collapse of culture. The innumerable stories of persons maimed, wounded, exilic, enslaved, posthumously crowned were in such hours much less alien to him than they had hitherto been, as concepts, or method in exaggeration. He did not see himself as a martyr or as one who would save the world; but he could at least, at last turn inward and reconsider the limits of excess and salvific, Augustinian aspects in moving against the current.

Such were the thoughts he brought with him by night into his cave. It was a miracle, he reflected, that he was even considering the possibility of seeing through base pleasures and mindless activity; and it was also an invitation to a cultural beheading. Therefore he kept the little flower within his heart well nursed with contemplative practice of higher viewpoints and began—every so nocturnal often—to reconsider self-destruction and its endless, futile wages of sin.

The Souls of Jupiter Arranged
like Letter-Lights

PHIL SPECTOR ALL THE way down that vivid coastline of infinite land and highway, windows down and life serene for strangers to the guided seas, questions drowned out with walls of sound, the sandy sight with its rich air of autonomy and adventure before that melancholic last instance of San Francisco slipping away though it'll be there in the evening beneath the faded, towering capsule of rich blue sky which implodes at sundown, the sole white whale of a cloud sifting by through highway mirror, dancing through one's seatbelt, on the way to Hallelujah where in flash of canopy shade with its streams of flickering sunlight breaking across the car as if an automatic camera snapping away, dew-glisten and distant riverbeds gelled tranquil with that revitalizing air of a hundred thousand striking oak trees. William cut his black pants at the knee and rolled the frayed ends up once, twice, singing each song and by heart as they tore through the backwoods street heading 60 MPH south to the Santa Cruz boardwalk.

Mary and William spoke at length of the mutual agony of growing up an outsider in towns of fools as William crossed his tennis shoes without socks, bare arms outstretched across the back of the seat and the wind swept through everyone's hair. He told her tales of the summer prior and of Jerusalem and of the future. Porcelain bowls went around, which the three others took to. Mary shared her bottle of champagne with William and they took a break from the smoke.

"You can't alter your sense of smell so bad all of the time!"

He threw his unbuttoned flannel too high and it disappeared into the forestry. The driver insisted they return as it was no problem whatsoever. William resisted, overcome by the wall of sound, the millions of others sweating it out in office buildings, supermarkets, and trench warfare:

"I'm alive! I don't hate it!" he sang, laughing aloud with his new housemates as the driver pressed on. "I don't hate it a little after two in the afternoon!"

Mary smiled as the weedwind pressed on, throwing the empty bottle of champagne into a paper-bag and unlatching a twinkling miniature bottle of Glenlivet.

They parked near the boardwalk and at once Mary led the way across sandy streets with the familiar warmth of one revisiting the city of one's youth, for the teeming boardwalk went with its redolent air of hot dogs, French fries, milkshakes, ice cream cones—big cables strapped to turning wheels while three dozen peoples cried out with in joy, the rockabilly music breaking from each overhead speaker-set before the dozens of multicolored rides and fountains. They spent the day singing and laughing out in neon arcades, colloquial ruminations outstretched upon warm sands with two grams of hashish, photobooths and rollercoasters and the photographic perfection with which Mary's eyes widened, shot forth with an ethereal joy at each corner proclaiming it was the greatest birthday she had ever had with the exuberance of Olympic javelins when at dusk she was presented with the biggest ice cream cone ever built, lined with rainbow jimmies and a cherry on top.

"It was a fine day," Mary reflected through bursts of innocent laughter, "And must end with Elvis Presley all the way home."

William thanked the stars that after-all his mother's fondness of the King would come into play. He waltzed into the store for a half-pint of Old Grand Dad, poured it into John's half-filled cup of soda and the two ran out to the others in the lot following that burning orange, distant bead.

He and Mary watched the moon-glow encapsulate the boardwalk growing smaller, smaller, and microscopic and then vanishing. The music came back on as the cool wind broke through their hair and William felt quite insane with bliss for ever—even but just for a moment—not wanting to exist at all, feeling overt pessimism, unaware of laconic despondency, laden with terminal doubt, irreversible metaphysical horrors because then he was singing aloud in synchronicity with matching triumphant faces, stranger souls in the night, his body wrapped in makeshift shawls of blankets as he'd never reacquired a shirt to wear and for that moment and all of that brisk car ride he could admit that to expect the worst was in part a plagued irrationality albeit steady dismay although for some, the revered and the nocturnal, it was the price of never being let down.

He wanted more. For that Summer Paradiso limitless as language was something else, he knew, the radiance of the self-recaptured, daydreaming through the forestry and back unto the city night: "I had Dame Fortune prostrate at my feet; my prudence seized on chance and never failed to turn to me, pulling with both hands—and your heart's on fire too!" Soaring 100 MPH through overhead aluminum green signs which say San Francisco x amount of miles and still mean so much more.

Stopping for gas the pilgrim observed light commotion outside of a church, Deut. 32:35 on the menu for this Sunday, and a man selling glow-in-the-dark flesh-colored Israelites. Beside the smiling man sat another, younger man, toothless and decadent, selling a pyramid of sponges and some books. William greeted himself and picked up a pocket edition of Kipling on the sidewalk, while beyond these salesmen yet another was now crying out in pain, screaming ,as he struck another with a piece of what looked like a brick. All at once blood ran down the once-tranquil forehead.

"Ambulance coming. Looks like they are voting on lowering the age of consent today, and now that's spiked crazy whispers of legalizing bestiality and incest too. I would get the hell out of here if I were you, kid."

"I am armed with sagacity, prescience, and the harmony of the heavenly spheres in the multiplicity of lights," resounded the pilgrim.

Then his peers zipped up to the curb and William leapt in, saying nothing of the incident.

"For the heart beats on," shouted the driver, "The world turns its hollowed inside aflame, and the past breaks away like disassociated ash from hexagonal porcelain," and William knew he was in good, albeit new company, his left arm across the leather interior, his right retracing the wind of western night.

Sunlight on a Broken Column

HE FOUND IT FAR easier to get down to work, and therefore drank instead, whence living out near the Pacific Ocean. There were bars and cafes in the Sunset although none of them generated anything evocative in terms of reoccurrence. He found a nice little café out on 44th although he found himself in a position to get to work at once in his room. Everyone upstairs worked odd-jobs and took summer courses all his first week there and when the bender wore off he sat down to the computer.

There, at the iMac, he realized two critical truths concerning his craft and art with the immediacy of a switchblade knife:

First, anyone using the computer for first drafts was damned, bound to the flaccid reality of digital life, of distractive mechanization.

Second, all first-drafts must be handwritten or typewritten. The hand works to the accordance of the heart, the typewriter is a machine designed for words. The computer is a fine invention, upon which strict typing is to become swallowed by that newfound eternity of disassociation, and all first drafts must begin elsewhere if they are to be considered serious.

Then what could be reasons for combating such conviction or referring to one who believed William 'Old-fashioned'?

Time-deficient? In such a case, that registration of time would be less killed by itself (Its concern bound by ruins) but bludgeoned for the sake of artistry, swept away like memory, the last microbes of vocal dust having fallen from the face of flint, some reduplicating vortex or another.

What mattered, disconcerted or otherwise, was to achieve through the labor of a thousand pistols the accuracy, calculation, the lens of the sniper. It would be a hellish pursuit of quixotic realities in a world of ruins and vipers, but couldn't the end-result be such memory-laden epiphany as to deconstruct that paralytic death of subservient days and poisonous nights, of unraveling the falsified systems of reason, to let it come down disintegrating before, within, and beyond the mind's eye?

If all was timed well, William gathered, he would in the course of one month have completed two packets of articles and another draft of something or another which he could then let sit for weeks as to reread with fresh autumnal eyes and make cuts, edits, the final draft upon the computer and begin mailing out copies en masse or begin circulating around the city.

It was a complex psychological acceleration and before business took hold William knew just what preliminary necessities and extravagances to call upon before that extended period of solitary sobriety which is concentration in the raging life.

Metempsychosis kneeled at one end of the line, to discard old friends and inspirations and yet to call at them in that long silent hour of recollection-between-dashes.

But then what did the past consist of anymore but reconsidered disciplinary failure leaning against the towering pillar of powdered incoherence? A preemptive strike on either spectral end rushed through his mind in the middle of the week, alone in bed past midnight when one considers that even the mind makes not a sound.

The following afternoon he arose, shaved, and counted his excess money. The action of thought became that of volcanic deliverance when beneath an old, beat-up hutch set on Mission Street packed with trading cards, tinsel, board games missing cardboard cover halves, electronics tied together by interwoven white and red cables, he came across an old typewriter on Mission Street in mint-condition cream blue, white keys and a black strip of background: Webster XL-500. The ancient instruction booklet, certificate, illegible inscriptions upon stamps of approval brought a smile to William's face, a spark to the fuse in his mind. $75.00 was a fair, if not low price for the machine, so when the fellow reminded William today was half-off day the summer seemed complete.

Still there was the matter of a good woman. He went into the neighboring department store for cheap notebooks and jars of Café Bustelo instant espresso. His heart sunk with brief, delirious melancholy to notice the aged yellow raincoats slumped at the foot of a forlorn ladder. She was long gone, William knew. And he'd never had her. Sweet cheat!

But then Daniel had mentioned something, hadn't he? And it would be critical, if not obligatory, to find a good woman before getting down to business.

"In a strange way she resembles a prostitute, man," Daniel said in the evening, smoking a cigar upon the fire escape of his Cesar Chavez apartment. "Although, well, she's not. I think she's from Nebraska or something. She drinks more than anyone I know. Henry Miller wrote about her before she was reincarnated, alas, back into herself. She's got feet like boats and all that rivals her bank account in terms of convulsion is neurosis—"

"Well you sure have got a lot to say. I don't know how I feel about this."

"It'll do you good." Daniel took on the cigar-clenched gesticulations of a businessman. "She is nice, a handful, two hands' full, but so are some of the best women."

"For a time."

"And you want something fleeting."

Daniel was correct. William had taken again to chain-smoking and wore a store-bought outfit parallel to that which Janine had bought him one summer prior. He couldn't muster it up to even go back to old Polk Street until some of the gang reappeared.

That night he and Daniel would hit Valencia up and down, and William hoped to see Janine and for her to see him in his white button up, black pants, new wingtips, the scar and the beard adding to his manliness.

"But you don't know any actual prostitutes is what I'm saying, I'm checking, I just want an actual prostitute," William said, following Daniel down the ladder, out to a zinc café-bar on Guerrero.

"I know none but the beauties of the Tenderloin."

"We'll leave them to Vollmann. Now, I'll take this other one's number."

"Just pretend you're overseas, two hundred years ago; her breasts are enormous, like melons—"

"And mention your name, then?" William asked.

"Yes, please do," Daniel said, readjusting the brim of his jet-black top hat in the reflection of a stalled police car. An auburn peacock feather projected from the side of its silken band as they began to mosey, and the night was a ball, although no one had heard from the like of Janine, Melody Nelson, Heather Daley, or Harold Smith in months.

He called the next day while nursing a hangover with mimosas and grapefruit in an unfamiliar bedroom, revisiting lines of an introduction speech he'd put together.

He was surprised and jolted awake to receive response. Her voice on the receiving end gave off a most interesting effect; instead of breaking through some chaotic surrounding or another, the voice itself seemed to contain the chaos of midnight in Amsterdam, in a sweet way, and William took deep breaths in noticing between her words an ordered silence in the backdrop. Meanwhile, he learned, through the woman's window paint peeled and flickered in the wind of Mission Dolores.

"Ah yes, you see Daniel Welles and I were just talking, and he gave me this phone number and said we—"

Trays of something or another crashed together on the other end as the woman shouted for more of something, her voice resounding and echoing through the contour of the room, then the receiver and the wires. "And said we ought to introduce ourselves at once."

"Oh, puerile Daniel; is he there now?"

"I was with him last night. He's around here somewhere."

"Oh." She yelled something in a foreign language and seemed neither pleased nor displeased at William's notification. Nor did she seem in the least perplexed. "Well I'm having a cocktail at the hotel bar near Union Square. I'll text you the address if you bring Danny along. We've been friends for years."

Then the chaos became underpinned within her voice although one retained the feeling that somewhere, sometime soon, violins would begin to play and before being smashed to smithereens in multitudes, just as the girl pointed with gentility to the entrancing shade of light glass-green reflecting upon the bar-counter.

The phone was addictive deception, second to the computer screen, in its race to the retinal grave of narcissism divided by waste book. Upon the latter, one could master angles in photographs, and grow to master the awkwardness in time of meeting strangers for dates who seemed displeased at such false advertising and yet were going to have an orgasm somehow that day and so then it might as well be with another person. 'Gosh', said the pilgrim to himself. 'I should really have stuck with Octavia.'

All what Daniel had said of the girl didn't seem to jell with her voice at all on reflection. William felt that he was exaggerating his initial reactions to her voice, that his head and body hurt, and that the best thing to do was make up a fresh cup of black coffee and hail a taxi.

He received the message at once: Fifth Floor 12 4th Street.

Down on the street a dark-skinned girl with torn stockings had her face in a book, her hand clutching an empty coffee cup upon her bare knee. William recognized her from last year. A tuxedoed transvestite walked by, dropping a handful of coins into the cup. The day was delirious with sunlight as she threw the cup away and staggered upright, storming down the street, not once meeting William's perplexed eyes.

"Perhaps she was just a student," the businessman suggested to William, then to the grocer, whose belly pressed forth like a hot-air balloon as he let go a smile that seemed as if sketched in chalk.

∾

As modernity is by proxy chained to the past in that all its molecular future is bound atom by lucid atom, microscopic and heedless, still yet linked by oblivion's reflective occult renaissance—so was William's chance encounter.

For she was young and old at once; a roguish, slight brunette, the sole patron of the bar and its wall-high windows, polishing off a bourbon cocktail of pasty elbows. Bourbon—even from afar—because a high-end quart of it reclined in the metallic bucket of ice cubes before her tattooed arms, empty bottles twinkling above to the still chandelier light. The chandelier looked as if a great angel's head wrapped in a hundred halos of quartz, for freedom from societal bondage's enslaved, martyred time is a taxation worth paying forward in all its ghosted lucre.

The room was long and dim, curving with tailor-cut tables and mythic silverware lined with designer cloth and signed, finalized in gold while faint chic dancehall dub music played on in preparation for nocturnal Sodom and Gomorrah.

She turned with slurred suddenness, as if to catch a pickpocket, with such an uncontrolled reflex William half-expected her head to pop clean off and roll along the sparkling marble floor.

"Danny," she sang, "Oh Danny *boy.*"

Her skin was wrinkled, as if her body had long ago proclaimed mutiny upon her sense of well-being, and her body did not match up with the birth-date Daniel had mentioned. On the streets it seemed clear that older people with bad luck were the ones who had once consumed alcohol, though at a certain point the tables turned and it consumed them in the end. Trouble with being born was it was it impossible for anyone young in days or spirit to ever fathom getting old. At least something of the sort had been recognized by Steinbeck the Village Idiot. 'Everything in moderation, including moderation.'

Here, now, William approached the sad mishap of a young girl and took Daniel's advice verbatim; he pretended he was in some old brothel or another. The severity of imminent sorrow filled him less then as he walked ahead, to pull a seat beside her as she pressed one wet lip against one another and swallowed a crack with two cubes of cheese. She advised the plump, Irish bartender that vicious minute's measurements with a loud snap of her fingers.

"I knew Daniel wasn't gonna come," she said to herself, advising the bartender to make William a glass of bourbon with ice.

The bartender glared at William like he was intruding on an important moment. He slid the drink ahead with fleshy hands. William summoned one random title to summarize him.

"Thank you, Sonny West."

"I knew—I knew Daniel wasn't going to come! He never comes around anymore!" She dismissed the bewildered bartender with a hand like the wing of an old bird, up and down, "But we'll go soon, soon, we'll go."

They drank bourbon in silence. William had regained his drunkenness from the night prior in one sip and focused on the colorway of the bottles. He drank himself into sobriety. She spoke in a raspy voice and breathed heavily, neither one bothering with names; neither opposite would remember, and on the chance of enjoyment one would feel ashamed to look the other up.

"You men are all the same. You all want the same thing. You even just show up! On a whim! And think it's alright!" She clenched his shoulder playfully, almost falling from her stool. Each time she laughed she shut her eyes. William saw this once in the reflection of the aluminum bar counter, and thereafter could hear it in her voice. "But it's OK—we'll go soon."

"Look at Sonny West there," pointing to the bartender transfixed with high-definition flat screens. "Hey Sonny!" William shouted, "Turn the TV off!" They laughed together as the stout man went for a ladder; they laughed at their sheer intoxication on a Sunday afternoon.

"Who still plays by the *rules*? I don't *care* what day of the week it is," she bragged. "My dad owns this hotel and seven others. There're two types of people follow the clock, the calendar, Jim, or whatever your name is, two types: the unsuccessful and the patriarchal. Don't you think so?"

"I don't know."

"I mean just think about it." She at last looked William in the eyes; through the long mirror before them. "Beethoven was deaf, Borges was blind. Don't you want to go now ridicule *everyone sober* on the streets, which is the *greatest* part of day-drinking, and then we'll get a cab to my a*part*ment," whispering, slurring every other word, "And get *high*. They always say that sex is the greatest pleasure! What a lie!"

She slid money ahead as Sonny West tucked the ladder aside.

"It is so to always just be terrible! Sex, of course, is nothing but an obligation. But that's what's nice about chemicals. They feel good, and for the first time, *every* time. They used to use guillotines in public, you know, guillotines, those strange machines with their elemental nostalgia."

It was a long afternoon in the tallest apartment building next to the cathedral atop Sacramento Street. William found redemptive qualities in the room's bareness; there was no overwhelming shelf of unread books, no series of unpronounceable paintings, nor two television sets and a laptop hooked up to several new recognizable objects. It was that sex, indulgence, the city had a dark-side, physical needs at the other end of the real.

Between wallowing and lunging and shouting he longed to leave and yet did not move. One thing he later recalled from the lazy orgiastic afternoon, as transcribed to Phil Cohen and Octavia Savonarola in an e-mail, was a statement the prostitute had made over postmortem cigarettes:

"You ever notice on labels of food, on commercials, those little teeny-weeny written messages you can't read? Like there is a health food, see, or a prescription that works for some illness, and then below there's always that print you can seldom even read that's warning you of potential death or that healthy doesn't mean healthy, touché? Do you ever feel that way about people in One Nation Under Baal, Divisible? They spewed off these recitative speeches and introduce themselves, and yet if you look even for a spot upon their shirts, or a break in their voice over a certain word, you can figure them out and realize they're hollow, which you knew all along, though didn't want to believe so—Have you ever considered that metaphor? Brother, see, I'm a poet."

When she started up her tablet to recite poems, he excused himself.

"No hold on, it's loading. Don't you want to hear a masterpiece? You don't even know who I am."

"Yes, 'tis true my fair lady. But please—let me go or my pants are ruined!"

Dame Horowitz was on the cusp of something uncomical concerning soiled pants when William crept out of the door, and leapt into a trolley, downtown in slow motion, time stalled by periodic brownbag porter.

At Embarcadero he looked out to the water, the ships, the Bay Bridge, and absorbed all of the sounds around him—the similarity of seagulls' wings and that of distant trains, the remembrance of things past within the echoing cartridge of the mind. He recalled his arrival last summer and inhaled the garden air of serenity.

Men put together a homemade drum set upon the ruptured concrete ledge as William began to walk back down the street. The sun had set. He was in no mood for jazz rinsed solitudes, nor even the night glowing in the dark. He walked to Church Street, and from Church down to Mission Dolores, where a doppelganger for Man Ray passed him in the dark with a waddling beagle puppy.

He lay atop the mild slope using his bag for a pillow and listening to the dozens of voices below. Fireworks exploded over the city skyline. He envisioned their reflection rippling with delayed reverberation in batches of two, three, and four successive roman candles across the Pacific Ocean and its harbors. Women and men of the cool Mission night screamed and laughed and for moments William fell asleep.

Angular chrome headlights ricocheted with their familiar distant pin-needle resurrection and still he couldn't shake the strange delirium from his mind. Little light beads drifted across the bridge, the voices receding outside of Columbus Café, till something felt wrong about all of being.

He turned off his phone, climbed the remainder of the hill, and turned back once more. Taciturn gusts blew in through leaning, shadowy trees. He thought of his life and death within such a furious slideshow of photographic memories that he fell over, sideswiped by the world's weight measured not in ounces, pounds, tons, but rather by belligerence and clairvoyance, creation and destruction.

Aberration called his name. There was nothing left in the world but motion, the nine-mile hike through enveloping fog, streams of which rushed through his body in rivers of distilled blood.

He turned the keys at last. He smelt the smoke, he heard the laughter, and he sat down. His senses felt deranged and he gave himself over again to eternity, pursued by that furious unspeakable voyage of the imagination. He thought once more of the living and the dead, and his mind entered a phase of acceleration that would not cease.

～

Although he spent the next 22 days alone at his sawdust desk and pacing the rungs of the basement squalor which had begun to take on that bucolic reverence of an abandoned cathedral, there were times when Mary came down to speak and marvel at how splendid a roommate could be; how quiet, how invisible, and how altogether sane in solitude.

Aside from the occasional machine-gun fire of typewriter keys, there was little proof of William Fellows' existence save the handful of showers and stragglers of the night as he awoke at dawn for a pot of boiling water. But as the water went untouched in preference to chilled wine and hibernation, his textual methodology no longer moved him. He knew it but did not admit it. He felt the spectacle-nature of what was in fact an earnest attempt to not just transcend the totalitarian tone of the times, but to ensure his first California pieces hit their mark right away, drafted away from screens for the sake of ensuring not a syllable was out of place, nor a word remaining which could have been bettered. Language itself giving way: *how can I probe a thing with itself? Shall I not let it be, remain upon her eyes of pleasure, fixed on paradisal words, 'look into my eyes and come inside of me'; the unity of bodies, we for a moment recapture what was split apart in the Fall: and through this comes sacred life.*

No doubt William was also, controversially in that gynocentric age, fast growing fed up with the types of bipedals he had taken to calling *spurious damsels*: 'Begone, thou whore', he announced, draped in his ominous cloak, "I hast my affluence of muses to protect me; thy mind is death, and mine affixed within the helmet of salvation; we seek the good, and thereby grow in goodness; ye seeketh evil, and each day descend further into the rim of Hell. Behold, pale woman, holy and true, form of my highest good, I shalt render thee unladen, shy, and turn my back on thee for comradely pipe smoke and chilled white wine. Sing, O birds! Even the birds danced about us singing, thou lowland lady of the penetration night, as I tied the wreath around thy tender, fragrant hair. But friends, you call me out, you say, for what I call beyond any city or kingdom, as logs burn in a winter solstice night, drowning fools and sparks of vision—a thousand nocturnal lights unfolding with mutated consciousness and the structure of eternity—pipe smoke, rays of light—fireflies and auguries—but I tell you all, drunk or not, we must seek the military of heaven, dancing with serenity through the halls of martyrdom, en route to the Truth."

But he likewise came to understand that whether his outrageous displays were taken in jest or fury, that there was now no turning back the tide. All the houses, indeed, had been built. Now sex dolls were on the table, and divorce as common as marriage. Now they either followed Carlin and converted golf courses or perished, as millions of rootless, jobless bodies joined in on the infernal charade, posing problems neither Solomon nor Gibbon had words for; and in the case of the former, they would perish, because the absence of golf would reinstall the idle rich's sense of mortality. For, thought the pilgrim, where there is love of money there is hatred of the truth; it cannot exist any other way, and so if there was no efficient means of changing things, no series of articles which could arouse the hypnotized public from its collective conquered stupor, there was nothing left to do but find what one loved and let it kill him. Somewhere between ironical obsession and propagandized emotional states lay the truth, desert island that it was.

Parties transpired and the trains to the city rushed through outside at all hours and yet William felt at last and again that intoxication far sweeter than chemical alteration in his enacted self-discipline; heightened consciousness and the deliverance of such into art.

He rummaged through hundreds of meticulous, edited pages and felt nothing profound nor presumptuous in either folder upon reflection; the story of the street had begun, the uninhibited articles being filed, trimmed, and reasserted. Soon he could set them up online, send them out, even contact Dr. Ober back east and such routine filled him with the utmost joy, joy upon tears, laughter, sorrow, and rejuvenation. In this society of bickering, hypocritical asphyxiation it would do men and women far better to cast themselves away from electricity and people for weeks at a time, to go through a case or two of good or bad wine as needed, and flush the soul out in a way the wars and films could never dream of; in a way reconciling its replenishing and rejuvenation.

He felt in no way he could evoke comparisons within his voice, for he'd been reading nothing and talking to no one. He eliminated, in a step he found necessary and more satisfactory than he'd bargained, all narcissism, and found himself at the end of it with a fine beard breaking through the skull that had contained the thoughts so long he at last read and reread on paper. Autumn would return soon enough; he would save his final edits until then, return to them with even fresher eyes, lock the folders away in fire-proof safe until then. The further one is to descend, the more glorious shall be the horizon on the long way out.

"Ah yes!" he cried, unlatching the blinds one by one, letting sunlight flush again into the vast room in glorious rectangular shades.

All was quiet upstairs as he shaved in the late, tranquil afternoon of August. He polished off the last spoonful of instant espresso and jammed his envelopes into an old trunk Mary had mentioned, dragging the ancient piece of equipment downstairs and latching shut the leather belt of broken rust. He applied his bicycle lock and lifted the dumb bell awhile.

With good money in his pockets he set out downtown for a new bicycle, and to find Harold Smith.

~

For last year, whatever that meant, at KoKo's, was the last time William had seen Harold. Before that it had been Blondie's, he recalled upon the subway, which was open in the later morning. He stepped in for a cocktail. At once the familiar faces commenced to pass in and out of the bar, through Valencia Street, in pursuit of carnality, superfluity, or mental enslavement masked in protest slogans.

The bartender recognized William; he expressed so with a sore squint of his torn green velvet eyes. He set the tumbler and hardware upon the table beside William.

"Haven't seen him in months," he coughed. "Buddy of his is stopping in though. Jean from over at the Beauty Bar. Jean should know. Their girlfriends are friends or something. You still doing journalism?"

"No, no."

"Me neither."

William ordered another drink and the bartender continued talking:

"There are two types of journalists," he explained to William. "Those who've failed at more serious writing and those unwilling to give it, themselves, a shot."

"Thank you for the information," William said.

He drank out on the porch and watched the women's faces go by, half entranced by headphones, the other half contorted, engulfed by sunglass lenses. That was a bad trend. The larger the lenses the less confident you could feel in removing them. The cocktail burned unmercifully in its little dark-yellow ravine, swirling about the pitted circular glass via cherry stem.

Jean came to the table with a shot of Fernet. William recalled him at once. He would have looked worn out if he hadn't always looked worn out, yet sudden streaks of gray hair seemed to heighten the matter. He looked much older and much less interesting when he was not beneath half a dozen disco balls.

He noticed William and bought him a drink. He took a seat, snapped his fingers with recollections of clouded nights, and the drunken afternoon began 74 degrees and sunny.

William gathered this much over a round of cocktails, two cans of Busch and two shots of Tullamore Dew:

H. Smith had last been seen one month ago on a porch in Lower Haight in a Groucho Marx mask beside a young woman whose description mirrored Heather's.

"I recognized him at once from the polish of his shoes," Jean added more than once. In brief cup-handed conversation The Shroud had revealed to Jean through the Groucho Marx mask that warrants had been issued for his arrest, the details of which remained ambiguous. "Each time I asked him to tell me more he handed me a bottle of Old Grand Dad and told me to shut up." His plan was to visit southern California for three weeks and return to Page Street at Webster if he was feeling right about everything. "And you know I had to at least mention that he might be drawing more attention to himself walking around in that mask, in daylight, but he just stood up and started ridiculing me in gibberish. He walked inside, put on a record. Hash smoke you could smell four blocks away burst through the open doorway, throughout the courtyard. I could hear him laughing a block away. It seemed as if the most ill-fated recluse I had ever borne witness to. He might be in jail," Jean concluded.

"And what was that girl like, again," William inquired.

"Oh, just a pretty dirty-blonde girl with this laugh, this precious laugh that tore the world in two. It was raining. She was wearing a funny yellow raincoat. You should have seen here."

William stood to go and to find them at once—For when the assessments grow vague, the mind idle, it is time to get on one's bicycle and ride into the city, in pursuit of lost friends and a round of Hamm's.

"We'll see you soon," William said to the bewildered man. His gray hair broke like a faded metal shield beneath the reemerging sunlight.

"Who's 'we,'" Jean said, bewildered. He motioned for two Fernet.

"Why old Harold Smith and I, if course," William said, any grave nature of the world cut off by laughter. He paid his tab and had a farewell drink. He bought another lock from the bicycle shop next door and rode out to the old, decrepit bakery on Van Ness and Market in the middle-afternoon.

The afternoon was already dying down into evening and the sidewalks and streets were jam-packed as he locked his bike to the post. He had coffee and listened to the choruses of laughter along Market Street, hands waving in the looming dusk.

On the corner of South Van Ness was the steel-blue gray panel of the thrift shop. Myriad faces broke to and fro through swinging doors of taxicabs and lobbies.

There was a painting in the window of navy yards, of titanic ships being lifted by cranes and crumpled men beneath castrated lights, slaves of perpetual victimhood's proponents, rusted valves and humming machines, ancient barrels stacked to the unseen.

The transsexual dressed as Peter Pan with bluish skin approached William speaking through rose-colored lips in a voice of vulgar recitation:

"Hey now I'm Clau*dette*. Can you help me?"

He, she, held out the stub of an arm, to which a Carl's Jr. soda cup was taped. Her, his stench of compact urine rose terribly through the crowds. The scotch tape unraveled, and the cup fell to the sidewalk. As coins sprinkled upon the floor:

"HA! That's change ya'll could believe in! That's it, that what you all believe in! Now get, get down! Kiss my piggy toes!"

The skin of the body that hobbled away was a diverse blend of blisters, scales, skin diseases seemingly originated in the Tenderloin, San Francisco, California, United States of America, one of thousands with both diseases and an identity unknown to anyone.

Disgusting children rummaged through for quarters and ran ahead to the 49 squealing with laughter, whence window-shopping for love there was Percy, or Brendan White, embracing his red-headed bespectacled wife farewell. William recognized him from the Geary Experiment.

She had an antique chair in her hands stepping into the cab. Brendan turned around, his eyes at once meeting William's. He was a shorter Maupassant in leather jacket, his arm rising with William's above the heads of the crowd. They weaved through the crowd toward one another in disbelief.

"What the Hell!" Brendan cried. "No way!"

They shook hands and William's warm feelings for the encounter hit him with delay. He stood in the midst of the crowd unsure of how to express his exultation.

"Now, let's go over there," Brendan said, pointing through the crowd, "To Lafayette!"

William locked his bike up out front of the apartment.

"They're trying to kick me out of this God-damn place!" He pressed several matches to a book and lit his cigarette with wavering blue flame, singing part of his mustache. "Let's get a drink! I—"

A window slid open overhead.

"What's that smell!

"That *smell!*"

"Hey, listen—shut up, you old whore!"

Reality set in with preliminaries out of the way, of attaining familiarity in chaos, and William began to feel comfortable; within moments he had forgotten there had ever been months he hadn't been in San Francisco.

Brendan brought out two six packs of Anchor Steam and patted William on the back with great zest. Something good was in the air, like a fuse, parades passing by on idle Sundays, and the company of an old friend rather than loose acquaintance was a refreshing spark in the city of unceasing deaths and entrances.

"Why are they trying to kick you out?"

"My girlfriend pays rent, the other two—a student and a translator—are never even here. I don't know. They just don't like me. And people don't like have to like or respect one another at all as long as they can dislike someone. That's enough to keep most people together. Mutual dislike. Ignorance is a group effort. They think I'm lazy, pretentious. Sure, I like to sleep in, drink too much, listen to music and smoke in my bathroom—it's the ideal life if you have the balls to reach for it and people that will lend you money when you are out of a job. But no, man, enough of me! When did you even arrive back!"

"Oh," William said, tilting the neck of his bottle to Percy's, lighting hand-rolled cigarettes, "Oh it's all simple—just the other day, a whim, I got bored, so I hopped on a train. Nothing better to do."

He knew Brendan had never traveled and wouldn't understand it much and seemed, no matter what the situation, far more concerned with what was just happening in his life, be it suicidal tendencies, bad roommates, or new variations on the peanut-butter sandwich; it all worked because William had grown sick of discussing traveling and didn't mind listening to Brendan yell about things, when he got going and referred to his plump wife as if a super-model, or a 'Damned fine woman,' when in reality she bore rather the awkward appearance of a dilated feminist vegan. She was common and dull and nothing more and William felt bad Percy had ended up with her once more, assuming his drunken compliments were some sort of adverse reaction to the realization that he'd slipped up in having to live with her again. Percy began again to ask of travel and to give his stern opinions on the subject; many people seemed in awe of the idea, but it was very simple—you were either seized by hollow eternities or otherwise.

William listened to him talk on and on and the beers went by, losing track of his complaints and realizing that Brendan would get drunk and begin referring to himself as 'Papa,' which was uncomfortable for anyone who had ever heard of someone named Ernest Hemingway. William recalled why he hadn't bothered staying in touch and still smiled to himself to recall that Brendan would continue to drink all night and begin talking like a Hemingway character which always went to show in the morning that the line between art and life, imitation and reaction, was as scorched and braiding as an equator.

"Let's digress about your situation," William interjected. "I may be able to help you. I've got an enormous room in the Sunset. 100 a month." Brendan spit beer through the garden in disbelief. "So don't go dying on me. Don't you know that the visible is nothing, and theological geography all? You laugh in public but weep in private; you must reverse this pattern. Ye Olde William Fellows hath returned to find himself in fine situations."

"Let's go then!" He leapt up. His eyes glowed as if it were the first bit of positive news anyone had brought him in months. "Because they want me *out* of here. They're not artists, they don't understand that during the process, well." He paused for a moment, looking to the concrete ground for the term. "It would be so beautiful to share a big studio. No one gets it."

"What you mean, I suppose, is that they don't understand that during the creative process it isn't that nothing else matters, it's that nothing else *exists*," said William.

Smoke broke through the perimeter like two fumigated chimneys. Night had fallen.

"And then of course one of them hates men. I wrote a little short story and left it half-finished in the bathroom. She ridiculed me. We got into an enormous argument. I told her that the Statue of Liberty is a pagan whore! We'll go, tonight—here, man, let's finish these drinks. I had a dream about you while you were gone. You were with a girl; we were at a tavern. She was a damned-fine woman.

"It was a damned-fine dream. I rolled up a joint. You were with a girl. She was quiet and boring. Still I wanted her. I was with my girl. She bought a chair earlier. You may have seen her. It was a nice chair. I picked it out. It was damned-fine in my dream. We split a bottle of wine beforehand. It was all damned-fine. We ate pumpernickel bread beneath a tree. She came in and called me Papa. I don't know how she knew my nickname. I did not give a damn. One cannot give a damn. One can never give a good damn. We went back to the tavern. It was damned nice. One must go to the tavern. Then we went hunting at the crack of dawn. I shot a lion in the head. It did not die. I strangled it to death with my bare hands. We ate him for brunch. You were with your girl by the creek. You may have been making tired love. I love to make love when I'm tired. Then you nap. One must take naps or go to the café. I always wake up at the crack of dawn. My eyelids are thinner than other people's. Then we hopped on a train."

The Flame of the Meteor That Goes

BRENDAN STUMBLED AWESTRUCK ABOUT the cavernous studio.

"I'd put—put a Chinese wall there and my desk, and Hell, I'll move in tomorrow!"

"Sure." William drank scotch. He did not give a damn.

"They won't mind upstairs?"

"I don't bother with them much," William said. "Except for the bathroom and coffee in the morning. Otherwise everyone except Mary is stoned. It's a rather sad business and it is rather easy to become invisible here."

On Brendan's laptop they listened to the oldies radio station and spoke all night beside the open windows remembering, forgetting, prophesying, and reading. He'd begun to mellow out upon arriving in new, strange quarters, slight envy curtailing his Papa routine. William felt confident in that some good luck would set his head straight. Although he knew not where Harold Smith was those days, he was a friend of his regardless, and William would always set out to keep that slanted community alive.

"You know what I hate about this whole new trust-fund, hipster generation," Brendan started, breaking into coughing fits, "Is that when your wallet is filled with money any seat is comfortable. All these kids with inherited money talk art and for all of them the schoolbook is the experience; the standard American education is less an intellectual seminar than a parental assumption. There must be more time for television; senility is a fine trait in professors." He poured whiskey into the glasses, seltzer water. William liked him more and more. Brendan was the sort whose ramblings seemed far more coherent than most people's studied speeches. Whether or not William agreed with him he agreed with anyone whose aura entailed a strict disregard for public opinion without succumbing to evangelical athesim. A short Maupassant in his leather jacket, speaking and dismissing at once: "All of the women run around the city with nose rings and general looks of horror. I tried to get a job at the sandwich shop; no luck. There, there, look at the moon. Listen to the crickets. My fingernails are darkened, chipped, stained with tobacco. I think of death as something to sentimentalize and not something that happens to people in the grocery store. I can feel the freeways of the world pass through my circulatory system." He paused, casting an anxious eye at William. "There's something wrong with me."

"You ought to dump that girl you've been clinging to and get the fuck out of California. And think of how you'll feel when that glass is empty. You'll care for nothing but how nice the singular moment is, the rustic breeze breaking in through these windows. And stop giving yourself nicknames. You can't trust anyone who gives themselves nicknames or whistles with any sense of regularity. You understand?"

"You don't trust me?"

"No. I know not where your hand's been, let alone your mind."

"You're right," Brendan said. "You're right. I've got to just be myself."

"You need new décor before your eyes. Dress the world up in dreams. No clinging to anyone. Women no longer depend on men and men no longer upon women. No dependencies, no physical contact—I am the good doctor, the doctor of affect!"

"Let me tell you!" Brendan shouted, laughing, "Let me—"

At sunrise William said at last:

"Still—still though—" He swirled his highball with a bent bookmark and daydreamt of the October wind. "We must find Harold. I know he is still in San Francisco."

"The shadow knows—an Indian Summer of the soul, nay, till we find Smith. And we will! The shadow knows. The shadow knows."

William believed him without question. There is that look at night in one's eyes, in the summer in the city, where the most casual confidences resound like cathedral bells upon instantaneous reflection the abandonment, the evaporation of chagrin. It was the feeling of knowing good, interesting, respectable people as opposed to the decades of lesser evils.

He could hear the old typewriter was being put to good use as William lost his battle against unconsciousness, drifting abstract into the unconscious through that symphonic sea of keys.

～

He awoke to a torturous, repetitive doorbell tearing through an indescribable dream from which a singular observation remained as he stretched out upon the mattress: If miscellaneous items are spread along a bed or ground of any sort and one happens to fall asleep upon them the indentation may enter the dream. For example, if one falls asleep with lower back wrapped from behind by long sleeved shirts in a pile, one is apt to awaken with memories of dreams of being almost held by someone. He thought of this, letting the second more interesting point unfold within his mind, when the doorbell turned to the bellowing of that ill-fated term 'POLICE' began to work its way into his shaken sensorial proximity. William swung the door open and felt as if he had been pummeled the night prior. His sight was tinted and foggy and offset by a sort of blistery, bleary film.

Brendan stood in a black bowling cap, Cuban cigar between his teeth, black sunglasses, and his wife standing behind him. Both she and William looked down at Brendan marveling his style, his stillness. Behind him were the simple belongings of calm, good room. William recalled he had insisted Brendan move in with him and shed a cranial smile.

By sundown bookshelves lined the walls, trunks of clothing and folders formulated in off-colored stacks, stand-up closets and fresh second rounds of cleaning and dusting made the exposed concrete ground sparkle. The whipped, wooden columns marked with thumbtack and nail holes stood in its new coat of beige polish like Roman pillars. From any angle William looked upon the room it seemed a gracefully shabby replication of an ancient library with vague roots in speakeasies.

Brendan's Chinese wall was the last piece of furniture to go up and proved a working division between the far corners of the ancient room.

"I've never been prouder to live anywhere," Percy said. They stood out front of the bodega. He and William walked up the disquieted street of fog, train headlights breaking uphill through the fumes and turning away out of sight, with a bottle of Johnny Walker and new wingtips. "This place is going to be our mansion!"

For a week straight William Fellows, Brendan White, Daniel Welles, and Phil Cohen hit the city and all its best bars and parks, restaurants and cafés, and still in steady pursuit of Harold Smith. At the end of it there was no trace of the Shroud and little remained save exhaustion and great, forgotten talk that proved important in the ways its details remained forgotten and engulfed in vague lights of dim rooms, the gentle touch and foreign scent of lost women, the green fuse that burns through flowers from the sky. Thereafter Brendan went to Lake Tahoe for a week to visit his mother.

William sat upstairs with Mary having breakfast, playing off his week as 'One full of productivity; sheer productivity.' In a sense this was true, yet he longed for one more of anything they'd spent their money on—Moroccan hashish, awful sex shows in North Beach, aimless cab rides which ended in standing outside of Janine's apartment howling at the moon, bottles of top-shelf champagne which made one insanely drunk, and in concealed reflection to his makeshift landlord he relayed that advent of progress and adventure in the summer until it dawned on him, in the middle of one sentence or another, that he'd already managed to spend all of his money.

"There's that little job you can do downtown that Daniel was talking about," Mary suggested, giving William a cigarette and sitting down beside him. She wore a black kimono with dark-red patterns sequined o'er one of her bare-footed legs over the other. "You know you can go to the food stamps office and sign up for welfare and get a couple of hundred dollars too. You just sign some paperwork and if you never speak with them again it is OK, you just take the money and never go back. My ex-boyfriend used to do that. You just go sign up to work the Muni buses four hours a week and at the beginning of the month they just give you four-hundred dollars and a month-long MUNI pass."

"I never learned how to drive. And *buses*—"

"No, it's sort of—" Mary paused with clear determination to recall what Daniel had said, how her ex-boyfriend had described it. Her face lifted; her eyes widened. "You work in the cleaning department and just sit in a warehouse inside of a bus with ex-convicts and bring back your soap and bucket an hour later."

"Oh, come on man, forget *that*," Daniel said. "Thom is coming to town in a week!" A light bulb clicked in William's mind. "He's bringing in an enormous shipment of weed and hash. Better late than never. We'll each be selling pounds. Let me come by and give you a down payment."

Open windows, small meals, cheap wine; even poverty was mesmerizing that summer. When Daniel returned days later from Monterey, he gave William $600.00 for spending money. William worked all day at the string of articles and afterward took Mary out to the Stinking Rose. Neither had ever been there, and aside from a bar or two, a sex parlor or two, there was no longer any reason to go to North Beach unless you were going to Sammy's late at night with friends, or so William liked to say. In reality, his nocturnal memories of North Beach meant so much to him that he feared his emotions might get the best of him were he to return and reflect upon Fort Mason, upon Isaac outside of the Hemlock Tavern—his empty room, Janine at Land's End—

He once again had that strange feeling inside of him hopping into a cab, longing for the unattainable, for Mary.

Perhaps he could just say it, so as to ease his load, or suggest it, as the waiters rushed to and fro with piping plates, steam breaking from the kitchen stove-tops, knives slicing cloves of garlic and great big dishes of pasta with hot breads and fresh bottles of red wine; serenity in the chaos of clanging porcelain and shouting voices. He glanced once through his window to the distant, luminous lights; in his mind North Beach resembled a great human reflection of its surrounding sea of light. He bit his nails out of longing to go dance the night away with friends and strangers in its bars and tucked his hands away and held them together so as not to show his anxious being. Mary was a calm, balanced girl, he was coming to find, and around her he often attempted his best behavior.

They were discussing the quality of the wine and the weather when Thom Stoykovich called from the mountains.

"William?"

"Delmore Schwartz speaking."

"Who?"

"Mikhail Bakunin on the line."

"What?"

"Macon Dead III here."

"Stop it!" Mary smacked his arm.

"Yes, this is William Fellows. I am half drunk and in a crowded restaurant. Thom?"

"Daniel wanted me to call you; I've got to leave tomorrow morning from Santa Cruz. The compound is being raided." His voice reminded William much of Nielsen's brother with its drug-addled pessimism attached to the slightest shift in tone, wherein all optimism sounds forced, as if coming from a vulnerable set of vocal cords. William stepped outside, overlooking the distant harbor lights, inhaling the Pacific's sifting multisensical breeze at a crisp sixty-seven degrees.

"Why don't you call me when you're in the city and we'll take it from there?"

"And you've got room, or at least somewhere we can break out a couple of pounds of it and well—I don't know how many—ounces of hash?"

"Sure."

"That is all worked out," Mary said, under the impression that a friend of Daniel's was staying the night and nothing more, who had also assumed, quite rational, that Brendan had just been staying the night. "And everything?"

William thought of selling the drugs with great danger and wonder and excitement. He'd have to clear off his desk for a week, but so be it, for this notion brought him back to more romantic things, to think of himself pushing Grade-A marijuana, because in San Francisco it didn't feel that way at all. It was just about legal by then, casual as a can of Coca Cola, yet its danger was implicit and always lingering for anyone who had not been born and raised in the Bay Area.

"It is so nice to think of money without taxes being taken out."

"I can imagine! And Daniel's friend is fine, I'm sure."

"He's got thy bearings," William said, wondering what old Phil Cohen had been up to. He would have to call him soon. "Ye Frisco, land of question-not lest yearn," he concluded as the check was delivered, Mary smiling, glancing into his eyes, William positive he was just about to take her in his arms and kiss her—either that or take siesta.

"I'm just glad you've made it comfortable down there," she said.

"I'll be around awhile, Mary—until my projects are done—that's all I know."

"Isn't it funny how life works out sometimes?"

"A good year or two—perhaps more!"

As they walked through the streets William could not bring himself to interlock his arm within hers. He hadn't felt that way in a long time. And who would have known the man in the wine shop had been such a fan of *Scott 4*?

It was another golden day in the middle-afternoon as William stood upon a ledge outside of the State University watching the students rush to and fro the doorways, daydreaming of Octavia in the university days, the New York nights, the outdoor train stations, the outdoor cafés.

In pursuit of the Muni, Thom text messaged, he had somehow managed to hop upon the student shuttle bus; they hadn't carded him at all and the drugs were safely strapped within two pieces of luggage, the scent subdued by an extensive wrapping and rewrapping process Thom had begun to explain over the phone. William worried little of anything, for just then were marijuana cards becoming accessible to just about anyone, whether due to chronic depression or a sore tooth.

Earlier in the afternoon he'd gone downtown to the barber shop to treat himself to one of those haircuts that receives compliments, new tires for his bicycle, fried pickles and vegan tacos with sangria out on Mission Street at the Weird Fish. The day thus far had been perfect.

He was stunned when the shuttle bus arrived and deported its batch of students, with Thom standing out in line less like a sore thumb than a broken arm.

First, Thom Stoykovich looked identical to the way he'd sounded; ragged, paranoid, with long and wavering dark hair, his outfit outdated by three and a half decades. He seemed inoffensive, yet he understood why Daniel did not want him around. William noticed the flowers embroidered on his shirt, the mushroom tattooed to his forearm, and breathed pretending to not notice the vehicle had arrived some half block away.

More, though, it was the stark difference in his appearance to anyone on the bus—either the tennis or rugby team in their headbands and pouches—and in short one was left with little to the imagination wondering what was in his luggage bags. William marveled the strange circumstance and stepped ahead, truncating the preliminaries and hailing a cab. Thom was visibly trembling as they stepped into the cab. Everything about the man seemed dark.

"Relax, relax," William said. "It's just a five-minute ride from here."

Brendan had set up a roundtable and had two bottles of Charles Shaw set out. Daniel Welles and Phil Cohen would come by later in the evening.

"I thought they were gonna catch me man, I think they were gonna. Where's your bathroom?"

"Well Daniel was right," Brendan said, pouring out tumblers of wine. "This man is dull across the boards, dressed like a hippy. Just make sure he doesn't play that God-damned guitar. Send him up to Haight Street if he has to."

"He's staying a few nights. There's money in this. Otherwise I wouldn't have accepted the offer. The guy's just passing through, going home to the country with good money soon."

"I'll give him a chance at sanity and self-respect. That or he can go buy a couple of 30-packs."

The color returned to Thom's face as he broke the drugs out on the table. The table was filled with mountains of lime-green, purple, and orange patterns, straight from the mountains of Santa Cruz. Altogether there was two pounds, Thom explained, and they broke it into quarter-pounds and ounces.

"Then at night with machine guns these psychopaths would be screaming and shooting rapid fire at nothing at all, hallucinating and going insane while the downtown area was nine miles away. The guy I was staying with was a megalomaniac who used to be a pro-skateboarder but broke his arms too many times. I knew it'd be like 'The Boy Who Cried Wolf,' and last night, man, they were tipped off the cops were going to come tonight. It's a strange business. Everyone is convinced that *this time* they're going to make a million dollars, but never to be had. Hey, you mind if I play a song on guitar? You guys like the Beatles, right?"

"Let's get this stuff ready, and the hash in the oven, and then we'll start singing songs," William said.

"Sorry, man. The wine—you know?"

"Tell us more about the mountains," Brendan said.

"Well all the crops were starting to go bad. I always woke up at dawn and there would be dead animals all over the place. I slept in a broken-down tin-rod shack out on a gravel road and listened to Woody Guthrie."

"Why'd you even go?"

Thom looked up at Brendan startled, frightened by the realization he might be leading an aimless criminal life, and that for months he'd been around no one but characters from bad films modeled after the sixties and that the whole peace and love gambit had died a long time ago.

"Well you know man, I thought there was going to be a lot more to it. Money, man," he admitted. "And to live. That's the main part, man. Because I don't care about money. I just want to live, man."

William got on the phone and called a poet from Berkeley.

"He's coming by in an hour for a quarter-pound. After that we'll hit the town. It'll be dark out soon."

Mary walked in through the open door, smoking a cigarette. Her eyes bolted open at the sight of the Chinese wall, the pounds of marijuana upon the table, and the bits and pieces of wine bottles glittering in the sunlight.

"It just smells so . . . *fresh*," she smiled, shedding custard-colored teeth. Thom handed her a fistful of weed.

"There you go, Ms. Mary."

She brought it to her nose.

"Oh, *wow!*"

"I'm—"

"His name's Sonny West," Brendan said, conjoining Mary's hand with Thom's.

Thom laughed and went to speak.

"He'll be staying with us a few nights while we take care of all this," William said. "And then you'll never see Sonny West again."

"Just be *careful* is all."

Sonny West brought out two licenses for William and Brendan. Mary went to go share her weed with the others.

"Why are you calling me Sonny West?" Thom laughed. He showed some disenfranchised tone, some level of dissatisfaction in his inquiry.

William considered that up in the mountains Thom had had enormous daydreams of the city after being isolated with disillusioned drug dealers who appeared held together more by their shared defeats and the reproaches with which they addressed one another than anything else.

"Because that is your name," William said. "From now on you're Sonny West. Now come on, this poet will be here in not too long."

The other roommates rushed down and threw three-hundred dollars on the table.

"Saint William!"

He'd never seen them so excited. Brendan readjusted his crackling radio. He lit a spliff and unraveled the second bottle of wine.

"No, no—thank Sonny West here."

One of the roommates' boyfriends was working the door at Elbo Room on Valencia and could get everyone into the acapella Leonard Cohen show. The poet handed over more money than was needed. Had the poet misheard? Good for him. When he realized his error, he could at least get a poem out of it.

William lent Percy a hundred dollars, had several hundred in his pocket, and he liked Thom Stoykovich, or Sonny West, just a little bit more. He locked up the trunk and even let, albeit with grave persuasion, Sonny West borrow his leather jacket.

"Oh, I'm cool man, I've got a coat!"

"No," William said. "Please, borrow some of my clothing. I love to lend people things."

Sonny put on a long black coat and a good pair of black shoes which concealed everything.

"How's I look?'

"Swell!"

"We'll meet Phil and Welles here later," William said, locking the trunk.

"But I've called Daniel already! He's driving one of the big taxi-vans tonight!"

Everyone had a block of hash and Brendan's flask was filled with Clan Macgregor as the old Soto van pulled up. Everyone squeezed in.

"Alright, ladies and germs!"

They yelled and sang along at the top of their lungs.

Kyrie Eleison, Kyrie Eleison
Kyrie Eleison, Kyrie Eleison

Theeuphoric high hologram of the city made its way into sight and smoke plumed through open windows, seas of voices out onto the open highway, Daniel and Sonny West reminiscing up front while the rest of the house roared and danced amidst the backseats.

Christe
Christe Eleison, Eleison, Eleison, Eleison
Christe

Upon arrival the place was packed, hashhigh, and they were rushed upstairs where the weed went. William ordered two private bottles of Fernet and took a roundtable for Brendan and his roommates. Sonny West caroused the streets with Daniel, getting rid of further ounces of weed and hashish around Dolores Park.

The choir men sang on as the serene late-summer winds rushed in through open windows and sifted around waxen candles like cool fluttering leaves past nocturnal lights. William looked over the traffic with Mary and Brendan at either side; then through a thick, twisting cloud of spliff smoke he saw Janine step to a taxicab and froze in shock; she'd only ever looked more beautiful when he'd spent the day upon Polk Street with her, or his first night in the city between she and Isaac, and now William could do little but raise his glass from the window and hope to see her again as she sped off into the vortex of the Mission. He longed to yell: Revolt against nostalgia!

"Let's hit the streets after the bottles are gone," said Brendan. "I've gotta fight the bouncer down the street."

"Where?"

"Zeitgeist. He gave me nasty looks last night. I'm going to punch him out. One clean hit. That man deserves a beating. Here, let me show you how to box."

William suggested to Phil Cohen that he meet them there for the brawl.

"I'll get behind you," he said, looking up from his phone, "Now be quiet and listen to these men sing and smoke hashish, drink Fernet, for a while you'll understand there's nothing to even say. Here, roll some cigarettes, Papa." He threw Brendan an unopened pouch of Bali-Shag.

"So," Mary said between songs, "Brendan, tell us all about you—you look so *familiar*."

A little while later he and William were outside of Zeitgeist.

"Hey, Butterbean," Percy turned around inside. "Tell me—why does anything exist?"

Someone at the bar summoned Bierberkof's severed arm—any number of collegiate prostitutes grimacing, skirts displaying their asses for all the world to see and yet aggrieved when one dared speak aloud that which they lived to hear; bottles clanking together, two dark drafts and darting to the backyard, to Phil Cohen and his table.

To William's bewilderment and sick pleasure he noticed that Melody Nelson in the crowd; one drink ago he would have felt excited enough to approach her. Then he was just past euphoria and felt more like speaking of the future than the past.

She was dressed as a fairy, selling cigarettes and candy from some portable tray harnessed around her neck. Music resounded overhead as if prolonged gunshots; Brendan had already finished his first drink as William noticed Mary had been correct—Melody had gained weight. Cellulite ran across the back of her legs. It wasn't all that bad, but William's eyes had followed the pointing fingers of raucous, outstretched hands. She was no longer Melody; Margaret, perhaps, was more apt, or something of the sort. Margery? 'Steph?' She had lost her mystique; William had lost his loving feelings. The death of dreams.

He thought once to when he'd met her in the subway. She had appeared in a red dress as the train rushed through; and now she was back inside of the bar re-shelving the dead souls of candy bars and cigarettes.

"Well, well," El said, extending his hand.

"You've shaved," marveled William, diving into a discussion on psycholinguistics.

Brendan had run into friends and then was across the yard hitting on uninterested prospects and buying cigarettes. Through the crowd he fell back as the people perpendicularly parted across smothered rocks. The doorman reemerged. Brendan pulled down his pants.

He shouted to William and El: "TAXI!" and the three vaulted outside. William gave El a twenty-dollar bill.

"About that drink."

The barback appeared at the doorway just behind them. William felt as if were in a strange film.

"Don't ever come back!"

"Hey, you fatso," Brendan said, crushing out his cigarette. "I'm going to kick your stupid ass."

William watched in amazement as Brendan, five foot four and 165 lbs., approached the barback, six feet tall and 275 lbs. Brendan took a can of beer from his pocket and threw it at the man's head. He missed and lunged in with an uppercut. The barback was knocked out cold in one punch.

"Drinks are on me all night!" cried William, throwing his arm around Brendan. "My God, you were not kidding!'

They walked up Valencia back to the Elbo Room as sirens and flashing lights dissolved behind them.

The Elbo Room was packed. The Marina crowd had begun its weekend outing.

"I'll go get everyone else," Brendan shouted, "And call you in half an hour."

"He almost reminds me of oh—I don't know," El laughed. "Who does he remind you of?"

"I don't know. How about Isaac," William said. "Do you ever hear from him?"

"Online every so often– nothing; it seems so long ago."

It did. William found himself disturbed at the prospect of how compact his past year had been with nonstop motion. Sleep was a thing of the past. Then he looked to the sky and reflected upon the words of his younger self, 'To absorb richness for the ordinary,' and El held the door at Casanova for a round of whiskey and pints of Racer-5.

Sonny West was on the line, drunk and full of color:

"Hey man, Daniel's taking me all around the city (Daniel blowing a kazoo) and we're going to have drinks in North Beach when it's all over—you want to meet around midnight? (Ibid) I made a thousand more dollars—"

"We'll be there!"

William tucked his phone away and raised his glass in a toast to the city. A hundred voices crashed together as William caught a glimpse of El turning to the lamp-light, to the mirror before him, say something Hebrew, take down a becalmed drink. There was December in Manhattan and Brooklyn and there was August in San Francisco, and there was August and September and October in San Francisco when where empty glasses towered—

"We've got to betting on horses soon," El said. "You know there's a track in Oakland with 'Dollar Days'—dollar hot dogs and dollar beer, right there on the waterfront, me lad."

"Let's go next Sunday!"

He turned to the beautiful girl beside him and looked away, she was no Heather Daily—but even that observation was mowed down by an overhead sound like rocks in a cigar box,.

"Because I think we both know by now not to make plans for anything sooner than 24 hours away after nights like this. And then after all this me, you, Daniel, Brendan, Sonny West and everybody can throw a party at my place."

"You ever hear that old Harold what's his name?"

"Not these days," sighed William, drinking from his pint glass, "But we're searching for him. We'll find him. There's no summer without him."

"Amen."

They walked down an alleyway where spliced cables intersected with crabapple trees and the passersby smoked pipes, drank from paper bags beneath the moon. The roommates and Mary went ahead home. Brendan stumbled to the corner, extending his hand and pursing, muttering to himself. He turned back around and caught up with El and William as the latter began a monologue on how he had come to think of Daniel Welles, and how much he looked to seeing him again tonight.

"We need to get damned fine cab. Come all ye heifers. The cab, yes. But have you two ever went fishing? I love fishing. Fishing is damned fine. You drink a bottle of rum and thirty beers first. Then at night you drink a cool red bottle of wine and slice bread under a cherry tree, and you read Turgenev. Turgenev is a damned fine writer. William, I bet you *never* went fishing."

"No, I haven't," William admitted, sobered by Brendan's animation. William guessed that something else was bothering him, or anyone could guess it. El rolled his eyes, then a cigarette, and he and William sat upon the decrepit bench people-watching; Brendan, as he staggered away and near, muttering to everyone on the streets like a bum. His hair was disheveled, his new denim jacket torn.

"People like you don't need to go fishing. You have all your money. You go to fancy seafood *restaurants.*" William gave El that sort of fleeting-squinted look which means: *If by the end of this cigarette he doesn't take to coffee or water he may not even notice us leave; I don't know what's gotten into him, but he is a good man altogether, with his problems, so let's see.* He longed to catch up with Daniel; if you hadn't seen Daniel in eons you had missed quite a bit, almost as if that first week upon returning home from some metropolis or another when you're walking to the supermarket and it thousands of memories come down on you all at once—

"Go around," he slurred, "Drinking and messing around and everything. I should just go back to the monastery, God-damn, God-damn. The Berkeley monastery. The city life is a lie!"

"Alright, look," said William, giving him first a dose of his own Hemingway medicine, secondly making an attempt to pry Brendan back to Earth as the passing people looked at him and laughed through horror when he vomitously relieved himself against the tractor trailer on Guerrero: "If you have any balls left cut them off and throw them off of a bridge before you do that. Second, you're unimportant. No one knows you." Brendan looked into William's bloodshot eyes beneath the blinking lights of the traffic, of Guerrero. "Nobody knows me or you and the ones that everyone knows can't bear it, so either shut up and keep moving on or stand in the street muttering about Buddha and what's wrong with society. You won't know what suffering is until you're faced with either eating your sibling or starving to death as bombs fall on the nearest church. This is also why we should put all Bolsheviks in gulags. Man up, bub."

"Thank you," Brendan said. "Thank you; you're right."

"Now enough of this insane drunken blues in the streets," El said, "Get me in a God-damned cab to North Beach! Ye drunken beach, ye drunken boat!"

They stepped to the cab and took off into the night, Brendan crying just a little bit back into sobriety.

The intoxicating lure of open windows, the trance of the city rushing by, that abstract paradise in the faces of a thousand strangers with friends at one's elbow, and in the distant morning to begin working out the details of tomorrow night's party, the voyage that never ends.

"Sonny West!" He pointed him out in the window, cradling a pitcher of beer, reeling them in from the cab with his cloaked arm:

They rushed through the mobs and into the bar, upstairs and beside the open window.

"Daniel's on his way!"

The waitress appeared as Sonny explained, slurred, that if he lived in the city he'd die. He while ordered two pitchers of Rogue to pass around. William thought of Anaheim and wished he had brought his packet at that instant. He would have recited his poems aloud.

The women of the world were out in peacock dresses and denim shorts, blonde hair breaking through the breeze of overhead antique fans like chimes. The music was roaring, rounds of applause, barrels and glasses breaking together with interlocked hands and eyes, the dissociative ecstasy of singularity regained, thoughts breaking together like voices that could never withstand the pain of black heavens, of ashen daylight.

The voices of the street sang:

Men and women ran through sidewalks and alleyways below like chickens with their heads cut off; bankers ate bacon sandwiches and spoke skepticism in unison of 'The effort against global warming' while automatic cries vivacious broke through the futile shades of teahouse drainage pipes; west, agape, aghast, aglow, the 421st blow, drunken so , no cab until later, to tell tales of past simple hearts, skull-crest towns where there is no sexuality or artistry but drained laughter caught in hallways; velvet capes, sentinel buttons being repaired for more than minimum wage; work is hard to come by; checkers and cheese across the concrete (Bread broken over basket); in the distance I saw peering eyes turn away to the walls of enclosed posters and newspaper articles where we may even get rid of the first pound by tomorrow if all goes well, swimming through the liquid streets, the war will never end, and what's cancer but some symbolic termination as insufferably ambiguous as the void itself? There is nothing to be afraid of when it all comes back to the blackout city, that unseen zone wherein the sickening world gets to die a little bit more on its own and leaves you alone for the night, there where television sets do not play and everyone is high.

"Forget it," Brendan said.

"Forget it!" Phil Cohen cried.

"What do you mean?"

"Oh just always, and always, man, forget it, forget it, forget it!"

He brought his hands down upon the old-fashioned tabletop. William overlooked the crowd below—he returned his eyes to Brendan's; they looked as if on fire.

"Forget it!"

Somewhere the television sets were playing television wars on a television night very far away; you couldn't even see it anymore. The voices were too loud, the lights too bright, and that, of course—

"Was damned-fine," concluded Brendan.

Daniel swooped in, clear for the night, 90 MPH across the highway back home, and the night fell like a grand piano as he took a seat.

"Let me tell you of my night!"

∽

"I've got a better idea," Daniel said at noon, the young men disheveled and listening through hangovers alleviated by that flash of excess free money. "Let's go out, downtown, and buy ourselves suits. We'll wear nice suits, second-hand or whatever, and it'll just be good to own a suit."

William nodded. Sonny West rushed downstairs to throw up again. Phil Cohen leafed through a notebook left upon the table and Brendan laughed, pouring out the remains of a fifth of Old Crow into cereal bowls. William and Daniel accepted.

"This is the best whiskey I've ever had," William said, his hangover dissolving into thin air. He counted the hundred-dollar bills and twenties over again in his pocket. Daniel turned up the oldies radio station.

"When did you all start calling Thom 'Sonny West'?" he asked.

"I heard it from William," Brendan said.

"I just couldn't take him in a thoughtful way as a person with his little Beatle-boots and mushroom-tattoo, so he became Sonny West. I called the bartender at the Hotel Bar or whatever Sonny West. If you can't stand someone who may be able to do you a favor, you call them Sonny West."

"God, I hope no one ever calls me Sonny West."

"But that's the whole point," Brendan said. "Is that even if no one can take you at least you've got a good moniker even if you can't take it. Think about it."

"Mary was telling me that you can get a job downtown—"

"Oh, the *bus* thing!"

El took off for the East Bay having made plans for the next weekend to bet on the horses. Daniel and Brendan and William were drunk and took the train downtown. Sonny West rested in the basement and sold more of his hashish.

Two hours later the three of them walked out with food-stamp cards to which $400.00 in cash had been activated. They rushed to the bank and withdrew it.

"This is splendid," said William, throwing his arms around Daniel Welles. Brendan had been sifting in and out of sleep throughout the journey and William and Daniel spoke for hours straight at a time.

They made their way to Larkin; Daniel to buy a gram of cocaine, a pellet of morphine, and for William and Brendan to retreat with pouches of tobacco to the Brown Jug.

"Two whiskeys, please," Brendan said. He looked at his money like he could have cried. William was beginning to understand that Brendan was a good man.

"He's not so bad, right," Daniel reappeared. "I mean and you're getting your money's worth with someone like Thom, or Sonny West. He leaves soon anyway."

"No problems with Sonny, but Daniel, now last year—Hey, man, get this guy a pint of the freshest beer you've got—Budweiser? Sure—What about this trip to Portland and Seattle and everything? I've been to every state and I never forgot you mentioning that last year and perhaps last week also."

His eyes widened as if no pain whatsoever were left in the world, the collision of traveling Northwest in autumn and that first euphoric rush of cocaine.

"We'll do that. I'm getting the bike rigged up." He rubbed his hands together, the look in his eyes emanating the rhapsodic beauty which is the rush of forestry in the northwest in October. "Oh, but first we buy our suits, get into a cab pronto."

The best feeling, William marveled, was to have a thousand dollars in cash and a crisp new suit, and polished wingtips, drinking orange juice with vodka and ridiculing world affairs by casting them off with the wand wave of a cigarette in the kitchen overlooking downtown San Francisco as night began to formulate once more. Hash was in the air and Mary told stories all night long. Her girlfriends came over for dancing and cocktails.

"You know what I like about her," Daniel said, combing his mustache in the mirror with a wax-kit he'd bought earlier on Leavenworth,

"Is that she has a good sense of humor. I always thought women were just born unfunny and that if I ever laughed at any of their jokes it was to further my chances of getting laid."

"We are all doomed," Brendan grinned.

Mary returned to the room and for a moment William thought she might sit upon his lap as two couples passed through the narrow hallway, pressing Mary's summer dress to William's knees. Instead she smiled, lit a cigarette, and stepped away to a group of diplomatic-looking men from the university who drank Johnny Walker Blue and wielded imaginary canes each time they spoke.

William watched Daniel slip away with Mary and made a disquieted toast to him.

"To what's her name, from the other day!" Daniel whispered, sniggered, and tossed a glance to Mary. "You, though, are the lucky dog."

Brendan turned around to the room:

"Yo ho ho!" He lifted a pint of rum to the chandelier with a twist and a crackle within a budding grove, and with that he collapsed upon the kitchen table. Then it was dawn.

The thunderous bout came to an end. For lucid days William showed Sonny West around the city and took him to the parties and either man made his money. Toward the end William liked the lost man, though still there was no grain of individuality, no shred of life to reach for. He seemed still, at the end of it all, most apt to live in the woods with machine-gunners and disillusioned drug dealers, memorizing his John Lennon songs in peace.

Still, one of the best ways to relive any city is to show someone around it. William longed more than ever for Octavia to come out to visit in his days recapturing Divisadero, Clement, Mission, the Sunset, Haight, and Golden Gate Park.

Brendan wrote short stories in the backyard with weeds that surpassed his head; William could never see him there, working, but he could hear it.

After a sandwich at Ike's the days—plentifully beautiful and undermined with the subtlest poignancy which added that imperfect bliss of reality to reflection—of recapturing the past came to an end. He took Thom Stoykovich to each possible destination except Polk Street; that would have to be saved in the instance that old Harold Smith reemerged.

William and Sonny West had a last drink atop Dolores Park before he'd get his belongings, go through West Portal and back to the airport.

His mother, Sonny admitted in a moment of confessional clarity, had just been diagnosed with cancer.

"I'll be back soon, though, I love this damned city—thanks for helping me out."

The subway doors clicked open as William stood to go.

"Take care, Thom."

"Thank you, again, for everything," he said. He shook William's hand with great zest.

He knew someday, perhaps across the country, someone like Sonny West would understand that he had been brought in for mere finances, and what further implications such realities entailed. And yet if he did not understand, perhaps he would return to San Francisco to look everyone up one day, and that was fine too.

The sun set and the pace at which such lives passed through one another seemed unmerciful. The train was out of sight, dissolved into the tunnel, and William took on up the long road for a drink at Terry's Lounge.

~

"The most irrevocable truths are those brought on by ambiguities," William said to the prostitute.

Two weeks passed. He sat at the good old desk, made calls, sent e-mails; nothing.

Where once, when struck by the overwhelming ineffectuality of it all, William could walk down to the University Library and end up sprinting home with ideas, encouragement, enthusiasm and proof that the creative task was life, this subtle trick no longer stimulated that particular region of his intellect.

In another instance, there were always dozens of pretty girls one saw on the subway trains reading articles and novels, their beautiful lipstick traces parting to the rhythm of words; hadn't you wished you'd written that very article, that very paragraph?

Summer became September all too soon. William looked to the northwestern voyage with Daniel, and yet still he could not shake certain melancholic recognitions from his soul; the lack of anyone doing anything at all, the war, the country's disintegration. Left and right the unemployment was running out and a good deal of the talk at parties turned to who had moved home this week, last week, or the next. Whether he liked it or not, California had changed.

So it was far easier to have breakfast in the morning with Mary, marvel her innocent motions, breathe in the cool air and go out to brainstorm (Which meant begin the trek downtown, to begin and end at the Tempest). William found day-drinking in the Sunset depressing. Downtown it seemed rational halfway through the first drink, where spirits were higher, and by the time the next drink came you knew you'd made the right decision. And so on.

Daniel arrived in the middle-afternoon. The two went on a long walk and mapped out the trip through Northern California, Eugene, Portland, Olympia, Seattle, hypothesizing the idea of staying put in one such place at least for some days or months, because both could admit that things were shifting in the city, beginning with summer's end, and while the end was not in sight, there seemed some colossal vibration crossing the country. Everything their generation had been raised to believe was true had ended up false; and while one could debate the innumerable reasons behind this, one could not debate it was happening.

"You know, I think what everyone needs is a break, so let's get our heads out of the city and return with fresh eyes!"

The next morning they took off at sunrise; the leaves were just beginning to go. Again, as soon as the wind began to burst through William's hair once more, he felt much better about himself.

∿

All the souls of days past, interwoven albeit yearning, crates clinking full of beer, Dionysian dream of forms, I/My, We/Our, tap of glass, and they of Jerusalem were like dirt caught in a sewer of clay, screams out in the summer night, Octavia a flowerbed beside glittering waters, when she spoke of the bread of life I witnessed dissolve that hovering corpse that had so long lingered about faith and reason—occult forces, hunger for truth, oceanic compass—the Spirit departeth not by stayed, in all its lucent splendor—the one who said she sought her faith, nailed to a tree, in search of lost time—I have long pondered what becomes of he who is born on an island somewhere, who never has even heard of Christ, and heard instead, 'The West will set me free. But not until it is finished with me'—Now we have seen this hypothetical before, in asking what becomes of such a good man? Ah cursed poets, full of wine and vigor, the bell is tolling—I seek to know, though, that for a man who has never heard of cosmic punishment, but follows his savage heart, raping and killing and suppressing in accordance with his ilk, never out of cruelty but out of his barbaric, savage stage: the evil is all he knows, and none has ever been sent unto him with news of another sort; and what of the kind-hearted Luciferian, in light of the endlessly greedy televangelist? Turn to Keats, who turned to Jeremy Taylor—for I know, said someone, the strength of camels' humps, and backs therein; but the sacred poor know how burdensome a displaced piece of mattress straw can be—set my pencil in motion, writing to the East, as for reasons unbeknownst even to I, pilgrim, raise a glass to P.B. Shelley—

Pale Misfeature

"YOU NEVER CALLED ME! I can never get a hold of you! I'm going to buy you a laptop!"

Octavia's voice breathed life into William's exhausted body and mind as he sat alone on the old mattress, taking buckets of water that had flooded the basement outside to the rain-saturated streets while he had been away.

"I just returned home from a week-long tour of the northwest—we stopped everywhere, met up with girlfriends of Daniel's, watched the sun rise, everything! What are you doing now?"

"Sitting here at the table, overlooking Manhattan, drinking a bottle of wine. Tell me about it! My angel, you struck me as wretchedly depressed, and it was intensified by knowing that, right then, I could not help you. I think of you always. What have you been *up* to?"

He again felt guilty about his lack of productivity although not for the sake of art; Octavia's voice seemed to resonate within him the conviction that true love was the real pinnacle of humanity, and yet she'd laugh at him if he were ever to say so. He cared less about letting himself down than letting Octavia down, for he knew at once in what had become of his life, his nocturnal pilgrimage, that still one of the sole consistencies in his life at all was the way Octavia spoke, the tone of her voice, and he felt idiotic to have waited so long in receiving her calls. In his heart he knew it was a prolonging of the pain he felt each time their conversations ended, and she was 3,000 miles away.

"I'll tell you all about the northwest," he began, "And—well, God, it's hard to explain, but just let me say one thing of all this traveling, this writing, this desperate longing to live—it's not just a thing of the past, Octavia, and I don't give a damn about the past—the cities didn't strike me as the forestry at the break of autumn passing through Oregon and

Washington. That, I think, is all I can say on the matter. If you've ever got the chance to see the northwest during the beginning of autumn, go—I urge you to drop everything you want to drop anyway and go, because even if I die a poor young death, I'll have died now with a trinity born in my mind: The summer of San Francisco, the autumnal Northwest, and winter dusk of New York City; that, then, is what my heart must be composed of."

At this point, this autumnal America begot, the best way to describe the market, the sources of income, would have degenerated from a cautious 'Severe' to 'Terminal.' No one had called from the east at all. None but Octavia, whose city was impenetrable in the light of the rest of the country. It seemed a startling disillusion.

"I wish I could have been there," she said. "We must read Augustine together. Let it ease in, tell me all about it later."

William contemplated expressing his near shock at the extent of Daniel's drug addiction but kept it to himself. He'd went through two thousand dollars' worth of cocaine in seven days, William noted, and even more startling was how well he'd kept his composure together. He seemed to save all his energy for mutual conversation and women. Once or twice did William grow tired of his pushiness, fleeting neurotic insistences, and in such a case William did a couple of lines with him in the morning and that solved the issue. Still he felt nervous as he watched Daniel depart for the Tenderloin, for more drugs, in his three-piece suit, at once upon their arrival home. All the time his mustache had stayed perfectly-set.

"The most awful thing has happened," William groaned, crossing his legs upon the desk and kicking several cans filled with dampened cigarette butts to the ground, listening to the relayed clamor and the rain pelt upon the windowpane.

"What happened?"

"Summer's gone."

"Don't scare me like that."

"I didn't mean to. It just hit me. Each summer goes by faster, each conscious second en route to the grave seems to snap in two with a more calculated vigor, entranced by the imperceptible chaos of abstraction and creation. I wish we were laying around and hadn't had jobs in years, go down to that Tandem on Troutman Street and have a fresh Bloody Mary in the daylight hours with the windows open."

"Oh my God!" laughed Octavia. "That's what I'm going to do now." Keys jostled, locking the door, and she began to walk down the street; wind and sirens came across the receiver. "Just a lazy old Bushwick Sunday."

"That's my fun day—"

"What?"

"Take a table with an extra seat and pretend I'm there! If I had just arrived, I would have kissed you on your perfect cheek, or just above your eyebrow."

"Why the cheek?"

"Because then later, when we kissed on the mouth, we'd both have been thinking of it for so long," said William, "And you're a perfect kisser. No, the perfect kisser, Octavia, for there's forever room for one in such terms, in our lifetimes of mediocre and bad kisses. Don't you wish you could tell a person's kissing style by the way they spoke? I suppose that is what makes certain surprises pleasant, though, like walking into a bedroom without a bookshelf. Or worse, a bad collection. When I leave due to nausea, I often wish I were faking it."

"Oh my sweet boy, are you getting things done or just sweeping San Franciscan women off of their feet and drinking?"

The sound of an emptied bar's creaking doors made its way across the receiver. William pictured the blue tile tables in his mind and the old, curved bar shipped from an Elks Club upstate.

"Few women, few words, many drinks. With some difficulty it's all coming together although not as quick as I'd like it, and I dislike myself when I am strained."

"We're still so young," Octavia said.

William considered this, tossed another bucket of water out of the back door.

"Age is not a number but an amount of knowledge, I think, but I see what you mean; there are no seasons, no years, but I suppose all of this is getting old, too," he paused, sighing, lighting a pipe and counting his coins from a mason jar. "I remember awhile back you told me about a job as editor for some journals—ever hear about that?"

"All I've been doing is working and sleeping. I was not hired at either of the journals for reviews editor. I suppose it had something to do with a joke I made, suggesting that Husserl used to frighten me, but now just gives me migraines. I am shocked, I tell you, that I am not the only epistemologist or phenomenologist on earth. I never even have time to sit down like this and drink." She took sips and sighed with immense pleasure. "Gin is like a Christmas party."

"The American way," William paused to laugh, "The dream always *almost* coming alive, the light never to be seen, but oh, though, this deadened phrase had grown most common long ago. I am all scrambled up, Octavia, in between emotions and all of that, exhausted although when I sit still, I feel as if I'm missing out and long to rush downtown. The days and nights I stay in bed and do nothing I feel as if some estranged city spirit is laughing in my face, or behind my back. I try to explain to myself that I am weary and oversexed and feeling terrible and promised myself in the morning that I would take it easy and yet I still feel this sense that I am not being a man."

"I've had no good conversation in this city all year," Octavia whispered. "Let us have summer and peace become one synonymous goal, getting you all established throughout winter and spring. It is terrible to run around the city in the dead of winter, and worse to start working in spring."

"Yes."

"What are you doing today?"

"I think I'll have a drink of wine, read a chapter of a book, then drink the bottle, and read the whole book. I've got about seven in a pile beside me."

"No, you're going on a date I bet. I got the pictures you sent me."

"I've grown a mustache almost as colossal as Nietzsche's," William exaggerated. "And I've cast off women till I see you." There was a hint of truth in this spontaneity. "This hasn't been a year of love, simple or otherwise, hearts or bodies or minds, for me. I feel every which way but comfortable around potential lovers, but you get to a point wherein you'd rather be comfortable than yourself."

"Don't say that!"

"It's what everyone does. No one impresses me. Do you know anyone that *impresses* you? I feel as if my life has been composed of photographic instances wherein people tell me what they are doing, I sip from a coffee mug, and give them an ominous look while nodding and pursing my lips. I cannot help it, even though I am unaccomplished and unknown myself. Oy vey. Why do we even still speak?"

"Because I care about you, because I want to see you again. It seems to me, William, that we belong to a long-extinct generation. Sometimes I am astonished that either one of us, let alone both, exists. I took a rented car up to Poets' Walk, north of the city, upon realizing I had and have no friends."

"Wait," William said, as if breaking with meditation, "The most terrible things have been happening to me as well. I've been in isolation too long. Even when I was traveling, in the cities and towns, I felt alone; beforehand I was spending weeks alone at a time. It almost reminded me of Pennsylvania. Each window I walk by makes me sicker than the last, some drunk tourists taunting me earlier on the streets near Embarcadero in their Caldor clothing and shopping mall personalities, Brendan's out of town, Phil's in the East Bay, Harold Smith has vanished, and all the others from last year, Octavia, I tell you they've been moved out. I miss them and tried to just let it go, but it's bothering me again. Then Daniel, we voyage all the northwest together, and when we arrive home something loathsome happens. A week of discussion and bonding and traveling and it all breaks apart the second we get back to San Francisco."

He took a breath and dumped another bucket of water outside. Octavia waited, unsure of William's seriousness, yet intrigued nonetheless:

"What happened?"

"He offered me something I had little interest in."

"Head?"

"No, no—more God-damn *drugs*! I'll tell you one night he was high beyond language, and I freaked out." He had to tell someone. "We hadn't even made it through Portland, and I was contemplating getting on the bus. A big party of rich, university graduates going through hundreds of nitrous pellets and taking MDMA, throwing neon Frisbees into the river. I hated all of them. I ended up telling some of them off and it got strange; I figured Daniel was so drugged he wouldn't have remembered in the morning, but he did."

"What did you say? Here, wait; let I, thy lexicographer and philologist step outside."

William envisioned the blinking lights of the bodega on Troutman and Wilson, its white and royal-blue sign chipped with rust visible from distances. He missed old New York, Octavia Savonarola's block and its scaly dark-skinned women slouching by with prosthetic eyes and shark-tooth necklaces waving Puerto Rican flags, smelling of chicken empanadas and yellow rice, while horn music rang out through the uncured concrete streets of bursting hydrants, strange white people in their twenties and thirties who despised attentions and wore outfits which begged for it, the biblical processions on karaoke machines at dusk and the secret bars one turned into to get away from it all just to return delighted, and surprised to be back on the streets one had learned and knew by heart.

"Well I don't remember it all so well—but I managed to offend and insult everyone at the party. Not at once, but the word spread, and it was spooky. This story is meaningless. Anyway, I feel the weight of desolation everywhere I go, as if the innocent beauty of life has been absorbed from my perception, oh, don't you feel terrible like this sometimes?"

"Every day," Octavia admitted with an uplifting air of confidence, "But what about drinking—are you drunk?"

"I sound drunk?"

"No, no—I mean I can never tell if you're drunk, just when you're not drunk."

"Well at the moment, no, and I either drink or not at all."

"But not every night for extended periods of time?"

"No, no—nothing like that."

"Because I've been drinking," she said. "For years, of course you know—it's just a matter of how much I drink, which is a result of how the day went. When one is doing it as a way of life, the chemical alterity lends itself to laughing off physiological reality. There are joys, of course—last time I was drinking I listened to Mozart's *The Marriage of Figaro* all the way up and thought of Edith Stein. But then the next day I had to pull over twice because of my tears; I wished a single person in the world longed to attend symphony with me. What depressed me further was that I am incapable of keeping my sorrow to myself: that it cast a melancholic glow on you. It is the same reason no one talks to me, and it makes the original problem amplified just thinking about it. But if one is blessed with an ability to cease, take a moment, and contemplate how life might be without it, I believe then a life dedicated to aesthetic, theological inquiry is in the cards. Nothing, I have found, is more intoxicating than waking up early to get to work on something one loves."

Despair took the form of a nagging in William's heart. Octavia knew very well he went out every night, for if she spoke to William at night, he could explain it made perfect sense. Even as he listened to the aesthetic splendor of care for the self, the pilgrim took to wondering what he'd drink that night. Chilled white wine, and a lot of it. He had not considered himself like this until it was daylight and he was alone, and he heard someone else admit to what he had been up to. At the same token, one immersed in hedonism is also immersed in a reality of fellow hedonists; and part and parcel of the condemned life is to let anything transpire, so long as one is hammered for it. Hence, the sole wager that seemed most absurd was that of halting to preserve one's heart and mind; it seemed bound to that offensive way of meetings over kumbaya and medication, which itself made one want to drink more. There were no answers. If one thought about it, the difference between being intoxicated and being sober was that intoxication provided the fine illusion of time slowed down, while in secret it pressed on faster. It killed the pain and enhanced the ordinary; it brought on pain and magnified the mundane. He looked at himself in the mirror and knew not what to think save that the agonies of hangover with drink were still not so heinous as sobriety with the intent of preservation. Just the thought of an A.A. meeting was enough to drive any sane person into annihilating relapse. And yet how many lives had they saved? It would appear one ought to remain silent until one knows, be it a house of worship or basement folding chair, what it's like to have one thing, and one thing alone in life, keeping one afloat. The old man in church, the young woman in church basement: let us now cease condemning that which is foreign and be thankful for right and just mercy. And thus it dawned on him that there was still yet another way, an aesthetic mysticism that left behind indulgence as well; one just needed to take the broom of the system and break it over one's vodkahobble knee.

"But what else can a young person do in the city," Octavia said. "But I suppose the Master was not all too keen on Edith Stein leaving phenomenology for a life of enclosed prayer, now was he?"

"I miss you right now. I always miss you."

"Ideally you arrive before spring semester begins, so we might talk about a million things in peace, or at least uninterrupted. And then you know about Nielsen of course."

William hadn't thought of Nielsen in a long time. His heart skipped a beat. Unclear emotions panged within his heart and fell away; he no longer had any real opinions of anyone from his past, he knew, for they were past.

"What'd he end up doing with himself?"

"He tried to kill himself, dropped out of school, moved back in with his parents and takes pharmaceutical drugs."

"Just like his brother," William sighed. "How did you find out?"

"He posted it on online."

He stood, opening the window wide. Then he took the old typewriter and threw it through to the concrete ground. It smashed like a melon, shards broken and sprawled across the littered sidewalk. An invisible dog howled.

He looked around the room for other furniture to destroy.

"But I understand it," William said, "For what is nobility but a presumptive characteristic when you loathe life and distrust death? We must go on, but why? I'll stop now." He cut himself off, wiped sweat from his brow. Hundreds of words broke through his mind in repetitious, dehydrated chaos. "I ought to go over to Oakland tonight and rest up, go to the horse races."

"You, betting horses," Octavia laughed. "I can't see that."

"El described it as most pleasant. I know he is not wrong."

"But please," she said, her voice balanced by an instinctual tenderness borne of conviction and experience: "You know I always think of you. Call me tomorrow. You never call me! I thought when we were younger, we decided on—"

"On what?" asked William, just to hear her gorgeous voice; then he realized what she had mentioned. Octavia Savonarola and William Fellows, he had recalled just walking through Seattle at dawn, entranced by idleness and thought, idyllic words woven by her simple heart, of when they had been teenagers and knew that someday they would be together again, when they were older and wiser. "Us," she began, before breathing as if to convey parallel thought, and William could hear a crack in her voice recalling childhood, that there was life before and after the complexities of young adulthood, and that the sun would rise tomorrow morning, and that the lungs of the earth hadn't collapsed just yet, that bombs could be dropped every single day, that Bolshevism, proving both William and Polybius right to the sixth degree, could destroy the American financial system, that the world could fall apart at once and everybody was a terrorist, and that did not matter—what mattered was the vision of the pursued heights of blessedness and paradise, and if you had not yet gotten there, you had to do what you loved, and do it. "Neither of us seems happy," she refrained, "Unless we are together."

"I agree; let us see one another again, soon! Let me give you my autobiography, Octavia: He was born in New York, never knew his father, grew insane with sitting still in the countryside, grew an occasional mustache and had fleeting hatreds for many things, indispensable loves for others—liquor and literature saved his life, for he had been contemptuously drifting through eternity before the advent of the illustrious duo. But at the core, and from the beginning, it was New York City and Octavia Savonarola, light at the end of the tunnel, proven with that unattainable quality of having the subtleties, the impossibilities of the transitions of life interwoven into her voice, and when she called him he felt confident once more, and he knew that when his world was dry, his personal libraries polished off, she would still be beside him. The cities came and went; she did not. When he saw her again, the entire world fell away, recaptured through embracing. He died one day, but so did everyone else. Death was the most uninteresting element of life. He took a crack at thought and knew a man was incomplete without his partner; you my love, you. How he longed to see her, to walk beside her in the streets. He was old-fashioned in multiple ways but one ought to not think too modest of the past in our generation tied to the technological future, for the past is inimitable, and the inimitable is all that is invincible in this life."

"I've got to see you before Christmas, William, I've got to! I need you around in my life!"

"No—I need you!" He paused to relight a cigarette. "Let me write you a letter tomorrow, hope from Oakland, and at dawn my final edits begin—I sketched out an old story about friends spending time with one another and some articles for journals, newspapers, and that way when we become lovers once more, I'll be a disciplined lover, a discipline learned from my craft and art."

"O but William, you always did what you wanted to and that—"

"But now, Octavia," as he stood atop an old shelf, "Now is the time to admit the value of exactitude as pertains to inherited traits! I apologize for all this chaos you've caught me within, my love, but God now I must go give old Phil Cohen a ring—what are your evening plans? Get to San Francisco as soon as possible!"

"I'll look at plane tickets tonight, I promise, and I suppose I'll return to my watered-down Bloody Mary and take it from there," she said cheerfully.

"But why watered down?"

"Because all of the ice cubes have melted by now!"

"Good Heavens!" William grasped his forehead. "Forgive me!"

"I don't mind—a lazy Sunday, I'll pretend you're sitting inside beside me. Though now I ought to go and I cannot stand goodbyes with you, William."

"Good-night," William said.

"Stop it!"

She paused; William apologized.

"Before I go back, and never hear from you again, let me read you something I wrote last night when I was drinking that reminded me of you; I was thinking of you when I wrote it."

William sat still upon the couch waiting to hear the sound of rustling paper. Instead Octavia began to recite at once as if she'd been skimming over her sentiments all the while: 'If one is to decide one's life the attested way to which we are brought up to believe, one ought to take a step back first, or to unplug the teleprompter, if you will; the first duty in life is not life but to maintain a good buzz throughout life. Going overboard is often a waste of time, glamorized in commercials, though often a serialized bout of headaches and anxieties. Knowing this much, one ought to go through life for at least a good while saying what he wants and maintaining a good buzz on whatever is available. For what are the other options? Variants of our dilemma: The internet, the gadgets, the breaking news, and the billboards, all for more fatal than any mere chemical could strive to be—so don't worry much at all about living the illusion, the spectacle, because those (The masses) who live such a way know nothing of themselves and can surround themselves with pathological liars and frauds of existence: mirrors of themselves. If there is a vital mirror it is art, and never physical appearance; thus I say as a painter that life is to have fine style, and survive surrounded by the few that understand, that remain. Otherwise you've got lines for useless films, job applications, and commercial breaks. 'I'd rather have a bottle in front of me than a frontal lobotomy,' and again, and when the whiskey runs out make a fresh pot of coffee and stock up on the classics. Study queer culture, study anarchism, study the founding fathers, study Serge Gainsbourg or Lee Hazelwood for God's sake—anything but Bill O'Reilly, coupon booklets, and staged lectures which stage for conversation in our futile culture bent on technological overload; the rebirth of Roman distraction; and while you're at it, throw your cellular phone into the river and pack up a suitcase filled with a spare outfit and a set of books. Meet me here; nothing can satisfy me.'

"What is that for," William said, concealing his heightened interest. "It sounds like a draft of something we co-wrote in another life."

"Draft? You think it needs work?"

"It is a little too cagey. The intensity of it takes away from the intensity of it. Turn it into a poem. Break it down into lines and publish it that way. Most poems are formulated, structured rants conceived by through and for idiotic boredom; thus thine'd be most refreshing."

"It's for an old journal one of the editors laid off from the *Village Voice* is putting together. She wanted some sort of biopic from my featured paintings. I figured I would write that there is no actual meaning in life at all but to have good style, and to face the fact that you're going to have to spend time alone to find it. The target is my family. One of my aunts is now a wealthy politician who has the personality of a tampon and the intellectual togetherness of match-lit anthills. She is also worshipped because she is miserable and has excess money and another unhappy mansion. Then the one guy who ought to be understanding about the whole thing, who turned on my father, has been working at a factory for thirty years after suffering an injury in a play he did in Los Angeles decades ago about the post office. The whole family's been severed, and while I never cared for any of them anyway, I find it astounding how they worship spectacle with religious fervor. At close of day if I wish for one last thing, it is that I was wrong. People can hate one another, but if one of them has money, he will have followers. Not even for free money and gifts, but to be within the presence of people with money. I expect more than the world from you; I expect you to overcome the world."

"I love you, Octavia, and don't forget it. It'll work fine for a paragraph prefacing prints of paintings. You'll see me sooner than we'll ever know. Our society remains nameless while you're not a household name, and the nameless societies of time lack comprehension of themselves in history, themselves in the streets, themselves in the afternoon."

"You'd better write me soon—the world's mutating, the second coming of that Petrarchan mountain, William, the Augustinian turn at last— Love you, and think of me before you go to sleep, thinking of you." She hung up the phone; her soft voice traversed through William's memory and flesh in a pristine echo.

He slouched upon the couch, began to undress. He sighed and closed his eyes. He thought he'd locked the door until it swung open; he had just finished.

"One moment, no, ten—wait!" he cried.

Whether or not she was something of a prude (Daniel had admitted in all his time around Mary they'd still done little more than kiss) she stood in the doorway transfixed. She looked around the room, her eyes returning once, twice to William. There was an equatorial plane torn between arousal and budding fear within the pale texture of her freckled face.

"What is going on!" She went to retrieve her laundry basket from the outdoor steps. "The window!" she cried, of all things. She pointed northeastern with her free, trembling hand.

That corner of the room did look as if a crime scene. Layers of dust had accumulated atop the unused desks and dressers, upon which an old rimless fan sat wrapped in its rubber chord. There was a clear shape where sweaters and buckets of paint had been, above which the rectangular window stood smashed all the way through. Fragmented glass shined on the windowsill and William felt as if he were acting suspicious although he, also, was observing the shattered window for the first time. He had never noticed that corner of the room until Mary had pointed its way and by then he was uplifting his trousers.

"Have you gone insane!" She still couldn't help but smile. "It looks awful down here! What have you *done*!"

White lights blinked off and on from Brendan's section of the room, providing William's inability to find the polite thing to say with a casual sort of catatonic appeal. The lights pressed and reflected on and off from his glass lenses. Whiskey bottles piled beside his mattress like little model pyramids set to crumble. He felt dizzy just looking at them.

He then felt offended that he had returned from his splendid northwestern trip to the complacencies of parental banter. He realized he had no true interest in anyone in the house except Brendan and longed to go for a walk.

"Why do men *do* that?"

"Do what, my love?"

"Keep bottles around like trophies, like victories! You'd even make a dollar or two if you recycled those!" She marched with haughty movements over to the pile. "How was your trip?" She sat on the arm of the couch in her kimono and smoked.

"Brilliant."

"That was hilarious when you and Daniel called me. How much cocaine did he do the whole time?"

"I don't know. I was busy looking at the leaves and singing songs with strangers and drinking Hamm's. What do you think of my beard?"

"How is the writing coming along?" Mary asked, shedding a threatening glance of skepticism and satisfaction in the wreckage of her basement. She shifted to the mattress. William had no idea if she was conscious of what she had walked in upon.

"Near completion."

"Already?"

"I thought you said it'd take years."

"I move when I am determined. If I would have moved even more just a minute ago, I could have spared us some embarrassment."

"Will you stop destroying things down here?"

"I didn't, yea, but nor do I have an explanation, so alright," William offered.

"Where's Brendan?"

"He'll be home this evening. We're going to the horse racing track tomorrow."

"Oh. I heard that place is disgusting."

"Me too."

"Look here," her face shifting with childish inquisition and delight, "You got some on the carpet." William leaned ahead, wiping it away with tissue-paper. "Why did you go and do that?"

"Something overcame me."

"That doesn't seem very, um, artistic."

"Seeming is the worst."

"Drink cocktails with me later."

"If I'm not going to Oakland."

"Go tomorrow morning. I'll leave cab fare out for you."

"OK."

"This is a nice chair." She stood and placed her hand upon the mahogany chair William had bought at the neon thrift store out on Valencia.

"Beneath every good man is the whole of society and a good chair."

"Oh please," laughed Mary, "And now you remind me I'm visiting home later in the week."

"I'm sorry to hear that."

"The suburbs."

"When the drugs are over with everyone just starts eating and become obese alcoholics or television-addicted derelicts and get divorces and buy expensive cars for quarrels in the drive-thru. They drive around in their cars as if they've won some war. The automobile is their medallion. Automobiles are disgusting. They look stupid, they sound stupid, and they smell stupid. I hate cars. I hate the suburbs. You go to rank bars, run into rank people, and exaggerate how swell the burnt pizza is with one eye on your defaulted counterpart, the other on high-definition reality television. Never go home, Mary, you're just too pretty for any of it."

"Oh, don't look at me like that."

"I like to look at you that way sometimes."

"Why?"

"You have special powers, Mary. Let me help you with the laundry."

"You are filthy." She pointed to a hole in William's tennis shoes, another hole in the mattress.

He looked over her legs with a nature beyond obvious. She smiled before standing to walk to the laundry machine and then upstairs.

"Mr. Cohen, I've had the strangest day thus far. Dawn voyage to thy East Bay is in order. To Mustard."

"Come, O lad, as I pry ye Old Crow from th' wall." He could tell by the tone of his voice Phil had received his microtexts in the mail from 6th Avenue and was at work with the miniature flashlight attached to his lenses. William packed his notebooks and socks into a bag and made for the door. Mary was outside in a long coat. William was in his long coat. She gave him a certain smile and they shared a wordless cigarette as the train passed through the falling rain, its headlights shining through the sifting fog of the street. Stopping before a storefront, the odd couple absorbed glittering crystals, a pulling on the rustic pipe, questions of love and hate, poverty, life and death—'how can I tell you what death brings, when I have not yet died?'—as well as two glasses of absinthe in a club where the glass changed colors as one moved past it, based on Goethe's *Theory of Colors*. From there Mary and the pilgrim rode out into the night from autumnal station to autumnal station in black peacoats, hypothesizing which bar to stop in next, in which part of the city.

She began to let William sit beside her in bars. She began to tell him all her life story in candle-lit corners, all of which seemed to stem from an overwhelming acknowledgment of inexperience. She was the sort of drinker who drank too much when she did, which was common enough anyway; but it was a specific turn of the arm, an exaggeration of the eyes that at first one thought was part of an act, till one understood that alcohol, perhaps genetically, really took her that way. It reminded William of Abigail Blake, and the tragedy that was a life which ended by way of corded rope and crate.

"So often have I heard of Calvin's predestination," said William, "but seldom does anyone speak of Augustine, or our pilgrims for that matter. And as we cannot literally go back but in our minds, predestination strikes me as a doctrine that I would say even the pagans could meet us in the middle on. A doctrine of Augustinian predestination infused with Georges Sorel could well do that most ostentatious thing, that is, make perfect sense—we spent the night drinking vodka and wine, listening to the delicious recordings of Renaissance lute, and I drink down the agreeable medicine of Octavia's voice, in memory, while conveying to you that forthcoming of vulnerability, that is research in the book of life, the new life coming into itself."

"I'm sorry—*what?*"

He felt detached when he looked over Mary's figure and at the same time, he felt dedicated to making love to her. Fall was a bad time to go unloved, but certain types of love seemed destined to come together through tragedies, the way specific restaurants and bars are crowded after specific funereal viewings.

～

Phil was calling at 11:00 to confirm and William felt guilty for not having gotten it together sooner. He could hear Brendan reading aloud to himself in the kitchen and frying eggs. Discarded by the steps, where no light shined, rectangular, frisbeed: *Tim Maia, Self-Titled:* Polydor 1980.

He set his blistered feet to the cold, dusty ground and recalled working as a hotdog vendor, more that day when Phil had come to meet him after a beautiful walk down Polk Street in the middle-afternoon of last July. Phil was then explaining to him news directions in the enormous novel he was writing, and it was funny to think friendships could be formed over misplaced chairs.

Then Brendan was texting him: "Come on, man, let's get going! The track! Coffee!"

He stood up and laughed with an increasing vigor at the idea of life, and more so the idea of a hangover, because one was coming to get him soon, in mere minutes, and until then he coughed and laughed in the daylight of a broken window until he thought his lungs might go.

A hangover seemed like a theatrical performance; one awoke shocked, as if this has never happened before, continued to breathe, focused on water, coffee, orange juice, pills, box office statistics, marijuana, or whatever gets one through. William was coming to find that everyone has the solution to a hangover but none of them work except in the sense of placebo. One feels as if a war veteran with purple lips and one can't be that handsome, singing thing from last night—my God, no, you've gained weight! You're an alcoholic! You feel like you might die, or worse, have a nervous breakdown! And yet no one has the God-damned cure!

The cure, William learned, is simple of course, and requires two accessible things in the predicament: a set of balls and a good tumbler of whiskey, and the recognition that agony and anxiety are not worth the admission price of the illusion of civility. If the night was that good, the day will be that bad; but then one ought to swallow the daylight down through the night recaptured, for the night is always on its way. He made a highball and walked, unchained, to the steps.

Brendan was looking good. He wore polished shoes, his three-piece suit, and read the Chronicle smoking a hand-rolled cigarette

He jumped. William was glad to be his friend and would have to execute his outfit for the day with equal precision. "You're back!" The two embraced, discussing Los Angeles, Portland, Seattle, Olympia, Eugene, and Northern California. The tranquil morning breeze came in through the window from the sea.

"Coffee. Pots of coffee," Brendan White said, and life was back to life. "I saw Daniel last night too—he looked like Hell. Drugs. Still, though, his mustache was—trimmed and curled."

"I worry about him," William said. He used a sharp tone that disabled further discussion on the topic.

Percy took out a bottle of Old Crow from his attaché and poured into William's coffee.

"It's just like the old days with Harold Smith. We would have Irish coffee and ride our bikes to Green Apple, spend sixty dollars on used books and read them in Chinatown dive bars."

"We'll see him again."

"I can hear the parade formulating."

"You excited for the track!"

"Oh, of course," William said. "We're going to strike gold. We'll be rich!"

"I plan on it," Brendan said sedately.

"I'm going to attempt to have fifteen beers and five hot dogs before sundown," William said, taking a crisp twenty from his wallet and pulling at it like a folding fan. "Everything is a dollar today."

"Well of course, but before we go have some of this bagel with avocado and tomato."

They took the MUNI out to Balboa Park and transferred to BART. Phil Cohen stood before the ramshackle barbed-wire fence beneath the sign which read DOLLAR DAYS.

"This is all damned fine," Brendan said, unlatching the Old Crow and stepping through the turnstile to the track.

They got situated outside on the bleachers with all the tattooed, ashen crew of ink-stained fingertips and graying beards, nets of oily black hair and loud lipstick, enormous breasts and flapping asses, broken teeth, and unlatched suitcases. William bet on Blade Runner and enjoyed drinking outdoors with three hundred others and Phil Cohen and Brendan White in Oakland, telling stories for hours on end.

At dusk one could walk out to the coast at the end of the parking lot where everyone smoked weed and listened to the Pacific crash at your feet against the boulders and ahead stood San Francisco. It was alright to cry looking at it, to consider yourself a citizen of the universe, and William noticed several people doing so that day.

He thought of old Harold Smith once more, of Fort Mason and of sitting on the dock of the bay, and let it go once more. They were great days and they weren't coming back.

Then it was back inside with your friends to the bleachers to bet on Cyclops, and after that there were several parties happening and you were proud to have been forty dollars less rich than when you'd entered because some day in the future you'd be much richer than that and longing to let it be otherwise.

"This hot dog is genius and damned good and genius one must know," said Brendan.

The Sacrament of Fragmentation

RAIN ARRIVED AHEAD OF schedule that fall, and everyone was in slumps. Someone's mother had bought a brand-new television set and William could no longer use the kitchen without catching admonished glimpses of the rubber horses at the bottom of in-ground pools on the television set or on television screens upon laptops plugged in around the house. Upstairs became a maze of wires and screens and silence interrupted by moving eyes cast in light, periodic laughter automated and otherwise. Then there were phones that played movies also, and phones with a thousand features. All of it seemed both surreal and banal and proved no one could draw the line between invention, necessity, and frivolity; it soared somewhere within the ringlets of marijuana smoke curling at one's shoulder in the morning. William wondered if the deafening silence that followed Brendan's narcotized suggestion that David Duke would have been a better President than Barack Obama were due in part to such all-encompassing digital absorption. Yet he was unsure if he'd said it aloud or dreamt it. With the urgency of shrugged shoulders, he checked out a copy of Quentin Lauer, SJ's *Hegel's Concept of God*, Rabelais, Melville's letters, and Hyppolite's *Genesis and Structure*. That week was a good year. There were the occasional evenings to speak some laborious semantics or another, the inauthenticity of jargon, although the rain did its number all through October. Daniel had vanished, Mary had taken an internship, Brendan ran out of money, the East Bay was so far in the rain, and still no one from last summer had resurfaced. At times William contemplated having a drink in the Mission to perhaps like see a familiar face although he could not bring himself to get out. He felt his immobility and stagnant train of mind less honest than harnessed and yet he could not find the answer.

Productivity was easy to not feel bad about as long as he limited his correspondence with Octavia although speaking with her was one of the events in those weeks which kept him optimistic:

"Explain."

"My self-confidence is shattered, and I doubt that solitude will mend it. But I have nothing else, and so what happens next is anyone's guess."

"We must keep faith. The country is a mess—this is no longer hyperbole but a real account of insanity coming down upon like a swarm, like demons. The only paradise left is the one that leads one to the One. But then I grow enraged and fantasize about throwing in the towel as far as peace goes."

"O William, why not follow Cardinal Newman instead? Such a man, who did the right thing and sought the truth, was inevitably led to its dwelling place: Roman Catholicism."

"I must make note of that . . . I need angels in my corner. Let a thing be scarce, so long as it is love, and borne of the natural law."

"Indeed the rarest, William, truly love life, and I mean love it in a sense beyond words and language's surface-level automations. What I mean by loving life is knowing precisely what one is living for; at that point death itself is made an entrance.

"But still I want to see less tinkering, and more solidifying."

"I beg your pardon," said William.

"You say you have read everything, and yet you have not even bothered with the Scholastics and have several library cards. This is no less sane, William, than a man inside a matchstick factory claiming he has no way to light his cigarette. Do not conflate fractal learning with enlightenment; you are a mere sophist working less with wisdom than presumption, the hallmark of stupidity. Even should every last public intellectual side with this insanity, you do not have the right to do so. The truth entails aspects of the simple, but it is not entirely simple; self-righteousness borne of rejection and simplicity borne of ignorance are two bodies at the same bridge: one is falling, the other diving."

"I read Psalm 14 as you requested. I believe I am beginning to understand."

"One believes in order to understand; one who does not believe only ever claims to understand. This is why it makes no difference whether the earth is four billion, two thousand, or eighty trillion years old: all that actually matters is the disregard for infinity."

"Yes," said William.

"A good plan would be, then, to sit down one day and decide, once and for all, whether coincidences exist or not. Then you might be getting at a beginning of the beginning of the beginning."

"This is what I want; and all I get are braindead oafs regurgitating 'social construct.'"

"A social construct is a social construct is a social construct."

"There is no understanding of solitude, and hence no understanding of freedom. The cities are filled to the brim with reversion."

"I spent my Thanksgiving at a convent. Do not fear 'reverting' me. All this does is show that you are absurdly mistaken in my way of life. You see, I well recall the part of my life when the blinders were still on. But then I read, studied, and learned that religion and philosophy were long inseparable, and still are although unpublicized, because there are limits to knowledge. Therefore I recognized the invisible cell walls that might be erected around me, a portal dwelling place. Love of this world cannot be the only love there is as space and time retain imperceptible technologies of critique. So now four invisible walls of freedom are forever around me . . . While I enjoyed the first attachment very much, the second was the most bewildering thing I have ever read in my life. I have read the pages three times now and still have no idea what you are talking about. One of the many dangers is that one cannot tell if you are just, well, screwing with people or not. Certainly, I understand that, if it's even the case—but I am your friend and the rest of the world isn't. While even the most obvious things begin as mystifying language ideas, it is seldom good to wonder if a writer is invested in torture rather than scholarship. Lastly, I know you so well that I know you are not a charlatan; but again, who else knows you in such a way? I'll be your virgin already past the altar. Remember to remember. Look at Corinthians 7:26. Soon."

Then for the first time in a long time he felt that he was alone, and it struck him dead in the middle of sleep paralysis.

He looked around his room: The humming boiler, cracked marble soap-dishes, countertops outlined with copper and wood as if splinters from an old man's cane; to place on the skeleton a singular suit, teeth of tattooed film, navy-blue brass and wordless intermissions through hallways. He listened to the flags break at night and longed to hike through the Muir Woods, spend the evening in the secret Yacht Club beneath the Golden Gate Bridge in time for sunset at the window-seat contemplating life, art, and triamcinolone acetonide.

The feeling of being alone in the universe was a feeling one could come upon, and a feeling that not ever after two thousand years could one shake free as if dust from boots; this psychological incidence was the dust, the boots, and the nail in the coffin of carrying on.

Somewhere far away crystal snowflakes would soon begin to stream past lamplights and past the windows of cinnamon shops and riverbanks. A child could study cursive with his mother by candlelight, she contemplative with the memorandums of Oceanside and ancestry, he contemplative of God. Silence from the other side, implicative of stalemate.

He got up out of bed at dawn and walked through the cold winds and fog. Sheepish policemen spoke gibberish on the marble steps of courthouses. William walked by.

'Morning due. There is no good mourning. Applause even amongst the passersby is a matter of presentation, delineation—the exterior quantum-physicality of disbelief.'

He listened to the metal clicking bracelets around the woman's wrists strapped to the wheel on Larkin Street.

"Get like in the like yo shut up I said get like in the car, you're under arrest," and so on. The Tenderloin was one place to walk in the wee morning, and the Brown Jug opened at six.

What had he said from all he had said? Those incapable of creating philosophies of their own—who amongst them but ruins; the ruins of gray, dismantled minds. What had Bertrand Russell said?

'But between theology and science there is No Man's Land.'

William dashed through his sleepless counter:

'Between theology and science is an alphabetical race to the grave in which any man alive can partake if he has discipline and sorrow and would like to rebel against either one with the other. There is no meaning to life; there is life, and you can often tell when something bad is about to happen.'

He walked past Sasha's old apartment on Post Street and thought of her and Daniel walking down the street, making tomato soup, and of those indescribable voyages and of reuniting at once in Dolores Park. It was wrong to break away from a good friend in need; one was better off trying to say something, even in the instance of seeming parental. He looked up at the old window where the grand piano had been, and the traffic passed through in the misty morning.

The Brown Jug had opened. The free jukebox was playing Nilsson—"Gotta Get Up." An old man walked by with an empty shoe box wrapped around his bald head chewing at a metal harmonica.

"We all have an idea when we think of a notorious drunk," a trans man calling himself Juanita explained to the pilgrim over afternoon vodka. "But think of this—never do we see it is ourselves. Every stereotype we conjure, when it is a single person, seems to us an open and shut case. But we are not even remotely close to understanding what seems, in delusion, to us most self-evident."

"Well that is why I had moved from the black cube death cult of Saturn into the revelations of one Peter Damian," responded William. "You mentioned medievalism earlier. Someone once told me that love was like a bottle of gin. I would add that it is a cross between a bottle of gin and medievalism more generally. Damian, for instance, convinced me that we learn from history that we do not learn from history: that even given the chance to learn, physiognomy may well make up its own mind to not give a damn, and persist in its release from restlessness and fragility.

"The Blessed Virgin has long been my celestial escort," said Juanita.

Such were the lost afternoons of spilled ashtray and thunderstorm, extinguishing the wicked disease of apathetic assumption, sharing photographs of Octavia's painting of the golden ladder. Then night walks, and letting go of one's desire for the temporal, thinking, *we do not go out and find the blessed life; for it we go in, and exteriority becomes in time inconsequential; have no fear that the truth render you hated, for now thou art entering the kingdom of righteousness, uplifted in a cesspool of incendiary automatism.*

But William on one particular night stared at the glass in front of him and felt an impending doom. It vanished along with his drink, and still all day short he could not shake that sense of impending doom from his soul.

～

The pilgrim awoke from dreamless, disjointed sleep to hands nudging at his shoulder with increasing firmness, consistent urgency. He was unsure if the sun was rising or setting through his window.

The sound of sniffling coincided with Brendan's distant snoring, left unconcealed by the running fan behind his Chinese wall draped with silken pajamas which blew to and fro. It was the first day of November and the day had been a chemical bastardization of dignity. A teardrop fell to William's lips.

He looked up and observed Mary crying in the dark. He noticed at once the swollen, reddish hue of her face brought on a sobering, direct sense of suffering and crying, clouds' reflective grayness which permeated in Mary's sullen, watery eyes.

"What—is it?"

"Thank God I didn't buy a new summer dress."

White ribbons fell in part from her black dress which presented her body in a striking manner, further tampering her grief with an irreversible pale beauty, her exposed shoulders under bits of strawberry-blonde hair which sifted before the open window, the edges held together dampened by tears.

She cried, breathless, refraining to sit down beside William, and in his arms began at once to sniffle again. The suddenness of this image panicked William, as if he were on a new drug he'd decided he ought not to have taken after swallowing it down. Still, he could combat such a notion, and whether he was dreaming: "Mary—"

"Oh, you're just not going to believe it, William," she howled awfully; her sniffling shifted into hysterical tears. She had, he felt, never called William by his first name before.

He looked over to Brendan and away, leading Mary upstairs by her shivering hand.

Just late last night, Mary explained, Daniel Welles had died; he had overdosed on multiple drugs. His blue, decapitated body had been found beneath the Golden Gate Bridge by an old fisherman after having been ejected through the windshield of a friend's car at like 110 MPH. Mary didn't recognize the driver's name and in her hours at the hospital not a single mutual friend had arrived. She'd called everyone she knew in the city and still no one came. William felt ill for having slept through her messages and a panic gripped him in the way it had gripped him last summer at dawn with Heather as she spoke of her childhood.

"The viewing is tomorrow, in Walnut Creek."

William spent the night drinking cocktails with Mary. Everything was sad. Melancholia was a wretched stimulant, driving one to fight sleep with coffee at certain hours and stay awake to talk and reflect, to be within the company of the living in the shadow of death. She helped him through a quart of gin and three long trays of ice cubes, two liters of tonic water and two whole limes.

There was even, at the numbest hour, disco music, and frantic cross-dressing outfits. Nothing worked; all that had hitherto appeared substantial was incrementally revealed as little more than a collective conceptual illusion of substance.

He couldn't cry because he'd seen it coming, though nor had it struck him down yet, so he said the thing he wanted to say for hours:

"If his head turns up in the Pacific at least we'll know in our hearts that somehow his mustache had remained intact."

Mary looked up to William through teary eyes and threw her fragile arms around him. The walls of the living room seemed to close in around them, and William sifted in and out of feelings not unlike that of sporadic suffocation.

"Did he repent in time?"

"Repent? What? Are you insane? It is you who should be repenting, thou whore!"

"How can I say where the soul is bound? Does it even matter what I believe—to you, that is?"

At 4:00 am Mary and William rustled themselves from vague unconsciousness and awoke and to the half-emptied glasses of gin upon the table. He reached through the litter of empty bags and cigarette boxes. Mary extended her hand into his and gripped a bit; she was wiping her cheeks although her buckets of tears had long dried, blowing nothing out of her freckled nose.

"He's dead," in a voice interwoven with tactile memory.

Then she nestled her nose into William's chest. Her body was warm as William held her, running his hand back and forth across her shoulder to show he was being asexual amidst this platonic silence. She guided his hand to the leg of paper-thin pajama-pants Mary had applied at some point in the emotional, alcoholic blackout.

"You'll come with me to the funeral—right?"

The trains went to and fro outside, rumbling through the house.

"Yes, yes of course," he said.

"I'll borrow my mother's car."

She pressed her lips to William's and held them there; neither one knew what to do but that. William took himself away and finished his gin thinking of nothing whatsoever save poor Daniel in that old Post Street apartment.

"Tuck me in," Mary asked.

William feigned exhaustion and stood up before her. He reached down to pick her up and carry her to her queen-sized brass bed. Nothing would register until William got to sit down alone and think about it; it was difficult make comprehensive sense of anything awful with company around.

He ran his eyes around the bookshelves, the multicolored garments strewn about bedposts and open dresser drawers.

He tucked her into bed. She looked beautiful, William thought, beneath the skylight, with reflected panels of lanterns spread across her incremental sheets. She seemed ready to fall asleep after one final thought. That was the look in her eye.

William looked forward to the night ending; to awaken tomorrow and face the despair in a sober state of mind that which he could not bring himself to say aloud: California *had* changed.

Mary took William beneath the warmth of the blankets.

"I am on birth control, William," she said. He was shocked although he did not move. "Do you know what that means?"

'My God,' thought William; 'My God, I have forsaken thee . . . help me, Lord . . . learn from Daniel lest I wind up like him . . . casket-dead in cold crushing waters, Christ help us all . . . '

⌇

The sudden couple awoke to Mary's mother ringing the doorbell, throwing old discarded newspapers at the window while batches of dampened leaves smacked the porch and surrounding puddles. Mary spoke with her in the living room as the taxi came to transport her back to Twin Peaks.

Rain fell upon the window and the porch. Damp air came through Mary's window and he slept until Mary began to show anger in his exhaustion.

They were running late to the funeral. William wore his knee-length black trench coat with black pants and boots with a white shirt beneath the silken coat. Mary wore an identical outfit without makeup and William was reminded of his earlier incestual feelings as she chain-smoked, looking for where her mother had set down the car keys. He was not meant to be with her. No one was meant to be with one another under such circumstances. The similarities, if one could put it that way, between

sex and death plagued his mind. With each deep breath he felt more astonished, more appalled, more lost.

Burned into William's mind was the image of someone's head at the
bottom of the ocean filling with parasitic vermin—or would it float? He
sat back and wondered if it were possible any longer to be bothered by
anything. His generation had seen it all: the multi-million dollar movies
of petty sorcerers and animated dragons, violent deaths and air-brushed
breasts, the politics of subliminal fascism and neocapitalism presented
from plump, giddy commentators, the emotional chronologies presented
in slideshows of profile pictures—what, to that generation, was a death
in the family? God was dead, but even attempting seriousness from the
other side seemed outdated. You could throw a corpse from its casket,
send chimpanzees to Neptune, and know that McDonald's had sold 100
billion hamburgers, and nothing mattered any longer; with the search
engine in their pockets, the whole cannon of human inquiry predetermined and broken down, one had little requirement to civility on the
streets, behind closed doors. Private life had become so sick that all of
the world's chaos seemed under the control of flashing imagery and text,
irrelevant one moment and forgotten in the next; where everything was
available nothing was retained, and it was difficult to get worked up about
anything anymore. The unreal city's artistry died its death, the last brave
men suicided by society, the rest irrelevant, yea, and a million had been
mowed down by malevolent sycophants with photographic guns to their
perverted, parroting skulls, wise men deemed irrelevant by the society
on its verge of reconciliation at the gates of Hell, and as skyscrapers fell
and Baal devoured Armorican children feasting millions of little limbs, in
death as in life delirious so it was, it was hard to get a good look at one's
self any longer. Moral relativism is not moral; it is the suicide of thought.
Now, William concluded, images were all that remained. The images of
death could haunt one, but life was too accelerated for any death to mean
much more than a frenzy of blog posts and comments, digital flowers at
a digital grave.

"Where did she put the *keys*?"

He stood out in the backyard and vomited several times into the
pelting rain. Then he brushed his teeth and washed up. Mary found the
car keys.

"Who puts *keys* on a *coat rack*? Who? Oh my God, it's raining. No
one's going to be there."

Forty minutes later, with slight traffic, the pair just so recently introduced by Daniel were arriving at his funeral.

Ten people stood huddled around the hole in the ground. Ferocious winds whipped the rain off and against the overhead tarp. Cold, metallic rain overtook any looming sense of reason and one could do little but stand transfixed upon the thousands of symmetrical graves running miles in each direction. William and Mary stood just far away enough to hear; not another mutual friend had come. From a distance they recognized no one.

A line of strapped umbrellas curved across the rounded marble enclave as the priest spoke his last:

> *Though he heap up silver as the dust, and prepare raiment as clay;*
> *He may prepare it, just as the just shall put it on,*
> *And the innocent shall divide the silver.*

They listened and met with fleeting unfamiliar eyes. Neither recognized a soul present. Then suited men stepped out into the rain and pulled the triggers of long shotguns which exploded vehement and dazed, resounding warmth into the frozen faces. It was so peculiar to ever imagine Daniel—even if just for a brief stint—as part of the military, but then William realized he knew quite little about his friend at all, or for that matter, most of the people in his life. The gunshots echoed through the saturated fields and water trickled down the aluminum drainage.

Bodies leaned over in disbelief as the wooden casket descended beneath the soil; the entrancement of the scenario made it feel as if it were a projection in slow-motion being shown from the enormous gray sky.

"I remember once last year we sat up in my old hotel room just talking—talking—for hours; I remember he told me, in the most serious tone I'd ever heard him take on, which is saying something, over Bob's doughnuts and coffee, that his ideal last words if he were to choose would have been 'I've seen enough.' And to have the epilogue to *Moby Dick* read at the wake, and here instead we have the Navy and gunshots." The tears came down. "Forget this life."

"I don't see why no one comes to this end of the pavilion," Mary thought aloud. She turned to William: "And what was your funereal idea?"

"I couldn't come up with anything," he admitted. "I suppose when I'm dead that's just it, I'll be back to where I was, or wasn't, before I was born. Whether it's good or bad is indecipherable, but it's soothing to believe I won't be conscious of any of it."

They walked through the parking lot, their arms interlocked.

"My mother is such a pain in the ass. She's drunk *already* and wants to the car back tonight. 'Why, mom! Why!'" Mary wept through clenched teeth, typing with rapid fire, and tucking her cell phone away.

Pallbearers took their final shot at the drained, pallid sky, and Mary grabbed William's hand with swift anguish. In the brand-new convertible they held one another.

"The poor son of a bitch," she cried, and the absolute sorrow of the whole affair did not manifest itself within William for another good 48 hours.

The living smoke of shotguns dissolved dying into the vermillion past of patchy sky, dispensed unto the Holy Ghost.

"He descended into Hell—"

Thereafter, naturally, a raucous night on Haight Street, something about a fire burning below, scent of wood, revolving and descending, all of vapid night merging into a sole form from which he, in the middle of a song, walked away, and awoke disconsolate, anguished, summoning within the grand, if obscure, historical narrative of the unknown soldier's life, something of a Machiavellian moment giving way to eternal recurrence, or life as literature.

Chromatic Transposition

WILLIAM'S FACE WENT PALE and remained so. He considered the casualties of his generation—the living and the dead—and looked upon the pouring rain from his window; the way it danced at such furious paces upon ancient concrete one could feel delirious looking into a specific portion of it for too long. Self-destruction seemed the sole reentry into the infernal land that ought to have been Paradise; subjugation and folly had blinded men from recognizing in another the spirits visible with burning charity. But this self-destruction that had consumed all levels of society seemed to say less about its victims than the system-builders: had the great soldiers and martyrs given up their lives for what one lived today concerning state and church? That there was something wrong was obvious; one could not turn without having to confront all of this voluminous stupidity, its onerous worship that had swept up the essence of the technological world; and yet that the apparent solutions to such problems consisted of a left or right matter of temporal leaning was a falsehood predicated in that most taboo of subjects, the hermeneutic facticity of taboo itself. In essence, William realized, public opinion is inorganic; it is manufactured. Self-evidentiality, in the digital public sphere, is a single mode of confronting conceptual reality. The mode, or technologicity, is perhaps the grand finale of a self-comprehension begun in Plato, whereby man gradually lost sight of who he is, concerned rather with what he can do with objects. This is why we are so often astonished to see that the ancients share so many of our problems: we have conjoined technological development with interior development, when in fact something like deterioration would be more far more applicable, comprehensible solely from a thoroughgoing dialectical historiography. The answer lied not in gadgetry but in etymology, through which one prepared a place en route to conceptual history.

But then, alternating between Gaddis's Harrowing of Hell and some articles on the Salvadoran Martyrs, and deliberate delirium seemed appropriate and bound to the urgency of lightning rods. There are images in this life that do not contain bolted-open eyes, and it is those certain eyeless glances within which chaos and descent exist in looming, emulated solace; that was the look William had begun to notice in the mirror. An eyeless despair marching to the heartbeat of lucid nightmares.

When the thunderstorms returned to slight drizzle it was as if the world were weeping over the fact that daily life had become agonizing, sterile, and aimless. One lost the energy to revisit the library reading Roman history, saying with Scullard, 'Here are my brothers and father, from Romulus into the desert.'

No one around the house spoke of Daniel Welles. If they could not handle his death, they most assuredly could not handle his life, something for which William was at fault. He longed to ask anyone if they felt haunted at all, but he did not, for he believed they felt and thought such things also. There were many things to do and say, so many that it left one crippled and incapable of anything at all, there beneath the western sky and its famous graveyard of stars, that remotest sphere of joyous solitude.

Instead there were series of nods which continued to converge through unraveling clouds of smoke and the periodical break of audience laughter while varied lights projected across the carpeting. The worst part about being poor is having to share one another's sounds, and William lay in bed for some time taking them in. There was but one focus, said Robert Walser, or was it Emily Dickinson's envelopes? Regardless one focus in the impossible object of the microscopic.

Mary and William took the train to the grocery store. She stocked up for the two of them—pears and imported cheeses, a case of Spanish wine and fresh vegetables, New York strip and sweet potatoes—and they spent most of the time thereafter in her room discussing and recollecting the past. She proposed a trip to Europe to clear out their minds.

The late afternoon and evening trips to grocers became the little highlights of William's forlorn days. Could it possibly be that his earlier agonies in Jerusalem were not exclusively tied to that place, and hence any place? He was beginning to reconsider theological geography. He had neither the energy to visit Oakland nor the composure to call East, Brendan had been staying with wife, and he let his phone die while actively rejecting its resurrection.

Mary appeared, in ephemeral looks, to express that William's despondency was not of chivalrous nature and conveyed this by doing things such as tossing cylinders of cinnamon-oatmeal into the shopping cart without looking as they walked down the aisle. She recalled William's drunken theories on the obtrusive lights of supermarkets and of the pains of large crowds and remembered them now and laughed to herself. The problem was that she felt unable to ask him if he were alright because she was nowhere near alright, nor was their situation, but there were also other basic reasons William's detachment contained the promise to blossom that day in aisle 9:

1. Daniel Welles.

2. His known, albeit unnatural incapacity for large stores.

3. Fear she'd sound heartless in admitting she longed for him to appreciate her efforts.

4. She'd just started to act on her feeling toward William, ambiguous as it was, and if she had been a virgin and she felt guilt at their physicality being brought on by death and indulgence less than a week ago, further guilt for not feeling guilty.

5. What obligation did he have to her all?

So they drove on, arrived home sighing, thoughts long locked in prelude to mutant roommate babble.

The roommates knew of a party. William excused himself, and noticing Brendan still gone, walked a mile back to the store in the rain for a fifth of whiskey and thirty cans of beer. The rain was coming down so fast he could have yelled at traffic and gone unnoticed. He arrived in the store drenched, his glasses so fogged he looked blind. Security was called.

"Are you any drugs, sir?"

"No—just Tennyson's 'The Lady of Shalott.' But as I first tasted the Bay air, now I long for the Brooklyn air, that I might find a home in her eyes, and a little trappist cell. There was excess at Hyperion bar, and revolution on the lips of the deluded. But that is all."

"Can you explain, at least, why you are so soaking wet and out of breath? You upset the children."

"Well then that's good training, as they're certainly in for many upsetting things in the years to come. Mine was a long walk, but the car is broken down and I forgot to buy the liquor for the big party, Sonny West,"

William explained to the middle-aged man and woman. The janitor came out growling from the back and dried the floor with an old mildew-wig of a mop, never taking his glazed eyes from the ground. "I have no umbrella and I must walk."

The security guards seemed too dumbfounded to carry on with questioning. They returned to the back of the store and sat down upon crates of coffee beans. William signed the receipt and began walking again up the road.

"William!" Mary leapt out of armchair with a weary cocktail, stopping short when she noticed the bags. "I told you that you could've gotten whatever you wanted with my mother's credit card," she said.

Brendan stepped into the living room in his bathrobe.

"I'm sorry, William," he said, walking past and tilting his head down and away. He helped William place the beer and the liquor upon the counter. He noticed Brendan had begun developing gray patches of hair throughout his head and the whiteness streaked across like whiskers. "What is the occasion," he asked, concealing his excitement.

Mary reproached William and stepped into the shower.

"Sickness unto death," he said, smoking, "I don't know. Sometimes, like today, I feel like deliberating breaking away from reality. I admit it, Brendan. Tonight, I do not want to think. Sometimes it is just too unbearable."

"Come with me," Mary said, pulling William away and into the steaming room. Brendan looked downtrodden at the palm of his hand.

She locked the door behind her and began to unbutton William's shirt; he was soaked to the bone and furious at how obvious she'd made his temporal irrationality seem around the housemates. Something about it seemed disastrous, the other half uninteresting; he feared not anyone knowing, or being kicked out of the house some day because there were several other houses to live in, but that it was that incestual notion of roommates sleeping together that clawed at his heart, and reminded him of Heather.

"What was the point of all of that just now?" She sat on the toilet bowl. William undid the towel wrapped around her body, leaning against the rim of the bathtub, and the two sat naked before one another.

"It seemed like a fair idea to walk in the rain."

"Now what if you get sick? You don't have health insurance."

"That's what whiskey is for. You never heard of the whiskey cure? It works although people are more interested in spending hundreds of dollars on appointments and medicine. If your throat hurts you ought to get ahold of some whiskey and ginger-ale. You'll be dancing in the streets in no time."

"I thought you were going to cut back on drinking," Mary reminded him. One sometimes said the silliest things just before sex. "I thought we were all going to take it easy."

"Well so did I," William admitted.

"Then what *happened*?"

"Well," he attempted, "I did think I was going to stop indulging for a moment. Then in the next moment I understood I would not. And in the moment thereafter I felt much better."

She began, with a dark intensity, to perform unusual acts. William closed his eyes and let her, daydreaming of Daniel, which mutated into a nightmare involving Satan, a clay body, climbing a ladder of dried excrement down to the bottom of cosmological pits.

He drank down his pint in one piratical motion.

She gave up and held back tears, going to her knees, giving him head. William listened to Brendan open a beer and walk downstairs. The trains passed by, headlights collecting each angle of the spacious room. He felt deranged and knew he should have never gotten involved.

Mary was fingering herself when William blinked, like awakening from a month-long trance, and looked down at her body. He took her beneath her arms and stood her up as she leaned into his chest and began to turn, pulling him to the bed. He took a deep breath. That was that. Water off.

Without awaiting the results William took his bags downstairs. It was as if Hell had broken loose within an initial Hell and that its sole captive had found it hilarious; such multilayering within his mind sprouted like reduplicating holograms. The world was a desperate joke and there was an answer and that was to get away from the world. He had a feeling that for a long time there would be no projects and no getting things done after-all and he would be thrown out of the house and on his own again. He welcomed this prospect, albeit regretting his violence, and did so because the situation seemed beyond words. He considered that slapping someone across the face you do not know very well is perhaps one way to never go back to the way things were with that person, which can be a good thing, whether his pacifistic culture, obsessed by murder and weather, admitted it or not.

~

"At least we have money," Brendan said. It was days later but all the days crashed together and by then it felt more like months. There was the next moment and the moment after next and little else in the universe of death. "Not much, but some. There are countries where kids eat mud and drink urine. At least we're not there."

William pulled on a pair of jeans and a sweater and a coat.

"I laid her the night before last and then I went ahead and just had to stop. No, how long ago was it? I forget. That was my poor decision. Perhaps she will forgive me. People may do irrational things when they think of their friend's body being eaten by earthworms. And I'm starting to wonder why the hell this year is so much lesser than last."

"It wasn't that bad. It's commoner for the woman to bring sexual relations to an end but what you did is good. In other words, you are a mad chill ass nigga. You're mad chill."

"In our society it's coming to rival the gunshot. She'll get a lawyer and have me imprisoned." William did not believe this but felt it sounded good for dramatic effect as his voice was raspy and marginalized from extensive smoke and he lacked even enough energy to sit up in bed. She could make something up and post it online. Then again, she was just another girl. Best to drink today and drown one's sorrow, lest one not make it tomorrow.

His phone had been dead over a week. "We must buy seltzer and ice and cups and dig holes." They laughed together. "Yes! And not face anyone until next Sunday! Death, who cares, the best of them are dead!"

"Having lived," said Brendan.

William contemplated calling Daniel's prostitute friend but even sex had come to seem a grotesque act; two desperate bodies reaching out for one another through scripted words, thinking of nothing more than filling holes and having holes filled. And to think, that was life.

Brendan, singing the Crystals, attempted to explain that sometimes hitting someone could feel like a kiss. It was a fine song but in real life it seemed unconvincing.

"Oblivion! Je ne comprends pas les lois! La vie est la farce a mener par tous!"

Hours passed in the alcoholic haze and yet within them one felt recaptured.

"How was the funeral?"

"Well not much happened save a conversation on eugenics between two middle-aged women, their eyes strapped together with straight-jacket tension."

"There is a bug in your drink."

"So what do I do?"

"Say a prayer for it and drink it."

"What if there are no bugs?"

It was again the cold, quiet morning, and William readjusted the notch on his space heater.

"Then you say a prayer for yourself and keep walking."

"That is dreadful," William said.

"But isn't life awful?" Percy became quite animated in his gestures. "It's almost like a drug, right? It kills you yet it keeps you alive, but why? Because sometimes it feels good, the way sex sometimes feels good, and that is why the world is. Because sex is intoxicating and people enjoy being intoxicated. It's a shame anyone would have to go through something so embarrassing as life, but now, I meant to ask you for a cigarette. You know, William, you look like an assistant professor of neurophysiology just now."

William looked to the mirror. He agreed. He wanted to neither die nor lie down and sat down still. That way as the dust broke upon the cold concrete ground he could hope that with it comes someday again that sense of opportunity, or an emotive state less comparable to solitary confinement.

He looked transiently to the mirror again: dark well-forming beard interwoven with shades of orange and blonde. The beard was getting thick and for the first time he looked as though the man he'd felt himself to be inside that afternoon, Engels, and was glad at that prospect, as the train took off across the dampened tracks, in which there were options and that the town he'd left behind had burned to the ground, and in no time he would get on with his life, but at least he could afford to maintain the chemical illusion that all was wine and roses. His personal life, and not the world at large, was not coming to end, and no one knew his name. This made him feel much better as he rolled a cigarette for Brendan White, who filled out crossword puzzles in hunting boots and had enormous bags under his eyes as he stretched out for a book of matches.

～

For three good days thereafter a miniature bar was installed in the basement, sessions of which went on interrupted by collapsing, vomiting, and running out to the bodega at random intervals.

Mary became sick of the house being divided. She expressed this by doing her laundry without acknowledging William or Brendan and by turning around to wait in the living room when either one was in the kitchen. Brendan complicated things further by sleeping with one of the roommates. This was not so much a big deal, as she slept with everyone, but it was all the information Mary needed to take action against William and Brendan and put the studio up for sale.

Footsteps stomped their way down the creaking steps connecting the laundry room to the kitchenette. William still had not turned his phone on. He looked a disheveled wreck upon his mattress, as if he were deserted, adrift upon some concrete island. The basement looked worse than it ever had and William did not comprehend this until he was alone and awaiting reentrance from someone stomping down the steps.

He pretended he was asleep. Mary stood over him. She cursed to herself and rummaged through Brendan's belongings as a call went through on her phone and she spoke in fastidious fragments:

"No, mother, he's been in bed for three days. We are all—yes—heartbroken and no, listen; his roommate has been sleeping with the engaged girl; yes, you met her. The weather is awful of course. I live a few quick miles away, you know. Not like Bermuda. *When* do we go back to Bermuda, anyway? They claim they're artists but just drink most of the time. I—no, I've read both of them. They leave stories out all over the place. I bother with William's journalism. Brendan's papers—here are some now—parallel his personal life: thin chaos. I think he'll be alright one day if he lives an ordered life, and I fear William is throwing away something. I read him all the time; sometimes it is handsome and intelligent and sometimes it is illegible. He has been kind since the beginning. He is devastated. I might—I don't *know*, mother, I don't know what to do. They don't care about landlords! OK? Well, he's a friend of William's, so I figured I'd give him a chance. We might just box his things up and when he comes home one day just tell it to him straight and have the room rented out by then. Look, mother, you're fine. Daniel brought William and I together. I don't want to talk about—al*right*, then; hold on—he's asleep— we'll just vacate the basement and he can move upstairs. I can't have this other one around. No one likes him. The weather is bad. I am depressed. I will call you later! Oh? Then hold on, I'm stepping outside—Shut up!"

William turned in bed, coughed, and reached for a glass of scotch and the remains of Rex Goliath Merlot. He said a prayer, nodded to the 47 lb. rooster, drank, and felt drunk.

He had been drunk too long, though, and could not kill off that sense of something awful burning behind him by any other means than sleeping. And when he slept he had nightmares—No nightmare of the usual variety, but dreams so realistic and lucid that he awoke in a state of disintegrating memory and collapse.

Mary reentered the room. She saw him move. From his pillow and through single opened eye he observed Mary lay upon Brendan's bed in exhaustion. Opioid traces burned through his body, and then his mind. He took another pinch of crushed Oxycontin, laced the bowl, and smoked. He felt enthusiastic and light as a feather. The wine had murdered him and the scotch was attempting to pry him from the afterlife. Each time he drank scotch he thought of dawn in San Diego.

Mary looked over and noticed William awake. She called out his name. He did not respond. She walked to him in her long black kimono. She must have come down, William considered, for she knew better than William where there was shattered glass and where there wasn't. He would have to buy a broom. The slightest bruise was upon her cheek as she skipped through the flickering white lights and he felt infinite sorrow rush through him.

She lay beside him and they kissed one another's lips.

"I am sorry," William said. "I lost control of myself. I am sorry, Mary. I have learned a life lesson."

For some time she expressed again and again, with words and the way she ran her fingers through his hair, how it felt so good to be back in his arms, so good that she hadn't bothered to question whether he'd heard the fragmented news. He kissed her neck, listening to the rain fall, and wrapped his arms around her.

"I just awoke as you descended the stairs," he later explained.

"You look better than you did, William." Her face was most unbearable in its childishness when it was very close to his. He longed to keep his eyes closed and dream of her and open his eyes again and catch hers looking into his. "It sounded like the seventh circle of Hell down here for a while."

She gazed about the gray room and did not mention their conflict. Again, it seemed as if for some time she'd forgotten; she was in the earliest intoxicating stages of love with someone who could never reciprocate, which without experience seemed to tug at the heart but lead nowhere, seeking concrete otherness and receiving instead lightness in the gravity of time. "But everything is better. Everything is better."

"Yes," he said. He took the belt of her kimono and untied it with one hand. He slid the quilt off from atop their bodies and perched himself atop her fragile belly. He overlooked her perfect frame and she pulled him down, guiding one another to the eruptive motions whose psychological fixity, monomaniacal consummation would ironically render extinct the lesser generations. Real life, perhaps because of its mortal inconveniences, was much more incredible than the digital life.

It was also enticing, sang William, to remain drunk all the time. It was a good way to fall in love and a good way to look at the world. It was the sole way the world ever seemed to look back at you; and there was even a bit of horrifyingly comedic relief when Mary violently shook William and told him that he was hallucinating, that no one had ever laid a finger on her, and he noticed that there was no mark, and that it was, literally, a nightmare that had officially crept into reality; and he was relieved although he never had even thought of touching the fairer sex that heinous way, and still ultimately disturbed at the state of reality, and he was no doubt possibly losing control but had lost control.

∾

Carnivalesque rain returned, full of all the colors of the rainbow and twice as many visual and philosophical-symbolic meanings around midnight, and the trains rumbled from the street out into the dresser counter tops and again their bodies were draped over with a thin blanket and there was a chill in the disorienting air of the basement.

"Good morning," Mary smiled.

Something was wrong. He felt bad about reaching for a drink but there one was, and it was an expensive scotch. Mary had given up drinking. He ignored the full cup.

"Listen to my dream," he suggested.

Mary interjected: "No!

"Do you know that there are classes for pregnant women in which you can learn of things like the differing periods of pregnancy for partners?" He knew not what she meant although through proximity alone persuaded him to nod his head with interest.

"Don't start with all of that bad luck. We should never talk about pregnancy."

He took the drink in two sips.

"Besides, I don't believe in karma, but I believe that sometimes preparing yourself for the worst can be a bad thing if you are not positive of what the worst is like."

"How can preparing for the worst ever be a good thing?"

"It can be a good thing when you're on your own in life. That way you're never slaughtered if you expect the worst. Bad things happen and they cannot bring you down if you're somewhat pessimistic. Then when the good things happen, you're happy. Otherwise you will be brought down and unsure why and that sort of anxious life will not suffice. You're too beautiful for any of that. In this world of abysmal longings, one must understand wit, irony, skepticism, and always wear a good pair of shoes. I think that's all there is to it."

"I think you're drunk again."

"I think if you were, also, you would regret having said so in a sober state of mind."

"Why can't you just talk like a normal person?"

"Because the lady is a mere Gemini; because Whitman contained mere multitudes; because Octavia demarcated the universe in her eyes."

"That's not talking like a normal person."

"I tried. It didn't work. But there are plenty of others. They are staring at a computer screen at Borders right now eating stale cake and drinking frappuccinos and explaining to someone in a nasal voice the charm of some television show or another. I hate them all. I'm either going to join the Society of Jesus or lose my mind in this material world. The world outside of a holy order is just insanity. Objects, chemicals, food, drink . . . it never ends this renegade consumption."

"Oh, boy. William, William, William—what will we do with you?"

". . . throw me out the way you plan to throw out Percy, invite some idiot to take his space and pretend you're happy?"

Mary stood up and made the face the rich make when they're just coming of age into amateurish snobbery and hatred of the truth. She longed to make a remark about the look of the room, or that neither Percy nor William had much money, but she was unsure how much control she had on the situation. William responded with a look which explains that you will move on and continue to pass through life no matter what happens.

"I put a spell on you," she said.

"He goes and I go," William said, although by then he had very little money and had come to grow nervous and bored with San Francisco, and that was always a bad sign. 'Did she not even care if he vanished and joined a religious order, not just any—the *Company*? Does *anyone* save the Lord care about my method of proceeding?'

He thought of Daniel, of Octavia, and then who would tell Percy first.

In the meantime, he stretched his legs, felt the looming end, and longed to see Harold Smith once more. He lifted the bottle of Cutty Sark to the sky and thought of everyone else, and even his father whom he had never met, and felt that strange old melancholia returning. He knew it would be best to move on, but then again it was always much better to make decisions in the morning.

There was a party forming upstairs and he thought of how odd it was to ever live with strangers; was any city that good?

Perhaps, but so was the good train ride downtown in the rain.

Janine, Janine—O Valencia Street at midnight.

Gone.

～

Sometimes, if a night were good enough, a shower seemed horrifying in the morning. His already-sensitive skin had developed blisters upon his feet, and he had taken to biting his nails again. He had the wherewithal to know something was wrong within his mind pertaining to his sudden aversion to water and thus dragged his corpse into the tub. Regardless, it lingered with him for some haunted days that whatever bliss he had experienced last year was part of a time that was not coming back . . . self-destruction was no longer romantic, cloaked in tinted mirrors and designer drugs. It was a physiological issue which made him swallow, scared to death he was in the process of breaking down in a torrent of wasted autumn days.

In his lap beneath the cold window two mason jars sat upon an old cafeteria tray from the thrift store. Each contained half a quart of gin with seltzer. His hands and his body seemed to have shrunk. He drank the gin and after some time paced about the kitchen.

Through the window all was covered in fog. William poured the rest of the drinks into an old plastic pitcher filled with ice cubes. The cubes cracked and broke. Someone had written the word 'Cyanide' on the back of a receipt for Good Vibrations. The party must have been excellent; there was nary an air mattress left inflatable. He was daydreaming in bed when the basement began to flood again, drop by condemned drop, and could do nothing but fall into a dreamless sleep. Such was the calling of the gods: desolation, vanity, and discomfiture; better to go in alone toward the exilic aesthetics of higher poverty, than to stay put because the reprobate collective says it is right and just to hang, photographed with zeal, only for the flashes to fade, the volume withered, to slip back into the disintegrative reality of empirical nothingness and carnal destitution.

∼

Before noon he awoke with enough false energy rushing through him to grasp clarity. Through this clarity rushed a single phrase through his mind with agonizing repetition: 'My mind has become a riot.'

The cold water was an inch high—William turned the radio way up—something new resembling Paul Simon—and in rubber boots he danced like Oliver Reed splashing and singing in the rain and drinking from the pitcher with energy searing through his blood.

"I can dance God damnit!" he cried out, leaping up and down to Paul Simon in the rain and splashing rainwater about the room. He turned on his phone as torrents of rain came through the open windows. Voicemails, and then a sudden yearning from Octavia—

"Octavia!"

He called out to the people whispering to themselves beneath umbrellas and asked them where they were going.

"Back to work!" said an old man beneath umbrella, surprised, and turned away from William's head protruding through the window.

"Well—enjoy it! Enjoy life!" He slammed the window shut, lowering the radio.

"Octavia—"

"William what took you—"

"I'm coming east, Octavia! My work is done here—all the envelopes' return addresses to Pennsylvania for all I *knew* was—"

"Oh but William it's just begun the coldest winter in—I don't know how long, do you remember the blizzard when we were children?'

"It's that bad?"

"Yes," Octavia admitted at once, "And everyone is just in misery." By her deep breathing William could tell she was walking through it.

"Oh but Octavia I already know all of this, all of the east's climate, its thereafter pallid psychological trapeze—what is Brooklyn anyway," he began maddening and hysterical at once, "But a miserable long face upon a beautiful woman in McCarren Park in the summer? If you, I, anyone cannot see this, see through it, there is no option but to quit breathing!" He outspread his arms and began to speak as the overhead subway dissolved on the other end of the line. "New York is a lost illusion in every literal and elemental sense of the term. Cities no longer, for now—as all I want is you—and until then comfort is but the bludgeoning of growth."

"Then come! Come to me! Stay with me and we'll find you a room of your own! Mine—it is so small."

"I'll just come for a visit and lay beside you through eternity, or the lack of it," William said. Euphoria rushed through him at once. "Because don't you know what a good friend of mine once said?"

"What," said Octavia, with that natural beauty inscribed as if designed to provide his life with meaning. "What he did he say?"

"That there is no such thing as a mistake for a writer. And then another writer said that, in conclusion, there are but portals of discovery."

Octavia laughed in a way that embodied her blissful atonement in walking the streets alone in Brooklyn listening to her best friend speak. New York was the worst place on earth to live in despair; anyone without money could tell you that. She readjusted the phone to her ear and breathed.

"Now you're considering leaving?"

"I'm no longer considering it; I'm going to leave."

"Now are you sure?" She grew serious—

"I've no longer a bank account and a couple hundred dollars in my pocket. My art has failed and so have my best friends to return. I don't know my roommates' names nor do I believe it's worth it." He cleared his breath and felt confident in the way he felt the first time we awoke beside Octavia half a decade ago. "Can you book the ticket, e-mail me the information, and I'll pay you back with interest?"

"But you—you know, are ready to just *leave*?"

He thought of Manhattan's nocturnal skyline and responded cautiously.

"We ought to talk about it tomorrow also. This will be a big step. If I return, I am returning will all my heart; hitherto have I been guided by the profane masses and their false gods; now I shall reinstall the solitude of exilic cunning on one temporal hand, but seek first the everlasting wisdom of the right hand.

"Just give me three weeks or so to see if anything happens here," he said. "I may read Aquinas still more, but I have learned that that which being seen, pleases, is the right sign of the good; and all I see now displeases me, is death, and temporality; and I must change my life, now, but I've been all shaken up and I am ready to reunite with you as we promised—with you and the first and everlasting wisdom."

"And in reality, then, San Francisco to JFK?"

He thoughtfully listened again to the soundtrack rushing trains.

"To Philadelphia," he said. "I've some unfinished business there—something I've got to see to believe which I'm sure you grasp. I abide by no single city, for I am limitless. But think, think of us together at Christmas! Even the blackest heart must shine then!"

William wept.

"Oh don't go crying!" She'd never heard him cry, said the angel; she turned down an alleyway and sat atop an upturned concrete block.

"But I think we all ought to cry sometimes for this tragic life, for the lovers fast asleep, for the forlorn families whose homes differ from prison cells in that their fences are not topped off with razor-wire, but through it all we are virtuous, we are right and were right when we were younger than we are now—shall we be innocent, seeking redemption in the nightingale precision of conscious eternity—each time I speak with you I know that I am alive, it's no longer any question."

"And to think I ever felt alone," she thought aloud. "I'll count the minutes. I was beginning to feel so isolated again. A group of friends of mine ditched me did I tell you–"

"You had mentioned it in an e-mail, but doesn't our kind know by now that there is no reaffirmation or originality and intelligence quite like being despised by the inane?"

"You're coming back from San Francisco," Octavia said as if to herself, and it was one of the rare instances wherein her voice seemed to encompass the fragilities and wonders of childhood; these instances had in their thrilling scarcity equated for the pilgrim ever since his freshman year in college as the sign of something good to come.

"And I'll count the milliseconds, for now infinite's search says farewell to San Francisco, O cosmos—in your retracing for missing children you've found just another orphan."

She then sent William the receipt for the plane ticket online. He bought a case of wine and Spanish rice and kept the news to himself. Octavia had noted it must be strange to take a plane for the first time and it could be, having done the whole thing in trains and buses first. William postponed any reply and knew that for the present tense at least it was the quickest way to determine whether Hell existed within or around him, amongst other things, and that he would now return to the first and everlasting wisdom.

Across the street there was a birthday party going on. An old man shouted something through confetti about a mint-julep before taking again to his tambourine. Children encircled him and screeched in joy.

He listened to the music and could no longer comprehend weariness. Rain. Thunder. Indifference, that fate worse than death, though elemental life pressed on, life lingering as much as anything else.

An NA meeting let out of the old protestant church downhill. A young man passing William's window stopped and taped a note to the skeletal tree below.

"How curious!"

William went out and looked at the note:

"The deadliest poison of our time is indifference."
—Kolbe

Nothing Ordinary Souls Learn

An afternoon in the life of a bird, out and about, returning to her nest at last, to the little upward gaping mouths—such was the sequence of afternoon solitudes, which gave way to evenings of sacred flame in the pillar of oceanic cloud. Lubricant and milk for sale—militaristic in its cosmic grandeur! And thus the pilgrim reflected in the lily field on matters eucharistic and divine, guided by the exilic genius of Jungmann and the history of the Mass of the Roman Rite. William was getting close. However, any of these thoughts colliding with memories of Schopenhauer or Feuerbach set him back some alchemical distance. He longed to pray in sporadic frenzies but could not bring himself to kneel. Who could he even talk to about these matters? Against his credit, he did not consult the nearest parish priest; he attempted to follow Tolstoy, and thence Mark, all the ragged way down to sociological martyrdom. By the end of the week William had a set of plays written which he found so trite he set them on fire and threw pieces of furniture out of the window until he ran out of breath. He considered buying a gun downtown and shooting himself in the heart, but there was a train delay whose bulwark came to him as a sign from Above and rendered him four hundred dollars richer. Percy had taken to living back on Lafayette Street and had no phone and Phil Cohen was in Chicago for the month with family. In solitude he would come close to giving in, but he could not get over the fact that millions upon millions of people had lived before Christ. What of them? What of unborn children? What of all the good people who had no interest in Jesus Christ?

After some days, the rain ceased at last. He left the studio although to neither his dismay nor delight everyone he walked past or beside or behind sickened him to near-vertigo. Within such deadened awakenings he longed to visit Percy's girlfriend's apartment just past South Van Ness where dim lights towered out toward the drenched, glittering perimeters of Union Square.

By now the ice-skating rink was being installed and generators hummed with electric light as William walked the crowded streets consumed by an unshakeable solitude. It was no longer a joyous time in reflection, but a way of seeing every last element of the world touched in morose, temporal tragedy. Memories of days past fell apart at each turning street corner, arched brick in the exasperated death of nostalgia. His bitter, unwarranted inabilities prohibited him from calling anyone at all and no one called him. The darkroom of the lens of life was to walk for cold, dampened miles on standby and yet to walk home alone again through the blissful crowds recognizing one's former self in the innumerable smiling faces cast in the glow of flashlights and storefront entrances. Through the metal grates below the battery-ram trains rushed into drained, unseen throats of iron.

There was a small flower he'd plucked in the Muir Woods before the poem he'd cut from a book and had kept inside which he thought of in accordance with his internal recitation of Joyce's "Bahnhofstrasse."

He felt spiteful and knew the way it felt to have no one in the world of the city and wished he were leaving its vortex tomorrow. He thought of ways to reconnect atop Sacramento Street on the staircase of the cathedral overlooking the distant Bay Bridge soon leaving the vanishing ornamental photography behind and still to study the heels of the sidewalk and die alone alive in life and still to know one's self at last so well that all else slips away.

The sea thrashed in a way that dismantled hope for reality. The beach looked no longer beautiful at night but a vast hallucination, some wavering mirror dimmed and breaking to and fro across cold sands. He lay down listening to the thunderous waves praying that one would crash down upon him and swallow him whole. Broken black waves crashed against the land and broke like thoughts in an overloaded mind coming back and forth, varied in degree, retracing, and recurring all at once. Was one just on a ball in infinite outer space? *Why does anything exist?* How was everyone not insane? Lo, everybody was!

He stood before the Pacific Ocean and let the wind burn his dried, exhausted eyes. The sky appeared hollow. Desultory reflections of experience raced through the winter streets as he walked home through the emptied streets where cars passed by anonymous, high, maligned. Sunset was another abandoned child, abandoned replaced with indolent prurience: His craft and love, both or either, bound like books upon the shelved paradise visible even to the sightless, of Babylon's ability to seize the day. The last sounds of the nocturnal ocean disintegrated at the un-latched gates and night-watchmen shivering in the wind. Pluming smoke ascended through chimney-tops and fresh-cut wood burned throughout the avenues. The world would perish and so must San Francisco and so must he once more; through indignation and the crashing vapors and the distilled, rustling wind by torn curtains, white giraffes, and the limitless future. And where is our Billie Holiday? Distilleries of the interior; the centuries shall fall where they may as that shiftless, incoherent Venn-diagram that is consciousness recaptured.

Church bells clamored rhythmic to the sky of drifting, cotton pearls, and William awoke alone to find the flood had ceased and he swept away the disfigured ash and dust of the weather-beaten ground. He pieced to-gether vignettes of the week and admitted to that purposeful descent, the urgently shrugging shoulders he had for so long acknowledged and loathed in others that now he had succumbed to, the drowning of dreams. Wind rushed through the gray windows. Kaleidoscopic tran-quility precluded the onset of any further agonies, isolations, terminal considerations. There was life to live, and to live beatifically, while the savage molecular ruins of incoherent livelihoods remained intact; he took the bus to Clement Street for the day and heard from Percy step-ping from Green Apple. He'd be home tonight, and he had great news, he explained. William felt bad at not letting him know he was to be kicked out soon when Percy mentioned it with optimism and yet without care. The biggest difference in life was claiming to not care and not caring, and it went far beyond appearance and soliloquy; it was broken down the action of thought in societal transparency, reduplication, and it was the best to know that someone once in a while did not care; it was the look in their eyes.

A marching band beat down the street as he stopped in for a shot of tequila and a pint of Pabst. He had another and noticed it was no march-ing band but a parade of some sort. Then the sun arose for the first time in months as flowed the meticulous, unrecognizable streams of rejuvenated tendency in the eyes of passersby from the old-fashioned terrace seat.

∿

William held Mary's new Scottish Terrier puppy in his arms upon the couch. The roommates were asleep as the little coal-grey dog licked William's face over and over, his miniature watery nose glistening beneath the ceiling light. She had rescued him from the shelter and needed a name.

"Call him Shakespeare," William said. Each time he turned away the puppy's tail went back and forth with the slight might of an eager child and William returned to petting him all over.

"Shakespeare?"

"Sure. His little beard here makes him look wise."

"Come on, Shakespeare!" Mary smiled. The dog wouldn't break away. William wondered when or if he would tell anyone that he was leaving. It seemed difficult.

She scooped up the dog, whispering into his flipped-over ear:

"Come on, Shakespeare—Just another night!"

William interpreted this as a casual invitation. His mind was shot, though, and he stood to wash up and go downstairs. At some point before the ocean Pascal's Wager returned to him for the first time since years past. He ought to borrow *Pensees* from the library . . .

Mary walked out of the room in her kimono. Shakespeare, howling, scratched at the door.

"Why do you always wear kimonos?"

"Because they are comfortable."

Two hours later when Mary and Shakespeare were fast asleep it was just past midnight and William, refreshed, dressed, and stood to go downstairs. Shakespeare's small frame lay sideways across the edge of the bed. Without moving his body, he set his tired eyes upon William.

"I'm sorry, but I can't sleep that well," William said. He kissed Shakespeare on the nose.

The dog bolted off the bed and began to wag its tail at the door. William rubbed his belly until he fell fast asleep again and tip-toed out of the bedroom.

Something was either happening or approaching, he felt, colossal in its own right. Some sort of flame burned through him each time he sat down alone. His mind would not cease. Streams of thought came, multilayered and multidimensional, through his mind. He longed to write an Lovecraftian letter or go speak in bars for the remainder of the night. It felt incorrect to sit so still as his imagination burst open.

William felt some sort of overwhelming feeling rush through his heart as the highlights of the Giants game ended on the radio and he noticed he'd caught wind of not one single pitch and he could no longer lay alone with his eyes closed unable to sleep. He could take no more and walked back outside into the damp, misty night as train bells resounded at the curving edge of the street, engulfed by fog wrapping around one corner and gone.

Hundreds of stars shone above and in bursts that obscure sense of consciousness reccurred, rushed through him. When he looked east he could recall Manhattan and Brooklyn's compressed madness, the angular brick and chrome and nocturnal voices and broken fields and walkways of astrophysical cement and Octavia grace drifting through some subway stop or another, somewhere like Grand Street or Greenpoint Avenue, and for she tomorrow to awaken beneath the winter sun of Morgan Avenue.

When seven days of ambiguity remained until anything important, William marveled, the thing became surreal and unbearable all at once, the daydream sanctified by a sort of clear, yearning tonality. Nautical air rushed through the streets of subway trains as William walked again in the direction of the ocean. It was past midnight and Brendan had never arrived back home. William knew not what he would say to him, by means of explanation, or to Phil Cohen, or to his mother, or anyone at all. He felt himself a failure and gifted for his insight at once. Although he had made the decision to return to New York City in a drunken state of mind, it was a choice he stood behind in sober melancholic hours.

He sensed the internal, colossal vibration once more, the unspeakable epiphany, as he locked the rustic gate behind him and set off in the direction of the ocean to hear once more the breaking of the waves, reflective of some black heavens, and to exhaust himself so as to sleep.

Quilts of fog seeped through each alleyway and avenue. Familiar voices came into stark auditory recognition. William sat down on a broken pillar and attempted to register the voices. The clicking boot-heels neared as if shrouded fireworks.

"N-n-no, no damnit, in prison it wasn't all like that, now, just big old books on John Muir and Artaud! Now stop in here, right now, and get matches! Matches! Brendan here, take this money and buy beer—you know how long it's been since I had a beer! Long enough to go blind!" William could taste the smoke breaking across the fog. Bottle caps fell to the railroad tracks and broke spinning through hazy headlights. "Now William needs company, you see, of course, because I *love* you guys, always did, damnit, right rather ripped, and you he—you know—he won't care if we wake him up! I feel bad enough being gone so damned long! Duane Eddy holding forth in a cheap hotel." He made an outrageous Indian call which burst through the long, empty street. The parade had not ended.

"Over here," Brendan motioned through hysterical laughter. He and Harold Smith, that erudite scholar of the streets, stepped into the lamplight of the nearest corner. White wore his denim outfit while Smith wore a tailored brown suit with a lemon flower stemming from its breast pocket. William had a good buzz just listening to them speak and decided, for whatever reason, to take a short-cut to the house and meet them there.

"And I tell you man, I was in the store first of all, a little café with records and books and everything, and I got the hell out of there because I don't even like bookstores in cities all that much anymore, hate to say it but now they over here, now, insist upon hiring these stereotypical, archetypical, miserable Faulkner fanatics who have never read Faulkner but in Idaho their father is a lawyer because you know of course that I'm not pessimistic but it was the first encounter I had right out of jail for Christ-sake—oh, oh—the bad timing of it all, now don't you have such fond memories of the womb? It hurt my heart when the nine-months' lease was up. Room service and everything! Heat!" He was talking as the shadows of his hands ran along the sides of houses and the middle of the sidewalk. Brendan had been clutching his sides and throat with exhaustive hilarity and William wondered how long they had been talking and drinking and wished he could have been there. "Now have you ever eaten cake as of late? I mean a good damn slice of cake, Brendan, and you sit still in a chair for eight hours drinking black coffee all day? No cigarettes or anything, no, he-he, and you get yourself a good piece of plain cake at the end of it all, see, now what? No? It is a long story. You know I was there after, or before, I bumped into you at Wreath Kinnards a secret alleyway bar with blank doorway on Guerrero and brick-heavy townhouses reminded me of something I can no longer recall like a long dream, a dream that spans for days, and yet when you describe just the way a single image is in your mind you see, for instance I was having a dream I was at the bus depot and there for hours mingling around and doing unexciting things, you see, waiting, some purgatorial connotation, but the main point is even as I speak to you about this there is but one image: Crowds of people crossing through aisleways at the end of which stand baskets of fruit. That's the whole thing. I even went back to school for a day, you know, in a lecture hall with a hundred kids listening to a bellowing, top-heavy lecture on Nero Claudius Drusus and my God—I swear, I swear it was like my mind could have imploded, I realized all of the American situation! We sit through lectures, sawmills, checkout counters, office desks, in what other hope of getting rich and doing nothing in the end! Then we get to the end, and guess what! All your life, I saw in the old professor's eyes, was spent reading newspapers and watching worthless movies and decades later you're an old man, you can quit work and go to Florida, but guess what! You've absorbed nothing but fictional violence in the meantime, and once the sun becomes boring again, you'll return to violence!"

"Harold, Harold—Where is this *going*? You're going to give William a heart attack unless you start making sense."

"No, no, just listen, Brendan, listen—you were at Fort Mason, you ran into William just outside of the thrift shop on South Van Ness, just listen: You ever get that feeling of anxiety so fierce you're quite positive the world is going to implode, and, get this—it's not much of a big deal? You laugh, you see—" They stood, finishing their beers at the edge of the block. "And then destruction, in the form of installation, looked my way as I stood up prim and proper. Then I threw my notes to the carpeted ground, blew my nose on a stale handkerchief, and told him to go to Hell. Then I hit the University library and made my way home. They never got the books, no, but right after that I got into the trouble with the weed and all of that and started wearing a mask and never leaving my porch till I had to leave and went south, got picked up, got out, tried school, came home. Tried Facebook. Didn't work."

Brendan explained to him of Sonny West and the pounds of weed and several other anecdotal tales. Harold looked on with his jaw dropped, uttering fractal bits of language:

"But of course before they got me what's old Cervantes say, the road and the inn, something like that, anyway I went *South*, because anything that is the same as ever of course sits still, stands still, remains still which is a matter of your *surroundings–*"

William stepped down from the porch and turned around the splintered white fence. He thought of his adventures with Harold last year, how they had been cut short and how they would be cut short again. Still no one knew a thing of William's leaving in six days and he thought it best to say nothing and remain optimistic and made his best attempt at coming off.

"Ah, comrades," he said, concealing his excitement by looking down and back again. He felt out of place without fresher clothing but made the best of his mechanic outfit, blue jeans, and a white t-shirt. "It's taken long enough but so it begins again." He extended his hand to Harold.

"I," he cried, stepping forth. He made his own attempt at dodging the overwhelming feeling. "I don't—hell, wait—ha, took, took damnit now long enough here, look at all of this fog out this way all the story is complicated quite complicated I was just explaining, I'm a little excited to be back out in society of course but complicity is well, we were just talking 'bout physiological degeneration you well ah," his voice elevating with proximity, "Ah you see of course, damnit Bill, enough of this, come 'ere m' boy!"

It turned out Brendan had noticed a young man in Groucho Marx mask as he stepped out of the Union Square hotel bar. Both were there for the same woman. It'd just been an hour ago. They hopped on the train.

"Damn young girl, in the car, hashish, red, white, blue signs over-running the God-damn thing, then Los Angeles burned to the ground." He spoke of bare trees and untouched fire escapes and admitted he'd drunk 13 cups of coffee that day and was hallucinating. He looked sharp, though, and one never would have known. All three of them looked un-moved since last year, as if they had decided against growing old.

Brendan's belongings hadn't been boxed up yet and he spoke little of the situation. Harold looked at the sidewalk and nodded along. William knew not the whole story.

Still, he observed, the sign of good friends is that way in which their company dissolves the world of problems around you, the way certain tones of voices dismantle banalities, and by existing prove anything and everything is going to be alright.

"The space," Harold said, "Between the buildings through gated windows in the compound, keyholes and oh, what a shame is prison, friends, what a shame it is. They want you to die there. Next topic!" Water rushed through the drainpipes and they drank beer, their voices echoing through the street. "Thought I was gonna marry the girl, you see, and now do you mind if I sleep here tonight?"

"Of course not," William said. He repeated himself, exasperated. He asked if Harold had kept in contact with Heather, Isaac, Janine, or any-one—he hadn't, though he knew just where to find all of them and more.

"We'll make a whole week of it!" he shouted, taking three thou-sand dollars in clipped cash from his pocket. His body seemed to shake with excitement as he spoke. "A whole week of it before I get a room somewhere, maybe out here, good old Irving Street! Who lives on Irving Street? Goddamn riot to be back, and then of course we'll ride out to Sausalito, have a sheer riot, go see Man Ray! How about that! Glad you're back, buddy, glad you're back because you see this whole time—"

"And San Francisco accelerates past its winter monolith now in this instance and at once procures an endless summer, see, for the seasons are of the mind in as much as half of a good meal is half ingredients and half location, you see!"

They sat along the withered couches recalling the past, predicting the future, standing and shouting with excitement, fever, and the past was unattainable although amidst such an utterance one could carve the future of better things and San Francisco was beginning to feel like San Francisco again where you fall asleep sitting upright at dawn as you notice the pencil-sketch of Olde Saint Mustard taped to the pillar.

"To the end my brothers, to the end—I overheard someone say that on the L train—don't you know, to the end, to the end!"

His words were like dynamite set off beneath a dam and everyone was in such high spirits it became difficult to sit still at all. They paced the room. William brought in Shakespeare and let him run around.

William, Harold, and Brendan took back off for downtown in the middle of the night. William looked to the morning raving with his friends until it was a quarter to nine and they were racing toward the Golden Gate Bridge.

But in a heavenly lucid dream he dreamt he had revisited Petrarch out wandering around the Sunset, abstaining from smoke and drink, ferociously praying to himself something he called the 'seven graces', which he could have sworn he had heard of in his adolescence. The seven graces were simply seven Hail Mary's, but with concentration fixed upon each word, whispered aloud. He was painfully conscious of not letting himself be seen moving his lips alone in public and he spaced out his sets of seven graces with interludes of the Jesus Prayer. And before he knew it he had missed the train, and instead decided to walk seven miles, whispering concentric prayers, all the way out to Lands End. And there as he stood on the cliff, overlooking the blinding rim of ocean light, a presence of angelic love filled his breast, and drew his right hand up onto his heart. And he breathed slowly, absorbing the distant oceanic crashing of the vast Pacific, seagulls, and the sounds of children laughing and screaming in the invisible distance. And like a song one has had stuck in one's head for a painfully long time that is at last blared from speakers, he felt the flood of the Holy Spirit enter into him, rushing through his body and into his mind, beheld in the hands of Providence, mutiny upon a wicked ship, demonic heads blown out of cannons, replenished by the womb of all our desire here in this flash of life called, in English, 'earth.' *I sing a new song unto the Lord; may never my eyes never lose sight again, and let not my forefathers of the faith and land have died in vain; theirs was the meteoric task of building, preservation; ours reinstallation, and holy war against the time and its assassins,* and the tears flowed from his eyes and cries from his lips, far away from the maddening crowd of ironical sickness unto death, and reunited with the One. White sand and a sky of cloud, submerged with the purity of a child at its mother's breast; such was the pilgrim's quenched thirst through the tears of exile, as the most ancient counsel is after all that of tomorrow.

And the Shadows Frame the Light

THEIR VOICES TRAVELING THROUGH the endless lot were sharp and cold as the wind and in a way it made more sense of the season and in another it made no sense at all. Cold—every single thing, living and otherwise, could be described so long as the word 'cold' was interwoven therein. Either was fine as one approached the Golden Gate Bridge on sleepless feet in November.

All grew silent as the towering bridge engulfed in white, luminous fog, stood just before them. Parades of pulled suitcases clicked over each crack in the road as white light hummed overhead and mist ran across and through each bulb in wavering, delicate sheets. They stepped onto the pathway and beneath the towering pastel-orange pillars were out of the city and channeling ragged across the Golden Gate Bridge laughing and speaking riotous, elegiac remembrances through shielding scarves.

"Here, now," Harold said, "We'll throw our arms around each other and walk the length of the bridge in silence! But look there—you can see Fort Mason! Say!"

Beneath the bridge there was the secret bar off a beaten path with window seating. They took a table and ordered martinis for breakfast. Brendan said little all the while. He looked through the window, wondrous and content, perhaps as if pondering how he would explain to Harold that he was moving out soon and that he had no money.

"After this we spend the day at the Hearth, you see, and then investigate Fort Mason, and ah, this is just the beginning of it all! Cheers, boys!"

From the window seat they overlooked the bridge, engulfed in clouds of white fog.

It was an ecstatic morning broken up by an old friend of Harold's who stopped by to talk about his new documentary in "That insufferable tone some young men who have," Brendan would later recapture, "Alas, been laid once or twice although not in years."

When at last he began to absorb the wavering energy from the table, the phantasmagoric view of the bridge shrouded in bursting fog, and on the fifth try no one could remember his name, Brendan seemed ready to say something. William gazed through the window and continued talking with Harold. He focused on his martini saying, 'Oh,' 'Ah,' and the occasional 'I see.'

"You see where the originality of the piece comes in, I think, is where, considering such a *malnourished* bit of *culture*—oh, now wait one, second." He stretched the 'one' meticulous as he dug his phone from his pocket. "Oh, screw it, I'll call him later. Anyway—"

"Hey, you," Brendan said. The abruptness of it brought laughter to the table although it did not last long. "You're like a lot of people. You asked us how we were doing, talked about your personal life, your new sneaker laces, your summons you received for drinking wine-spritzers on the hill in the park, and your little documentary. No one cares about your little documentary on the untraditional landscapes of cottages in Switzerland! Go home, Lazarus! That would be damned fine of you."

"You've got to be kidding me. How rude!" He turned to William. "How rude is your friend! How vitri*olic*!" He turned to Brendan and brushed the waiter away with a flimsy hand before he could set down his glasses of water. "And don't you dare speak of my documentary! You don't know a thing about film, about the life of a documentarian! I'm making discussion, and you're some asshole brooding in the corner drinking whiskey and not talking to anyone!"

"No, no, you see I'm just not talking to you is all, because you've been the sole bipedal talking for ten minutes. I just want to save everyone time. It is nice to sit here. It is damned fine. Go get into your father's pickup truck and skedaddle back the Marina or wherever the hell you document things. Harold, why did you invite this bozo? Yes, you, are a bozo."

William observed the quarrel with indifference. Sunlight was creaking out of the sky beyond the bridge and shined upon the water in a way he had not seen since the evening he arrived in San Francisco.

"You know, you're an asshole," the documentarian explained.

"Alright."

"You're alright with being an asshole?"

"Coming from you? Of course!—What sort of asshole wouldn't be?"

The documentarian got his pamphlets and disposable baggies back together and stepped to the doorway. He got back into his pickup truck and sped off to the Marina.

"Some people change, boys," Harold said. "Suppose I was so drunk I called someone I didn't care about."

"He was insufferable."

"D-d you have something against documentaries," Harold stammered, "Or did you not like him that much?"

"I think he just rubbed me the wrong way. I longed to say what was on my mind. I did. People seldom do that."

"That is true," William said. Harold shook his head and coughed.

"It's just, you know, these days I don't care what anybody does—if you're gay, green, political, celibate, revolutionary, pacifist, carnivorous, or something, anything else, I don't care at all, what matters is that you don't impose yourself upon strangers and then claim that they are prejudice against your beliefs. All I'm prejudice against is a culture of egomaniacs with nothing to offer but unbearable detail concerning their person lives which are all the same and all irrelevant and uninteresting. You see?"

"Oh, well."

Harold looked.

"*Now*! *Hell*! I was saying!! What was I *saying*!!" He paused for a moment, ordered another round of martinis. "Some epic grandeur or another, built and sustained by the seething energies of Lucifer . . . O Lucifer, light-bearer—shield me!" he implored, gazing out with William to the Golden Gate. "Git drunk, my God, just git drunk!"

He snapped his fingers in the midst of readjusting the yellow flower upon his brown suit jacket and turned to Brendan as if he'd just recalled something he'd been attempting to catch in his mind for months.

At noon they took a cab out to Geary Street and sang through the open windows across the bridge and the city. Sunlight still attempted to break through the day, succeeding in fine intervals.

At the Hearth they sat with bottles of Miller High Life and glasses of Jameson beside the old men, the young women, and had gone past drunkenness and hysterics and exhaustion into that contagious ethereality wherein everything seemed hilarious and tragic at once and yet one had not the energy to deliver sentiment to any such thing.

"An old girlfriend of mine lives on Polk and Market now, you see, and is having a party tonight and I think we must go," he said. William knew that Harold was feeling fine. William was here and had taken to mixing the whiskey with coffee. Brendan appeared on the verge of collapse. He raised his hand as if in a classroom, and like that collapsed onto the counter.

Resurrected, he arose at once, his glass lenses smeared, his dark hair flattened with grease.

"Brendan, m'boy, what's the matter, old bud? We're just having a little weekend drinky drink."

"It's alright, hun," the bartender said. "He looked exhausted when he walked in." William recognized her with a smile from last summer. She did not seem to recognize him.

"Now my boy, my son," said Harold, "We'll have a big lunch, dinner, and go down to Polk Street, old Polk Street because I haven't been there in well, well, a long time, long time, recall even now just as what's his name old, old Isaac up in Portland all that last summer, left you a note to meet me here, missed you by a moment, a mere moment, and, ah, my son, the time," he said, "The time is, I don't know—God—God-damn!" He looked away, then at his hands, and to the ossified men around him drinking cold split-pea soup with pint-glasses of brandy. The bartender had gone to the back to make food. "Where do all these highways go, my son, where do all of these highways go?"

"I don't know," William said. "What sort of highways you mean?" He leapt up and sprinted to the bathroom. He splashed cold water on his face, observed the bags beneath his eyes. When he returned Smith was looking more composed, although caught within some psychological frenzy. "Now what were you saying?"

"Oh, oh—I don't know. Just get tired and talk sometimes, lonesome in prison, lonelier than life. Wish we were back in the summer, the summer before last, my son, out on the docks, the broken docks you know, at Fisherman's Wharf. But I guess those times are gone and never coming back."

"We can make it tonight though I'm sure."

His last offering hit William with delayed impact and filled him with sadness.

"Truth is I called from jail and talked to the old supervisor Mike. They evicted the house, the whole thing is done. Possums living upstairs. Went to investigate the whole thing and both of them fell through the roof. Clean straight the damned roof. Can—can you believe that?"

But the comical note did not work well and both knew it. Fort Mason closing down took on an instant, tragic tone. William looked over at

Harold and Brendan, at Geary Street through the opening door, and he knew he had no one else left in old transient San Francisco. The rest were somewhere—in the city, the country, back home, in foreign lands—some shooting machine guns, others volunteering, others wining and dining—but it were as if after the initial golden summer the state was ready to give in, the dream of America, its finest citizens ready to move on or collapse, and the personified, glorified, illusive California Dream had died just as any natural person does in the obituaries.

There were always statistics to accompany the tragedy, but the statistics were neither here nor there, and always a day late. The studies found something out each moment, but then what did that say of studies? The study found that the studies found nothing.

William felt the chemical ardor rushing through his body in waves. He excused himself and stepped out front without looking up from his dirty fingernails for recognition, his arm outstretched for a door handle.

It was dismal and raining and traffic till the end of the line. On the tarped path it was Segways all the way down.

He looked out to Land's End and called Phil Cohen.

"How's Chicago, old bud?" he said, taking great effort and precision to sound as composed as possible. At 20 he'd felt 30, at 21 he'd felt 31, and then at 22 he felt 22, a mortal young man, a figurine in the atmospheric grid wherein reality was disheartening, disengaging, quixotic.

Chicago was going fine, fine as could be. El was in town another week and was ecstatic to return. He'd reunited with old friends in the windy city, gathered much material, and had been enjoying himself all the while.

"Still, as you know, there's nothing like returning home to the Bay."

William was gladder than anything for El and they kept the conversation short and by its end couldn't bring himself to say he was returning to New York for good. It was the way one sometimes had to downplay the descriptions of diseases before light-hearted types, just now it was the raw power of nature against lost young men in the multidimensional generation of worthless art, plagued condominiums, and technological futility. There was no escape but to swing doors open with crossed fingers, and if you lacked conviction in any such sort of whim or temporality or lofty nihilism you could return to the computer and investigate a thousand worthless images and opinions at once. The simultaneous, virtual sex-death shined in the sunglasses or passersby, but what did it mean? No one knew anything but that asking questions seemed unfathomable,

offensive, and implausible, which is often the direct connotation of corporate fascism rising, developing, and conquering, for in the land where
everything is some mechanical laughing matter its citizens are either
dead on arrival or automatons strapped to IV bags peddling through the
streets en route to the next futility, be it emotional barometers controlled
by sports teams or the cutting edge becoming television realities, there
wherein the land of manufactured culture and subculture, and there
where everything must be celebrated unceasingly looms that violent
purge at the core of such masked devastations, guided by commercial
breaks and conducted by the military's vipers, that make everyday living seem an eternal struggle rather than past time. And in the land once
noble that had burned to the ground one would have to suffer without
shedding tears, stick to his soul of precision, his art, and refuse to bow
down, to bend, to that which he could not help seeing straight through
the beginning, the first and everlasting wisdom.

He smoked butter-rum tobacco from an old Scandinavian pipe he'd
never bothered with and brought himself together. He feared the one way
out was perpetual motion but knew still that there was nothing rarer in
life than good company; so, he turned around, blew out the pipe, and
watched the orange embers blow and dissolve down Geary Street round
about noon.

"Well bud, I'm about ready to hit the hay. Now help me get old
Brendan here back to the cot. Needs a nap." He readjusted his wristwatch
for dramatic effect and lifted Brendan by the shoulders. The poor man,
grayed and suffocating under the weight of mounting child support bills
at 25, was a weary balloon blown-up with a sort of alcoholic helium.

Harold pressed down his crinkled coat and stood for a final pro-
nouncement and directions later on to the apartment. He'd had a strange
encounter on the phone concerning someone whose voice he did not
recognize.

"You cannot trust anyone that tells jokes all the time," Brendan said,
in his sleep, and fell back again into unconsciousness.

"Poor old fellow, bud, ain't he?" He thanked the bartender as she
poured two Bloody Maries and declined Harold's money. "But, Hell, we
got things to do! People to see! There's a city out there!" He whispered as
if he'd just realized this for the first time, gripping his temples and biting
each of his nails once, "We can't sit still! We can't sit *still*! Come on, now,
Bill! We've got to *go*!"

"I thought you were going to take a nap?"

"To Hell with it!"

After the Bloody Maries balanced everything out it was crowded Clement Street, dinner in the Mission, and an enormous party on Polk and Market where half of the people were dressed in costumes and smoking unpronounceable substances out of antique pipes, the other half dancing old-fashioned dances until the wee hours of morning, smoking cigarettes through long plastic holders. It was a true ball. Brendan had arrived late and looked much healthier; proximity to departure, rather than the company, kept William at Bay: he found peace now not in chemical arrival but in private Seraphic charity and Cherubic truth.

Hours into the slurred, trancelike party of costumes and dancing, Harold took off with a girl; the party by then had dissolved to a circuit of older couples around the vaporizer.

William awoke in another strange bed with a girl he did not recognize. In those morning hours his departure seemed as realistic, in its looming at last, as his arrival once had; only now he was fully clothed, and less anxious to fall back asleep than to depart.

He sat up in bed, sweating—it had been a delirious dream, one which he again fell into, his arm around some beautiful stranger and his mind felt as if a vacated mansion even through sleep filling up each room with peculiar half-dreams and lucid images—upon the couch he saw Brendan, snoring, and something about the way the ashtray went up and down on his chest was comforting and he reluctantly fell back asleep again for some hours.

◦◦◦

Octavia had undergone an experience like William's, on a trip she had taken alone down to the Abbey of Gethsemani. William read through her handwritten letters with tears of joy in his eyes, as he read of visions, monks and mysticism, and one Brother _____ who had said to her on the Last Supper, "how I would have loved to have been here when the Lord cleansed the temple." Thus the pilgrim stepped out into the sleepless night William saw an apparition of righteousness above in the form of a comet, sifting across the concept-sky. Thus blinded by the tint and hue of his interior speeches on ardent love, he returned to the nocturnal sea to contemplate the formation of the land. Hadn't Jacques Maritain decried Americans who knew not what walking was? America could have its highway self; let one keep Maritain, and the growth of the soil.

"I didn't wake you up, did I? I thought you slept with your phone off?"

"No worries, my angel. Can't sleep and saw the light of the phone over on the desk. How lovely to hear your voice!"

"Well my boy, you do sound sleepy, but I just wanted to say: *faith is substance of that which we hope for, and evidence for that which is in a sense unseen—we must turn to the place of divine names, and mystical theology—holy spheres of recognition, and the apostolic light.*"

Fading out, the pilgrim had his greatest sleep, or golden slumber, in what felt like since childhood: peaceful, plentiful, with the innocence of that Latinity which taught '*Imitatio Christi.*'

Some Velvet Morning

Mine is no matter *of returning to Jerusalem a conqueror of the land, coronated with a crown of leaves, paid for my opinion as parades go by; no, I have learned from my rejected forebearers how all of this goes; I am against the current, but never deluded into thinking I shall change the course of tyrannical waters—the altitude of doves, murmuring affections, our invectives trickling across the land—I can see the warfare that began in Jerusalem coming to its end, with neither whimper or bang, but hermeneutics and judgment—we have seen enough examples, my love; now let us become examples—stopping into Happy World, where nothing costs more than ninety-nine cents, but is this Queens—a dream, a drink, furnaced trial—ah, now I awaken, Lord forgive me, take this cotton from my mouth—*

William threw himself awake at 10:11am in the unfamiliar studio apartment where, piece by piece, dripping tapestries, fused with floating broken incense and some pipes, spliced by scattered and Persian rugs lined the walls connected with dream fragments in the mind of he who whispered, *whither Lazarus?* And as one can love in the city none but the city the city loveless, he knew what had happened and he knew he was in downtown San Francisco although he was unsure of what to do next. He eyed the masks and bottles and costumes strewn across the mantelpieces and the kitchenette and felt as if a dazed victim of excessive hopes. An immediate hangover came on, no temporal intoxication about it. He recalled his mother telling him to become a professor. Professors had the summer off. It felt like summer and yet it was still November.

He peeled old newspaper from sore elbows. It seemed incorrect that Harold Smith and his girl had made it out. Awakening alone in a once-crowded room is, he reflected, par excellence, the cusped essence of *looming.*

Downtown San Francisco pressed on as he set his ankles beside the radiator and coughed at length. Everyone had gone out and he felt weary. The last he remembered he was lying beside a grand piano slouched over in vague delirium thinking of nothing but his birth rippling into context.

The sun was shining in the rhapsodic autumnal light of morning and the city brilliant. His phone had died.

There was a café or bar open, he knew. He reached over the coffee table for the finest novel in tow, tossed it aside, and daydreamt of taking off for Polk Street. That novel was a hundred years old. He was jealous but he was more interested in having a fine Tuesday, because no one ever had such an affair.

Brendan fell through the punch table and destroyed at once the last of the punch bowls and the plates and cups and the sheets and the carpets. The girl slept through it or pretended to. He stood and fixed his glasses. "He was a damned good man," he imagined Brendan commentating his own being in the third person. Brendan pointed at two naked women sleeping in bed and pointed to the door.

"William, now, come," Brendan White coughed, "Let's go. Let us seize the day. For Daniel Welles. For humanity. For something to do. To Polk Street."

They washed up and walked out to Market and Polk and watched the American scene go by beneath fading advertisements. The air was freezing cold. Down the street traces of echoes of chants regarding a Presidential candidate came into perceptive agony. William looked to see the marching band but buildings were in the way. Flags waved, thunderous fluttering, atop the buildings.

"I feel ill," he said. "I can't believe they've all made it to work."

"Everyone from last night? They went to brunch. We're meeting them tonight."

Brendan lit the end of a cigarette. Two legless men, selling stolen diabetic socks, crawled on arthritic hands asking for a cigarette. He gave them the butt-end and they walked off on their hands smoking the filter before several free-newspaper stands.

"Where? Teleology Ave.? To the trees of wooden clogs?"

"I don't know. We have to keep moving though or I'll throw up."

A gasoline truck roared through the long-red light amidst the didactic infancy of an ambulance siren, four simultaneous car horns, the wailing of taxi cab tires, the deep bellowing THUMP of the gasoline truck bouncing over a concrete dip in the road, the rattle of loose manholes, the illegible screams of beggars broken-down who walked in line with the se-cret-agent stock brokers waving down cabs with a polished pinky nail as William looked out at that enormous silver oval within which one could see himself flashing by, twisting and stretching with erosion, before the gasoline truck fell away somewhere unseen around Leavenworth Street.

He stood out and let the oceanic air cleanse his body, his blood, and straight through to the bones as clinking trolley cars traced across Market Street. North: 000 Polk. He and Percy hooked a left and barged forth toward the parade of people in the middle morning.

He stretched out and yawned at 000 Polk, then hooked a left and went.

~

There was an old, rickety bench of torn red paint outside of Arch-stone Fox Plaza's automated spherical entranceway. He'd never noticed the building, nor the bench existed.

The building barreled toward the gray morning sky in an enormous faded brown of brief rectangular windows, like a table set of singular dominoes, through which long bulbs dangled from the ceiling of surveil-lance cameras. Tenth Street stood next to a wasteland, a fenced off pit of destroyed concrete and broken metal tubes. Diagonal, SF-Mart, upon which a clock fixed on 10:11 was displayed in this case being just some minutes behind.

"Oh, thank God," William recalled.

"What is it?"

"I have two hundred dollars. I had a nightmare I had spent all of it."

A cut out of a Mondrian print blew down the sidewalk, twirling and heaving into the air of racing Market Street traffic and disappearing.

"I have twenty dollars," Brendan said. "Let's go up Polk Street. It will be nice to walk the whole thing."

Torn overhead tarp stretched from Market to Hayes through spray-painted orange corridors. Fresh coffee brewed, leaked into the air. Stamped crates of oysters clicked and clacked like wind-up teeth before shop window displays while a hissing 19 bus heaved toward Market Street.

"I swear to God I think the horns and sirens have gotten louder," Brendan said. They smiled and walked ahead up Polk Street. "Do you know where a morning bottle of wine leads?"

"I do."

"We could turn around and go to Dolores Park and drink a bottle of wine and recap the night. By the time we finished we'd be working on another."

"Another bottle of wine?"

Brendan paused to light another cigarette.

William texted Harold:

"?"

The immediate response:

"!"

"No, another night. We'd be getting to work on another night. What do you think?"

"I would rather seize the day, as you put it, on Polk Street."

"Why."

William looked down at him and then ahead, to the distant unforeseeable tip of Russian Hill. His beard and mustache was in disarray. Emaciated women rushed the discolored walls, slipped down their sweatpants, and ran half naked laughing down the broken concrete alleyways.

"Because Polk Street is the truest American street," William resounded, "Wrack the mind open timeless let it barge; either that or a boozy nap on the beach. Fulfillment of such general serenity as motion, a momentary reflectionless concept vast in scope, to sleep beside afternoon waves of salt drunk on the basis of enjoyment harming not a soul and to the left ancient buildings before a string of sifting little clouds," he began to sing and dance in homage to Daniel Welles, as Brendan joined him in delirious falsetto weaving through scattered passersby, his voice rising like vertigo inverted, swanlike motions, "Over from the Golden Gate Bridge, puffy and white, like cotton candy drifting by in brisk motion! Woo-hoo, I feel like hell, and still I shall survive! Taste the air, from Embarcadero, otherwise daydream! Rich white lines strewn across that bluest hue, that soft distant air and array of San Francisco! Beyond this tunnel connecting two towering, teal buildings and now to the right I could go! Diago*nal*! *Against* traffic! How sweet it is! My sorts of people hang out in pubs, due for yet avoiding love; we long for more intelligent life, and yet conflate juxtaposition with mediation; and when it comes we throw a fit, the wine goes so fast, doesn't it?"

Brendan sang along as the twosome straightened their rumpled coats, shuffling ahead and spilling ash, "And get back to Market but instead I follow the distant tip-top of City Hall! Coming into view if you lean a certain way, across this yellow barrier!"

"Gimme a call!"

"Held back in order to let the automobiles spill from the underground garage against the sound—of approaching and passing tires, endless here, rolling over cups! Papers! Plastic bags! Cigarette, here, well alright, I'll smoke, have a coke a smoke with you—I'm singing in the rain now I don't feel so blue!"

They jogged through the colorless maze ahead where Civic Center spread out at the end of Hayes. No soul lingered at the foot of the Tenderloin but the men who'd climbed steel-rimmed steps to die beneath bolted doors that say DO NOT ENTER as newspapers blew against their motionless shoulders—

'And the sun fills the faces like mine'

"You know," began Brendan, straightening his hair and walking ahead, his eye upon the spreading fields, "The men and women will be at work and at school right now. I'm bored to death with both. My paychecks arrive courtesy of twenty hours' worth of tea drinking per week, while scrubbing the occasional dish. I believe life will be alright."

"You've found work?"

"Some old dingy café on Haight Street."

"O Tenderloin," William said, "And what thoughts are to be had on the dying men who fade out before your banks? What is the bank but an avalanching failure? There should be riots every day on Wall Street. The age of the peaceful protest is not dying, for it never even began. We need something more! In order to access your money, you've got to pay money, and in order to appear normal you've got to be in debt! Goodness gracious I am in bad shape," William exclaimed, clutching at his ribcage.

He slouched against the plastic planter for a moment. Brendan looked on at the buildings they had gotten to know by heart all summer and last summer and there was a strange ecclesiastical look in his green eyes.

"Donations please"
—Emaciated Puerto Rican naked except sock and denim vest

City Hall, that most magnificent failure, stood one way, The Public Library another. Along granite wall at Grove there stood, carved, ANNO DOMINO MCMXIV. Bill Graham Auditorium and distant headless skyscrapers stood beneath clouds soft with motion, open fields before them wherein the living dead rested on their ancient cloths of wet cardboard, seventy-five flags rustling overhead and cars coming to and fro every direction beneath massive gray gothic architecture encompassed by distant buildings which overlapped in a strange tinted holographic fence as if reemerging tidal waves.

"Say," Brendan began, looking to double-check William was paying attention, "It's as if they've come to the beach. They are on vacation from the Tenderloin. Look at those couples and loners stretched out."

"It is a nice day for the beach. I haven't gone swimming in two years."

"Me neither." He looked again across the field and ahead as packs of cyclists whizzed by in a stream of whirling chains and reflective lights. "Let's go eat something good. Let's go eat a damned good Vietnamese sandwich."

At the set latched up subway entrances and flickering walkway lights Polk became Carlton B. Goodlett. It was a still day for Civic Center walk and talk, the last long green field for some time; a young couple with backpacks drank wine from a mason jar.

"How do you know it's wine?"

"Her lips are purple." The roaring Five plowed past, down McCallister. "Look here—at McCallister as you pass this big parking garage and Goodlett cancels itself there is a sense, William, an unspoken sense of being locked into Polk Street. Do you ever feel that way now?"

William looked ahead and around, City Hall behind him emerging into the ghetto, and responded mutely.

An encroaching diagonal collage of deformed, heaving faces with clouds of eviction on their foreheads, bustling shoulders, swaying arms, and discarded lids of coffee cups trembled or sprinted through siren echoes as soon as they had stepped off of Goodlett. At Polk and Golden Gate gusts of tepid machinery breeze blew forth from the flower shop air conditioner. Light-posts of lost dogs and missing persons, cigarettes burning to the filter, cracked white lips which dangled from haunted faces treading with flimsy metallic walkers and plastic canes and rattling shopping carts filled with crushed cans catalogued by aluminum shades of rust.

The yellow neon sign GOLDEN-1 blazed in the daylight.

"Have you ever eaten there?"

"No," William said. "Have you?"

"No, sir."

Beneath the neon sign groups of men burst through swinging silver doors. Sunlight came through skyscrapers and reflected off the flashing sheets of angular chrome.

Down the street there were ten, twenty, fifty-something people dressed in rags on each block, wrapped in linoleum sheets, woolen fabrics, drinking rubbing alcohol out of enormous soda cups. The large cups were most convenient, William had grown to consider, and used later for collections trudging forth to Polk from Larkin.

An aged Indian woman played dominoes with a chicken. *Goodbye Vishnu—I'm flying of over you*—William and Percy shared a tall can of beer and continued down Polk Street. The stories of those streets were not told in any tone of voice; the stories of those streets were told in the glances caught within closed shop windows which reflected and shined, tinted, like mirrors.

"The men to our left, outside of the restaurant, are pimps. Dressed in shining purple suits, hats with feathers, they live in decades past and do so well enough that no one dare says a word but behind their tailored backs."

"I never thought of it that way."

Taxi cabs tore down the street. The men in feathered suits waved them down and stepped inside. William thought of Daniel, of Post Street.

The distant light turned green; the uphill trudge from Ellis to O'Farrell became visible through the briskish wind. Slanted, discolored government and rehabilitation centers seemed to moan with age, their shadows stretching out into the street like frozen black sand.

"I know," said the first officer.

His partner spoke in code through his walkie-talkie and wiped cake crumbs from his protruding stomach. He looked as if he were pregnant and pried himself from a bottle of Diet Pepsi.

The vacant 19 bus passed by. William thought of when he took it to work one day a year ago when he first arrived in San Francisco. Brendan must have been living on Mission Street and 19th then and William had his room on Polk and Sacramento. When he thought of that summer he thought of being in love and Valencia Street and the smell of fresh food in the air, the smell of cafes and bars and the hot coffee fumes sifting, then pressing past bodies to another candlestick-lit bar, the serene smell of wet oak and leaking kegs of beer when it was so crowded, and in a similar way to that bus and to the present-tense where you could see the lines in the passengers' faces pressed against the window when you walked past and all it took was the proper look of beauty from a face never to be seen again.

Car alarms went off in channeled, echoing, seismic metal cries. They passed slabs of marble to sit along and empty silences of still alleyways, torn pages of telephone books and broken staple-guns and vocal requiems of life retained; then somewhere those distinct helpless screams projecting animalistic agonies:

"Outfits, outfits, I got outfits."

He limped past, flashing a kit which gleamed beneath the twirling soda-bulb of the barber shop. "Outfits, outfits," and his tactile Oakland Raiders coat was torn at the cuff, reflecting within black sunglasses behind which an unfathomable slate, and unfathomable life history, stood still.

Market Street exited stage left and those men and women passing through now did not walk but drag their limbs along the ground in search of something that no longer existed, never existed at all, which could be described in the texture of brain tumors, war stories, broken down coughs, belches of hot dogs and pickles and two-dollar vodka and potato chips and the look in their prosthetic eyes.

Brendan walked ahead past Turk, as if caught within some private Hell, sifting uphill to Eddy past the ravished faces in their shades of white, brown, black, blue, pink, all of them agonizing and swollen. Their faces resembled imploded hand grenades rather than the mask of any skull. They wept beside cardboard beds and argued with wallpaper. They walked naked through alleyways, hunched over, and screaming by the dozen, stepping on glass and screaming bloody murder, like emaciated ghosts sifting through a never-ending concrete nightmare.

William looked to the array of shop signs. He inhaled sudden fumes of burning rubber and glanced down to notice the trash can beside him just catching fire. Each time he looked up enough he mistook the MASSAGE sign for MASSACRE.

The air transformed noticeably at Eddy Street. The air became thicker, the walls of buildings and bodies closing in on one another and compact with agony; the ingredients, or invisibilities, of complete ruin. But still they did not stand out. Brendan fell quiet once more when William reappeared at his side and the pair walked ahead.

Sensorial bodies heaved past William there where the air supply was made of chains and fire. He felt as if he did not to exist along the intoxicated dream-state of a street and longed for something else, anything but the feeling of having died already and having remerged in some chaotic zone familiar and foreign once one settled in. Brendan stood ahead at the light observing four Asian men across the rickety street of bicycles, bottles and fog, whose heads turned toward the rattling dice upon the splintered table. William turned his attentions and energies to the gambling table.

Interweaving strands of ivy ran along the faded brick donut shop beneath its torn lime-green canopy of chalk-white letters: D O N U T S C O F F E E E T C. They once sat at that table at sunrise each morning before going to class or to get drunk or to the library or something downtown, always behind those immense clouds rushing through the colossal orange body of Golden Gate Bridge. William crossed the street.

One of the men clad in brown jumpsuit covered in cigarette ash and varied tar streaks to the left of the steam coffee pot rolled his clicking dice into a gasping spiral. With an exacted, sharpened inhale, then clenched fists of filthy fingernails, and at last exposed nerve-teeth, it is over.

Another packed bus roared by, and upon a cracked red stoop Brendan sat down.

"Look at that woman," he said, "Beside the man who's rolled over her through poison ivy, her back is of sweat and turned now—there— are the wet-white spots of perspiration. Her hand movements are like a rattlesnake's flickering tongue. She has wild, fine spasms using her right hand as a rake with which to deliver herself the winnings!"

She raked in a batch of coins. William smelt their collective sweat and stepped back. The scent contained that figurative nihilism appreciative upon memory.

Diagonal to her another man, at least 85, blinked his eyes and swallowed several blue pills with bottled water. The last man faced William and Brendan and wore identical jumpsuits as the other man. He held up an edition of the San Francisco Chronicle over his head.

Upon her counting the winnings he placed his newspaper down at his lap and extended his free, limp hand to the coffee pot. He placed his cards down and asked to double check her hand.

He stood awestruck, sweat breaking from his forehead down into his scorched, sleepless eyes. He threw the newspaper to the wind with a sigh of defeat. Obscure agony existed within his outspread arms; he appeared to be wrapping his arms around a nonexistent world while the pages of the newspaper fell apart and came down wavering and across the sidewalk and the street palpating like the wings of crooked, stuck birds, each rustling out maddening into the wind of automotive breeze. The stray paper rustled home toward the white-checkered street, strapped to the foreheads of gutters. With his palms to his forehead he smiled, and then everyone smiled, and he let down his hands.

"Across the street there is a bar where men dance the tabletops in underwear packed with money after midnight. Techno music pulses and two high definition television sets play homosexual pornography," William said.

"How do you know that?"

"I used to live upstairs."

The doors swung open. Three men stepped out and began conversation debating the differences between being and becoming a drunk, or lush, as opposed to an alcoholic, all with that cheerful sentiment one could take on a funeral with if he were in good company beneath the San Francisco sun drinking during the day.

"Oh don't be absurd," one reassured the others, "We know nothing of hallucinations."

William rubbed his hands together, yawning, cupped his hands, and breathed warm fog into their open crevasse to heat the tip of his watery nose. He retrieved newspaper pages from the street. Snow had begun to fall in New York City.

"How do you feel?"

"Fine, how do you feel?"

"I'm fine," Brendan said, looking into William's eyes. "But I mean here, in your head, do you feel fine?"

"Yes, why? Fine. Do I look unwell?" William looked over his long,— torn black coat, his black jeans, his black wingtips, his cardigan with collared shirt, his beard, and checked his parted hair in the reflective glass panels of the candy shop. He looked better than he felt and could not understand if Brendan were alluding to something.

"No, no," he explained. "I just mean that sometimes people look fine, but they walk around, you know, thinking miserable things. Sometimes I walk down the street in a tuxedo contemplating suicide. Sometimes I hold the door open for aging women with an erection that won't die. Sometimes I have coffee with a friend although I am positive, I must go to the bathroom and still I sit there laughing through agony! I think friends ought to inquire one another's state of mind at random, but not in an overbearing way, you know? I don't know."

"How do you feel today, then? The weather is perfect, my appetite gone."

"I always lose my appetite when I walk across Eddy," Brendan explained.

"So do I."

An exhausted, eye-patched mailman barreled by with his click-rolling, ticking crate of mail. The racket of black plastic wheels broke below the indented blue canvas. He dragged another rectangular pouch as if it were an anchor, rattling and scraping down the street, lunging ahead from Van Ness. A stocky police officer with blue-white hair then jaywalked past a transgender parade toward indistinct, miniature spray-painted murals near the front window of Napoli's Pizzeria.

"Let's go there," William said. "I'm buying you a slice of pizza. I am hungry again. I am always hungry. Nothing can satisfy me."

"A good woman," Brendan stated. "A real good one that you loved and loved you. Not the rare usual kind where you either love their body or the mind but not the two. Occasionally you can strike gold and you will meet someone whose body and mind drive you mad. You will be deranged forever. Goes for men and women. That would satisfy you."

"Some day when I'm older and wiser, good friend, some fine day."

They sat and had the pizza with a great can of beer and another, all of which was bought with food stamps, and watched the whirlwind pass by through torn circulars and broken sunglasses tumbling down the ancient November Street. The eyes of passersby appeared absorbed by some sheet music to theatrics to be produced upon the occasion of a Roman Orgy.

"A Spanish woman recommended I read Christopher Columbus's diaries in Spanish last night," William said.

"Have you yet?"

"No."

"You ought to."

"But just because she kissed so well. Did you hear us in the bathroom? I understand. Now, this pale ale works, I will give it that much."

"It is damned-fine beer."

"No, it is not," countered William. He took another sip. "Oh, right— now I see what you mean."

William spotted his old landlord ahead locking the door behind him. He could spot Anthony from a block away. He was a short, stylish man with a grand, never off-kilter sense of humor. The two always went so well together.

He wore a sky-blue sports-coat, tilted tan detective hat; Dick Tracy gone casual in blue jeans and spotless Keds. A new pearl earring shone beneath the worn-out entrance sign, home to birdsong, nests of shade, and adjacent dwelling spiders spinning webs.

"We'll get a drink at Bob's," Brendan said.

"No, no not yet. Not at all. Besides, it is overpriced."

"They're going out of business, though. That's why they're overpriced."

"?"

Somehow this saddened William; he knew at once it was the night he had moved into his hotel room the first thing he saw through his window was the diner lit up at night. It had come to represent a sense of life to him in those occasional black ass midnights of the soul.

They sat down smiling at the counter and drank Fernet with Anchor Steam.

"Last time I saw Anthony a friend and I had met at noon to buy a twelve pack of Guinness, six bottles of Blackstone wine, a six pack of Bass, and the complete works of Shakespeare. As Phil Cohen gave me a interesting history lesson on the Black & Tan his car was towed. We were drunk in the afternoon of Earth and did something bad somewhere and some cop came looking for us down the hallway and Anthony just shooed him away." William laughed. The waitresses laughed with him, and the rest of the diner was shedding teeth. Brendan laughed. "I remember," William said through tears, "I remember hearing him say, 'Oh *Gawd*, don't you know by now that I can't help you? Leave the boys alone!'"

"Thank you!"

William set ten dollars down for a tip and walked through the worn back door as the bell attached to it by yarn rang.

Brendan asked what had happened as they walked back down Polk Street.

"We sat listening to a little tape-desk I had bought because I had saved all of my mix-tapes and drank Dante wine and then stole books from an old-news bookstore across the beach but the cops were not there for that and I was yelling out in the streets or something," began William, recalling the audacity with which the police officer and his bowling-pin legs had chased them inside. "See, if a man keeps to himself when need-be and expects nothing from anyone, let him succumb to pleasure. Habits are habits because the voice of flesh is want. What matters is that you make rent, and that I did; is there anything more loathsome than policemen and their bowling-pin legs?"

Anthony noticed them a quarter-block away. He extended his Buddha belly and yawning, shed a wave, meandering about as Brendan and William approached. William went to speak.

"You look like Hell," Anthony said. "What rooftop were you raving about last night?"

"It was on Market Street just there . . ."

Anthony reminded William of a big film coming out that he had a role in. It was like the good old days.

"Oh I'll keep an eye out for you indeed," Brendan nodded with hopeful air. Multiple conversations cut around them with each passing batch of streetcleaners, butlers, strippers, senators, cashiers, teachers, and vagabonds in the afternoon.

A man with golden wristwatches and the worst belt you have ever seen in your life from France asked for directions to the museum.

"It's the beginning, I'm smoking in the café," Anthony relayed, elevating his pitch over cement trucks running red lights. The look on his aging face was that of the interior design to his dream; the truthful claim to filmic presence, and its wayward, beautiful hope, that irretrievable light at the end of the tunnel. "Stop by for a martini!"

"We will!"

"Tonight! We're having a big dinner party at Moby Dick! Come out!"

"See you then!"

And everyone turned to go.

"He seemed like a good landlord, a good guy. I'll go see that film. Validity is a personal equation, notion, and is found within concepts, influential feelings and realizations, debate. There is no fact, just outrage."

William noticed blueprints of human feces streaked along the side of a molded dumpster. He looked over Brendan's shoulder down Geary straight through to the Union Square vicinity, toward thicker coats, scarves, umbrellas spilling out in numbers and loud conversations on phones in brief traffic. The bad weather did not exist if one had something good in his stomach. Summer as more of a feeling than a time of year, William thought, and be they gray skies above or otherwise, I feel right now as if it is summer; and therefore, it is.

A fleeting sense of mitigation and decay and delirium passed fleeting through him and hovered above the gum-struck sidewalk as the sun microscopically pressed on through the wall of rain clouds. Brendan spoke of making another trip out to the East Bay:

"It's the afternoon," he marveled. "We'll meet Harold right over there!"

"Wisdom builds herself a house!"

Polk Street noon had passed on with further, heightened gusts of cold, oceanic wind. Several steam-caps released heat. At night men and women could be found curled above these circular grates; when a specific

November moment clicked it remained damp and the junkies and insane of San Francisco recoiled to their afternoon and evening homes:
the metal sewer grates which emitted hot steam. It was rare although not
impossible to see lesser beings cross Geary Street on that side of Larkin.

The terminal tone of their voices was never fear but despair. Violence was never antiquated with homeless inquiries the way it might be
on the East. No one was going to get hurt or die but someone was going
to walk on and someone else was going to fall back against a cardboard
box dampened with morning dew. William thought of these things every
time he saw steam rise from the ground. The fetal positioning of metal
drug-induced silence reminded him of bad memories, or of his organs
tying themselves into knots within his stomach. He recalled last winter
spending all his food stamps on sandwiches and handing them out in the
late night to the homeless spread about Geary and Post Street.

'Winter time is where these dead souls come to evaporate for good,
arms and necks by now mere grids of sexual diseases and flesh-torn
needle scars, flailing blood and saliva. Specific stenches encompass the
perimeter of their near-air; it is the stench of defected cells committing
suicide,' he thought, daydreaming of writing that down before letting it
go, forgetting just what he had meant and if he could not please everyone
then he would please himself. He thought it funny to think just about
everyone wrote a book a day within their minds.

At Bush Street Harold emerged amidst passing automobiles, the
smell of donuts and coffee and hot dogs and hamburgers, toasted wheat
buns and opening bars, windows closing and opening, chairs and tables
being turned and pulled into position and signs clacking along the corridor of flimsy stamps, windings of an unraveled chain, smoke signals in
the midst of volcanic avenging.

Smith, out of the myriad of a hundred or so in sight, appeared
the sole triumphant young man on the street. He walked as if he had
triumphed over life in his peacoat and penny-loafers and could find an
ample name for unknown heroes in a land where the dead rule all. He
looked at them saying nothing, and then grinning, which said more than
most people say in a lifetime.

They shared the fine agonizing feeling on the beautiful day and
dragged their carcasses along. William crossed the street to shake Harold's hand and to compliment his developing mustache.

"I exist through words, words of which exist through me! Let's go
to the deli!"

Brendan gazed into the vat of a Gap advertisement encompassing the exterior of a bus and as it passed he crossed the street to join William and Harold at an aluminum table outside of the infamous deli.

William had once ordered 45 sandwiches from the deli at midnight to bring back to Fort Mason for a party. He remained a customer during his stay on Sacramento. The owners liked him and his friends. They tipped the sandwich man. Houston Street and Metropolitan Avenue taught you things.

It helped that William had already been long-fond of the type of people who work in delis in cities. Those people and garbage-men who smoked cigarettes on the back of their trucks at midnight in the rain down Market Street seemed liked the best people.

The owners let him sit outside whenever his legs were weary when William lived down the street and had been standing for a long time. They had not seen him in weeks and were elated when he stopped in with Brendan and Harold. Brendan bought a bag of caramel.

"Do you mind if we sit outside while the tables are empty?"

Faye came out from the backroom, enquiring: "Is daht Bill!"

William approached her and received a kiss on his cheek. He felt elated. He made sure all was well with her and agreed the sun ought to return.

"It will, honey, it will! Go, relax! Go relax with friends!" She shooed William out as if he were mad to have asked to take a seat without ordering sandwiches.

Then little Jeremy, Faye, and Edward's son, set off a firecracker and threw confetti in the air and lit one of the snake fireworks which looked like long spiraling waste. Everyone laughed and danced a moment and it was perfect and everyone continued to laugh until their eyes and throat hurt and then little Jeremy did it again and threw confetti all over the snake droppings and pulled the string of a popper until Harold told him, "Go now, watch out your mother may get the broom!"

"There is a party tonight," he announced, readjusting himself along the table, rubbing at exhausted temples. He took a bottle of Old Grand Dad from his bag.

"Where is it?"

"The East Bay, I think. I'm waiting to hear back. It would be nice as Hell to make it out that way! Oh and William, did I tell you, I'm glad you're back in town!"

He patted William on the shoulder as he placed the bottle of Old Grand Dad upon the aluminum table which jangled as if a minute tambourine.

"It is good to be back. It has been a good year thus far. We're all getting laid, and moving around, and riding bicycles on Saturday morning to Sausalito, and drinking in the afternoon on Polk Street. They say the prime of your life is what, 40?"

"I think it's something like mid to late thirties."

"So we've got 12 or 14 years until our prime? Our odds are fair."

They made a big toast and looked out on the street as the sun rose and fell upon the street. A neon-bespectacled campaign-worker approached them to ask them to vote.

"Oh come on, guys, just sign the clipboard."

William dismissed his khaki-shorts and electric-yellow visor and turned his attention to his miniature cigars. Harold took a puff and blew rings of smoke at the sky.

"I don't vote," Brendan said.

"Why don't you vote? You are lucky to have the right."

"Because the President is an ape of wrath," Brendan shouted, grinning, "And all politics are tendencies caught within the wheels of a chain-reaction, and politics are dead!"

Meanwhile one merry gentleman passed wielding a wicker cane at the group of pigeons huddled around a fallen castle of breadcrumb. His face sagged like the bottom of a bag bearing paperweights. His Brooks Brothers suit was auburn, and crisp. His top hat was felt, and from its beige side stemmed a bluish peacock-feather. He looked good for his age. He passed by, walking toward Market.

Brendan observed the little glass bottle of absinthe William set upon the table as he and Harold discussed women and records. An Indian man across the street at the tobacconist smiled at them sitting there in daylight drinking whiskey and absinthe.

"Hey, come on! Come have a drink with us!" Harold shouted.

The fleeting gust of warm wind blew leaves down the sidewalk.

"Ah, he never comes over!"

They sat out there awhile quite discussing the nice singularity of whiskey, the embrace of momentary recognition, retelling the best stories from last summer. Each time one began to drink whiskey one was sure it would be the best day of your life thus far because at last it was impossible to care to bother, and then even remember, about tomorrow. People drank because for the time being tomorrow did not have to exist and the past was worth recapturing. The country had spent so much time on propaganda concerning physical health it had gone insane. Indulgence was a fine rebellion against this. Good friends and taste and wit leveled the experience clean off, like a bad memory being tossed down into the Grand Canyon as one plucked good memories from thin, chaotic air, like petals from a pastel flower.

The seafood shops were windingly coming to open, and the dense smell of lobster and clams and squid ran down the street.

"Why don't we go down to the aquarium on Clement?"

"I don't want to move."

"We could take the buses around and drink whiskey until something happens! Come on! William, I'm glad you're back! I love you! You too, Brendan—give me a God-damned hug!"

He returned with three glasses and a bottle of Perrier as to cut the absinthe.

"I like it when nothing is happening," William admitted. "Something is always bound to happen, so I like it when nothing is happening. I feel fine."

"We'll go to the party later. Let's just sit here for now. I never get to just sit anywhere anymore."

"I will need to take a nap before-hand. Can I sleep on the floor of your old apartment building for an hour? Would Anthony find that strange?"

"Take a nap here," suggested Harold.

"I can't."

"Why?"

"Because it is not warm and there is no good music to listen to."

"We could go to the Hearth. You like to sleep there."

"But we could get silverware inside here and fall asleep clutching it and when we doze off, we will drop the silverware and the clang will wake us up. All we need is the initiated feeling of unconsciousness. We will feel much better then, and less to sleep all through the night which is a waste of time."

They drank the whiskey and no one was tired anymore. The sun had disappeared behind a set of clouds. William smoked several consecutive cigarettes and felt like smiling although his jaw was sore. He smiled anyway and listened to everyone talk.

"I need to use your computer."

"I don't have a computer."

"I just borrow other people's computers. Sometimes people get sick of their computers and lend them out for a couple of days."

"We are all doomed."

Rain fell upon the tarp. The men and women in the streets opened their umbrellas, lifted their newspapers, and began running full speed in every direction in a stampede.

"Where is everyone rushing to?" Harold asked.

"I don't know," Brendan said. He studied the simultaneous compression and elevation of passing eyebrows and said that they did look as if within a collective rush. "What did you think of high school?"

"It was good," Harold said, outstretching his arms.

"What was it like? Tell me all about high school. I dropped out in the ninth grade."

"My high school was fine," Harold said. "I think, see, I never asked for anything during those years of living beneath my parent's roof because it seemed wrong to. I let my parents have their dreams and I stuck to mine," scratching his meditative chin as raindrops fell to the tip of his black shoe. There in a bus window, a head hidden within the contents of Kafka's *Metamorphosis*. They scooted the table and chair further beneath the tarp and dried the table with napkins. "I like my life here though, and I like that the people from home and their stupid personalities drive many good people to certain cities at certain times. A lot of times, boys, ridicule, see, is erstwhile the translation of reflecting one's inferiority. A lot of everyone who was nice looking and popular in high school was obese or pregnant or dead in a few years. The American Dream has failed in more ways than one!"

William watched the wet cars pass through the dampened afternoon street.

"And the coffin longs for another nail!" cried Harold, running his fists across the table.

Brendan passed his caramel cubes around.

"I keep thinking about a reoccurring cavity that's been bothering one of my back teeth every time I've eaten candy or ice cream in the past two years," William said. "I have been chewing candy and ice cream on the exclusive right side of my mouth for the last two years. I ought to reapply for food stamps."

"Where do I get food stamps?"

"Burning yellow urinal cakes."

"Over on Eighth and Mission."

"My philosophy is that food stamps is like a two or three hour-long job you get paid for if you can withstand it. It is like a reality TV show. It is horrible."

William confirmed this as to why he hadn't been there as of late and was letting his food stamps stretch out. Harold drank whiskey and wanted to hear all about it before he went. Brendan began in a magnificent story-telling voice as the city in the rain dissolved for a moment, clearing his throat and crossing his leg over his knee, and guided by absinthe:

"Well you walk through a concrete maze of handicap railing and a hundred human beings who are often outside screaming, projectile defecating, and being thrown into police cars. Beyond the maze there is a metal detector and several armed guards. The violent beeping echoes through the building all day long. Immediate smell of excrement and rotten food."

He pointed to a brown banana peel slanted over a rustic fence plastic fence before the café and continued.

"On the discolored walls are posters for self-help groups in several languages, anti-drug ads, suicide prevention bulletins, abortion clinics, all of which are smeared with handprints and ash. In the center of the main building is an island filled with dishes of forms and free condoms. You choose your form and take it to a window for instructions, what to fill out and what gets filled out without you or later on. The forms take just a few minutes to complete and in the second room are the various windows, one of which your papers are brought to. The curving lines take up all the enormous room at all hours of the day, and multiple security guards stand by ignoring everything except physical contact. Women tear scream into the bulletproof windows holding their children's hands, prostitutes adjust their loud makeup in shattered handheld mirrors, older men and women lean against the wooden posts staring into the tiles of the floor, their heads making silent, circular motions of terminal depression. There is an occasional young looking person somewhere in the midst, swallowing, taking deep breaths and avoiding eye contact at all costs, as the majority of the room glares at this person, waiting to see who will say something first and most imperative of all if the young person will respond, at which point all corners of the room will focus on attacking said person with the most extreme vulgarities. Whispers of broken coughs, seas of yellow teeth, an equatorial stench of Night on Needle Mountain: DMT Symphony. And then at the window, unless you are denied, the forms are overlooked, questions are asked, a meeting for either the next day is arranged, as are fingerprints. They sent me to the waiting room I'd heard of. The form said if I wasn't called up in three hours, to let a deskman know.

"The room is filled with putrid salmon and yellow wallpaper that resembles one enormous stain more than anything. It is the size of a cafeteria and filled with hundreds of plastic chairs and one television set. There are no fans overhead. Certain rows smell more of excrement than others, and to make eye contact is to cheat a severe beating. Men sit still with keys between their knuckles, carving signatures into the chairs. The women scream over one another's voices and often at one other, resulting in physical fights and beatings that require multiple security guards to control and break up and many janitors to clean the aftermath up. Even the security guards get beaten, and this is the one thing that gets a unanimous rise out of the lifeless room.

"Oh, and one more thing, last time I was there as a fight wore off and a man in a trench coat slumped against one the front desks, before being sent towards another bulletproof window outside of the waiting room entrance. I took a seat and watched him. He was denied of anything he'd applied for and put his head down in a motion of finality. The clerk resumed her conversation behind the window, which could be heard, discussing politics. The man grabbed his black leather trench coat and turned around towards the exit. On the floor he squatted down wrapped within his leather cape. Something like a homemade hypodermic kit lay beside him, like out of an old lunchbox, same gray shade as the cold ground. He let out a scream that overrode the beeping metal detectors and fell over. He lay there for about fifteen seconds before packing his needle away and walked out of the exit door smiling. His farewell scream echoed over the speakers calling names.

"The TV in the waiting room is small and plays the exact same ten-minute-long video all day long. The video is nothing but talking heads discussing their problems, and how the state helped them. At the end, there is a speech made by someone in a suit. Everyone in the video is referred to but by their first names, even in the credits. It is disturbing as it is endless.

"Meanwhile everyone stares at the ground or reads over their forms for hours. There are scattered seizures and violent outbreaks as dividers, but that is all. I was called in ten minutes before the three-hour wait was up. The thoughts one delves into in that zone are not too horrible to relay, as no thought is, but as your name is called, there is instant erasing from all that has just happened. The near impossibility between deciphering daydream from wakened instance is too unclear to deconstruct within these confines of another institutionalized Hell. Everyone is sweating and moaning and going through withdrawal. The 30th looping of the film is not so much a breaking point, but a realization of psychosis followed a synthetic mental indolence. After all, this is free money we are talking about. It is all unpleasant. Damned unpleasant. Still, like life, worth it in the end."

"That is all gloomy, boy! I am in no rush!"

"Look, there is the sun."

They looked toward the ocean and the sun began again to emerge through fractal rain clouds.

"I feel wonderful," William said. He bought a pack of cigarettes and a bottle of Chimay and returned.

The sudden stillness of the city overtook them. The wind stopped blowing and for a moment Polk Street was silent save the tires cutting through small puddles of water and rainbow-colored oil which flipped and splashed onto the edge of the sidewalk. William thought a moment of the wars taking place, of the newspapers being delivered filled with nothing but death and weather and wished for a moment to speak of it. He no longer knew what to say.

Harold and Brendan looked down the street in a golden moment of contemplation. William looked at the peeling wooden window-frame of a boarded-up corner store and at the last to the final drops rain breaking from leaves, and then beyond the window, and through the rain. The church bells of the cathedral were ringing.

Through fractional openings between buildings the looming sunset was on its way. The rain had stopped hours ago.

"I feel as if the busiest man alive when I am sitting still, meditative-high, unable or rather unwilling to move, for I've realized there is no reason to move. There is no reason for reason, save reason. We learn from history that we do not learn from history, and from mistakes how not to make mistakes. Satisfaction is a mythical disease, perfection one lamentable side effect."

"Yes, I know, I taught you so. I'm getting hungry," said William. He inhaled the fumes of the bakery.

"We should go somewhere in a few minutes. I don't want to get up just yet. I've molded into this chair."

"I am in no rush."

An exhausted whore limped by. Her clothing was torn to shreds except for the President Obama cap which had been kept in mint-condition. She had makeup smeared all along her face in darker shades of blue, red, and yellow, and she looked quite sad. She leant down to tie her shoe and the cuff of her acid-washed pants ascended. Her left leg was made of wood.

"Barack Obama, everyone before and everyone after, is a dispensable idiot. They master the art of lying only so long as you master the art of justifying it."

They laughed as Faye came back out.

"How is the caramel?"

"It is the best caramel I've ever had."

"It melts in your mouth."

"Here," she said, stepping inside. "Jeremy bring three cup and two ginger ale! And you boys need eat!"

She turned to the young men, shaking her head.

"You can't drink that by itself all day! You get sick!"

"It's an old tradition, Faye."

"Here you go."

She placed three ice cups on the table and they made up three highballs.

They finished the drinks and stood up and bid farewell to everyone. The rain had stopped and everyone felt warm and blissful and the streets were coming back to life and they walked with their arms draped over one another's shoulders to Bob's Doughnuts where the concrete began just to slope back downhill and made a left inside of the old-fashioned doughnut shop.

The foghorn sounded, echoing and spreading across the ocean and into the storefronts.

Harold ordered three coffees, Brendan a bag of rainbow-cookies, crullers of toasted apple and pumpkin pie, and coffee cakes. William took a table near the back behind two old men in black leather jackets and matching flat-brimmed hats who worked together on crossword puzzles. He placed the package of four small bottles of wine of the table.

"To my brothers," Harold said, dropping a tumbler of whiskey into each steaming cup.

"Irish coffee is the best with you two," William said.

The other old men stared at the television set through trails of coffee steam. The steam trickled to the overhead fluorescent bulb. A beautiful young woman made sure everyone was alright and went in the back to fix a hole.

"Try this," said William.

Brendan took a piece of the maple-doughnut and nodded and then.

"This is the best doughnut shop in the city. There is no other doughnut shop worth going to."

"After this let's go to the apartment. I need to pick up some things and I want to make a big steak."

"I have to stop by my girlfriend's house too," Harold said.

"How are you getting there?"

"I have my bike around the corner."

"I'll meet you there then," Brendan said. "I want to go for a walk. I feel drunk." He turned to William. "Want to go for a walk instead of going home?"

"I'm going to visit Mary tonight in Fisherman's Wharf and get a nice bottle of wine for tonight she has for me there at the restaurant and then we'll go to the party."

"I thought she hated you now," Brendan said.

"Good hatred will never get in the way of good extinguishing," William announced.

"Then Saturday morning," Harold interjected, "We ride out to Tiburon and eat wild berries and get back in time for Dolores Park at sunset! Yes! Those are my favorite days! All of these days are my favorite!"

"Let's have women meet us there," Brendan said. "They can drive out and we'll meet them there and have a picnic."

"Brendan, when do you have work again?"

"I don't know. I think I quit."

"Good. Work is a waste of time."

"Oh come on," deplored Harold, "Routine is not so bad and you have money."

"You don't even have a job! Neither do you!"

"I never said anything," William said.

"Well you do what you please but I—"

"Not quite. It is a bad trade. One must never wander around searching for routine. There is no higher plateau, or pillar, in the realm of contradiction. I want to live and sing my life. Till then have a damned good time. This wine is nice. Thank you, William."

The men at the booth discussed lotteries and looked on at the announced numbers.

"Go to the Green Door," one of the men whispered, "And get the pussy."

The cashier gazed through the window while sending out rapid-fire text messages. Her reflection in the glass was beautiful and William considered at once asking her out and daydreamt of having children with her. He wondered just how soft her face could be and that he would never know until he put his hand along her neck one night and kissed her after taking her out for a nice evening at the movies and the restaurant and the quiet bar. She was the type of woman he would like to take out on dates. There were quite few of them in San Francisco. She was so plain and precious and looked longing for the perfect love beside the pastries on Polk Street that all his money would still always be spent on nice dates and things with her and then someday a family.

In his brief daydream they walked around holding hands content and he began to live a refined life. Her dark hair would always still remind him of lifelong mental and physical chaos, and of its potential beauty.

The man in the bomber jacket held a crayon in his hand and said:

"Let's go to Bob's Diner and get a cheeseburger. I am famished. Then go to one of them bathhouses." He spit phlegm into an empty cup. The other man turned to him with a toothless grin and told him he had no money. The leather jacketed man took his wallet from his secret coat pocket and flashed him two dozen hundred-dollar bills. They got up and left.

Harold was on the table laughing. William told him W.C. Fields jokes to keep it going and soon William had coffee coming through his nose. He chased whiskey with a glass of lukewarm water, the lukewarm water with lukewarm wine. That was the best feeling. Then everyone started to laugh and someone lit a joint. They drank their coffee and whiskey and electric lights began to buzz in their brains. Everyone was high and drunk and full of food and life.

"I always wanted to go to the Green Door," said Brendan. "I was just thinking about this in bed the other day, rubbing one out, analyzing commercials on television, realizing this constant pressure to become a harmless, defenseless citizen was the big goal everywhere. Big money is buying and selling big fear right out in the open too to be true. It's like dropping a mouse into burial grounds. I almost rode over to the Green Door and spent my last one hundred dollar one two massages or however much it costs."

"I will go to the Green Door with you as soon as I have money. This weekend; here, shake on it."

"I won't have the spare money this weekend but the next."

"I'll lend you the money," William reassured him. "We'll go to the Green Door this weekend and then walk through the Chinatown tunnel at night and make a night of it and hit a couple others in North Beach. We'll go to the dollar-shows at Lusty Lady. Here, shake on it."

Brendan shook his hand and either man knew he meant it and felt good and getting there and talking. William sensed few people had ever bought anything for Brendan. He understood poverty. And while that is not beautiful, it had happened and had happened in their youths, and in the real world they could just persevere. That, then, was beautiful; knowing you were not alone.

"And we should go up to Portland next year again when the leaves are changing and visit some people," William said, blowing on his coffee and not knowing what he was talking about except that once upon a time Harold used to often get high and drunk and begin to tell a tale about Portland that no one could remember two hours later. "Harold, weren't you just there?"

"It was something like a year ago, I think, no, two years ago. Wow, I'm high."

The rest of the patrons left. They stood up and took their places at the counter.

"?"

"Yeah, that was last winter," he said, smiling. He gripped his temples and drank coffee. "I think I know what it feels like to be insane."

"This year or last?"

"I think technic—it was . . . last year. I would like to go again though. Weren't you there?"

"I was there on business during the first week of autumn, driving through Oregon and Washington with our late friend Daniel Welles."

"I heard about that."

"That poor boy."

"We made stops in Portland, Olympia, and Seattle, and spent ten days or so. I want to go back and visit one of them women I met."

"No, no!' Harold cried out—"What happened to the other, my God—"

"Janine?"

"Janine, Janine!"

"Never saw her again."

"No!"

Newspaper bits were strewn across the old counter and the city went by through the closed door beneath the steady hum of the air conditioner.

"There where the trees are lime-green, ruby-red, dim auburn, flash of forest green, petal yellow, right, the atmosphere of colors! I met a fun group of people in those cities, always do."

"I must go sometime," Brendan said to William. William excused himself and walked into the bar next door.

"What can I get you," said the bartender. Invisible men whistled from dim corners exposed by bursting disco balls.

"Fernet and Anchor Steam."

He gave the bartender a buck, took the shot, drank the beer. He stepped out to call Octavia, his mother. Their phones were off, and in a flash that high encroaching upon his auditory incapacity fixated on the perilous, hypnotizing hum of an overhead air-conditioner's dripping drone. He felt perfect and returned next door to the counter after a cigarette. Last night was today was last night, then. His torn paper stool had retained its warmth.

"A friend and I spent the night at this young mother's apartment in Portland. She was the same age my mother was when she had me, and her child, one year old or eleven months or something, looked just like me as a child. I awoke with a vicious hangover and went grocery shopping with her mother who lived next door. I bought a Harp and drank it for breakfast, and no one minded at all. In fact, they seemed to encourage it, as everyone had a hangover but did not dare begin drinking it off. Over this beer I said to the young woman, with whom late into the morning I had been discussing personal philosophies and psycholinguistics: 'In his unawareness of alphabetical instinct the child has become your body; one of zest, immaculate nourish. The coordinated seasons which we've done nothing but name; are they God?'

"And—we had been talking about work or something prior—she sighed, 'Against nature! What is it that we with memory, we the revered, respond to?'"

"What did she say?"

"'The unfathomable.'"

"I do not understand," Brendan said.

William could have sworn it a clever moment and still in his current state of mind it seemed to make little sense. Harold waited for further stories with squinted eyes. He readjusted the yellow flower stemming from the breast pocket of his brown suit and uncorked a bottle of wine.

"Well I'll tell you more about the young mother later. Sometimes I am so clever I have no idea what I am saying."

"Hell, last time I was in Portland there was the most beautiful homeless girl outside of Powell's looking for food—"

"I saw her too!" cried William, punching the countertop. The cashier looked over again, smiled, and caught his attention. She returned to her phone.

"No! This bothered me the whole time I was there! What were you going to say to her? I couldn't come up with anything."

"I don't recall," William said. "I just drank coffee on a concrete bench at dawn on Third and Couch near Chinatown after I got out of the bookstore and wished I would have said something sooner, lifting my head to the blows of the rain."

"Didn't a bunch of us go to the theatre the day you got back? This all sounds familiar," said Brendan.

"Oh, but I never knew that girl in Portland at all. She was married and I wasn't attracted to her. If anything, there is a woman in New York I love, that intrigues me, if we want to dig into the vaults of our sexual interests and just take a trip and go somewhere, gentlemen."

"We should go to New York," Harold said.

William's heart skipped a beat:

"There are some women there, east, that I once loved, and it's funny because I remember not so much each of them as individuals, but the images each woman had to thrust into public view, digital and world, solidify, in order to justify the decisions and chance of her life. They were all different and yet all lived by an unspoken obsession in presenting the opposite of what was in her heart to the world. I could say some of them loved me and I could be wrong, though it would be fairest to say that as each faded from my life, dejected and aloof as I was, it was the image of the Beyond-Woman in each case that I and she fell in love with. We loved the prospect of her great image if we loved at all. I had nothing to offer but a few dollars and a young mind, but just a fool could expect less from more. There was nothing more than what she had to come off as, blossoming into adulthood. Anything else was disgust, and I loved her one by one, the last goodbye on a yellow bicycle. But that was they, and I was so much older then, still yet marching with however long is.

"There is one, though, as I've said, whom is the finest woman I know, gentlemen. Octavia Savonarola is New York City; she is artistry; she is the fabulous artificer, the enabled ascension, the acceleration, the sole woman I've felt complete besides. Some may disagree with my lifestyle, but to they I would inquire: Don't you know that most relationships are someone being loved and someone loving, or two people loving one person? Once you understand this, you can detect it at once in other people. Thus, I know straight out now which women lack that rare trait of eternal question and beauty, confidence, and wit. So far out of the hundreds I've met just one—but still, boys, Brendan White and Harold Smith, you must say now, how sweet it is, how sweet all of it is, don't you find life enjoyable just once in a while?"

"Cheers!" cried Harold, and the three lifted their glasses to the overhead electric lights. The cashier laughed to herself and the people began once again to flood back out onto Polk Street.

For a time they sat at the counter laughing as the sunlight returned, blanketing the slick concrete, shining upon dampened ground, in one fell rummy swoop, it went back down for good.

DEATH, MIDDLE EAST, COMMANDER, CHIEF, CRISIS, SUICIDE, SAFETY, BOMB, SUSPECT, TERRORIST, TERROR, FAME, AWARD, CONTROVERSY, TIGER WOODS—MISTRESS—GENERAL—YEMEN—NOBEL PEACE PRIZE CONTROVERSY

"As long as the descent into Hell is hysterical in its visual roar we will laugh," Brendan said.

"Are you going to finish that doughnut?"

"No."

There stood a porcelain bowl of multicolored, assorted flowers between which piles of sugar packets and napkin dispensers and paper menus leaned. Harold lifted a dead lilac from the soil and propped it beside the largest stem. An unrecognizable blue flower began to tilt. He took a phone call and walked outside.

"Today has been a great day. I need to go by the bookstore later."

Brendan rose from his stool in slow-motion. He walked backwards to the door gazing into the screen of his phone which glowed within his glass lenses and motioned for a cigarette.

William sat at the counter alone with eight songs stuck in his head. Buses swept through the street. He touched his fingertips to the counter. The coffee and whiskey made his mind race like ideological chainsaw sparks, ideas and thoughts bolting out of certain corridors at random, some like pinballs and other like light.

'Contextualize my mind into a permanent action film. Then I realize I have in a sense done nothing all day, which brings a vague smile to my face. I feel as if I'm in a film this moment, a notion I shall be laughing off tonight. Polk Street is an allegorical street. You begin in Hell, sift through purgatory, end at the Pacific Ocean, Heaven, though no allegory is complete without irony: Heaven is a tourist's trap.'

"Your friend reave wallet," she said, pointing to the wallet. "You know him?"

"It is alright, he's just outside."

"Oh."

She looked at the carpet, the television, the pastry display before the window. She adjusted and arranged them. William had never seen such thin arms.

"Did you just start working here?"

"I start two week ago."

"I used to come in here a lot."

She walked back toward him.

"You not come now?"

"Today I came."

"The rain stop."

"Where are you from?"

"Mongolia. You know Mongolia?"

"Yes," William said. "I always wanted to go. When did you move here?"

"Six month ago. I study Engish language and try save money for college."

"Have you been having fun in the city?"

"Fun?"

"Have you been going out, and having fun, and meeting people in San Francisco?"

She looked down, a grid of concern crossing her face. She canceled it and responded, albeit with strain: "I have not a lot of time for fun, I think. Study a lot, work all night. Do you all have big fun?"

"Oh," said William, "I think so."

"That good. But it too cold here. Very *hot* in Mongolia." She cooled herself off with an invisible fan and breathed. Her breath smelled like a wintergreen mint.

She and William smiled together. One day she would read a sonnet at a dead man's funeral luckier than any living; her favorite song may have been Enya: Trains and Winter Rains.

"I don't know," she continued. "Airplanes other day, I don't understand it," and pointed through the window, up at the sky, "Vroom. They wake me up out of bed. Big planes. Why they do that? What is reason?"

"They work me up too. They are loud. I dislike those planes."

"Why they do big show?"

"It is entertainment, and the army, and everyone loves it."

"Like big expensive action."

"And everyone looks with hands on shoulders and cameras clicking and go, 'Ah, wow, boy, oh.'"

"Why?"

"It is a celebration of the military."

"America celebrate military?"

"I think so."

"But don't Americans know their military is dee-gusting? Other day I see, by liberry, big protest. Lot people. World hate America."

"They do that a lot," William said, "But nothing ever happens."

"You like military?"

"I don't pay much attention to it. It's not worth anyone's time. You and I, we don't care about the war. We are too smart."

She let down her hair and turned to the framed family portrait beside the wicker coat rack and William's heart raced with longing.

"That terrible! America is big compricated! What you do?"

"A job?"

"What you do for living?"

"I am a journalist."

"Oh wow! You stay in San Francisco?"

"I live up the street, babe."

"Oh wow! You like live here?"

"I don't have anywhere else to go."

"Did you ever go anywhere else?"

"Most of the country."

"No outside?"

"No."

"You want?"

"I just don't want to do it alone. I don't want to cross the ocean alone."

"You bring friend."

"I'm working on it," William smiled. "Someday!"

"Some day! I—"

Two tall, well-dressed men come in for a dozen doughnuts. Their words sounded like varied chain links upon a dented lock and William felt ill listening to them speak through their noses. He finished his drink in twenty seconds. So many people rented films and never watched them and returned them and got fined and still never watched the films.

The men hit on the woman and asked her identical questions to William's.

'I cannot allow myself to care, this notion being a reaction to the fact that I care.'

"Sorry about that," Harold said, stumbling in through the doorway, "Hadn't talked to him in a while." He drank his coffee and wiped his face with a handkerchief. "But I need to get going soon, I have to drop my bike off and do some stuff around the house, but we should go to that party later come by around nine, bud!"

"That sounds good. I will do that."

"Is anything happening with that girl?"

He sat beside William, picking up his wallet from the table, and peeked inside of it. He tucked it into coat and buttoned it up halfway.

"It's strange. It seems obvious that I could be interested in her flesh and flesh alone. She knows basic English and has only lived here a few months."

"I think that's all of it, though. Sexual. Everything, sexual. Come into the world through a cock, that type of thing."

"Shot out of a cock," William said.

"Yes, well, see I mean it's fun to pretend otherwise, but things seem less magical than they do animalistic to me."

William nodded.

"It is November."

"Don't you think that's the case?"

"It is the case."

"So, make the best of it."

"Alright."

"Brendan is waiting for you on the corner."

"Why on the corner?"

"He got into a fight with Carolyn."

"See you soon!"

Harold threw his arm around William:

"And you know what we'll do tonight, old buddy?"

"What will we do?"

"Go down to the damned docks of Fisherman's Wharf and talk till dawn!"

He threw a dollar onto the table and bolted outside into the evening.

William waited around for the young woman to come out from speaking with the older woman in the back. After five minutes she had not come back out and William stood to go. He did not want to meet Mary at all. He stood beneath the old-fashioned television set and watched its reflection run along the Plexiglas encasings. She still did not come out. He felt most awful when the door opened, the bell rang, and still no one came out of the back room.

On the street he did not see Brendan and began walking downhill.

"Hey," his voice rang out from steps. He stood, dampened and disheveled, arms spreading out the creases in his crumpled jean jacket.

"What happened?"

"I have to go see Carolyn. We got in another fight."

"That is a shame."

"Let's go to a bar and then I'll go see her and we'll all go over to Harold's and then go to the party."

"There are no good bars between here and Carolyn." William did not want to return to the bar next door.

"We'll go drink out of the bathtub on Van Ness."

"I have no desire to do so. I have to go meet Mary at the back of her restaurant and retrieve an expensive bottle of wine and take her out to dinner and tell her—"

"Tell her what?"

"That I'm going to move out of the house soon."

"Where to?"

"I don't know."

"Do you have money?"

They continued walking down the street. Brendan knelt to tie his shoe.

"We'll go to the Rex Café. It's right over here."

He finished his beer and stood to go.

"I would rather go to an alleyway and carve my initials into the ground with thumbtacks," William said, "Than go to the Rex Café."

They walked downhill until Brendan began to explain his financial problems and correlating philosophies.

"You know why the poor are looked down upon, William?"

"Why?"

"Because they may need a dollar sometimes and as our minds were developing we were told nothing beyond the value of money and entertainment. That is it. Don't get me wrong, it has value; the value of emptiness. Emptiness. And now it's in our pockets; the money and entertainment are in our pockets and we are on indefinite standby. We watch TV on phones. We watch movies on phones. We have 946 friends. That is the truth. That is damned truth and the truth is damned fine. Why? Because no one wants to be the one to question this because anyone who stands alone in honesty is destroyed by the darkness of those who know they've been programmed, and the program entails a violent opposition to any other way. It takes a while to understand things and most people understand them too late if at all. So, realize what is happening now, not what may happen, and get beyond it," Brendan inhaled, walking beside William with his hair in disarray. "Wow," he concluded. "I have no idea what I am saying."

"You should get some water before you go see her."

"I don't need any damned water. Hey, let's box."

Brendan took his phone and his wallet out of his pocket and put his fists up in the air.

"We've got a big night ahead of us," William said. "You seem in bad shape. You're making midnight-sense at sundown."

"Don't talk about the way I talk. Don't be hypocritical."

"No, no, I don't mean it that way, I mean—"

"And anyway, I don't drink water."

Night had fallen.

At Broadway, a hundred cars raced to and fro the glowing, echoing tunnel, and Brendan began for Carolyn's apartment. William took off alone down Polk Street.

He looked over his shoulder and let the cold wind spread along his cheekbones. Sheets of cold wind raced through flashes of red and blue headlights, ground level cornerstones of yellow tape and traces of a faint siren. The foghorn sounded as Brendan dissolved into the light of the tunnel.

He passed by La Boulange with good warmth burning within him and looked through the windows at all the couples and acquaintances drinking Chimay and iced lattes and eating fresh vegetable panini. He and Harold had spent the good last summer there when they knew the staff and everything was given away for free and went to the roof at night, or when Janine had taken him there, or when he had taken Melody Nelson there.

Passing through, he marveled, it was always the strangest to catch a glimpse of someone who looked identical to someone else, and in William's case someone whose soul he'd once loved because it had mirrored his own in its obscurities and indescribable depths.

'Anything else was disgust and I loved her, bought her a yellow bicycle at sunrise some years ago, and I loved her, and though the window grows thin from a distance, I will never forget such gentle translucence at dusk. Ah, Abigail!'

Next door a man, made of tin rods, threw imaginary machetes at the seeping moon from an anonymous restaurant's stoop. Hundreds of them screamed all day of their waking lives, limbs thrown like rags, languages created because the world didn't understand such provocateurs of starlit telegrams, no one could, and his eyes were bolted open and looked damned. Looming headlights flashing past, grave as the torn feather in his corduroy cap amongst the ironic drowning motors of the ritziest automobiles and bass blaring from apartment buildings, an enigmatic mashing through the shopping bags and ringing telephones with his hands in his pockets feeling nostalgia for the present. Thick night fog grew immense and began to pass through Polk Street in its great gust of frost, like walking through a cloud, and behind William and to the right dissolved the light and echo of the Broadway Tunnel.

Beginnings of another deep foghorn resounded with each quarter-block toward Beach, its vivid sound rich in ominous texture. Out front of the voodoo shop someone played electric guitar blues on storefront mats for a collection of rubber skeletons.

Then ahead through the fog in scattered rags were the men who've made the same walk as William, they were in the near-distance stumbling and coughing and crying, crawling back up Polk St. from Fisherman's Wharf, the Pacific Ocean, six hundred crushed cans being dragged up the street and all the way out to Church, as there is nothing ahead within a circle but another slight bend.

Outside of sky-blue mansions William stopped to observe what appeared a fresh, positioned corpse; there were no swarms of flies yet gathered. He had seen a dead man once last year on Geary Street the third night he was in San Francisco, but even that had not registered at all until he'd seen the next. The mansion towered behind him as if a frozen tidal wave given to come crashing down and fall upon anything caught its shadow at any moment and the enormous gated house instilled William with less awe than anxiety.

He looked over the strange familiarity of the dead man and knew time slipped when one was faced with out-of-nowhere, absurd images and the image was interpreted, or indoctrinated as fact, there where the weightlessness of sound stood right up and extended its lucid hand.

'. . . a new reality is hatched; one wherein my uncle's teeth have become coal-black, his wardrobe that of a blind man whose aid has left him. I think of this man below me in silence, the sounds that break through around me are mutated blurbs of a discarded soundtrack.'

He stood to walk.

'Ahead, to the ocean, to the riverfront docks of shops and neon lights, to the wine, my key to the city for the sky is folding up, closing for time, Mexican children behind me shrieking, giggling with laughter and eating ice cream cones, and an anonymous man, myself, walks before them thinking of his aloneness in the universe , and to think of as a child ever longing to grow old, although I can say never have I longed for youth much once it had been absorbed from me, their palpating leaps up and down with their dark-skinned father with jet-black mustache who lights a cigar between his teeth, smiling, they are heading to the water and by the time they get there it will be night and the sand will be cool and they walked on this side of the street where no man has died but ahead to the Pacific, death then is nothing but some rumor, onward to where the children can cast stones into black water watching their reflections ripple, father with a faint tear in his eye that will never be known, but for now I let them pass me by, the father nods at me, still smiling, and the smoke is rich, cream-like as it levitates into the shape of a disparaging cone funneling in its light blue evaporation beneath nocturnal street lamp to the etherized sky.'

He neared the end of Polk Street as the moon came out at last from behind the buildings and for a moment appeared as if a papier-mâché oval run over with rolling grayish oils, white oils. William tilted his sights ahead and prepared himself to blend into the crowd below, weaving to and fro until fog horns hammered through the nightlit layout of the city, groaning whirlwinds, auditory stampedes.

There was the laughter of a thousand distant voices, three blocks or so until Beach Street where funnel cakes filled the scent of ages, sand rustled in the organ-echoed winds of fire. The last shops shut down and those who came to panhandle on that side of paradise now began to slouch back toward Market Street or fall into the holographic hole of its ground, to again fold up like human accordions and to have their minds rearranged.

Autumn leaves were blowing by the last blocks of mansions.

"Most of us have written a thousand books," Nielsen had once shouted into his ear over the raucous cries of jousting ecstasy and careless movement of a dim, packed bar on Passyunk Street in Philadelphia with a transmission signal of a look in his eyes, shaking off a winter-beaten cough to add: "And why not? Art is simple as long as it does not leave the head."

'Bless his—damned soul, bless his soul this very moment, you who have no ears nor arms nor template.'

Trolleys and double-decker buses heaved uphill. Tranquil gazes over twinkling glasses of wine with the lure of a traveler's windmill at midnight spun around and heaved into flightless trances.

His hair was blown back by the ocean beyond and all its vibrant dreams which created facial indentations of age that drifted by the windows of vision like whirling smoke. He walked ahead, microscopes within his mind, gazing up again at the moon which shone above the blackened sea of glittering starlight.

At North Point William watched the children play baseball. An old man walked through automatic garages of beige beside pink and through a maze of trimmed hedges with hatred burning in his eyes. William thought of the city and of being born and what he would do tonight and knew not what to do in life anymore but enjoy himself. He would think of that young woman from Mongolia, he would break up with Mary again, he would go out again, and it wasn't all too bad. He had mere days in California and he feared nothing. Mere days were all one needed. Men and women could do such much in one day and one day if they were reminded they would not have such days and nights soon.

He had not gotten down to work in San Francisco and it was not last summer and still it was just more normal a life than he had anticipated when he arrived in the city. It was aesthetic dissatisfaction and still he had made a return trip, one which prompted his ultimate return to New York City. He thought of his first year at the University, of meeting genocide survivors, children who wandered the Earth in our lifetimes who had seen their mothers and fathers have their heads sliced clean off by masked swordsmen on horseback, who had wandered for years living off of urine and mud, who had been eaten by lions, who had broken their legs hopping fences through rifle fire, and this was one issue of a thousand we'd dare not discuss in fear of now dispraising famous men.

Another 19 roared past and uphill as the near-sea night shaped itself proper, dissolving into the Aquarium where the last Polk Street sign, END, was in sight as he began to tread downhill.

There was something about the street, he knew once again, that was allegorical, perhaps, when stopping into the bodega for a beer. He drank outside as to time himself for that brief meeting with Mary and contemplated invention, desolation, hunger, beautiful ugliness, the mist of a sky-blue tip whenever he thought of youth or of the day, the world, the roses, the beautiful minds and the damned, the old friends remembered, the scents, the songs, the ecstatic commotion of the city, the kaleidoscopic riches of dreams and ambition, internal disintegration and the rebellion against it, the exuberant chaotic hue of one towering nocturnal skyscraper after another, the misaligned and deformed land which surrounded that city, peeling within which were the radio broadcasts, one million ringing telephones beginning to draft suicide notes as transient victims of another false war, the inheritance of spiritual invocation and mass bells at noon up on the Sunday Hill, and the anonymous lovers' arms, draped like a quilt across one's breast, at nine o'clock clear in the morning.

Birds broke in swarms across the rippling immense ocean to the torn curtain of the twilight sky. Through his mind passed uncoordinated ex-lovers, friends, new loves, new friends, and all the lifetimes of memories bound in quilt-rays of sun-blasted color as the sounds of the city break and rose around him. He walked ahead with the warmth of the sun inside him as the oceanic fever-air ran tranquilly across his face out front of the aquarium. Echoing sirens slipped into silence and he looked out to the distant crowd coming and going beneath street lamps beside the Pacific Ocean and wondered where the lost loves all went, where were they now, and if they would remember him, and what would happen in America, Polk Street?

He looked up at the street sign again: END. He drank his beer and began to walk ahead to the light and the enraptured nuance of the November crowd.

He thought of Harold and Brendan, in no time within another bar discussing the solution to the problems of the world over whiskey, Harold readjusted to the city life and filled with sudden indispensable knowledge:

"The texture of such fresh air of today, you see, seems to say the audacious dehumanization of our times is possible against only a population convinced its best interests, individual and intellectual, sexual and vocal, are unfashionable, and though I concentrate upon this moment, this very moment—Ah see it's gone, no now again, here, I've got it! Ah, no—the excursion's over with, we've broken up for good this time, love's out of my life, my tears still streaked across my face and now I keep an ear out for what's what and so I don't know what I want, but I think I know what is needed, and there's William marching forth in some ominous barge down Beach to get his wine to share!—Then out into the distant lights of the city here where we all meet again, do you know?"

"Ah," Brendan would have said, nibbling on a toothpick, "The look in my eyes makes me more of an outsider, my eyes which are the frontlines of my mind, than any outfit I could string together! We'll all be alright!"

"No, no, enough of ye metaphysical rambling," El announced. "And back unto the ominous barge of life."

"What have we even done today, William? Bartender! What have we done?"

"Ah, my boy," William would have said, "Just know that the chosen route's Polk Street, in San Francisco, and that is the end of it, for the night ahead is a bending collage of light-bulbs and bodies, briefcases and vocal lanterns, broken-bottled dreams and brilliant minds and songs to sing and songs that can save one's life, so you'll turn the next corner and go again, and I'll go ahead and turn another corner raucous, and we'll meet again amidst this languid universe of death and within it I want to swing like a wrecking ball into things and I will have it no other way! Swing like a wrecking ball into the people of this street, this colossal gravity! Millions of multicolored lights and people and voices in this here city ahead, see look at it glowing through the window, the men and women out there between the shops and docks of the Bay and if you fear you're dreaming and wondering then know it is the highest task to shun the perverted dreams jammed down our throats on a basis, gentlemen, and so what time this place close Sonny West, and everyone will feel better tonight and tomorrow!"

A tall, darkened man began to play drums in the middle of Beach Street as a tugboat crept across the sea, its rippling liquid shadow of light rushing to the shore. The percussionist's pace accelerated like a racing heart and William stopped to pay complete attention.

For a mile at once everyone heard the man warm up with a percussive gunshot before leaping, escaping, projecting an internal explosion. His percussion sounded as if auditory form being stripped from gravitational synthesis, particles from an imploded disc shattering throughout the atmosphere, each vein of each passing arm a nocturnal stream rushing and over-flooded with ferocious water. Hundreds of people sleepwalked in the direction of the furious sound, that of harmony in chaos, that of cathartic simplicities.

The police tried to no avail to have the man stop his playing. Everyone on the street got together and screamed at the police and threw rocks at their windows until they went back to Hunter's Point and the man did not stop playing drums for a standing ovation instead standing to prolong a raucous solo and continue.

His song beat on still more and echoed all throughout the crowded, lit-up streets of stands and restaurants and bars beside the ocean. The man paused a moment; through choruses of clapping hands William looked once over to Fort Mason looming atop the long hill.

Then a massive collage of contact rushed through the oceanic air like bomb after bomb that fell in lands no one had ever seen before, and the rising of a frantic percussive preemptive strike. Everyone turned their heads again to the drummer, entranced.

"Where do we come from, where do we go?" William liked to think old Harold Smith was asking from afar. "And yet, my son, no matter! For to the contrary belief ours is a new generation after-all; it lacks any sort of mirror, although if there were to arrive one it'd echo through to the new pathos, William, as I said long ago upon the swaying docks of the Bay:

"All gods haven't died, for they've never even existed but within the imagination of mortals! So all finite wars have been fought giving way to our infinite warfare routed in subliminal-fascist human emotion! The faiths of men and women have long been shaken and now begin disintegrating into the unquestioned realm of technological impulse, and faith in the western world had become emotional capacities set in the hearts of emerging, trivial gadgets, the stage directions of modern coliseums!"

"We come," William recalled, pushing through the crowds and lights of Beach Street, "To bury Caesar. His ides of March or June. He doesn't know who is here nor care."

"So we move on into the next world, and if there is no such thing it's not our fault, and in such a case we go on into nothingness the way we came into the world; breathless and with neither remembrance nor reconciliation, conceptual hallucination; if conscious eternity exists it might quite be Hell, and then thus our lifetimes some flawed paradises to begin and beget all falling ash and dust and such spectral angular chrome—"

Ye William Fellows, Bard of Polk Street: Moses fit in a little basket, thee out on the sunny side of the street, cadging a multicolored coat, and the dreaming moon.

William turned right after a time and away from the sound and water, looking once to the moon. It looked as if made of the collective leaden wax trimmings of Orpheus's "Hymn to Jove" and Roger Bacon's miscellany, souls animating stars. Then he looked to that city he loved, in some sense his home and in another figurative sense his father and walked back into its night.

Should Lanterns Shine

IT DID NOT HAPPEN the way it should have happened, but then that was the way most things happened. For William knew he should have gotten in touch with everyone that mattered on the east coast and west coast to check in, to inform, to talk, but it did not happen that way; en route to the bookstore to retrieve a book on John Milton he had tripped, fallen, and gone blind.

∾

Sightlessness caught him off guard less than his immediate reaction: *I suppose now I must suffer in earnest if I am to escape the prison of nothingness and make an attempt at the One.* He was blind for three days, recovering bits and pieces of vision like a terrible delirious puzzle, his heart dependent upon Octavia's soft voice of healing all the while.

"In all seriousness, William, call the ambulance whenever you are ready. Let us not be outrageous here—you can chase after the Thomistic good and the Gospel of St. John without decisively destroying your eyes."

He found himself with a brain less exhausted than bewildered as he read the Gospel of St. John with what felt like new, stronger vision, never bothering to return life to his phone that had, alas, passed away, as through dreams and visions the pilgrim entered into realm of blind seers, Ignatian cave, blind language on the conditions that he would preserve the secrets of the rites with the One. 'There are simply no more philosophical arguments to be had, as they are unfit for what I am after; philosophy has led me to this point. Let me never waste my time again in such mirages!' The way it happened was a weeklong party with Harold Smith reminiscent of last autumn and a thousand other characters. Again, it culminated along Geary Street with unspecific plans to go back to the races in Oakland for fun. Everyone was feeling too ill save William and

Harold and William could feel pleased when the day of the race, the day of departure, arrived gray and drizzling. He hadn't the energy to make up some story or another and could not bother saying goodbye to anyone. Brendan had been shopping when the day of departure arrived cold and gray and William decided to leave him his few belongings and his bicycle behind, everything save a spare outfit, folder compact with papers, toothbrush and a half-drained bottle of wine on the old mantelpiece.

Mary had been passive-aggressive, one of corporate feminism's various forms of mental illness, throughout the week and with finals approaching she seldom left her room. People were moving in and out upstairs whenever William stopped in. The passive-aggression seemed as if a predictable act in a play running far too long off Broadway; the technological subject of which seemed the sole consistency of their generation.

He looked about the studio and knew he'd achieved nothing as an artist, as a revolutionary, or a spokesperson. He laughed. It was less a matter of throwing in the towel than a matter of realizing life was not worth being spent trying to create something immortal which would dissolve into the abstract, finite catacombs of thoughts in mere years regardless. Dust to dust, and a reconsideration of spiritual matters, as he daydreamt of bringing his dreams and desires up to the Bronx of his mother's childhood, and Fordham University, Martyrs' Court.

He liked to think that in New York he could absorb the western experiences from his memory and get to work and yet he could not help but die with a smile on his face when he thought of how little money he had left.

Light spread across the reflective streets of the cold, dampened city. 'Holy, holy, holy' cried William, running a fresh apple under water.

Harold, despite cold rain, had insisted upon meeting outdoors:

"Well come on, now, you're going to the Eastern Bay, the East Bay, my son and everything and Hell, and who'd rain ever hurt! No one! No one at all! I'll be in Duboce Park in the misty rain on an old bench with my old waterproof bag! Come on! I leave the second this phone call ends!"

He had mustered the energy to produce a white lie to Harold in that by evening he was going to the East Bay. He did not mention that he was heading to the airport but instead to El Phillip's apartment, as the Rockridge stop was also on the way to the airport. He packed his folder and his bottle of wine and looked at the old house from the street. It was as if he'd never lived there. He wondered if he should have lived in the East Bay after all, yet that he would never know, and for that reason he could now realize he must sever himself from the material triviality of fate cloaked in human form, as a thing of the past. Eternity was not a thing of the past. And so he read until the train came in.

At West Portal young adults walked single file from SFSU through brick pathways to winding streets beneath enormous umbrellas. They walked past, shedding colorless eyes, speaking of celebrity encounters and profiles and reality television characters into headsets; their automatic eyes and bodies had come to overtake the city as few else could afford it any longer. The most noble were finding that there was no longer much substance worth starving over. Once the bridge had gilded textures shining upon either side of its embodied form and now the bridge seemed to lay in ruins beneath the emptied, godless sky of vacated vocal cords and disease-plagued carnality. Utopianism was in the end some perversity, preceded by its pathetic doctrine of convenience.

As if out of thin air Harold stood before William in his long, navy-blue raincoat on the bench in Duboce Park:

"Hey—hey, old pal. How are ye? Let's go down to this new café!" He squinted, outstretching his hand toward Church Street.

The distant bells of the train passed through its clay tunnel. The silver-red train crept by as his finger shook in the rain like a speedometer latched to a bullet.

In the café William had no trouble hiding any sort of emotion nor reflecting. Harold spoke his mind at once with a near psychic precision as they sat in the crowded café in the middle-afternoon.

"All go well with the roommates and all of that?" Something caught his eye as he removed the raincoat and hung it to the wooden hanger. "God-damnit," he whispered, leaning across the rectangular marble table, looking back and forth: "Everywhere you go everyone is the *same*! They're *identical*! Plugs in their ears, arrogant all their faces, their eyes," his hands shook as if he voice rose , descended, and cracked, "They are all just staring into the void, lost—now, m' boy, you know why?"

"Why?" William asked.

"Because we're all brought up, damnit, to believe we're special these days, and none of us are!"

They sat in the small, dim-lit bar on Market Street by the window drinking beer.

"What—what do you think Brendan will end up doing?"

"If he goes to southern California he's doomed."

"How," Harold said, nervous.

"Because anyone that leaves northern California for southern California just seems doomed. No one, well, it is just the sort of place where one finds nothing. They didn't during the Dust Bowl and they won't during the death of western civilization. In southern California one cannot even find an escape."He recalled Heather with sullen clarity, she whose words he had just paraphrased, and reflected upon her old yellow raincoat and nocturnal Dolores Park. Someday when everybody's older and wiser—

"Then where, where," shouted Harold, "Where can we go anymore?"

"Either inward, or wayward, or something, just to remain in some sort of motion, psychological, the mind on fire as you've said, or traveling, just moving, moving to the rhythm, as a man named Gideon once told me when I was much younger and much fuller of energy."

Harold glanced at him in the antique mirror as trolley cars passed through the emptied, rain-washed streets.

"What rhythm, my son, what rhythm?"

"Oh I don't know," William said, "Just drinking in the afternoon on a rainy December day is all I'm thinking about, what I'm doing." He took out his phone as memories began to flood his mind with aching clarity, a crystalline counteraction to his fable. "After this beer I had better be on my way."

Jerusalem, William Fellows knew, had never been his home. And so that explained, or began to explain in ways, that in departing now from Harold Smith upon Market Street in December he felt a way he'd never felt before: As if he were leaving home for the first time.

Harold bit his nail. He knew everyone in San Francisco. He would have a thousand options once William left, and still it was most difficult to part ways.

"Well I'm not doing too much today, you know, and I was thinking of course, Hell, I'll ride out with you to see old Phil Cohen and help you get situated and then we'll ride back out tonight, of course, it'll be nice out tonight I hear, and we'll come back, then, and meet—Saturnalia! The God-damned Parade!" He leapt out of his stool, his skin, and grabbed William by the arm. "Don't you *recall*! We used to say—"

"Don't worry old bud—I'd better go alone," William forced himself to say. He looked down to his reflection in the glass and finished his beer. Without warning Harold leapt to the bar counter and brought back two glasses of Fernet.

"Well I know all of that, but I've not much to do, now," and his voice trailed off. ". . . still why, why do I feel that time's running out? I'll take a ride out with you to see Phil! I'll pay for the subway, bud!"

"You know the sensitivity of arriving places—I had just better go in it alone."

Harold looked through the window at beggars dragging their blistered, discolored feet through the rain, crying through reddened eyes and moaning through toothless mouths, picking up old saturated cigarette butts from the ground and preserving them in uncovered soda cups. He looked on, and for the first time since William had met him, he seemed as if unsure of what to say.

"It's that damned feeling, you know, as if you're going farther than just the East Bay—See well, I've got a good head now, I'm getting silly, but it's always nice to be able to ride your bike to a bud's house, I know you know my son, it always just seems further away than it is sometimes, on old Market Street it seems further away, further away than it is." He lifted his Fernet high, wavering, and continued, "The city won't be the same without ya, but man, I know, I *know*, I just got into town too late but I knew then also, when you arrived, I knew I could call on you, you arrived under the same signal as me, my son, so a toast! We are blood brothers! Never knew someone whose life had been so like my own! We'll be alright! Just a commute away, bud, right—we'll do Dolores Park the first nice day we get! Toast to that, to you, to San Francisco old bud! And New Year's Eve—"

Nauseating guilt filled William with the impact of instant sobriety at the end of a long bender. Then he knew, raising his glass one last time and faking a smile, that there was nothing to do but just let him know, no matter how painful it would be. William felt he would be admitting something to himself. Twenty-five minutes would pass and he'd be at the airport, and it would be better at the end of it all to settle everything with Harold Smith. Their timing had been misaligned the second go-around, but then that was the way time worked. It worked for and without being, like a soundlessly tolling bell.

Outside, at departure, he began:

"I suppose we ought to talk a bit before—"

"We'll talk later, tonight!" Harold cried. "It's raining, m' boy—we can't stand out here now and get sick and get pneumonia! We got places to go, people to see! Long night ahead of us—long life ahead of us! Yee-hee!"

William tried to shake off his drunkenness and speak before he convinced himself that it was fine to say nothing at all, but it was too late.

"Yee-hee! Yee-hee-hee!" Harold sang through cupped hands, dancing in the sidewalk through passersby, doing a circular jig and kicking his heels together. He went out into the street and made Indian calls and yodels. "Hoo! Hoo-ha! Ha- ha—hoo! Yee-hee-hee!"

An officer on the other side of Market yelled for him to get out of the street. His suit was in tatters and he violently, in a pattering corkscrew, clapped his hands together. Several madmen on the street began to clap with him and overpowered the officer's voice.

"Yee-hee-hee!"

The policeman drove off.

"And anyway," he returned breathless, "You damned nut, half of your things are safe and sound with Brendan anyway! We'll see you tonight, my son!"

William could no longer laugh. The bums dispersed and Harold's sudden facial recognition of sorrow was a look he'd never seen the old vagabond wear and it made William worry perhaps he looked a bit too morose.

"Bud? Bud, you alright?"

"Ah," William sniffed, "You know sometimes I just get down, down in the dumps." A tear fell from his eye. Harold handed him his handkerchief:

"Well, Bill, now you listen here: It's just begun, all of this." He outspread his arms to the city. "And the odyssey of, of our lives—because we're not statues and we never will be but no, no now I'm saying things I heard you say, remember to remember but now, no, I was correct—it's all just beginning—for our types of people, you see, it's always just beginning! Never cry, old bud! We've got portals of discovery in this life, of course, and so when you feel down, now, what did old Nietzsche say, what would that old lunatic have said—or no, damnit what would William Fellows have said? What would *he* have when he was deserted in San Diego for God's sake, what would he have said when the whole country was at the dawn of a police state? We know the most when we are alone, now of course, and oh Hell, now I'm getting all sentimental! It's the ascension, old bud, the acceleration in life, the art of living so of course we'll have to suffer a bit more than other people, but damnit I was in jail, now I don't mean to dwell—but people like us in that old Book of Job, what did it say? 'The innocent shall divide the shall.' That's it bud, the innocent shall divide the silver, and the highs we know could wipe out entire coun-tries—the psychological highs, the drinking sprees, the traveling, throw-ing caution to the wind! No longer are we martyred slaves to time—leave that to other people—and never again shall we be, old bud, my old bud William Fellows!"

The rain had paused a moment prior and at the end of Market Street which had been a somber gray wall in the sky all of the month the sun crept through and at once relinquished William's internal misery as light fields in consonance reflected in the hundreds of windows and brought warmth to the street. A new dawn would rise where another had fallen; clouds made way for a rainbow, and all the reemerging persons of the street turned their collective attention toward its sudden brilliance in the shrouded winter sky.

"So now you, you old bud, you call on me when you're all situated and we'll take it from there—because now, in this case, I'm going to Do-lores Park! Good old Dolores Park! Ought to be drying by the time I get there! Yee-hee-hee!"

They embraced; they departed. William walked to the subway, glancing back every nine or ten steps. Harold walked with his overcoat thrown over his shoulder until he was up near Polk Street growing small-er, smaller through the street of mutilated copper linings.

Market filled up at once, crowds rushing to and fro the trains and buses, the shops and the newspaper stands spilling forth with people, and it was as jam-packed as William had first remembered Market Street some summers past, when all of the streets were alive with mystery and rapture, fate and wonder, life and death, then when there was so much more than routine and man was limitless and man had built the railroad tracks across the country by hand for other men to travel as similar men and women had constructed the communicative language to transport knowledge and experience and innocence and to reflect and learn, to and live and burn and the streets were alive again as he fell through the cas-cading voices and the jewel-soaked sun remained shining through little parting clouds.

That was the last William ever saw of old Market Street, with night just beginning to formulate through uncontrollable, bitter tears, and Har-old was off, and that was San Francisco, as William turned around once more to the dampened subway steps.

He never saw that just at Polk Street Harold had turned around once more to wave although that was fine because William heard him cry out something, anything, but something, his voice echoing and resounding above the collage of voices of the street, yet when he bolted above ground one last time through dozens of people Harold was gone. That last farewell cry from Market Street seemed to contain the inner auditory landscape of burning stars, or the heart pumping blood into the body.

William looked at San Francisco for the final time through fierce tears, and felt salvation burst through his heart. He turned, descended the staircase, and could feel the tears burn his throat, and for the first time in a long time. Carnivalesque, or Saturnalia, had, at last, come to an end.

The poets from across the water recited in the subway:

"As the sun cannot set without perceptive permission, instructions written still as the hospital lens, our lives outlined by nocturnal ends. Hence one steps toward Eden as cracked skulls spit toward platoons—the wound willow weeps as the dead must sleep, for she is more alive than I who awaken parading to the ramshackle corner of my choosing, and by night and by plight the hour of my life was me rewound, unglued and wandering concept-planet. Light-bulbs break needless as any hours' wine glass, and silence becomes this grave."

He threw them a coin, thought of New York City, all the highway lights en route, of re-arriving and living there in the shelter of his lady's arms, and hopped the turnstile. For all the chaos, mistakes, and sorrows, the pilgrim had long ago promised himself that those first six hours in San Francisco alone, the night he had arrived last summer, were worth whatever transpired next. And while his heart was now set on higher things than the night alone, he kept this promise between himself and the One. Thus William Fellows tipped his hat to the Bay, teary-eyed and worn out. She, and all her blinding fog, had fathered him well.

One Way of Proceeding

He retrieved his ticket and stepped out; vomited, drank, vomited, proceeded:

"There's something ever egotistical in mountaintops and towers," William incoherently espoused on Octavia's answering machine, as the angel appeared on the other line. Pouring rain fell outside of the airport and his flight was set to leave in ten minutes.

Her voice, that of artistry, was all that remained of William's future, and it was all he needed to hear any longer. Wherever he would go, moral abyss or palatial structure, he would go through and with her.

"William! Is all set to go?"

"Aside from the inestimable frivolity of modern airports I believe I shall arrive on time." She gasped. William exhaled. "No, no, I'm standing outside of the line just now, as I speak. I brought some little bottles of Old-Grand Dad to mix with seltzer water. It'll be a good, boozy flight."

"Have you eaten anything?"

The sincerity in her voice relinquished the sorrow and longing latched to his blood.

"I had some coffee ice cream just now, a whole-wheat bagel earlier. I'm fine."

"Are you excited?"

"Yes."

"How good was the ice cream?"

"Oh, Octavia—let me tell you—if your cells had a doorbell it would have rung with all of that sugar as if Bach had sung of Christ in the bathtub while lightning struck."

"So soon! I'll see you so soon!"

"Run it all by me again, deary."

"I leave for Europe tomorrow with my father and return in a week. During the week I'm going to set you up with some friends and one of them has a room opening up."

"OK."

"Otherwise you can stay with me, but it's always nice to have your own room."

"Yes."

"We'll spend enough time together, you know—how long has it been since we lived down the street from each other?"

"Years," William said, at once dumbfounded in his contemplative numeric.

"Years! I just can't believe it even though I know it to be true. Isn't that always funny?"

William took a sip of whiskey and felt drunk. He shivered, bumbled his lips, felt God tighten the halo of innocence around his overloaded brain in pangs and knots of measurement. He stepped out from beneath the overhead panels and stood in the pelting rain.

"The seconds tick by in life, Octavia, but with you at my side each second is golden and matters, because I love you." He slouched to the end of the metallic barricade and let the rain fall upon his head, then parting his hair to the side as if she could see him.

"You couldn't get here sooner, William—you couldn't! I've bought the worst bottle of wine. It was expensive, too. The first taste was like discounted honey, the next burnt bratwurst. The next—"

"My God, Octavia, what have you become!"

"I am a fool without your presence!"

"The incompatibility of *absence* within the erratic originality of genius," William said, "Will bring us together—more than the bombs that dear old red-faced fools with multiple chins debate on placid sofas—has brought us together—I will always remain at your side, O muse! Our sole responsibility is to our art. In Washington, a glass of white wine is considered adventurous. We'll have no peace until our dreams are fulfilled and everything will go on by until then—except one another, the rarest such as ours."

"William—has the line started moving yet?" He looked behind him in horror and threw his cigarette into a puddle. The line had already boarded. "William?"

"Yes, Octavia, don't mind me; I am a little scatter-brained. I was struck with a torrent of sorrow that was enough to die of starvation beside a ceaseless creek with a filtering stick in hand; thus has so many tears flowed. I thought that I had squeezed the Bay dry, vice-versa, and that we would sever ties like a pair of spurned babes. Nay—I shall miss her tenderly. Should she go further into depravity then I shall say that I'll always missed the spirit I knew in Saturnalia hours, and all the thing her wind said to me. Oh, but the line—of course, just as you speak! I must go. I'll call you from my mother's. See you in a week!"

He raced to the entrance ramp and was smuggled in just as the door was halfway clicked closed. He sat beside an old man and refused to look through the windows upon take off. He ate potato chips and drank whiskey and had two hundred dollars to his name. He felt somewhat lousy until he thought of Manhattan's skyline, and of San Francisco's. He felt limitless and slept an immense, dreamless sleep straight through the first half of the pilgrimage.

The woman across the aisle pulled a bottle of champagne from her corduroy purse. They drank. William told her all about his life with marvelous irony.

"Consider God as limit, ma'am, perceptible in mind and cosmos by comprehending holy amalgamation."

"How about I just drink champagne? My daughter is blind; I just ordered her Homer's *Odyssey* in brail. Her brother's bar mitzvah is soon. Joseph—'he will add.' But tell me, boy, more about the philosophy you speak of."

"I have come to understand that the fine thing about throwing yourself toward everything at once is that in doing so you move as though you have no time to feel hurt any longer, for when you see agony and wretchedness on the horizon you then understand it is no longer a horizon and you must leap to the next option, far beyond the thousandth plateau, into the dawn of a new era."

~

William's last dispatch was a long poem he'd written after several nights revisiting Boswell's *Life of Johnson*. He knew that it could use work, but for the time being settled into the prospect of its containing at least one fair line, and, minimally, guided an appalled reader back to Dr. Johnson:

"Brooklyn": A Draft
By William Fellows

For Octavia, Percy, and Samuel: Three Who Never Let Me Down

The City of God waves goodbye
From the burnt-out docks of Red Hook;
Splintered, spectral, glittering fond,
Closed microscopic like a book.
We were here and there and everywhere,
Though most importantly we were here;
Armorica gone in the teeth
Though once the Bridge was O so near.
Her sailor's striped, well-handled cap
He cradles in his hands
She trades his glass in for a map
Turned denim back to humdrum lands.
This borough had not open arms
Its arms had been cut off
Yet he felt these waters had their charm
As thy muted captain scoffed:
War, infinite, everywhere
And so I took a train;
Hatred, death, insanity fair,
These hidden streets shall kill this pain.
O I wandered far and wide,
Weighed but still found wanting;
To make my home horizon-wide,
This needled, narrow haunting.
The City of Orgies downcast, dire; We land in Brooklyn; meet the choir:
For who here has never scaled Brooklyn Bridge at hours odd,
To throw a champagne bottle through nocturne at Gog?
The suffusion of fog horns and dying lights,
Cast over the railroad the black heavens turned right;
Tulips and chimneys and Klopstock tattoos
Born broken in Bed-Stuy; give me back my blues.
I shall sit upon this stoop reading Horace, till taken away
For this evening is summer; I shall die another day.
Brownstones and bricks and a bird on a wire
With my eardrums cracked, Choral Eucharist Choir.
Free and easy, in the cathedral afternoon, &
Into this Brooklyn night: Another voice, another room.
The wise men drowned in rivulets of gasoline
Still these brutal columns stand, fractured and serene.

Towering majestic, deranged, like complex at Wyckoff;
We had good intentions, Neptune, as sand is soft.
And at the gallery, electric candlelight across her face,
As I standeth to speak, pissing in the fireplace.
The long march toward Evergreen, autumnal mediation;
We stop in silence, plant our seeds of contemplation.
Psalter for the living, wilderness unto bread
Wolfe's exegesis, for only the dead . . .
We spoke of history, friends, someday Gravesend
At the soup kitchen on Chauncey Street, we made amends.
We walk together again, but just to the train
Before a single flowerbed lies untouched by the rain.
Diagonal ruins and a cheap hotel
Amputation, wheelchairs, the sewer's ornamental smell.
Men high above, hammer at wires
While hundreds of the idle photograph another fire
Limbless men, 'neath screaming trains,
Dying to live, they've been driven insane.
Van Gogh, and the smoking skull;
Relatch this hook, replace in full.
Serenity in ghosted streets:
Second-hand box-springs and a pound of meat.
He's got a garage filled with motorboats and grills
Even his son has a trunk filled with pills.
They're way out in Flushing, no Sheepshead Bay
And it is best to miss one's alarm that day.
Through Prospect Park, smiling at her feet
Pregnant girl pushes carriage uphill concrete
One day this winter, a snow-white maze
Walking among Gods, one's soul recaptured;
The blinding blizzards best seen in books
Through which I walk, for the greatest look.
To march across Brooklyn Bridge at sunrise on New Year's Eve
To Grand Army Plaza; we meet, spend the day, and at night we leave.
Back into this kaleidoscope, colossal and tough as nails
Yet at its heart this town wants peace, lest go off its rails.
Outside of the Brooklyn Ale House
Where aging trust-found children espouse
'It's no wonder nobody likes her,
'They're bored to bars with Frida Spicer.'
Enough! Don't look back but ahead!
The voices fade, remaineth the Bread!
The best bread this side of inferno
Greenpoint, U.S.A, solicitude & hitherto.

Saint Kolbe on Bushwick Avenue—
Truck-stop food shall cure thy flu.
J.F. Powers and Spanish leather
'The bartender's great, her name is Heather.'
Stands of straw hats come Jay Street summer
We reunite by this river—Rodriguez: "I Wonder."
Overheard, overhead, windows open wide
Fourth story's clothes line, leaves rustling like tide;
Yesterday's children window shop, do their hair
Tonight the next riot which got us once more nowhere.
The eternal Brownstone hallway
Reminiscent in the dim-wick day
Where elsewhere's simply far away
Linoleums, which curved like clay;
I like a Trappist in his Cell;
Exterior darkness and the wishing well.
I remember you limitless and adorning;
And now all I see is 4 o'clock in the morning.
I don't live in Williamsburg anymore
Eve resides in Flatiron, an old curator's whore.
I just do my thing, sing, read in Prospect Park
Till it gets dark.
Go home and drink, and sing,
Now that my phone no longer rings.
I've found silence is the silver scripture of eternity;
For even I, clanging bell, have heard enough of me.
We're quitting now, it's too much sorrow.
Morrissey through bar door, porch—We quit tomorrow.
Never mind that digital prayer for Israel,
I've an East New York-sized water bill.
Here I stand with chinaware
So that my Greenpoint lady'd fidget
She loves me but abhors my friend
Thrice-great Catholic and a midget
We drank and spoke, and later drank
To twenty thousand leagues of rope
I told her that when Rome got me down
There was in waiting another sort of Pope
Some people called him Alex
The others lyrically insane
Swift had caught his drift at first
Back when he whinnied in the rain.
One day I dreamt I had a job
And woke up in Times Square

That same lady friend she left me
With multicolored coat so fair.
Down in Gravesend there's no poets
Just an owl named Rabelais
He's selling pumpernickel bread
And parking lots in Sheepshead Bay
We meet beneath Manhattan Bridge
Sit down atop a fallen fridge
Where flowers fold through needles fair
Severe mercies, cab horn cavities of air.
'The night is my woman, pale and thin,
'Christmas on Earth, lips like gin
'Prophets of exaggeration flee
'Swimming through some libraries
'In a Psalter's breadth, stilt serenade:
'Balustrades and cavalcades,
'Nineteen black market hand grenades.'
Selling tissues by the box
Smoking glass and cooking rocks
Genesis and Clinton Hill
Unmade beds and head and windowsills.
Schoolchildren squirm toward class dismissal
A widow writes her last epistle.
Scattered souls, primeval schisms
Love defined at last: Medievalism.
Bodega men, prosthetic lore,
Tis a pity I'm a whore
Mother Nature, my landlady
Platonic lust, eye long lazy:
Mother Nature's slinking blouse
Landlady of a haunted house.
Coney Island Baby's lark
No longer sees the end as dark
Walking autumnal Prospect Park
Pocket knife initials' bark.
This little piggy needs liposuction
Cathedral builders scale destruction
John Ashbery's weeping boat
Will you let me wear your coat?
Epigraphs and epitaphs
Cemeteries' cider naps.
Prosaic death to vile tyrants!
Enter kaleidoscopic silence.
Scrape the sky in heartwork patch

Another box, another batch
Eggshell prescience, spark and hatch
The cognition of a world to snatch.
For perhaps you could be my bodyguard,
I could be your Mona Lisa;
We'll move elsewhere for our psyches
Just return for pizza.
Enter ballad of a thin man:
Look how he threatens to dance;
He went to redial mother,
That's when he tore his new pants.
In the end they even came for irons, &
Some ominously encased aprons;
We need a dog to run for President,
Paw-signing peddles bilocation.
When I grow up I'll be an Argonaut
And live in age-old bath tubs;
Santa Claus brought me handguns
From the queen of Flatbush Avenue back-rubs.
Now somebody suggests language
This public luminary
In the night's great chain of being
I told her no, nigh, nary.
Get me to the library
Or I'll go eat a hot dog
She's got McDonald's on the brain
Exhaling mentholated smog.
Stapling pamphlets for the protest
Up against Kent's splintery pole
Nobody warned her about absinthe
She was the Human Asshole.
East New York needs not your prayers
Nor does it need your wishes.
Just a suitcase full of Oxycontin,
And maybe six knishes.
To perish well through hustle
Why I am not a Bertrand Russell
They see Satan fall like lightning, &
Listen to guillotine chords tightening.
For I saw the buildings burning down
Ashen hallways, ghosted towns
Striving forevermore, Euclidean,
Flesh perish through oblivion
Another caustic marching band

Bones collapse and words doth stand.
Remonstration's raped writ wall
Sacrificing life to Baal
Inferno, Adorno, Andante, Pope
Robespierre selling rope
Eyes burning at sunset beach
Truth and method cease to reach
Finality, or a pleasant life
Cardboard boxed up guns, a knife,
Tools of a false cinematic trade
Credits drawn at battery's raid
Drowning in Kieslowski's lake
We're here for war, first cake.
For another day in poverty, weeping
Giving up on jobs, or sleeping
Implode malignant voting booths
Tell her anything except the truth
Dialogue's hermeneutic cage
Sleepwalking through a secular age
There across the bridge and down
Domino, and thrice torn gown
Ring of glass, midday Mass,
After virtue, after class.
Drowned dry, in harbor light,
Long lilt toward solicitude;
Reality is not quite right,
Last goodbyes now framed, imbued.
For I sought by starlight consolation
Through cunning landmine aberration
Some cumulative restoration
Whence stilted, viz. emaciation
Past this funereal subway station
Verisimilitude, our conversation.
We make haste, toward utopian facility;
And thus waste, repeat; G-d damned, futility
Let me sing me land life with sound, vision
Immortalized, sidewalk precision.
Weary with machinery,
And paralyzed by lies,
Questioning congruence swiftly,
She looks down at the crowd and cries.
No more shall they fear for their children's future breath,
For now I am after the death of death.
And Octavia through cloud, a kiss,

Save us alterity and bliss. Midnight
In the Brooklyn garden; reminisce.
She uplifts disruption to the living dead, end of land:
Out there in noontide damnation, she led me by the hand.

Be Ye Transformed by the
Renewing of Your Mind

IN PHILADELPHIA IT WAS six below zero. The dimly lit station lounge was deserted. The city was cast in snow. The lights of Chinatown twinkled like belated ornaments. The hiss of sifting trucks and cars sliding through mountains of exhaust-blackened snow could be heard from the automatic station doors slid open upon detecting strangers wandering, passing through in the barren night.

William took the long walk down Broad Street to find Nielsen. He could not explain how or why, but it was as if his old curmudgeon's voice was calling him out of some indecent anthropology. The pilgrim had trouble remembering what he looked like, and longed to know if he had ever finished his novel about Russian peasants. Would Nielsen know, for instance, that it appears as if it remains unknown whether opposing forces can coexist as per a modern treatment of identity and difference? Or all of this yearning for novelistic discourse: was this mere appearances, formalities, constructive intentions paralyzed by technological commandments as the totality of being as after all a gilded process of opposites colliding and thus producing unforeseen effects, suggesting that there is no absolute control, but rather the implementation of a tautological pathology that is permanently over before it ever begins?

There was no answer at the door.

William stepped away from the apartment and back out along the Avenue of the Arts. Somehow he found relief in this, he considered, for in approaching an old friend one may at times come up with fine fantasies and optimistic hopes; yet upon lack of avail one recalls the truth: William considered Nielsen's most unflattering decline in appearance and dialect; his contempt for the society within which he was most privileged too interwoven within his most basic inquiries, be it hours of the record shop or the noticing of an untied shoelace, and all of it coinciding to prove that he was no longer a friend, one of the last good men waving by, but a symbol of the past, that past which William had grown emotionless whence to consider. He recalled their last uneventful afternoon that began on Dickinson Street with Nielsen taking several Xanax with mineral water, the riot on Passyunk, where William waved goodbye and walked to Mc-Glinchey's for several pints before onto the bus to see Octavia. But now he felt it cordial to try to see the old friend who'd once pointed him in the right direction, and now that it was over with, he felt good to never see him again. The state of Pennsylvania seemed unanimous with bereavement, less a state than another symbol whether one kept attachment from afar or chose to live there. The pilgrim contemplated Old St. Joseph's, a moment before church candles, and blinding sunlight through the windowpanes. Instead William walked through a light sunny snowfall coming down through streetlamps in the Philadelphian dawn. Farewell, O city! Fare thee well, O lost comrades of dialectical mythology, who sought to break the chain of magnets! May love and light in the temple of texts be thine! until the distant headlights neared into the lot and William was returning home in the morning to his mother's small apartment, and off again, and at last, to New York.

The encounter was devoid of emotion which William attributed to Ms. Fellows' recent addiction to tranquilizing medication, anti-depressants, and various other unpronounceable names taped upon sky-blue and gray stickers wrapped around orange cylinders. At breakfast, the surrounding television sets did the majority of the talking. His mother could no longer look her son in the eyes; she seemed afraid of everything that was neither commonplace nor the past, and in wordless reverberating such neurologic hallmarks and neurotic behaviorisms, William knew it best to say little and to speak of the weather and of the beaches in California. He would like to advise her stop biting her nails, but should one be left with a lonesome apartment and the occasional feast of nails, leave well enough alone. Critique of judgement was no longer worth leveling at the dispossessed despite the noble level of intentions.

Ms. Fellows grinded her teeth between pallid conversation and had attempted numerous times to contain the twitch developed in her right hand; William learned not to look. He felt sedated through incarnate disgust which was the town, the distant lights of the casino, the decaying steel mill as if some abstract set of rotting lungs, as he longed to rest upon the air-mattress and had a seminal feeling he would be unable to stay for more than a day before rushing to Brooklyn on his appointment as the anxiety compact within the microscopic household became insufferable right off of the bat. He could not believe his mother's hair was almost white and gray, just as he could not remove his eyes from the bizarre painting of a pale-blue rocking horse upon the wall. She cupped her face into her palms and appeared to be weeping.

"What is it?"

"I may as well tell you," she wept, as if delivering the closing lines in the episode of an outdated soap opera. "I may as well tell you."

"Tell me—what?"

"It is about your father."

"What about him?" William could not help but sit still and restrain from further internalization and regression. Upon hearing the term, he longed to brush off the concept of a father as if ash from a ledge; he knew that his mother had not spoken of such a person in years, and even then through berating difficulties and drunken lost illusions.

Now, in the sober hour of young adulthood, he listened on, swallowing and wiping sweat from his forehead.

"He passed away."

She stood and took their coffee mugs to the sink and washed them. William felt part ill and parts inquisitive and disinclined; he was in sum just another thief in the lifelong night of chaos; perhaps the shroud that was his father had seen the children of the future, and it was enough for him to take a willingness to die young from text to action. 'Perhaps he saw', thought the exhausted pilgrim, 'like Henry James, that the forms presenting themselves as manifest progress and light are in fact the eternal recurrence of ignorance and stupidity; and that which is uncommon may in fact be nothing more than a matter of what is called time.' His lack of order, structural, coherent living crept up on him like bats screaming in a nightmare, hovering and descending winged images reminding him of the unorthodox ascendancy of others as he'd wandered New Babylon having times so swell he could be bothered to do nothing but embrace the good times killing him.

"When?"

"Just a few weeks ago. I called you; your phone was off."

"What happened to him?" He could feel the breath being squeezed, crushed out of his lungs and out of his brain.

"Cancer of some sort out in *Michi*gan," his mother turned around, her eyes bolted open. "The newspaper man called me. How do you like that—oh, and in the bathtub. He died in the *bathtub*. How about that for a fool?" She polished off the kitchenware and began to strut around, rearranging the kitchenette while dancing the dance of a ballerina. He noticed her outfit odd-colored, misplaced—like the décor of a rebellious teenage girl's. "The bathtub—refused a doctor—see, now you know why I left him so long ago. Typical of him. Typical of *him*. We'll do dinner tonight, right?"

She jangled the copper car keys around her finger with a smile and left for work, slamming the door behind her. From the window William watched her get into the old sports car, reverse through the lot, and take off for the highway. There was something in that gesture which seemed like one of the most infantile futilities he had ever seen, and that image seemed to him to absorb, pained, a collective, spiteful reaction to the sudden consciousness of all the metaphysical horror entrancing the land, the psychological horror he was under the impression he alone had escaped.

The smokestacks pressed on beneath the breaking orange sky. He took a bottle of red wine from the countertop, unlatched it, and sat at his desk in the storage room. His mother had bought him a new air-mattress. He wondered what the feeling was inside of him, an illness of sorts? Nay, thirst? No matter: wine and bread.

Locomotive trains passed through, their whistles resounding from an unseen distance. He attempted to read the newspaper, but the text ran together as if liquefied. Then it passed, as all things must, and he realized that what he dealt with now was the greatest despair of his life; neither contextual nor in terms of contentment, but that he had seen these things happen in everybody's life around him, and now it was happening in his own. If anything, he felt as if his father would have wanted him to go on living if he were ever to have cared for his son at all. William was determined to do so and began at once to pack his bags. He would have cried had he not long ago left his heart in San Francisco, and he would have given up, succumbed to nothingness, had the madness he had experienced in the town earlier in the year not already prepared him in its own obscure way for anything whatsoever.

Still, he could not comprehend the death of his unknown father and the psychological decline of his mother. To the contrary he understood that he could but ever attribute a lack of comprehension to such events and he may never know just how to explain or whom to explain the feeling to would he ever be able to transcribe such agonies from his heart.

He sat back down at his good old desk and pulled down the blinds and wondered if his mother had wanted William to come home last year for any other reason but company, and if her inability to express such sentiment had led to her current crisis. He wondered what a young man could do, then or anytime, besides live nobody's life but his own. Thus he set the gift he had bought his mother aside, St. Therese of the Child Jesus's autobiography, to let her one day see it and pick it up if she so chose. Little cherubim, St. Therese! Soothe the Dionysian fire that burns, in the architectural construction of light, and the supplement of all-encircling truth, for they who have lost everything in order to gain all. Who know, like the one who sent thee, that nothing tangible shall last.

"The last anchor is lifted, and I am without foundation, money, or societal structure. All that was a given to the rest, became a mystery to me. The visible is restricted, its opposite a canvas of the sacred mysteries. Shall there be an angel in my corner? The muses set me in a basket, then threw me down a well. O blossoms of heaven, ashes of hell, be with me, Spirit, there when the temple was cleansed; let me immerse myself in the real presence of things by way of mystical annihilation. Be with me, savior, thou hath vouchsafed my life."

Sea and Land a Haze

An evening with Octavia's friends in the city turned, guided by whiskey, into a week-long extravaganza. He knew the instant he left the city to return to his mother's home he would have fell from the loop although he could not bring himself to rely upon Octavia. Her friends were a fine group of people, but she was the one, and she would be the one when William was able to support himself.

On the sixth day out he sat at the long wooden window tables of Harefield Road on Metropolitan Avenue drinking in the afternoon and watching the snowflakes fall as nightfall descended and everyone walked to and fro beneath the ashen sky. In hours some new friends were to come by; he had been staying with some of Octavia's friends on Skillman Street and Humboldt Street where he was to take a room in late-January. He thought reflectively of California, of intellect and love in light of the divine, and still the fuse within him went out bit by bit, as if dampened or defused by his pint of Guinness. The spark had died.

Upon the array of old bar napkins he mapped out economics and drank Brooklyn Lager as the snow came down. All over the city spread horizon like the last agony of days, days of sunbeams cast aglow through crystals at the county fair, where still the political religions reigned supreme in its box of chrome, their megaphoned desires rendering them not a new lease on life but well-handled extinction. Where and whence one turned one's back on the crowd forevermore, walking out of Hell's Kitchen and into St. Vincent Ferrer's, visions of the new life that sang to him on the Manhattan streets like a symphony of angels at the hour of incensing. Whereby a vision struck the pilgrim with furious zeal, as he wandered as an orphan, pondering where next to turn for structure: go, a light shined, against all ideologies and take overnight work at the factory in Jerusalem.

In all of William's idle hours that day nothing else had registered with any similar sense of coherence. He returned to Brooklyn to retrieve his items, bid temporary farewell, and watch the snow fall on Metropolitan Avenue alone, knowing next just what to do without any further instruction.

He wrote postcards explaining his irrationalities to everyone out West, concluding with a parallel effort to Phil Cohen and Harold Smith, whom he just then revisited in the crisp morning hour of summer at Fisherman's Wharf:

"I cannot be your equal; I am humbled by your prowess, your noble deeds, your fame, for you, like me, have gone and lost your mind. William Fellows. P.S. Visit East soon!"

The street was covered in a quilt of snow, structured by the light of overhead electronic lanterns. He stepped out for a walk as the voices mounted over candlelight, wandering down McGuinness Blvd. where the cars and buses rode to and fro Greenpoint, the snowflakes rushing in the blizzard past their headlights. The sky was a purplish gray in one direction, that of Bushwick, and yet when he looked again the tint had evaporated.

"Yes," he knew in his soul, coming back around and approaching the BQE, "Yes, I will make New York the final destination and begin piecing together the events in my life which have transpired and celebrate the days and dreams enriched with the splendors of innocence and experience and I shall write this down once and for all and because there are those who believe it insubstantial and they are for whom the bell tolls then and now unlocking eternity's bloodstained gates."

Seas of conciliatory ideas broke through the night, the flux of omnipresent rebellion, the encapsulation of singular artistry, the pursuit of pleasure and of fury colliding along Kent Avenue in the abstracted light of old Manhattan, walking along the water until the sun reared its commonplace head upon alter, the stage, the enriched men and women whom walk the hollowed streets.

Someone lit fireworks from invisible rooftops just as Octavia was checking in and they exploded straight through into dawn. He'd miscalculated. It was just 3:35. They dashed off to Berry Street where William borrowed the girl's phone for a moment to promise Octavia that he would be moving in mere weeks.

"Greeting from Prague!"

"Angel—I shall take up work at the matchstick factory of Jerusalem, and return soon, reinstated. This shall be the final step before we can the live the aesthetic faith together forever."

"Yes, I love it! We shall teach a new song to the world. For my dear William, I do not recall reading, 'Go forth, and teach the world stupidities'—no; we are to reject lukewarmth and build a holy place in our brief time here on earth, so that the next generations might feel less alone, even closer to the holy lights."

"Where memory dissolves into the One, and the wicked, less than pigs, are left behind to their own devices."

"And where the angels absorb the holy light differently, and love is set to the illuminative capacity for its reception; and the altitudinous hierarchy, with its reign of infinitely mirrored beatitudes, shines in the light of Christ, seated at the right hand of the Father, and voices in the streets are singing glory, glory hallelujah!"

Along the bus ride home William refused any sense of doubt that flickered within him. It was time to understand what exactly an old friend had meant when she had noted the life one saved may be one's own.

A Sea of Glass Mingled with Fire

WILLIAM STEADFASTLY REFUSED ANY reality that came between himself and Octavia. He looked with contemptuous clarity upon the passing land which had left his family and his friends jobless, insane, depressed, suicided; and yet now there was no call for self-destruction or despair, but to take into account the philosophical ceiling: there are questions that language can procure—but this does not mean said language can offer the answers. Only in that realm of Ideas or Forms, or in that clear glass that St. Paul wrote of, would a perfect language let itself be known. This would be the language of theological geography, and it would render one a double choice en route to the grave: Whom shall I serve? How shall I serve? Everything that did less than bring oneself closer to the light of *Logos Incarnate*, one's self and one's Creator, was an idol of distraction; and if this meant excising family, friends, and material possessions, obsessive carnality from one's life, then good, prayed William. *Do with me, O Lord, as You will, my Maker. Your Spirit entered at Lands End, and you have brought to me darkness for the sake of luminescence, for now that I have seen that which negates, I can follow in the mystical theological of your divine names. Should I need trek nother six thousand miles, at six o'clock in the morning, by foot—stay with me, Christ, and I shall set out. I turn to my eyes to Octavia, symbol of mortal beauty with her eye on the divine, to the vision of that second Edith Stein. And the light of lights that even Nathan the Prophet knew, holy lights that shined, when she said to me, "love of true light, replete with ecstasy"; and the veil of light that swathed me at the riverbank, there shoveling skeletons have been definitively buried; and in the new Elysian field of classless society, where a house of flowers stands. I abandon that which is profane, and shall follow Thee down any path, no matter how harsh or dangerous. Unto the Second Renaissance!*

In the most private cell of his heart he sat reflecting upon *The Wisdom of the Desert Fathers*. He knew now that should Octavia laugh off his vocation then it would be the entirety of the world he would reject for the sake of his recurring vision. One who is seeking in earnest to return to the Triune God cannot bend even if every single person on earth is against him. To return to God one must be willing to face head on all enemies of the Church to the utmost end of extremity; this includes everything from surviving chemical self-immolation to being mercilessly against the world itself should the age fall captive to tyrants and charlatans. Although he kept his 'Fordham Notes', they were neither exclusive to that university nor copious; in his childhood he had learned of St. Ignatius, though, and in his private reflections hypothesized he would either follow St. Ignatius's Company or start his own. One could no longer be upset at anything with the ancient theology in control, for everything was in His order. Everything made sense. Fear was but doubt in Him or contradiction in one's heart. But before all of this there was work to do en route to the home he never had, New York.

Returning home his mother seemed disengaged from his prospects although she had seemed disengaged from anything for some time. The most character she let off upon his return home had been hysterical laughter at his prospect of finding work, at that, in the town. Her intellectual points of reference had become newspaper headlines and cracked actors. He walked two miles to the factory down the old country roads and saw nothing for an hour save packs of deer and pairs of rabbits. Life was rushing by faster every day.

The factory glowed in the dark and could be seen from a mile away amidst the moonlight through the pines and ran over 500 yards in length by another 225 yards. He had seen the factory throughout his life. It had always retained its initial qualities of ineffectuality, despair, and mechanical humanity; a place fit for ex-convicts, drug addicts, and other shattered souls containing fragmented memories of life who had entered the drug world or the criminal world or some other fringe world and had been thereafter locked in its cage of sand and had arrived at the ominous building worn out albeit incapable of much else but severe manual labor. It was fast money and did not allow one to think. He would need to think and pray through his nocturnal hours, but no more than that for the time being. He would usher in an extreme asceticism, he thought, reflecting on the Kolbe note attached to the tree back on that forlorn rainy sidewalk.

The drills and trucks resounded from half a mile away and the temperature remained below zero in the frozen twilight morn.

~

William stepped into the stale office and was met with expected, suspicious glares. Although he looked worn down, beaten down, and exhausted in his enormous second-hand overcoat and torn black work boots with that hangover equivalent to some obscure form of shock treatment, on some unconscious level the ladies and gentlemen saw through it into his soul and began to laugh at his appearance. He arrived looking ragged and yet he was not the sort to work in the factory. It was something his aura permeated; he could not even arrive in filthy clothing to the factory and appear believable.

He completed his application and, minutes later, was rejected.

He sat and reapplied filling in the abyss of empty lines with lies. No, he had never been to college nor had he further goals on his mind than working as much as possible nor did he think of much but to climb the company's ladder nor had he graduated high school nor had he a single reference. He wrote with his pained hand breaking several pencils in half. The room was surrounded by television sets and multicolored posters peeling at the edges and revealing loops of adhesive tape upon which pieces of hair and dust stood still trapped within the winding tape. The secretaries switched. Bankrupt phraseologies, inane slogans, blinding bright colorways which, like the uncovered spherical light bulbs, stood marred and chipped and began to burn one's eyes in the little room which smelt of unwashed clothing.

William stalled until the second secretary clocked in and handed her his application.

"We'll call you if anything comes up."

That was his worst fear. He enquired an on-duty manager and a man behind him covered in third-degree burns answered for the middle-aged woman:

"Man we all in a God-damn bind. This a God-damn recession. We all wanna see a manager."

He used the bathroom and afterward marched through the entranceway to the factory through which there was not yet indefinite congregative grounds but a sort of emptied locker room with vending machines, blinking beside TV sets lining the walls.

A portly man in a maroon suit with a lazy eye stood before a bulletin board of arrayed company slogans. William persuaded him with a collection of exaggerations. The man at last responded. He made a quizzical face. Metal doorways with sealed latches seemed to drift around them as if some carousel of salmon-colored wallpaper.

"Do you know how many applications we get a day here? Do you even know?"

William decided it was the most violated he had ever felt in his life and felt quite ready to die. He had now not even enough cash to catch the bus home and as it was daylight, he would be ridiculed by every passing car for walking down the road. He struggled with the energy to stand upright. The interviewer sneezed and wiped his hands out in his pockets.

"I can't just give you a tour or anything, of course. Everyone wants to get hired on the spot. We're the biggest distributor in this part of Pennsylvania, bucko. We want the toughest guys we can get." He rumbled, crackling, through an asthmatic cough. William wiped cold sweat from his forehead and asked to have a look inside. He said that he'd always been intrigued by the company and that he had always had great respect for the company. He honed in on work ethic and the immediate need for money. Transportation? Of course (Feet)!

The plump man let loose something of a sympathetic sigh which signaled registration that he had little else to do and that he could use the exercise. He waved William through dual sets of swinging heavy doors and the sound of one hundred thousand machines, trucks, the circuitry of loading equipment, rushing boxes, cracking crates, buzzing electric lights, and humming heaters engulfed his senses in its unfathomable industrial cacophony. William stood still, appalled, and could not believe his eyes.

What he observed was the most atrocious exhibition he had ever seen in his life—beyond science, beyond science-fiction films, beyond nightmares, beyond tales of bad hallucinations, was the worst apparition of horror he could never have conceived and still, still, it was mere reality. The inside of the factory was like the inside of a giant's skull, that through which one seldom looks beyond the mask thereof.

This world, he knew, was one wherein desperation roared at deafening volumes, through structures so unfathomable one could not begin to question them. This was the heart and soul of automation, and this was the catatonic world Anaheim had spoken of so long ago.

Thousands of reduplicating, towering metallic orange shelves which ran six stories to the ceiling and 200 yards in length towered over the working men on forklifts, pallet-jacks, and foot. The structure seemed a blueprint for replicated cities founded in Hell. The electric extent of the ten-thousand ovular lights lined along the ceiling burned one's eyes awake at once. William struggled to not let on his fear and nausea as the man told tales and kept his sensitive eyes open in observance. In another step the ceiling seemed ten stories high. When he looked in any direction of the factory, he could not see the wall at its opposite side, its end; and the factory's sense of infinite, its trancelike, mechanical-timeless aura—this, more than anything, seemed most daunting. Innumerable cardboard boxes and cracked wooden pallets filled each available decimeter within the towering fixtures; their shadows ran across the dust-polished floor of fractured cardboard and tape.

'My detractors may come against my craft or art,' William thought to himself, 'Though what I am saying in presenting my descriptive formulaic is that freedom is objective in the sense of historical blindfolds and scripted symposiums; our options are limited when they ought to be limitless.'

Another harrowing feature seemed the intricacy applied to that most lucid nightmare, and the way young men spoke through headsets and broke violent sweats rushing from contour to contour at lightning speed. Of the hundreds of lost men there seemed not one who had not been long brainwashed, or etherized, and in his proximity, William felt himself their equal. He thought of his mother's laugh at his prospect of finding work in the town and knew that it took stepping foot inside of the factory, the same way a surgeon in the depths of his work cuts through and sees within and understands the human body, for William to understand the predicament of the ontological situation of his country.

When he came to, George, as he was, went on explaining the history of the company and pointing this way and that between subjects and predicates with rosy, gesticulating fingers:

"Now you see the net-worth of a place like this is, well, it is a lot of money, a *lot* of money. You say you've seen this building all your life, kid, and so, assuming you have, you'll know that this, this," turning a 360 degree spin with his arms outspread, "Is worth more than either one of us could know. We'd have to trek on up to Hartford, Connecticut for all that! You see!"

William carried on his act and nodded to the breathing of cold air, streaming white clouds of fog, robotic janitors and tractor trailer drivers working in the frozen air as others zipped in and out of aisleways talking into headsets, transporting multiple pallets' worth of boxes stacked seven feet high and bound by clear-wrapping paper, swaying narrow with each cautious turn around the steel bends, distant and at one's elbow. The dissonance of buzzing lights, ventilation, truck motors, loudspeakers, shouts, horns, and falling crates crashing together made one feel as if he were if some sort disjointed nightmare, feelings similar to being explained Satan as a child. William recalled his years of Catholic school, of being explained Hell, with fleeting specificity crippling dread, and felt the nausea eating at him inside as he conjured that Hell must be something like a factory that never closes . . . whereby tearing himself from this horror the man stopped and leant his tattooed arm against the iron railings. He knew for a number of people it did not matter if you went to college anymore. The dream was dying and would either die in its sleep or awaken at some incomprehensible moment in the future.

"You know, guy, we got a training course interview tomorrow. Stop by. I was your age once; you got a good head on your shoulders. Name's George, George Cruz."

William shook his dampened hand and his surroundings seemed more dangerous to the fragility of conscious than that of prison cells. He listened to George's teeth grind with speed. He spoke again with inaudible concision, his teeth chattering, and vanished through sliding doors.

"I'll be here," he said, feeling distraught, damned, and thinking of nothing but solidifying his craft in Brooklyn.

By night he sat at the kitchen table with his tea, with his wine, reading and writing letters, e-mails, and messages never to be sent.

He was engaged within the twilight hour whence his mother stepped inside. She seemed pale, exhausted, and for a moment as if she'd forgotten William had ever returned home, and then walked by with a smile that indicated depression akin to his own.

He looked to the river from his desk and marveled that often at the end of that kaleidoscopic urban filth of the finest cities was paradise, and at the end of every white picket fence was soil. There was something within him beyond cities, though.

His mind returned to the factory, to the packages that fell with swift crashes from the skies of pallet jacks and pillars and which seemed physical symbols of the falling scattered faiths his countrymen repossessed which fell lucid from unforeseen emotional heights upon absolute yet dustily penitential grounds.

⁓

'. . . following my anonymous departure from the west I have received many phone calls and messages enquiring as to where I am, what has happened. I cannot explain. What is the desire to retreat, to move on, to be alone at last once more? And yet it is not an absolute loneliness; for now I know what a calling is, and that mine may entail celibacy and interiorly vigilant sobriety now that I know the wages of sin. Still everyone I have spoken with has understood, albeit in a saddened way, and has promised to visit me on the east coast. Harold, Brendan, Phil Cohen, even dear Mary—None of them have seen New York before. I look to the day I can show them around. The lack of surprise at my sudden departure, the sense of understanding conveyed, perplexes me less than brings to light aesthetic solvencies within myself.

'Perhaps someday I shall see Janine, Isaac, Heather, even Daniel again—Perhaps not, but I am coming to find that what matters most is the things we did together and the way we did them. There is that anonymous notion, that sudden or prolonged feeling of something coming to an end; a relationship, a lifestyle, a point of view, an opinion, a long bit of text at the end of a deserted day—Sometimes we stop , knowing not whether we'll return again, knowing that for the time being something has come to an end. That was the West for me—I blame no one, nor myself, nor any of the things I did or didn't do—It was more so that pale moment of clarity wherein I realized at once I would leave, to return another unknown day, and to arrive somewhere new and familiar at once, less a place than unto myself.

'Octavia arrives home tomorrow. What will she think when I tell her my mother has fallen apart? I don't know who is rich or who is poor anymore, placated cup of tea.'

⁓

William attended his training interview with a multitude of characters. He sat observant through several hour-long lectures with the didactic scope of pre-kindergarten concerning his company's history, modern economics, preferred methods of loading trucks, always concluding with a team rally and chant.

Men young and old tightened at the mouth, grew teary eyed at the talk of bonuses. Their speaker sketched out maps in blue marker upon white boards between mouthfuls of McDonalds sandwiches.

William reverted to his imagination and lost track of the instructions in the way he had learned to lose track of time while traveling and daydreamt of himself for hours on end of doing other things in the wintry boroughs of New York. He daydreamt of being interviewed by magazines that did not yet exist, of brothers in the spirit who might guide him whom he had not met, of subway routes not yet constructed, of attending universities which he could not afford, and of getting in his hands that occasional classic novel he had somehow missed and to read it on the benches of parks the way one read occasional eyes in the dampened streets. He would take to his long black coat and let his cynicism steer the wheel; to return east was to return to the death of false optimism or as he had written, William concluded, the rebirth of one's self; the crystallization of western dreams. He longed to indulge further in mystical annihilation, to apologize for nothing and thus let unwind, spiral, and formulate the creative psyche—To paint the psychic volcano.

Nihilism by night, dementia by day, to the orchestral soundtrack of screeching subway trains and distant tolling cathedral bells: this was an education no ordinary soul had undertaken.

He marveled in that no one in the meeting room took him when he answered a question concerning his ambition and work history and ethical inclination as to deliver without hesitation the swiftest magnitude of dedication and vigor to the work team. The young manager nodded his skeptical head, threw a crumpled yellow plastic-paper ball to the wastebasket, and pointed his brass-ringed finger to the next man.

Such were William's thoughts and experiences throughout the long walks to and fro, beginning at 9:00 pm and ending at 7:00 am in that state of sensical blackout, the burning spherical whirlpool welcoming all who had died or been born dead, a psychological exile all that one could turn to, turning to the desolate walkways whereupon outlandish and exhaustive walks home through the countryside with sunlight streaming down upon the glazed-over yards and mountains and forestry whence dozens of cars and trucks passed to and fro staring as if one was diseased rather than down on his luck for advancing by foot and the feeling carried on ahead through the frozen dawn when he was bound by artistry and lost in love and the combination and there was in the late-afternoon Octavia's voice to explain the needlessness of explanation and there were many hours ahead to stay awake all night kissing and one image left itself to his mind and for weeks he stuck to it, for as the nights dissolved he felt at moments that San Francisco was too painful a process:

Brooklyn dawn, he dreamt, to watch the snow fall from one's bed, lover beneath your arm just asleep and to kiss their lips and to know that life would be worth living, exhaling cold air and to look once to the desk and away and tomorrow with memories and to walk the battered streets alive hands clenched in torn coat pockets sanctimonious and justified, and the last glance could be the longest as the midnight sun in the shadow of an echo of a memory when the hands of one's memory thrust themselves devoted to the sky and the sun came in through windows at dawn as one fell asleep.

Time passed at a reasonable rate if one was willing to attempt to give up on the present moment and slouch through the fragmented automaton hours while the pounding of machinery haunted William's dreams, meals, his soul emptied from the memories of the men and women who sat around the lunch tables at midnight of rusted gloves and ravished eyes and warped minds locked within the racing wheel and fleeting up, permanent, toward the tip of their topless ladder. They believed in the company, in the slogans, in the nickel-raises, in the financial climax, and William now and at last understood them although still the irreversible contempt lay at his heart. He despised every single one of them and went in it alone. Pity had fallen by the wayside of bruised hands, discolored collages in stale locker rooms of blisters and sliced flesh, clothing torn and stained with sweat and blood and whatever chemicals broke through those anonymous packages with the sound of machinery racing somewhere in his mind.

For two weeks he spoke with no one at all. He had all but forgotten how to communicate. His mind had become a slate polished off, wiped clean. Brief letters, messages from Octavia kept him afloat, he never saw his mother, and everyone else was either locked away or in a faraway land. His reoccurring derealization was thus upon his walks to and from the factory:

Modern life was a transmission which worked at such an incomprehensible speed nonexistence could no longer register within anybody's soul. Mere thought anymore had become far too much thought, and wherein one cannot compare his life or anything within it, to its precise reflection, its linear opposite, life itself must suffocate.

Then came the day that one of the men on nightshift severed his arm. This bothered William less than the nine pounds he had lost in nine days and the trails of blood in real life were much darker than in films. The workers seemed to anticipate atrocities; it was all that could bring them together. The factory's mechanical way of humanity was the unfathomable collision of sheer sobriety and violent intoxication and its periodic tragedies gave someone something to talk about, an unconscious moment to consider the reality of materialistic vanity unto interior destruction.

During the hazy days of sleeplessness and physical torment William began to consider, as if for the very first time, the suicide of Abigail Blake. He had not known her as well as others although he'd known her from the beginning. He had first heard her use the term love and encountered some of his first sexual experiences with her. She had been manic-depressive and that was of course something considered unfathomable, to those without the disease. William pondered in the roaring, screaming nights of factory machines and ceaselessly cacophonic blend of blaring robotic voices with morals', that he too was now experienced in the dark night of the soul, recalling his memories of her presence.

Specific images haunted him: A hanged young girl being found by her mother in the basement he had spent many afternoons. She ties the noose. She holds the rope or wire in her hands and considers death. Even if there is an afterlife, she is convinced that it is no worse than life, and if it is, it is not her fault. If there is no afterlife, that is also neither her fault and at last she will feel painless.

'What, then, *is* the structure of such an evil modern commonplace by and within suicide, society?'

She contained a functioning mind and artistic inclinations in the land of morbid, obese alcoholics and men and women willing to die for ventriloquists. She observed the rooted bread and circuses of modern culture: People of all ages begging to have inventions and images jammed down each last orifice in order to speak of their ambitions while intoxicated and to regret those fine visions in sober hours; that had been our inherited code of American ethics. Relevancy is measured in terms of the past and the future and never when it is relevant. Hadn't Nielsen tapped into this light over pitchers of lager? But Abigail, Abigail—She had attempted, then, to indulge in drugs light and hard and became dependent upon such drugs. Her fault? Never. Her choice? By the skin of one's teeth.

Explain:

'In middle-America every citizen loathes their life, despises their neighbor, and cannot see further from the day. Most who see further than the day see so in terms of vacation, in terms of elastic, magnetic anchorage, and are most attached to the gray disease one feigns: the continual, pressing need to escape. Part of their permanent misery is not that they cannot resurrect, to sleepwalk through life, to sleep, perchance to dream, prospects within their lives, but that their stationary mode is discontent enhanced by illusory plans and self-inflicted agonies.'

Why, then?

'We are taught to trust scripts designed to distract. Most Americans long to leave home and despise the rare few who do.'

What did Abigail Blake say the last time she spoke with William Fellows?

'That she longed to leave the town and longed with desperation to see her country. He told her to drop her bags and do as she would please as it would bode well for her to see the country so as to realize the endless possibilities of her finite self and the microscopic infantilism of one's hometown.'

Why, then, was she unable to leave?

'The society of the spectacle: Those who leave miserable situations in America in search of themselves are berated by those incapable of understanding that someone has done it before their very eyes and find it offensive that their dreams can be actualized if one is willing to throw caution to the wind.'

Why did William not attend the funeral?

'He felt it hypocritical to cry at the funeral and tell drunken tales at the after-party with the very people who had weighed her down.'

When did he think it would happen again in the town?

He did not think of the town, nor of suicide; he would never stay long enough again to redevelop another elementary relationship with another soul there. More young men and women, he assumed, would kill themselves given the settings and impulsive synchronicities of the air-brushed generation. 'For example, look to the suicide rates of the veterans concerning the War on Terrorism. We acknowledge them with bumper stickers.'

How could the country begin to acknowledge this?

By acknowledging itself: Monomaniacal, megalomaniacal feelings of pride and luck and freedom in a time suffering its worst from conformity in centuries. By acknowledging that such thoughtless psychological uniformity leads to complete disaster, or fascism.

'Kill youth on sight, ridicule what you cannot understand, and celebrate that which is tomorrow.'

Such were the entrances of William's isolated reflections and sorrows. At their core he felt a sense of triumph colliding between his heart and mind. At times he knew nothing, at other times he knew not even what he was saying, and at yet other times he felt as if on occasion there were answers, or steps in the right direction, to colossal problems of life and time:

> 'We cannot fathom what we cannot see,
> 'As what we cannot see we cannot acknowledge;
> 'We cannot acknowledge what we cannot face,
> 'As what we cannot face we cannot control;
> 'And what we cannot control we cannot dismantle.'

∽

The weeks were coming to an end. He seldom made in at all. He felt as if a wounded soldier struggling forth through some sickly winter night limping pain down the most peaceful road to have be invisibly embedded with landmines.

One of his managers brought William to the office and showed him the month's numbers. William Fellows had finished last of the hundreds. He laughed for the first time in a long time. He was well pleased with himself.

The odd couple paced about the factory shouting over the noise, stepping out of the way of speeding forklifts and falling packages and crashing machinery. The stout man fingered his clean-shaven bundle of chins and brought up specific days where it appeared as though William had done nothing whatsoever. He remembered nothing specific from weeks prior.

"Here is the thing," Dave Shoemaker said. He adjusted his baseball cap, coughed, swallowed mucus in a gesture concealed by loose fists, and raised the front of his faded blue jeans up above his barrel chest. "If you want to stay on board, kiddo, you've got to start using the preferred method. You know the preferred method. See, look at Skyler there." The middle-aged man with tobacco stained-fingers was careworn to stack anvils and fish-tanks into a rumbling, well-tagged tractor trailer. His emaciated face was turning royal blue. "Now him—he's gonna make it."

The violent wind channeled through the factory. Dave Shoemaker told William a story before he went to lunch:

"These new headsets we got, you see, on a million-dollar loan from the government. What we're going to do, to try them out—you talk to an automatic operator and set in orders by codes. What they want to see is—and they're doing it not many other companies besides ours, now, you see—is if it works we're going to try to have the software used in future wars. *Now* you get it, right? These little imbeciles, these little headsets, are going to be the way of war if we have a successful year here with them. We won't even have to ship out any more troops in the future! Isn't that exciting!"

In a strange way, between midnight and his state of mind (That which cannot contain itself any longer as it nears in upon a final departure from a reality unfit for itself), William believed him.

He took a walk through downtown Jerusalem on his day off and passed the shopping centers, parking lots, for-sale signs, abandoned buildings, and further dismal memories and further enhanced by his looming departure. One decade ago there had been nothing but nature and fields and now there had been thousands of acres bought and identical shopping centers had been erected in a perpetual convex mirror of decline and bellicosity. Progression and regression were figurative in that either vision precluded the viper's nest of on the one hand, eternal return, and on the other, salvation.

Familiar faces passed on the street and from their cars. No one stopped to speak anymore; William found it most fitting, most interpolative. He walked across the bridge and to the old library.

He looked ragged, worn, exhausted, clad in dirty clothes and a beard as he observed his reflection in the mirror of the Jerusalem University library one last time. He spent hours at his old desks rummaging through photography books and others picked at random. He wondered if he was unrecognizable now, and hoped that he was, and he saw no one he had recognized, faculty or staff, despite staying all day and night.

He needed a good outfit and had all the money he needed and more. He could not wait to sit out on Metropolitan Avenue once more on a winter night and watch the people pass by with Octavia Savonarola at his side.

He bought a black leather jacket, checkered red flannel shirt, cuffed black jeans, and worn wingtips. He ran his hand through his enormous beard and pushed his greasy hair back, to the side. He liked to think that the scar across his forehead had summoned a sort of Dostoyevskian James Dean from within. The radio overhead performed its vocal waltz, guiding listeners through glittering ballrooms of frivolous music and interjecting tales of death and war; Libya was next; meanwhile, drug the customers with music.

He lay down upon the air mattress down in the boondocks and pondered in earnest whether he would ever see any of the western friends again. If not, then why not? But he could no longer wrack his mind on such matters, turning rather to interiority, to the litany of humility.

'I can see that when it comes to the same grind nothing is worse than more of the same on the occasion one is not bidding the soul's will. What does it profit a man to please all and abhor himself for going against life and holiness? If one must get up in the morning for any other reason it is terrible. Our parents are incidental, God transcendent. If one wakes up with an agenda it becomes glorious in any form, whether real or a dream.

'I have had my fill and I have contemplated it in the past weeks of my solitude. I have had my fill of life; but this was not life itself, rather the not-life. Aimlessness is not a call for celebration; it is a call to begin exercising one's mind at once. The calling of the gods, ancient and today, demand that one reject society and devote oneself to what is truly right and justice, and to despise temporal political religions of deformed righteousness and justice. If life is lived well and wise there is no use for another, not one fixed in eternity. We speak of eternity as if it is an option while our option is a matter of recognition. Abhor distraction in the name of a divine dedication to bodily and mental health, but do not worship these things either; make your life a mirror of divinity, in the name of the natural law, and you shall never be psychologically subjugated again. Solitude, yea, is the first and last freedom; with another or alone, that which is not contemplative solitude, with a heart forever open to the *virtue* of charity: make this thy life.

'Be it clear-headed or rowdy, alone or amongst great company, in and out of seasons in Hell, concentrated or absent minded—I shall be no victim of the world but the world's conqueror—

'My mother has spoken of moving away from the town. I hope she will be happy. I know not what else today as the morning sun is in ascent.

'For, sometimes, I drink endless cups of hot tea at my desk. That seems as if my purpose in life. To drink tea amongst my papers in silence. Sometimes I get so sick of music.

'The silence is not beautiful or overwhelming or dreadful; to the contrary it is silence. I have seen the meaning of life and yet it is a sound. It deals with being young, but then that is just because I am young, and it deals with experiencing life by any means necessary, which anyone can do. Anyone can do anything, I've come to find, and it is a matter of being reminded or reminding yourself, and sometimes it takes no more than listening to the words people speak—Because sometimes something is put in such a way that you always knew and yet you never did put it that way yourself. Men and women are limitless. We must be reminded of this, as we must be reminded of life and death. Then we choose one or the other. Neither is selfish. And discovering such axioms, such predilection, adds graphic detail to our conception of being alive.

'O Trinal Light, guided to the city and my lady, the one with a crown of light around her head, preserve me that I might escape to tell thee more in all our days ahead, and try to make known to thee with kisses and verse the story of a soul. Western flame, burning brightest in its center; somewhere it is three o'clock in the morning, and the monastery bells are ringing. I do not feel like contemplating the meaning of life any longer. I can guess at things, knowing that I don't know; philosophy begins right where it ends. Anyone doing more than guessing with regard to temporal, finite matters is doing nothing. There are no facts. I no longer pass judgment. I no longer debate God and politics and philosophies and science. I can't act in those plays any longer. Now I've been promoted to the light booth.

'Such was a moment hitherto unknown, when bliss was made tangible, real, and the good people of this world played their part in clutching to the eternal rather than the temporal. One parts ways with adolescence of the mind and steps forth to meet she who has stepped into the room. May the saints and angels, known and not, walk beside us though unseen, smiling; my lady and I, in the house of light, the city of destruction, the country of beatific vision, the universe of death, far from the profane crowd, shall at last see the angels. Let him that is athirst come.'

The First and Everlasting Wisdom

THE LAST DAYS OF anything are often most glorious when the intensity of any means to its end is propositioned as inception rather than abyss, its simultaneous past and future memories and possibilities absorbed, and time at last and again breaks itself down into nothing. William had by then no dash of nostalgia for Jerusalem. He was at wits' end after two weeks in town. He no longer recognized the town and went for long solitary walks in the mountains.

When he descended in the evening light, he looked upon the streets as if looking upon photographs of dirty fingernails; that was Jerusalem's desperate longing for culture and growth, money and fame, notoriety and recognition—a misaligned hand extended toward the northern quilt of stars. And like most other American towns, unequivocal in yearning to waylay historiographical interiority and philosophical critiques of (its) nature in the process—This, William knew, was something that must have separated his country from any other: Its complete architectural and psychological inability to fathom anything more than the immediate future, and its unconscious obsession with deconstructing any sort of rich, vital culture, in lieu of the next obscene shopping complex and condominium towers to remain half vacant until they were vacated, at which point the hollow towers would then just stand still in the middle of fields that seemed more like the drugged, open-jawed faces of shock treatment than the land where any farm had once been. There had been too much pride and false optimism invested into the town and its clearest failures would remain symbols of progression. This he thought and more, overlooking the steel mill's absurd neon lights from the top of the mountains, and he knew that Jerusalem was more allegorical than an individual case, and that everything in the country seemed as if on stilts and set to all come crashing down again sometime soon, the way it did less than a century prior.

He saw at the foot of the cathedral a Starbucks in the making, and he wished there would be bricks thrown through its windows every night.

~

William walked untold miles down the old country road, observing the interior of tractor trailers, fingers across layers of dust paralleling an unclear calligraphy within long-forgotten metal canvases, and down below stalked a single buffalo; uphill one could purchase eggs or milk.

The factory was for a final time, descending the mountain, before him; contrasted with nature either contained mammalian insight he both sought to hypothesize and leave behind, never to see towering factories or farms again. He clocked in and got to work within the bread truck.

Mr. Shoemaker stepped inside of the truck, observed the obscenities, and smiled. William stood from the crate, marking the first time he had ever observed something other than a stoic, or possessed, trait upon the face of someone in the factory.

"Roth is going to want to suspend you. You can't be drawing out of dust on doors. I'm sorry. The preferred method, you see—"

William placed his hand on the man's shoulder:

"You're a good man, Sonny West. Call me tomorrow afternoon with the details. This issue is beyond our control."

"Well you guys are all off tomorrow, too."

An obese man walked over proudly displaying a Puerto Rican flag tattooed on both his arm and on his t-shirt.

"Man, I always see you on the road—where you live, anyway?"

"Two miles north," William said.

Driving through the valley at dawn, Jose spoke to William about his raise, his family, and an extensive grid of statistics concerning mortgages and minivans. Snow rustled across the fields, their ends collected by the sky in one vast whitegray wall. William watched the deer halt, tilt their heads, and pass through the snow, listening to the driver's dreams.

Jose spoke with uninhibited enthusiasm for the headsets.

"He told you, too?" William asked.

"Hell yeah!"

"It is something."

"Ah man—it's like some virtual reality—you know, because I was in the war, long ago, before you were born," he laughed, "And it's not the number of people you kill—it's the number of people you convince."

They drove on.

"Every man for himself," William sung aloud to the rising sun.

"Good meeting you—see you tomorrow, William."

He collapsed through the doorway with exhaustion and was free from the damned and from the implicative countryside. And still, somehow, life was moving faster, though the last big check would be directly deposited the morning after the pilgrim's return to Gotham.

～

William got his bags ready to go at noon. By sundown, the snow was to pick back up again. He called Octavia; she would meet him at the Port Authority. He went out for a beer, changed his mind. To the university library, to the mountain—again neither drew him any closer than intended. Looming departure: recaptured a time to keep recaptured silence. Everything flowed. Ms. Fellows would take him to the bus and that was that.

He configured a mass of sketches, articles, and organized them within envelopes and folders. Any last-minute, aesthetic-theoretical, albeit dormant, wistfulness had been absorbed, withdrawn from him weeks prior.

He could do little but wonder what Octavia looked like now as they geared toward their mid-twenties, where much happened in the matter of months. He longed to explore Woodside, Astoria, Gravesend, and other outer realms of the city with her, whose spiritual awakening was also a reality developing in William, who prayed she would forever be his guiding light, an angelic romantic love between them that unfolded itself by way of life in the spirit; she in her braided blonde crown actively with William not just participating in a relationship, which is to say the unfolding between two beings, but that it would itself be synonymous, or predicated upon, spiritual development.

Manhattan Avenue in the Greenpoint morning, fresh coffee and bagels upon plain Sunday, the restaurants and charm of the village in the morning, bicycle rides to and fro each last bridge intoxicated with wine, virtue, love, lust, and artistry interwoven within each breaking moment. He imagined the springtime wind rustling through Octavia's hair along the old broken-down piers of Red Hook, and to be caught within that harsh compass of New York City a new man.

Night fell and he tossed his two small bags o'er his good shoulder. Ms. Fellows told him to take the beer from the refrigerator and for a moment she seemed as if herself again; it was not of that which she spoke but that the color had returned to her face, that it had been there all day, and William marveled at his delayed awareness.

There seemed, he considered, much more of an archival finality in traveling small distances to wondrous cities than to go as far west as possible; 100 miles was much more believable, comprehensible, and wondrous in its own nocturnal right. He was returning home, to the home he'd never had, to the home he would create, the first and everlasting wisdom.

She helped him place his bags within the back seat. Each was quite light although it was a perfect gesture.

William could think of nothing to say, feeling content and refreshed with vigor for life, when his mother began to speak:

"You know I remember when you were a child, and one Christmas Eve I held you in my arms all along the train ride to Manhattan and you were the best child and the people always stopped to admire your curling blonde hair, your blue eyes, your little outfits. You never cried, you know—but smiled, gazed observant out upon everything."

They passed through a succession of green lights and approached the bridge. Streetlights shined and broke in patterns across the windshield still dashed with fragments of broken ice. Ms. Fellows paused to switch lanes and William listened to her and watched the town vanish behind him as if exiting one world and entering another rather than following his heart to another raucous city of night.

"Let's pull in over there. I'd like to see what that man has for sale there out front of the reptile store."

"Are you thinking of a pet?"

"No—I think he sells little trinkets and rosaries. Just a look before the bus."

They moved ahead in the still winter night, cherishing the ornamental snowfall.

Before the reptile shop stood a weather-beaten foldup table, chipped wood, broken metal lining, one leg held up by telephone book, where an elderly man sat selling rosaries and whistles. William observed a teal rosary, with beads of red and blue.

'I'm unsure what shall become of the woman. But I know compassion, pity, magnificence; I sought these in the lower depths.'

"I have found many things stopping by street persons," said William. He observed a cigar cutter and some beads. "Most have better books to suggest than the professors and publishers themselves. For in my continental investigations I have learned that the simple hearts are in it for the books themselves. And there is something about a handmade rosary, with beautiful colorways, that I have been thinking about for days."

Then suddenly there was darkness all around he who was transfixed, and the piercing sound of shattered glass. He both winced and shuddered while, for a second, he ceased breathing. Everything went pitch-black, except for the light that drew him forward, his mother—but even her narcotized voice, all at once, sounded as though it were being transmitted under water.

And at his foot a winding scorpion; for the pet shop owner, screaming, had dropped a glass cage containing also under a net two snakes that hissed, slithering, and lunged. William was floating in space weightless, gilded with beatific vision; but then with the force of history and congenial retribution, the pilgrim swiftly relayed his foot, crushing the snake's head underfoot with a savage crunch; he looked violently about for the scorpion, but could hear nothing but the man screaming "Crete! Orion!"

And William Fellows wiggled loose his shoe, took the one the scorpion had bitten, threw it into the garbage can, and stepped down from the high sidewalk toward the darkness of the car; and he stepped forward, looking not back, but ahead, into the car's interior.

And a light shined in the darkness.

William's Death and Funeral March

THERE WAS A CLARITY in his mother's voice he hadn't heard since he was a boy. He recalled at once that she had raised him, that there had been good times and bad, and all that remained was the future unknown, wherein the name of God was mercy. The pilgrim double-checked he had everything; and as he went to affirm, before walking to the bus, the poor woman spoke:

"And I don't know, I don't know what will happen when I die, but I always look back upon that moment, those days of my life, when I was just older than you are now and you were so young, and the way the church was with its organ songs and choirs and incense through the air—you'd fallen asleep in my arms, I remember, and it was no religious experience but it was much more important than that—I knew then that *life was worth living*. I was never rich and often we were poor, but the memories of youth always reinforced, I guess you could say, right," she laughed through concentrated words, "That I keep going, we keep going, and keep passing through life, and do the best that we could do. We're all just passing through life, William, and everyone should have a specific moment—if they're lucky, I think many—but one at least, that always reminds you that life is worth living everyone should have, and for me it was the two of us walking from St. Patrick's Cathedral on Christmas Day, wiping the snow from your little hat and little boots. Then, now, I went through pain so immense I may never be able to describe it, though it always seemed much more important to overcome it before anything else. I'm getting older now, you can see—I'm approaching old age, if I'm not already an old woman—but what I have, even in my loneliest or my last hour, what I have with me is the memories."

The bus was rumbling outside of the station. Passengers loaded in their luggage beneath and stepped up the steps through gusts of thick fog.

A light stream of snow fell across the fluorescent bulbs and thick funnels of smoke plumed across distant towers, factories and chimneys ascending beyond and through the mountains.

"It is a crystalline memory," William said, "And there is nothing more beautiful in life. Someday I will recall one of my own, and you will be the first one to know it, mom."

"It takes time—you may not know it, it may not be until years down the line, but someday you'll know it—you'll know it when it hits you, and life will never be despair ever again. Now go, go on, that man looks cold and ready and to go."

They embraced as the headlight bulbs burned before them.

"I'll visit soon—and oh, give Octavia my regards—that sweet girl."

"I will, mother. Should you pray, please pray for my vocation, or craft and art, that it unite with Providence, whatever it shall be in life. I must go speak to the priests and theologians, mother; my heart is on fire. I see the innocents as flower petals, as in a holy garden, replenishing rain is the holy minds; reality is one's choice, rendered in methodology of approach: His grace is sufficient for me."

Ms. Fellows did not look as stunned as her son had thought she'd be. They embraced once more, she promising to keep him in prayer, his woolen shoulder absorbing the tears she could no longer fight.

Their final phrases spoken, William walked to the bus and handed in his ticket. He placed his bags overhead and sat down in the far back.

The bus driver called out, "LAST CHANCE F' NEW YOKE CITY" before starting up the engine and taking off for the highway entrance; Ms. Fellows waved from her car, the windshield wipers intersecting, and William waved back to her before turning out of sight, onto the highway, and into the winter night.

Upon the passenger seat the pilgrim had left a little prayer card:

> And God shall wipe away all tears from their
> eyes; and there shall be no more death, neither
> sorrow, nor crying, neither shall there be any
> more pain: for the former things are passed away.

~

William stepped from the restroom to the dim contour of the bus. The bus was half-packed and everyone was in a gay, Christmas mood.

It was as if he was stepping from an irreversible past into an irreversible future with each step he took and the radiant hour burned in his blood.

The snowfall racing over and through the forestry around him produced a sort of tranquilizing, aesthetic effect, wherein life appeared to the pilgrim synonymous with prayer. He knew Octavia would be the one to recognize him in his new religious-philosophical investigations, away from the profane crowd, and that she would understand the clear break in his life from romantics, metaphysics, and cinematic inquiries.

The motor rumbled below and children slept within their mother's arms, couples read USA Today, the others gazed out upon the infinite stream of light absorbed within the checkered white and yellow dashes racing below, headphones wrapped around their ears. In their eyes and upon the windows beside them reflected the light of cell phones.

He thought little but of his arrival; within that moment he understood there were no longer windows to look through, nor yearnings to reconsider. He had ascended into becoming a young man in his own way, and now he would break back into the metropolitan world. He allowed himself at last to reflect upon the kaleidoscopic West, from the Canadian border to the Mexican. He knew, in some strange way, that he was being taken care of. And should even Octavia at last need retain her privacy, he would return to Grand Army Plaza library in Brooklyn and revisit the writings of St. Ignatius of Loyola. He no longer feared being alone and was ready to take to his feet across city and suburban landscapes should the nocturnal pilgrim have to do just that come Spring. With such thoughts he fell asleep.

Sudden thrashings awoke him from a vague dream. In towering capital-red letters to his left he made out THE NEW YORKER. The driver tore past accumulating traffic and all of the New York skyline gave itself over to William Fellows; he felt perhaps that would be his moment and his reason to live—he admitted to himself that the Bay Bridge had long ago taken that initium within his heart, but nonetheless cast his vision across the skyline.

The tunnel was a flashing maze of transfixed shadows and anticipation, and it arrived at 9th Avenue, veering left and parking. It hit him then—when the bus came to a complete stop—and he could not explain it to himself, but it had hit him, whatever that feeling was.

The streets were packed, alive, and everyone laughed in an ethereal chorus of vocal lanterns and a thousand flashing lights' enigmatic insanity and in the streets of Manhattan nocturne he stepped forth into the familiar blackened-dust and wooden concrete ledges of Port Authority entranceways and burst through the automatic door and straight to the subway entrance, carving his way through the ceaseless crowds, overhead announcements, newspaper stands, twelve languages at once from the benches of brown paper bags as his heels clicked and echoed in the chorused unison of a dozen others when the hand met his shoulder and her voice came through the disorienting sensorial cascade of Port Authority.

"O, William!"

Octavia soared forth, bursting with elation, her arms opened wide. The bags slid from William's body at once. The pilgrim kicked them away to embrace her in a glorious, triumphant way he had never done before. She reciprocated as they swayed back and forth through the mob.

She had grown more beautiful with time as a tear formed upon her pristine face, the unmatched complexion never to require makeup, her radiant beauty magnified by the halo of blonde braids, graceful figure beneath white duster, a smile with the striking flare of love, and she pressed her lips to William's with all of the New York come-go insanity revolving around them as they embraced pressing their hands upon one other's backs, interlocking and squeezing their hands, taking one another in as Octavia wept like William had never before seen her weep. He knew in some way she had recalled being younger, when they had lived in Jerusalem together and vowed one day to come together again, when they were older and wiser and could admit their love for one another.

"You're here," she said, "Finally, you're *here.*"

He was overtaken with joy and toppled over, opening an eye to peer out upon smiling passersby who cut around the couple, the golden-lighted station giving way to a collective jubilation, and streams of holy lights.

Octavia ran her hand through William's beard and looked awestruck as the two stepped aside. He kissed her lips once more, inhaling subtle apricot scent which broke forth from her hair and winter coat. The warmth of the sun twinkled in her eyes. She was the best memory William ever had of the east. Now that proximity to his mother had been recaptured, along with a striving to serve God Almighty, he could again hold his mother in that vacant cell of his heart, sending physical and digital letters describing the life and works of St. Kolbe, Bonhoeffer, and a thousand more.

The tip of her index finger ran across his lips; she looked into his eyes as he wiped away her little tear.

And he too looked hard into her eyes, and the brown speckles therein, each with its own contained shape and form.

"You look so—oh, I don't even know, William—"

She blushed, dashing her eyelashes.

"I've never seen you blush."

"I'm not that sort of person."

"Well of course not," William said. "That's why I love you. I dreamt about you last night, and the night before, the night after, and the always-night. It's like walking through a diamond mine."

"Oh, I love you too!" She wrapped her arms around William again, whispering, "But you know it feels nice, it feels nice to become over-whelmed sometimes: affect, grace, and the tender heart on fire." She looked down to his bags, lifted them up and laughed through sniffling tears. "This is all you've brought?"

"It's all I need!"

Five pairs of socks, two bottles of Spanish wine wrapped in boxes, a fire-proof safe, two notebooks, six pencils, Augustine, Benedict, spare pouch of pipe tobacco.

"We'll get you some furniture."

"That's all secondary," William said, "What matters is that you arrive. And you, you look like heaven—we must head out to St. Vincent Ferrer before they close the doors. Then we'll drop my bags off and go into the night at once! Anything for you!"

The pilgrim threw his arms around her, free at last, once more, before they interlocked their arms at the elbow, ascended the escalator, and walked straight ahead to the mob beside the subway. Islands of travelers split like a little sea before them.

"First we'll go to St. Vincent, then to the apartment, unload your things," Octavia said, drawing out a map of the night, a map which William took to be one of her life, the young-woman coming to in her masterful artistry, humble streams of thought, her furtive contemplation, sacred and pale gentility, visions of the future gilded as golden bracelets beneath ballroom chandeliers, somewhere in the new interior castle. "Then oh, Brooklyn, all these spots that have come up—there is so much, so much to do! To see!" William smiled and placed his hand within hers as a bath of interior light illuminated his line of sight.

The pair stepped through the doors to the subway, bought metro cards, and walked to the turnstile. The uptown train was rushing in.

"You take the C or the E," Octavia said, as if William did not know, "To 14th, the L—then to Graham Avenue. No, wait—but wait—we're going to St. Vincent Ferrer's! We'll get you all the things for your room and in the summer visit your friends in San Francisco—But oh, now, let's hurry! You're here! Let's go!"

William's heart raced like mad. He and Octavia waltzed, laughing, through the turnstile.

And she was right, anyway: He'd become so adapted to San Francisco street cars and trains he'd forgotten the precise routes of the New York subway. Octavia too had a secret: for all her years in the city, she had never once been to the church on Lexington. Meanwhile William at once began channeling through his mind for such memorized codes, numbers, and letters, rummaging through his memory for that zone wherein the subway remained mastered; for mastering the New York subway is a fine small feat as any in life, something either unfathomable or self-evident. Octavia thrust one of his bags over his shoulder as they slipped past the crowd formulating about innumerable synchronized gypsy dancers to the beat of an unseen synthesizer and slid into the car as its doors clicked shut. William wrapped his gloved palm around the steel pole and felt as if his imagination, his vision of the artistic life had long been a wavering pool of gasoline and now, at last, the lit matchbook had been dropped to it.

The thick slush broke beneath a thousand polished heels as they walked up. Octavia interlocked her arm within his once more and either one was too excited to speak of the world, of jobs, of infinite nights, of travels, of anything at all. They knew; they knew.

William halted at the foot of the ancient staircase as seventy-five souls cut around him.

"What is it, William?"

William looked into her beautiful eyes still dampened from the tears, luminescent with tender anticipation.

"Oh," he laughed, wrapping his arm around her and walking downstairs, projecting through the train doors, "There's just so much to do, but even more to be done, I believe. Miracles abound; and may you contemplate the fragility of consciousness, O ye lost pilgrims, and rectify thy life!"

Across the platform another train rushed screeching to its place. Octavia planted a smiling kiss upon William's neck; he placed his hand to her upper arm beneath her jacket and kissed her once upon the temple, overlooking the crowd. From the far end of the winding tunnel, glancing leant over the track-edge, a small light formed, building, and crept, distending, along the ancient subterranean wall.

The train pulled in. Octavia took William by the hand at the station and they walked out onto the platform with his luggage. They pressed ahead through a dozen jostling bodies, their inadvertent fixations.

'Stand clear of the closing doors, please—'

The subway doors closed in, out, and again, retracting backwards to the ring of an electronic bell.

Through the sea of bodies breaking from the car across the track a side-profile shone ragged like a pearl.

William squinted ahead in doubt and then in awe and rushed off the train at once. Octavia gripped his arm although he had not yet made a move—it was the sudden frantic look in his eyes that seemed to portray a relay of memory so intense his body could not react any other way to burst full speed ahead on foot.

The doors closed, opened again, clicked once more—he knew without question that young man's face in the crowd.

"Gideon!" William cried out through cupped hands: "Gideon!"

Multiple heads turned within and outside of the subway car as last-minute crowds pushed forth, pressing William and Octavia back, and back further. He let go of Octavia's hand to press ahead as she looked on in wonderment, reaching—

"William!"

Gideon, in all his ragged glory, turned and skipped down the steps as the doors retraced once more—but the door clicked shut before he could get his hand to the window. He stood in awe, glowing a moment, before yelling at, then pleading with, the driver:

"Let me on!" Gideon rapped at the spray-painted window, "Let me on!"

The subway train started moving as Octavia stepped ahead to again be at William's side. He stood transfixed; his look of fever had been drained, turned into one of shock, as buried albeit foundational memories broke like a the light of imploding stars across his mind, sweat breaking from his forehead, recapturing some winters past and the few photographic details which remained lucid and chaotic at once as crates of colored paints crashing against some untouched, limitless canvas. Gideon turned and jogged alongside the car, his face familiar and warm and yelling at the top of his lungs mad deranged bloodshot eyes and a well-handled volume of *Philokalia* beside winter cap tucked beneath his free arm, his old torn winter coat ends flailing, singing at the top of his lungs, jogging, and beating on the accelerating window.

A pianist beside him stood, bent, and tossed a pile of books into the air as he and Gideon cut through shopping bags and maps and outstretched arms and baby carriages until the train accelerated out of view and began to burn through the underground and through each window one saw colorless angles and through all of the windows broke only fleeting, cavernous bulbs, and William knew he would never see him again. But then in the city—

And Gideon, he had just said so much without a sound; it was the look in his eyes, and hadn't he been there since the beginning in his own way, he who spoke of his own way and lived it, and had found William in the withered rungs of Port Authority when everyone was much younger, dreaming as much as ever and yet so less conscience, and still what was the answer?

Octavia and a dozen others looked on with wide, wondrous eyes as William returned to her side and the train roared en route to St. Vincent's.

He looked at his face in the reflective windows as the lights streamed by in timeless flashes.

And he had said, old Gideon, he had said so long ago, William knew at once and at last: 'While there is no specific answer, thus while we are alive, there can appear but a single direction—But our direction is that iridescent lack of direction, you see, wayward, my son,' Gideon had said so long ago, 'Wayward.'

The pilgrim looked to Octavia and before he could speak, she responded to the look in his eyes:

"You've arrived William—You're here, and home, at last."

Octavia retook Williams in her arms.

"The beginning," William marveled, looking again into her eyes, "To think it hasn't even begun!"

"Tonight we can listen to Vaughan Williams, and "Prayers of Kierkegaard.""

"Yes, my love! O, I tell you, you I tell, thee, like a montage of emotions unaware of acrid sensibilities, the western roaring sun and the eastern dreaming moon, figurative-then and indefinite-now, they roar on through the alphabetical nights whence death shall have no dominion amidst and within the acceleration of artistry and the winter sky spills forth snow until dawn upon all of Brooklyn, upon all of America, walking ahead to where you can see the bridge's spectral, glittering entrancement upon any winding nocturnal angle of Metropolitan Avenue from which to get a drunken sleep, a malnourished salvation, and in the face of the future-past burn like autumnal leaves 'neath summer lens, from death to night encompassing the body language of dreams—"

The train jostled to and fro; the pilgrim smilingly clutched his angel, light in their eyes and woven into their words.

"I pray my latest paintings will be my masterpieces at last," declared Octavia, "And that, further, I don't desire to give off the impression I'm above putting myself in others' shoes, but rather that mine are broken in, double knotted, and swell as is; and last, that.someone would go play Samuel Barber's 'Living Prayers of Kierkegaard' on the jukebox—such would be paradisal.'

William and Octavia exited the train.

"And the art of art as in the art of life, Lord, we pray for the wisdom to always remember to remember that one glaring misconception concerning art is the idea of creating a masterpiece; a masterpiece has nothing to do with creation, and is in fact a matter of external judgement. There are no ingredients for a masterpiece; rather, it is a perception gathered by the masses, who do have elemental ties, that being a thorough-going, collective lack of individuality. Let us not despise them outright but learn, for in my life the doctrine of personal aesthetics' basis of perfection has been revealed to me through a development dictated by fate; let us rejoice and be glad. In the name of the Father, Son, and Holy Spirit. Amen."

Stepping out of the 63rd street station, William looked upward to the countless blinding lights of construction works involved with the back of the church, which now appeared as if a sight he had never seen, like one last multicolored gem itself contained with the light of the sun, illuminatingly hidden behind a tower; now he would live in the sphere of theological geography. And the book of life would now be bound up with love in a single volume, scattered Homeric leaves in the universe of perpetual and heavenly mansions of light from which an interior light is impossible to consent to severance; the light that shines in the darkness is eternal, and cannot be extinguished, but retrieved, by men.

"Yes, I have transformed," William said to Octavia, their hands interlocked, "the Love that moved me, the city, the stars and cosmos, was all One, to move from time to the eternal—"

"I chose you because you are a poet", Octavia whispered, as a nearby mumble turned into a scream that jolted one right out of poetic being, and rendered one paralyzed with arctic cold and trembling.

William Fellows looked Octavia Savonarola in the eyes to explain, but it would all have to wait until the night, until dawn, until the sun broke down, and in her eyes, he knew himself to be that much younger in the reflected soundless light.

"I'll tell you all about it in the morning."

"Yes, William," she smiled.

Octavia led William up the slight flight of stairs. She held open the door. He stepped into the church.

There the pilgrim was absorbed at once; his mind and heart connected and were absorbed, as if by a sacredly intricate, intricately sacred magnet. Its enormous arches of varied gray-beige stone, chained glass tubes of descending light as though frozen hourglasses, towering columns and a scent that transported William into another realm, that of the most subtly intoxicating grace of a Gothic masterpiece that, in light of the age's instruments, may as well have set one in antiquity, or another planet. Sifting incense, the last dissolving wisp of which ascended across stone, wood, and iron. Parentheses of smoke rose through shafts of workmen's lights a million ovular millimeters of it as crystallized by master craftsmen. Centering his eyes upon the altar that was drawing him near, the pilgrim was overcome with a sense of overwhelming holiness—William would see the rest of the church in time, but just then dissolved from his line of sight, giving way to an indexical glass symphony of perfect colors: purple, teal, yellow, red, blue, arranged in holy persons and forms, intricate stone tracery of a great rose. Shining with the last blast of blinding lights, William felt as though he could both touch and taste these holy lights. Their perfect arrangement slipped into the very air he breathed. Towering symphonic silence absorbed the pilgrim into the realm of woodcut, sacrament, and the choral light of sound; before the altar as her left hand felt for, touched, and interlocked with his, connecting with what felt like an explosion.

"Being there, or presence, has commenced," said the pilgrim, "And so we might light three candles, then journey back into the beginning and end of the night."

"Thus," whispered Octavia, squeezing, resting her head softly upon William's shoulder, "concluded the poet's pilgrimage?"

William squeezed Octavia's hand back in response, the poet and the angel then turning together toward the candles to solidify by flame their symbolic offering to thenceforth bear death and abide by it, separating the rational soul's desire from matter itself, that matter structured into stars and galaxies, stellar nucleosynthesis the source of generative energy, to together depart from matter, and merge irreversibly like unto the indestructibility of absolute spirit.